Praise for *The Cursing Stone*

"Historical Fiction at its best. This story is a delight. Set in 1884, we are introduced to the tiny community living on Tory Island off the north west coast of Ireland, with barely enough to sustain them. Cue a British naval vessel assigned the task of transporting a sheriff and his men to the islands to evict and burn the cottages of the families whose rent is in arrears. This is already a potential powder keg and the makings of a great story. Add a smorgasbord of fascinating characters: a one-eyed young man and his psychic aunt, a lonely, diminutive schoolmaster, an alcoholic priest, pitching his Christian dogma against pagan beliefs thousands of years old, and a fractious lighthouse crew. On board the naval vessel, we have a captain confined to his cabin by his infirmities and a portly sub-lieutenant, learning the ropes while bedevilled by self-doubt. The scene is set on page 1, where we read the monument on Tory Island that commemorates the sinking of a naval vessel. Providing the reader with a limited, but definitive knowledge of the outcome works beautifully, and the writing is exemplary. Highly recommended."

– JJ Toner, author of *The Black Orchestra*.

"Beautifully written and compelling story.... The interweaving of the characters and the tragedy of the HMS *Wasp* are masterfully handled. This is such a good read."

— Lissa Oliver, author of *Chantilly Downs*

"Every character just comes to life off the page – through both the interactions between them and the skilful sketching in of their back-stories. The various settings point up the different worlds Ruairi is drawn into – the way of life on Tory is so clearly drawn, including the slightly separate life of the lighthouse, and it seems a long way in time and place from the very different world of Westport, and again from the life on board the *Wasp*.

"But beneath all that, and bringing the stories together is the step-by-step portrayal of the historical background – we learn about it slowly, as Ruairi does – never too much information, but enough to allow readers to come to a realisation of the potential for ugliness of a world in transition from old communal ways to a new one of ownership of land, of rents and violent evictions.

"These various strands in the story link so naturally with each other, the different story-lines each building its own momentum as they move towards the shipwreck and all mesh into place. Nothing in the story is unnecessary, but there is a fund of just the right detail to bring everything to life and make the characters and their fortunes so deeply interesting. Gubby, Ruairi, the various crew-members on the *Wasp*, the lighthouse cast, the map-school and of course the island community – all are painted in with such light brush-stokes and yet there is a sense of each having a full life-history."

– Rosalind Duke, Lecturer (Retired),
Development and Inter-Cultural Education, DCU

Also by Tom Sigafoos

Code Blue: A Frank Chandler Mystery
Pool of Darkness: Raymond Chandler in Ireland

County Donegal, Ireland, 1884.
Your island home is threatened
with mass evictions.
What would you be willing to do
to stop them?

The Cursing Stone

a novel

Tom Sigafoos

This book is dedicated

to the people of Tory Island

and to King Patsy Dan Rodgers, 1943-2018

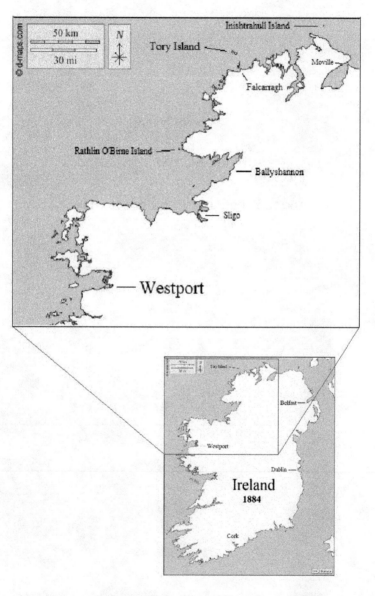

Tory Island, off the coast of Donegal, is known in ancient writings by two distinct names, *Toirinis* and *Torach*, quite different in meaning, but both derived from *tor*. This island is mentioned in our bardic histories as the stronghold of the Formorian pirates, and called in these documents *Toir-inis*, the island of the tower; and according to all our traditional accounts, it received this name from *Tor-Conaing*, or Conang's tower, a fortress famous in Irish legend, and called after Conang, a Formorian chief.

In many other ancient authorities, such as the Life of St. Columbkille... it is called *Torach*, and the present name Tory, is derived from an oblique case of this form (*Toraigh*, pron. *Torry*). The island abounds in lofty isolated rocks which are called *tors* or towers; and the name *Torach* means simply towery – abounding in *tors* or tower-like rocks. The intelligent Irish-speaking natives of the Donegal coast give it this interpretation; and no one can look at the island from the mainland, without admitting that the name is admirably descriptive of its appearance.

– P.W. Joyce, L.L.D., *Irish Names of Places, Vol I,* p 400.
Phoenix Publishing Co., Ltd., 1869

Tory Island, or simply Tory (officially known by its Irish name *Toraigh*) is an island 14.5 kilometres (9.0 miles) off the north-west coast of County Donegal, Ireland, and is the most remote inhabited island of Ireland. It is also known in Irish as *Oileán Toraigh* or, historically, *Oileán Thúr Rí*. The word Tory comes from the Middle Irish word *Tóraidhe* which means bandit.

– Wikipedia, 2021

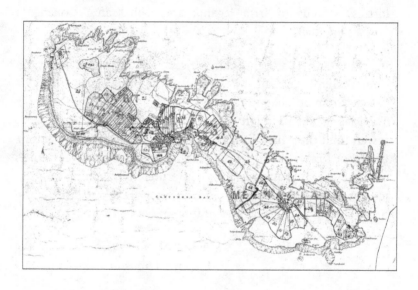

Map: Tory Island
Wikipedia Commons, Deutsch 1835, Irish Ordnance Survey

Book One

WITHIN
THIS ENCLOSURE
ARE BURIED
EIGHT BODIES
RECOVERED FROM
H.M.S. WASP
WHICH SHIP WAS
WRECKED
NEAR THIS ISLAND
22nd SEPT. 1884

Grave Marker, Tory Island

21 March 1884

Ruairí knew the path by the way it felt under his feet. The grassy walkway from East Town curved up through the sloping fields toward the cliffs on the north shore. He could see dim outlines ahead where the grass ended and the granite began. He had been out on the cliffs on other nights when a bright moon and stars lit the way, but the light had made the cliff-birds restless. The egging would be better, he knew, on a night like this one when the clouds covered the stars like a wet wool blanket.

He heard Eoghan following close behind. He knew that Eoghan couldn't see well in the dark – his shins were scarred from running at full speed into the rocks and iron ploughs that littered the fields of Toraigh Island. He could hear Eoghan's heavy breathing. Ruairí wondered if his brother realised exactly where they were.

The grassy walkway ended, and he felt the narrow dirt footpath begin. The path ran along the narrow granite ridge at the eastern end of the island, inches away from the sheer cliffs that dropped straight to the sea on both sides. He could hear the waves washing against the rocks hundreds of feet below. He shifted the bag of straw from one shoulder to the other. A gull flapped by, the sound of its wings disappearing into the darkness.

He saw a flickering light on the path ahead, and he kicked the ground in anger. He'd wanted to be the first one down.

"Hey, look," said Eoghan. "Pádraig's already here."

"Yeah, the bastard," said Ruairí. "That's twice tonight he's beat me."

"Twice?"

Ruairí was tempted to snap at Eoghan, but he didn't want Pádraig to hear them. "Don't you remember? In the match?"

"The match?"

"Remember when you got the ball away from him, and you broke away up the field?"

"Yeah, I scored a point then."

"That's the time. When you scored, he hacked me down from behind. I still got a sore rib."

"I didn't know that, Ruairí."

"Nobody else did, either."

"If you'd told me then, I'd have got him back."

Ruairí stopped and turned to his brother. "That's why I didn't tell you. This is just between him and me."

"Well, sure, Ruairí…"

Ruairí stared at Eoghan without saying anything. Eoghan fidgeted and said, "I'm sorry. I mean, I know you can take care of yourself. I just want to help…"

"If you wanted to help, why didn't you come up here faster with me?" Ruairí said, surprised by the harsh edge in his own voice. "I could have beat Pádraig up here if you hadn't wanted to piss around back there after the game."

"I didn't even know we was coming up here."

"Didn't you hear what he said? *It's a good night for eggin', if anybody's got the nerve.* Didn't you hear that?"

"No, I didn't…"

"He's been pushin' me since I can remember. Don't you see it?"

As they walked along the ridge, Ruairí could feel Eoghan trying to decide what to say. He didn't like to boss his brother around, but there were times when he ran out of patience with Eoghan's slow thoughts.

They approached an ankle-high pile of rocks where a dry, long-abandoned bird's nest smouldered. A rope was looped around an outcropping of stone, trailing over the edge of the cliff and down into the darkness. Far below, they could see Pádraig dangling at the end of the rope, holding a burning stick in one hand and a cloth bag in the other.

"Hey," said Eoghan. "I'll grab that rope and scare the piss out of him."

"No, don't do that. I got a better idea."

Looking down the cliff-face, they watched Pádraig shove the burning stick into a hollow in the cliffside. Two puffins came flapping out, and Ruairí could see a flash of their bright red beaks for an instant before they disappeared into the dark air. Pádraig reached into the hollow, pulled out an egg, and slipped it into the bag over his arm.

"I want to go down tonight," said Eoghan.

Ruairí put down the bag of straw and looked at his brother in the firelight. Eoghan was swaying back and forth, mimicking Pádraig's dangling dance at the end of the rope.

"Ah, now, Eoghan," said Ruairí, "you know what Aunt Eithne said. She'll skin us alive if she finds out we was eggin' up here."

"She won't know unless you tell her." Eoghan was still swaying, imagining the pull of the rope and the rock face under his feet.

Ruairí tried to size up his brother's mood. It was impossible to talk sense into Eoghan when he got one of his stubborn ideas, but sometimes he could be distracted. And he liked it when people confided in him.

"Come 'ere, Eoghan. I got an idea."

Eoghan grinned. "What's that, Ruairí?"

"He don't know we're here. You rig me up and lower me down. Not right beside Pádraig. Over here." He stepped away a few feet along the cliff-edge.

"Sure, Ruairí." Eoghan unslung the coil of rope from his shoulder and wrapped it around Ruairí's chest three times. Ruairí watched while Eoghan tied the bowline knot. Sometimes he got it backward, and it could slip.

Ruairí looked up at the dark sky. It was the time of year when the nights grew shorter and the days longer – Aunt Eithne said that the winter and the summer touched each other twice each year as they passed. She always lit a candle on the night when they touched. Ruairí imagined a boy and a girl walking toward each other on a path, too shy to look into each others' eyes but close enough to let the backs of their hands graze each other.

Eoghan wrapped the rope over his own shoulder and once around his chest. Ruairí picked up the bag of straw, and Eoghan's face clouded. "Why do you need the bag if you just want to scare him?"

"Watch this," Ruairí grinned, and he leaned out over the cliff. "Let me down there a little below him."

Like Pádraig, he kept his feet on the cliff face while he tilted back against the rope. The mossy rock face was slippery, and he tried to find solid purchase with one foot before moving the other. He looked up as he made his way down, seeing Eoghan and the cliff-edge recede against the sky.

The face of the cliff was pocked with deep holes, perfect shelters for the sea-birds. Gulls and gannets, graceful in flight, became puffy duck-like creatures in their shelter-holes, squawking like indignant old women when the island boys raided their nests. He wondered if they squawked and complained at other times. How would anyone ever know?

Pádraig didn't see him. Ruairí knew what it was like to grow absorbed in the in-front-of-your-nose details of egging. It was a way to keep yourself from thinking about the steep drop to the bone-shattering rocks below.

As Pádraig turned sideways to reach into a nesting-hole, Ruairí pushed himself along the cliff with his feet and snatched the egg-bag from Pádraig's arm.

"You fecker! Who's that?"

Swinging away, Ruairí grinned. "It's myself, Pádraig."

"Gimme my bag back!"

"Ah, it's only half-full. You can get more in this one." He threw the empty bag at Pádraig, who caught it and glared at him.

"Come on over here, you red-headed prick!"

"Nah, there's more eggs over here." Ruairí pulled the rope sideways, and Eoghan moved along the cliff edge, swinging him away from Pádraig.

Pádraig started climbing his rope. "I'm going to throw your fecking brother over the edge."

Ruairí put a friendlier tone into his voice. "Hey, Pádraig!"

Pádraig stopped climbing. "What?"

"I'll bet I can get six eggs before you do. If I can't, I'll give you these back."

"And the eggs you get?"

"And the eggs I get."

"All right, you piss-arse."

Moonlight broke through the scudding clouds, and Ruairí could see the silhouette of the granite ridge they were hanging from. The island looked like it had been tipped by the pounding of the ocean, exposing the unyielding layers of rock below a few inches of weedy soil. On this end of the island there was no soil at all, only a ridge of bare rocks jutting up out of the sea. The islanders called the ridge *Balor's Army* – Balor, the one-eyed king of the Formorians who could kill his enemies by staring at them – Balor, with his bloodthirsty army of mutilated and one-legged men, lined up to repel invaders from the east. Ruairí thought the ridge looked more like a row of rotten teeth.

A squawking pair of cormorants interrupted his reverie as Pádraig raided their nest for eggs. *I'd better get busy,* he thought. He pushed away from the granite wall and let his feet dangle as he swung back. Pulling himself sideways, he reached into a hole in the rock face. He felt a flurry of beating wings, and the webby feet of gulls slapped awkwardly at his arm as the birds scrambled out of the cleft and flapped away. He slid his hand over the crumbling sticks of the nest and reached inside. He could feel three eggs, still warm from their mother's breast. He slipped them one by one into the centre of the sack, separating them from each other with the straw. He hoped that they weren't ready to hatch, because it was disgusting when the eggs contained pink half-formed birds.

"I got three!" he shouted to Pádraig.

"Feck you, Mullan. I got four."

Pushing himself to the right, he felt Eoghan moving with him at the top of the cliff. He would beat Pádraig if he could find three more eggs. He scrambled toward the next recess in the cliff face, a perfect nesting hole. Reaching into the blackness, he was surprised to feel only dirt and pebbles under his hand. Had Pádraig already been in this one? Not likely – with his fixed rope, he couldn't have swung over this far. Pulling himself upward with one hand, Ruairí leaned into the hole and stretched his arm into the darkness. The narrowing cleft smelled of wet earth. He began to feel short of breath in the confining space, but he grinned when he felt the twigs of a nest.

Claws tore into the side of his face, and a bird-shriek filled the space like boiling water. He shoved himself out of the hole, swatting desperately at the thing that was digging into his skin. In the half-light he saw the glint of an eye – the eye of a hawk, a hunter – before the bird stabbed its beak into his eye and the world flared into hot red waves of pain.

≈≈≈≈≈

The peregrine falcon returned to her nest. Her leg hurt. The boy who had invaded her lair had bent her claw-joints when he pulled her away, and they would be slow to heal. With one claw she could capture only small birds. If her two eggs hatched before her foot healed, she would be able to bring back less food, and only one of her chicks would live.

Bits of the boy's flesh adhered to her injured claw. She picked and cleaned the claw with her beak. His blood tasted salty, like rabbit.

Below the falcon's lair, the cloth sack floated in the water. An incoming wave slammed it against the cliff, smashing the eggs. The loosely-woven cloth snagged against the sharp edges of the rock-face, and the waves tore the sack to shreds.

22 March 1884

The schoolmaster walked up the path to Eithne's cottage, fighting the exhaustion that weighed like wet sand on his shoulders. It surprised him to see the rising sun in a cloudless sky. In the night, clouds had blotted out the moon and stars, forcing him to sail to the mainland by dead reckoning. It had seemed to take hours to reach Magheroarty, and then to rouse the police to move Ruairí to the doctor in Falcarragh. But the clouds had vanished in the morning sunlight, and the sun shone like an indifferent, self-satisfied deity.

Eithne opened the door before he reached the cottage. The schoolmaster could tell that she had not slept either. The lines in her face looked more sunken, and her hair seemed more grey than white. She held the door open and motioned for him to come in. "How is he?"

"The doctor said that he should recover well. His concern is to keep any infection from spreading to his other eye."

"And his injured eye?"

The schoolmaster shook his head. "I'm afraid he will lose it. The wound is a deep one."

Eithne said, "I feared as much," and she busied herself with the kettle and cups. "I'm deeply in your debt, Mister Geraghty. Eoghan did not come back with you, no?"

He sat on one of the low stools near the hearth. "He wanted to stay with his brother. I imagine that he is sleeping in the doctor's barn."

They stirred their tea and sipped it in silence. He looked around the tiny cottage – the open fire, the few dishes in wooden boxes near the hearth, Eithne's bed beside the table. A low doorway into another room, separated only by a bit of worn cloth hanging from the door-frame; and beyond the doorway, Ruairí's and Eoghan's beds on the floor. His mug of tea felt heavy in his hands, and he yearned to go to his quarters in the schoolhouse and sleep. Still...

"Eithne," he said, "there is something that is puzzling me. You sent for me last night..."

"Yes, and I must remember to thank the Rodgers boy. He was half in bed when I went to their door."

"And he ran all the way to the West Village to rouse me, and then it took – what? – nearly half an hour for me to come here. But I arrived several minutes before Eoghan and Pádraig came in carrying Ruairí." He looked up from his tea to see Eithne adding a piece of turf to the fire. "How was it," he asked, "that you sent for me before the boys had got here?"

Eithne continued feeding sticks and turf into the embers. He felt a stir of resentment that she was ignoring him, but then she turned to him with the air of someone who has made a decision. "I felt sure he was injured," she said.

"But how could you possibly..."

"I knew. I can – I can *feel* what Ruairí feels."

He looked into her eyes for signs of tale-spinning. "But that cannot be, Eithne."

She looked back into the fire. "I'm sure you are right, Mister Geraghty. I am only a mad old woman, as Father Hayes tells me."

"No – please, Eithne, I don't mean to contradict you. But it – it is outside my realm of experience." He looked carefully to see if she had taken offence. "Does this – have you always...?"

"Not always. But ever since he was a wee boy I've known when he was in trouble. Or uneasy in his mind." She stirred the fire with a poker. "It was the same with his father."

"Did he know what *you* were feeling?"

"No, he was not able. But I had a sense of his mind."

The schoolmaster looked at the lines around Eithne's eyes, and the wisps of grey-white hair that brushed across her face. She had an air of self-possession that was rare among women he had met. Most had seemed nervous, apologising in advance for shortcomings he had never thought of. *I'm sorry that my Kieran isn't a better reader, Mister Geraghty. His eyes are weak, like his father's.* Eithne looked like she had never apologised for anything, or needed to.

He realised that his hands were shaking with weariness. "Thank you for the tea, Eithne. I must go and get some sleep."

"It is I who should be thanking you, Mister Geraghty."

"I'm glad that you sent for me. I'm very fond of Ruairí. He is an exceptional boy."

"That he is."

They stood, and he realised that she was no taller than himself. He said, "I hope..." but hesitated to start another thread of conversation. He felt exhausted.

"What do you hope, Mister Geraghty?"

"I hope that you will consider sending Ruairí to the mainland for an education. He has opportunities that are – that are..." He wanted to say *unprecedented*, but he had learned to avoid elaborate language with the islanders, who sometimes took offence.

Eithne resolved his dilemma by saying, "He is needed here."

He stepped to the door, torn between wanting to pursue the subject and wanting to leave. "I hope we can talk of this another time."

"Of course we will. Thank you again, Mister Geraghty."

He found himself clumsily trying to re-latch the gate that led from Eithne's front garden to the road. As he walked the weary mile back to West Town, he half-regretted that he had not made a stronger plea about Ruairí's future. The boy's life would be wasted as a fisherman on this remote and backward island... *And you're a fine one to talk, Peter Geraghty,* he imagined Eithne saying. No, he was in no shape, mentally or physically, to argue any important issues on this groggy morning. He could imagine himself and Eithne, the two smallest adults on this island of gangling six-footers, debating the future of the fifteen-year-old boy who already loomed over them. To convince Eithne to send him to the mainland would be... The phrase *no small accomplishment* ran through his mind, and he found himself half-smiling.

≈≈≈≈≈

By late morning, clusters of island women were at Eithne's door. *Mother of God, isn't it terrible about Ruairí. And how is his eye? Where is he now? We'll make a turas for him, we will.*

They left Eithne's house and walked to the East Town shrine. After they repeated three *Ave Marias* and three *Pater Nosters*, they all touched a stone near the base of the statue.

They walked on to the cove where the devil-dog had split the rock. Two stones in the cove looked like mirror-images of each other, and although the two halves were weather-worn, it was plain to see that they could still fit together. The women touched both halves of the broken stone.

They continued around the island, touching the stones at the Grave of the Seven, at the well, and at the seat of the cursing stone near the lighthouse. They were relieved that Father Hayes did not notice them as they passed his house. If the priest had asked, they would have told him the old story about how they were doing the Stations. But he did not appear.

The sun was high in the sky by the time they had circled the island and touched all of the stones. Some of the husbands and children complained about missing breakfast, but the women told them that they had been making a *turas* for Ruairí Mullan's eye, and that was that. Everyone spent the day wondering, and talking in groups, about what it would mean to all of them if Ruairí became half-blind.

≈≈≈≈≈

When the children arrived at the schoolhouse, the schoolmaster assigned the older ones to read to the young ones, and then locked himself into the upstairs room that served as his sparsely-furnished sitting room, library, and bedroom. He lay on the bed, too exhausted to fall asleep, listening to the soft voices of the children below.

After leaving the doctor's house in Falcarragh, he had ridden back to Magheroarty with Constable Gormley in the police-wagon. Gormley had talked the entire way to keep himself awake. The schoolmaster had fervently wished that the man would shut up, but out of gratitude and necessity he had listened to the Constable's stories – how he cursed the day that he'd joined the police, how he was weary of dealing with the scum of the earth, and how the Irishmen in the constabulary were despised by officers and townspeople alike. And how he hated doing evictions. It made him feel dirty, he said, throwing people out of their houses.

And Gormley had said one thing that echoed in the schoolmaster's mind. *Now they're bringing in the Navy to help with the evictions. The islands won't be safe no more.*

23 March 1884

Sub-Lieutenant William Gubby stood on the foredeck of *HMS Wasp*, exhilarated by the spray that surged up from the bow. As the gunboat made rapid headway past an island on the port side, he could see people, tiny specks of people, stepping out of their doorways to stare at the ship.

He fought an impulse to ask Petty Officer Carlisle the name of the island. He knew that it must be Tory. He had studied the map of the Donegal coastline when the *Wasp* had set out from Westport, and he had seen the tall black lighthouse perched at the top of the west-facing cliffs – and yet he found himself groping for a question or a conversational gambit that would prompt Carlisle to confirm the name.

He also found himself distracted by thoughts of the lighthouse. Something about the lives of light-keepers appealed to him deeply – the orderly routines, the unflagging dedication – but he pushed those thoughts away. He could imagine his father's scorn if he dared voice them. *Is that the height of your ambition, Young Willy? To live like a bloody monk?*

He shook away the thoughts and gripped the metal skirting that surrounded the foredeck. He could feel the North Atlantic wind at his back and see it churning the waves before the bow. He turned to Carlisle and said, "Why aren't we under sail? We ought to be running before the wind!"

Carlisle hesitated before answering the young officer, choosing his words. "We have better control when we're under steam, Sir. This channel can be tricky. There are sand bars..."

"Ah, but we must be a mile off that island – and even farther away from that one!" He gestured toward a distant low-lying land-mass, barely visible off the starboard bow.

"Oh, I warrant that it can be done, Sir. But we'll need to heel around smartly to come into the harbour at Inishtrahull, and the men would be scrambling."

He scanned the horizon and saw no sign of an island to the east. "Are we near Inishtrahull, then?"

"Another two hours, perhaps."

Gubby wondered how much coal would be consumed in the belly of the *Wasp* over two hours. He could try to draw the Petty Officer into a thoughtful discussion – *Might it speed our journey to lay on a bit of sail until the island is sighted?* – but he could imagine his father's rebuke. *What makes you think you are fit to question the judgement of an experienced man like Carlisle?*

He wondered how Carlisle saw him. A self-centred young officer who would work the men endlessly for his own amusement? With a shudder of despair, he wondered if he would ever be accepted as a man among men, sought out for his knowledge and judgement. Until that distant day might arrive, he knew it was better not to ask irksome questions. "You're quite right, Carlisle. I'm afraid that I was born too late for the great days of seafaring. Do you remember shipping out under full sail, yourself?"

"No, Sir, that was before my time."

The two men stood in silence as the *Wasp* passed the ragged row of sea-stacks at the eastern end of the island and headed into open water. With the air of someone making an important announcement, Gubby said, "Well, I think I will see what business is at hand on the bridge."

Carlisle suppressed a smile as he watched the boyish Lieutenant work his way along the deck, holding his stomach in, trying to appear less pudgy. There was no harm in young Gubby, Carlisle thought, but he wondered if there would be any steel.

≈≈≈≈≈

Gubby pressed his way along the deck, squeezing himself between the brass cannon and the canvas-shrouded pallets of cargo. He knew that the crates on the pallets contained provisions and spare lenses for the Inishtrahull lighthouse. Sailors were working everywhere, and he tried to stay out of their way.

He wondered how they had learned their roles. If someone had piped a command, he had not heard it.

He looked up at the masts where the furled sails were tied in neat bundles. Yes, the men would have needed to scramble to turn the ship toward Inishtrahull harbour, but he would have loved to see it happen. He had read Robert Louis Stevenson, and he pictured himself at the helm of a four-master, bringing treasure back from the East Indies or duelling with Spanish galleons off the coast of Cuba. Beyond the stern he could see the Bloody Foreland, the rocky shore of the north-western Irish coast where an Atlantic storm had destroyed the Spanish Armada three hundred years before. He chuckled to think that if the Armada had been successful, the *Wasp* might well be called *El Avispa*.

He drew himself up in his uniform. His father and brothers would certainly respect him now – a commission in Her Majesty's Navy was as worthy a career as medicine. They had been impressed when he told them that he had accompanied the Princes on their round-the-world trip as part of his training. It occurred to him that it would be a fine turn of events if, after he achieved command of his own ship, he could recruit a member of his family to serve as his ship's doctor. *That day will be a sweet one,* he thought.

"Beg pardon, Sir?"

Two sailors were standing beside him, and he realised that he must have spoken aloud. Feeling a hot flush on the back of his neck, he said, "No – nothing intended..."

"Sir – if we can reach behind you, Sir, we need to access the hatch..."

"Oh, right! Absolutely!" He muttered *Carry on* and stepped away from the sailors, reluctant to meet their eyes. He drew several deep breaths and pulled himself together. He was still new to the *Wasp*, he reminded himself – still finding his feet. He would have ample time to outgrow whatever discomforts he might feel. After all, he was only twenty-two.

24 March 1884

"Damn it, Eithne, this is the last straw!"

She could not resist a smile. "So you're a man with human feet after all, Father."

"Don't provoke me!" Father Hayes paced back and forth across the kitchen of the small house. "I've indulged your nonsense for too long. I told you that Rory would come to no good on this island..."

"Ruairí," she interrupted, pronouncing her grand-nephew's name with the throaty *rrr's* of the Irish language.

"Call him what you like, he's lucky not to be completely blind. He's lucky to be alive, for the love of God!"

"Thanks be to God," said Eithne.

Father Hayes scowled, listening for a hint of mockery in her tone. Her eyes were not the eyes he was accustomed to seeing – parishioners' eyes, anxious, quick to look away. Instead she met him with a steady gaze of her own. "I will not tolerate insolence, woman."

"I mean none. And my name is Eithne, Father."

Furious, he looked around the room. A black iron teakettle hung boiling over the small turf fire. The chimney did not draw well, and the smoke mixed with the steam from the teakettle to fill the room with a choking vapour. It was beyond comprehension, he thought, that one old woman could aggravate him to speechlessness.

With an innocent tone, Eithne asked, "Will you be having some tea, Father?" *Dear God,* he thought, *can she read my mind?*

"No!" he said. "Nothing at all!" His throat ached for a cup of tea, but he would not give her the satisfaction.

Eithne poured herself a cup of tea with elaborate slowness, and he wondered if she were taunting him. She took a sip and surprised him by asking, "So what is it that you would have me do, Father?"

He closed his eyes and massaged the bridge of his nose between finger and thumb, trying to regain some sense of balance. Was her question an honest one, or was she trying to draw him into a snare? The anger, the sense of righteous determination that had brought him to her house seemed to have evaporated in the smoky room. He felt weary and half-defeated, and he found it hard to find words that did not sound like pleading.

"Rory..." he said, wondering if she would presume to correct him again – "Rory is a very fine boy. There is a world of opportunity for him..."

Eithne took another sip of tea, but did not respond.

"The Word of God is being spread around the world," he continued. "The Christian countries of the world have a duty to bring the light to all of the heathen, and we need soldiers – smart young fellows like Rory – in the front line of that battle."

"So you'd have him become a priest, then?"

"It's a fine calling."

He stared at her, defying her to disagree. But she stared into a middle distance, without any hint of quarrel. "As best I can remember, Father, no one from the island has ever left to become a priest."

"Then it's about time that someone did. You practice a fanciful version of The Faith here, without many duties..."

"But is it not the faith of Saint Colmcille that we practice?"

"Saint Colmcille lived a thousand years ago. And you and I both know that over that thousand years the storytellers on Tory have – let us say, *reinterpreted* his teachings."

"We've had many a priest here that I can remember," said Eithne, "and none of them ever give out about our faith."

She is a sly one, he thought. *Now I am reduced to the posture of an old fishwife, "givin' out" about things I don't like. And the other priests – surely this island has been a dumping-ground for unfit priests since time immemorial.*

He decided to change tactics. "Eithne, what future do you see for Rory?"

She paused, as if deciding whether to turn away or to enter into battle. Finally she said, "He will be the Keeper of the Clay."

"Do you truly believe in that ridiculous business?"

"Well, Father, it has come down to me as Gospel that Saint Colmcille blessed the clay from a grave at The Church of The Seven..."

"Named after six princes and a princess from *India*, no less..."

"...and Colmcille declared that the oldest man in the Mullan family would be the Keeper of the Clay. And with Ruairí's father and grandfather gone..."

"Yes, I know all about the blessed clay. All of the fishermen come to old Sean Mullan for a tiny bit of clay..."

"That's my brother, Sean is."

"...and they keep it in the prows of their boats. But it seems to me that a good many of those *currachs* still overturn, and the men drown..."

"...and when Sean is gone, Ruairí will be the oldest Mullan man."

He drew a deep breath. "It smacks of paganism."

"And what is that, Father?"

"I think you know perfectly well what I mean. It's what the savages do in the East Indies, when they worship a volcano."

"But the rats, Father. How do you account for the clay keeping away the rats?"

"There must be some other explanation. I imagine that there never were any rats on Tory in the first place..."

"But could they not ride over on the ships, Father? And surely you know the stories from the mainland, how the rats won't come into a barn if a Toraigh man has sprinkled the clay there..."

"All I know is that it smacks of paganism. And Ruairí has a higher calling in life than to parcel out bits of clay."

Eithne took another sip of tea. "So you would have him become a priest, Father...?"

"Yes..."

"...and go to the East Indies?"

"No! That is not my point at all! He might well be sent to serve right here."

To his surprise, she smiled. "So he might, Father. So he might."

A gentle jibe occurred to him. "And if he served here, would you come to Mass, Eithne?"

"Ah, Father – you know I'm not able."

Eithne had not attended Mass in the five years that he had served on Tory. He was tempted to press her, but decided to return to the subject that had brought him to her cottage. "So you will not object if Rory chooses to become a priest?"

She looked out the small window of the cottage. "If he chooses..." she said, and then seemed to begin again. "I have seen young people make choices that they regret. If Ruairí chooses to become a priest, will he have a chance to change his mind?"

A long-buried memory flared up. *Michael, you cannot disgrace the family...* He coughed and forced out words, any words. "Of course! It is always a free choice..."

"Father," she said, "I've raised Ruairí to be his own man. Whatever he chooses, he will have my blessing." She looked at the priest with a sudden intensity. "He'll have my blessing if he chooses from his heart. But not if he chooses for any other reason."

His chest heaved with the effort to breathe. "You're not suggesting that I would press him unduly..."

"I'm not suggesting anything, Father. I'm sure he'll want to talk with you when his eye has healed. Now, would you not have some tea after all?"

≈≈≈≈≈

Madness. Sparring with a sacrilegious old crone. He stormed out of the house and breathed a deep lungful of sea-air. A spatter of rain stung his face, and he bowed his head as he hurried with long strides along the road toward West Town. Eithne Mullan - damn her and her insinuations!

You cannot disgrace the family... There was no earthly way for her to know of those terrible days so many years before, when he had come home from the seminary full of doubt and confusion. His father had nodded in understanding, but some hard facet of his mother had emerged, something impersonal and unyielding. *This will kill your grandmother if she hears...*

No, it was impossible. Eithne Mullan, who had never left Tory Island – what could she possibly know of his family disputes in Cork? She, who could not read a printed word – could she read his thoughts?

Ridiculous. His mind was his own, and under the firm control of his will. And his world was larger than hers, with ties to power that the ignorant souls of Tory Island could not imagine. The islanders might be eating out of her hand – or, he suspected, they might fear the secrets that she knew, the stories that she could tell. But he was not one of her creatures, even as she was not one of his.

And there had been a time, he knew, little more than a century before... He held back the thought, but then he decided to permit it, if only for his own grim satisfaction. There had been a time when his predecessors would have burned her as a witch.

28 March 1884

His face itched. Ruairí rubbed at the bandage, fighting an impulse to stick his finger under the cloth to scratch at the skin. His neck felt dirty and his muscles were stiff after days of dozing in bed. To distract himself, he stretched out his arms and tried to touch the tips of his index fingers.

"Ruairí?"

His brother loomed in the doorway, half-in and half-out of the bedroom. Ruairí raised himself up on one elbow. "What do you want, Eoghan?"

"Do you want to come out with me to the lobster pots?"

The light was dim. "Is it morning or evening?"

"For feck's sake, Ruairí, don't you know? Or are you coddin' me?"

"No – I really don't know. Where's Aunt Eithne?"

"She isn't here. Look – it's the middle of the day. It's raining, and I can't do nothing in the fields. The lobster pots been out there a week, ever since you was hurt. They'll be full of lobsters, either fighting, or half of them dead. Unless they tore up the pots and crawled out."

Ruairí swung his legs out to sit on the edge of the bed, and a wave of dizziness flooded over him. "Do you need me? Can't you pull them in yourself?"

"Aw, come on, Ruairí. You haven't done nothing but sleep for a week."

He looked at Eoghan's large, trusting face and realised how much his brother was missing him. He stood up and said, "Okay, I'll go with you. But you've got to peg the claws. I already lost an eye, and I don't want to lose any fingers."

≈≈≈≈≈

The *currach* bobbed and rolled in the waves, and Ruairí wished that he had talked Eoghan into setting rabbit snares. His stomach was churning, threatening to puke up the bread and jam he had eaten. He had never felt seasick before, except for the night when the schoolmaster had hurried him over to the doctor in Falcarragh. *No, please no* he thought – *I can't be one of those eejits who gets seasick.* Wasn't it enough to lose an eye?

He looked at the cliffs, trying to regain a sense of stability. They were passing the outcropping called Balor's Prison, and Balor's Army was coming into view – the tall, jagged ridge of granite sea-stacks that looked like rotten teeth in the dark. By daylight he could see the coral-coloured stone of the stacks, and the patches of green moss that clung to their near-vertical sides. Towers of small stones sat along the ridge, triumphantly built by island boys who had dared to scuttle out along the narrow path. With sacks of stones, he and Eoghan had made their way to the farthest point of the ridge, only to discover that someone had already built a tower there. Pádraig had bragged that he'd built it by himself, and no one could dispute his claim.

Ruairí looked for Balor's Fort at the top of the cliffs, but the upward angle made it impossible to see. The salt water stung the skin around the bandage over his eye…

No. It's the hole where my eye used to be.

Balor's this, Balor's that – he felt increasingly dizzy as he tried to look up at the cliffs. Balor's Fort was nothing but some old ridges in the dirt, anyway. And somewhere up there, everyone said, Balor had buried a fortune in gold. He and Eoghan had scraped at the thin soil with shovels, turning up rocks but no doubloons. They had trudged home in low spirits, wondering if the entire buried-treasure story was a snare to make island boys look foolish.

He felt the sea-change as they rounded the eastern tip of the island. He closed his eye and listened to the never-ending roar of the waves against the sheer rock cliffs on the north face. The feel of the water – the currents, the waves – everything changed.

They could drop me anywhere, he thought, *and I'd know which side of Toraigh I was on. I wouldn't even have to look.*

"There's our pots!" his brother shouted as the red-and-yellow cork floats came into view. Eoghan rowed across the path of the incoming waves, and the *currach* rocked violently. Ruairí huddled in the front of the small boat, embarrassed for his brother to see his helplessness but too miserable to care.

The curl of a tall wave drenched them and Eoghan laughed, trying to dissolve the tension between them. "Is that all you can do?" he shouted at the sea. "Hey, Ruairí! Better see if our clay is still there!"

Playing along, Ruairí reached under the prow of the *currach* and felt the cloth bag tied there. "Sure, I can feel it!"

"Then we can't sink, can we?"

"Feck, I hope not!" Ruairí ran his fingers over the sides and bottom of the boat. The cowhide felt precariously thin, humming with the force of the water beneath it. *Damned old cow skin, with a little bit of pitch smeared on it, and stretched over bent saplings...* Ruairí had seen his Uncle Sean making the *currachs* out by his lonely cottage, and he knew that Toraigh men had taken them to sea for generations. But something in him had changed, and he'd never felt so vulnerable.

They pulled close to a cork-float covered with red and yellow blotches of fading paint. Eoghan shipped the oars into the boat and reached for the long gaff that was lying by his feet, but the waves pushed the *currach* away from the float. "Here," he said, handing the gaff to Ruairí, "you'll have to get it."

Ruairí took the handle of the long pole and turned over onto his stomach. He reached with the hooked end and missed entirely, skimming the water in front of the float. Surprised and embarrassed, he pushed himself forward, swung the gaff and missed again. "This feckin' thing is too short!"

"Wait!" shouted Eoghan, rowing furiously.

Determined not to make the same mistake three times, Ruairí leaned forward and swung the gaff. A wave tipped the *currach* sideways, and he fell into the sea.

≈≈≈≈≈

They sat across the small table by the hearth, both of them embarrassed and exhausted. Ruairí could not remember when he had felt so utterly miserable. To be dragged to safety twice by his brother was humiliating, and he wondered if something inside himself had gone profoundly wrong, something that would make him helpless forever. Even after changing into dry clothes he was still shivering. Tea would help – anything to warm his insides. He reached for the teapot that hung over the hearth and lifted it over the table to pour it into his mug.

"Ruairí! What the feck are you doin'?"

Eoghan jumped away from the table as the boiling water spilled over the edge. Dumbfounded, Ruairí realised that he was pouring the water onto the tabletop, missing the mug entirely. "Feck me! Did I burn you, Eoghan?"

"You come mighty close!" Eoghan grabbed a rag and mopped the table furiously. "Can't you see what you're at?"

"I can see, but – it's not the same."

Ruairí took a deep breath and tilted the tea-kettle slowly. Hot water from the spout dribbled down the side of the mug and onto the table. He moved the kettle until he could see and hear the water pouring into the cavity of the mug. He would need to hold the mug in one hand and the kettle in the other to be sure they were lined up with each other.

"Can't you see with just one eye?" asked Eoghan.

"Sure, I can, but everything's..." He groped for words. "Everything's *flat.*"

"Flat?"

"I don't know how to tell you... Look here. If you reach out with both hands, can you touch your fingers together?"

"Course I can." Eoghan extended his arms and tapped his index fingers.

"Now close your eyes..."

"You aren't going to try any funny business with that kettle, are you?"

"No, but I want to show you something."

"All right." Eoghan closed his eyes.

"Now just open one eye..."

"All right, just one..."

"Now reach out and touch those fingers."

Eoghan brought his hands together, but his fingertips missed each other entirely. "What the feck...?"

"It's different, isn't it?"

Eoghan opened and closed his other eye. "I see what you mean."

≈≈≈≈≈

Sitting on the wall outside his aunt's cottage, Ruairí looked across the water at the mountains on the mainland. The setting sun bathed Mount Errigal in a golden glow, but Muckish and the other mountains lay mostly in shadow. He and Eoghan had once climbed Errigal. Exhilarated, they had stood on top of the triangular peak and looked back at Toraigh across eight miles of land and another nine miles of ocean. The island had looked like a long, thin ship sailing on the watery horizon.

"Ruairí," Eoghan had asked, "you know that story Aunt Eithne told us about Saint Colmcille? How he threw his stick all the way from here to Toraigh?"

"Sure, I know it, Eoghan."

"Do you think it's true?" Eoghan picked up a stone and threw it in a long, curving arc. It landed on the sloping rocky mountainside below and skittered another few yards before it stopped.

"He might have been a powerful man," Ruairí ventured, not wanting to burden his brother with his own doubts.

"It don't seem possible."

"Maybe he fitted it up with Chinese fireworks."

"Ah, sure! *Fazoom!*"

They had laughed and told each other that they would make their own gunpowder rockets. Sitting on the wall, thinking of the day on Errigal, Ruairí wondered if his brother remembered any of the plans they'd made. Eoghan had wandered over to West Town to see if anyone wanted to get up a football game. *For sure,* Ruairí thought, *it'll be a while before I'm back in the goalie box* – and then, sick at heart, he remembered that he couldn't judge distance any more. He'd be useless as a goalie – he might never play football again.

He felt the rough gauze bandage that covered half of his face. What else wouldn't he be able to do? Plant barley and potatoes? Oh, he could manage that, like the teakettle and the cup – but he'd need to keep touching everything. He was going to be one of the slow ones, no longer able to rip through his work and finish ahead of everyone else. Salty tears welled up, stinging his bandaged eye-socket. He knew how Eoghan must feel.

He sat for a long time, listening to the distant cries of the sea-birds. Was it true what the schoolmaster had said – that when people lose one sense, their others develop more? He hadn't lost his sight entirely, he reminded himself. He could still see. And read. And draw.

At the horizon, the ocean reflected the orange glow of the setting sun. Red and violet highlights were shimmering on a scattering of white clouds. *Watch the sunsets this year,* the schoolmaster had said. *A volcano has erupted on the other side of the world, and it blasted a whole island into the air. The island was called Krakatoa. It doesn't exist any more. Its dust is scattered in the air all around the globe, and when the sun shines through it you'll see colours in the sunsets that you've never seen before.*

Could Toraigh be blown up by a volcano? one of the students had asked.

Krakatoa was four times bigger than Toraigh, the schoolmaster had said, grinning wickedly.

Looking at the clouds, Ruairí found himself wondering what would happen if the dust particles of Krakatoa drifted back together. Would the reassembled island fall out of the sky and land in the ocean with a huge plop? He waved the thought away – it sounded like something that Eoghan would ask – but he felt sad that there had been a place on earth that he would never be able to see now. The schoolmaster had also talked about The Lost Continent of Atlantis, a civilisation that had disappeared into the sea. Ruairí felt small, overwhelmed by the sheer size of the earth and its islands and continents. And the earth wasn't standing still – it was washing away its seashores and blowing up its islands without regard to his wishes, or anyone else's.

He gripped the stone wall as a wave of dizziness washed over him. Toraigh didn't feel like a fragile sand-spit of an island in the Pacific Ocean. It felt hard and deeply-rooted, as though the granite under the soil reached down to the centre of the earth. Toraigh had always been his home, and always would be. He wanted to travel – beyond Errigal, even beyond Ireland – but sooner or later he would come back to Toraigh. He knew all the islanders in the same way that he knew the West Town road and the grassy path to the egging cliffs. He knew how everyone felt – how they worried about a too-rainy spring, or how the herring were running. He knew how they lived fiercely alone in their own cottages, refusing to ask for help but ready to offer it to their neighbours. He knew how shy they were with each other, how lonely – and at the same time, how they would come together to pray at the church or to drink at the pub and dance at the *céilí*. He knew them, and he knew that they knew him. He couldn't imagine that people felt this way about each other on the mainland, especially in the cities that he'd read about. On Toraigh everyone seemed to be part of a tribe, a clan, a living thing.

He squinted and looked directly at the sun as it touched the horizon, creating a red glare that made his eye ache. It looked like the fearful eye of Balor, who could kill men by staring at them. *And Balor was a King,* Ruairí thought, *and I will be King.* Of course, it was up to the islanders and their vote, but no one had ever doubted the outcome. The schoolmaster had always said he would gladly continue as King as long as necessary, but he would step down when Ruairí was ready to become King. Everyone knew the stipulations. The King must be at least sixteen – and his sixteenth birthday was less than a month away.

In his heart, Ruairí knew that being King would mean many joyless hours, listening to long-winded disputes about land markings and boundaries and marriages. But he knew that would be a price worth paying, because his life would be intertwined with the lives of the other islanders like roots in the soil.

As the sun sank into the sea, Ruairí felt a stirring to follow it beyond the horizon, to the Americas and across the Pacific to China and Japan. He had felt that surge in his heart before, when he stood on the peak of Errigal, and when he had seen distant ships sailing beyond Toraigh into the foggy North Atlantic waters. Without being told, he knew that a wise King would undertake a journey, a quest, before he took up his duties. He would see the world beyond Toraigh, and challenge himself to rise to its power. The islanders would wait for him. He would be stronger, and he would serve them better, if he tested his spirit the way a fisherman would test a new *currach*.

A fierce itch flared under the bandage near the corner of his eye-socket. He lifted the gauze and rubbed his skin carefully to avoid poking into the disturbing void where his eye had been. What will happen now? he wondered. How would they feel about him if he became the half-blind boy who could no longer stomach the rolling of the waves, the pitching of a boat?

"Ruairí?"

"*A Dhia,* Aunt Eithne!"

"I didn't mean to frighten you, Ruairí."

"No, no, you didn't. I...I didn't hear you coming."

"I came through the field." She stroked the bandaged side of his face with her hand, which smelled like soap and ashes. "I thought you'd be asleep."

"No, Eoghan and I... We went out fishing, and..."

"I know."

"And I – my stomach went into my throat, and when I tried to pull in the float..."

"I know, Ruairí."

He marvelled at the frail-looking wispy-haired woman who had raised him since he was a baby. "I can't keep any secrets from you, can I, Aunt Eithne?"

"It's not like that, Ruairí. I don't spy on you." She stood back and looked at her grand-nephew. "It was the same way with your Da and me. You're cold out here, aren't you?"

"No – well, it don't matter. Aunt Eithne, what am I going to do?"

The sun had slipped below the horizon, but brilliant colours still glowed in the sky. Eithne slipped a cloth bag off her shoulder and rested it on the wall next to Ruairí. "I was with Grainné McClafferty today. Her baby come, but it was in her backwards."

"Backwards?"

"Babies should come out head-first, but sometimes they don't." She reached over to push Ruairí's hair away from his bandage. "Grainné will be all right, but the baby died."

"That's awful, Aunt Eithne."

"It is and it isn't. Grainné and Liam has a hard time feeding the ones they already have."

Ruairí thought for a moment, hesitating to ask a clumsy question. "What happens to the baby now?"

Eithne shook her head. "They'll bury it in the graveyard down by the church."

"I wonder..."

"What do you wonder, Ruairí?"

"I wonder what it would have grown up to be? Was it a boy or a girl?"

Eithne ran her fingers through her long white hair, pulling it back from her face, her profile sharp against the fading sunset. "Anyone who's alive is lucky to be that way," she said. "I never had any children, and I never understood why it had to be that way until your Da and Mam died. Now I'm glad I have a place for you and Eoghan. Come inside."

She started to pick up the cloth bag, but Ruairí said, "Let me carry that, Aunt Eithne."

She smiled and shuffled along the path to the cottage. Following her, Ruairí realised how tiny she was, and how old and tired. He resisted an impulse to pick her up and hug her. Losing her would be too much to bear. "Aunt Eithne?"

"What, Ruairí?"

"The other night – after Eoghan and I..."

She stopped and turned to him. "After the bird stabbed you in the eye."

"Do you know what I want to ask you, Aunt Eithne?"

She smiled. "What is it?"

"Why did you send me over to the doctor? Wasn't there nothing that you could do?"

She reached up and touched his face. "When I saw your eye, Ruairí, I knew I couldn't fix it. I gave you what I had for the pain, but that was all I could do. I thought the doctor might have a chance."

The raspy call of a corncrake rose up from the field on the other side of the wall. Ruairí looked at the dark-red glow on the western horizon. He said, "I feel so tired I want to cry."

"Get yourself some sleep, Ruairí. Things will be sorted soon enough. Tomorrow..."

She seemed to be groping for words. Ruairí said, "What about tomorrow, Aunt Eithne?"

"Go talk with your Uncle Sean."

He lay down on his straw mattress, welcoming the waves of exhaustion that rolled over him. He turned onto his side and jerked back in alarm when a straw poked his cheek. *I better be careful with this eye,* he thought. *It's the only one I got.*

29 March 1884

Sean Mullan lived alone in a cottage above East Town, near the entrance to the summer cattle-fields. It was easy to keep the East Town cattle away from the barley and potato fields because the pathway could be blocked with a single gate. West Town had no natural barriers between the crops and the grazing land, and the men spent a Sunday afternoon every year building and repairing a long stone fence. Still, the West Town men celebrated with a *céilí* after it was done, drinking and dancing and telling stories. There were no *céilís* at Uncle Sean's cottage.

He found his uncle with a pitch-bucket and brush, applying a coat of black tar to the bottom of a *currach*. Sean nodded a greeting but kept working. Ruairí sat on a wooden crate and waited for what seemed like an eternity while Sean touched up the seams and edges of the boat-bottom.

"So, Ruairí," he finally said, "we'll go and look after the herd."

Although he was itching to ask questions, Ruairí knew that his uncle would only mutter until he felt like talking. They walked through the gate to the cow-pastures and closed it behind them. The pastures ran to the edge of the sea-cliffs, and Ruairí wondered if the cows got dizzy or worried about falling into the waves below.

Sean inspected the bellies and mouths of the cattle, sometimes grunting at what he saw. Ruairí followed along, avoiding the cow-patties and trying to see what his uncle was looking for. As Sean bent over to probe the udder of a large brown cow, her calf came up behind him and licked his ear. Sean laughed and patted the calf on its shoulder. Other cows turned their broad, blank faces and stared. *He is one of them,* Ruairí thought. Living away from other people, he had found a clan of sorts among the slow-moving, mildly-curious cattle.

Ruairí's stomach was grumbling by the time they walked around the pastures, and he wished that he had taken a bite of breakfast before hurrying to his uncle's house. Sean finally announced, "They'll manage for another day, they will," and headed back for the gate. Ruairí realised how little he knew of his uncle, and he wondered why Eithne's brother had chosen this lonely occupation.

Over tea and biscuits, his uncle launched into conversation without preliminaries. "How are you faring with one eye?"

"I'm doing better with it, Uncle Sean. It's hard to tell distance, but I'm learning. It itches sometimes, too. I mean where it used to be."

Sean held up his left hand, where two fingers were missing. "These yokes itch sometimes, but there's feck-all to scratch."

They sat in silence. Ruairí could hear the waves and sea-birds, and he could see the pasture-gate through his uncle's grimy window. A smell of sweat and unwashed clothing hung in the air of the cottage. His uncle sat in a rocking-chair, nodding his head in a steady rhythm.

"So what did you come to see me about, boy?"

"Uncle Sean, you're the Keeper of the Clay…"

"That's right."

"…and Aunt Eithne has always told me that someday… I mean…"

"You'll be the Keeper after I'm dead."

"But what would happen if I'm not here to be the Keeper? If I went away someplace?"

"Then it will be Eoghan."

Ruairí liked his uncle's unsentimental directness. *Yes, Eoghan will stay on Toraigh,* he realised. *He'll marry and have sons. He's like one of the boulders down by the shore.*

"Then what about King?"

He was surprised when his uncle stood up and poked at the hearth before answering. Sean sat down and looked directly at Ruairí for the first time. "They're not going to make you King."

Ruairí felt the ground slipping away from under his feet. "But everyone has always said…"

"That was before. Before you lost your eye."

"But sure, I can see to read the maps as good as…"

His uncle interrupted him. "It goes back a long way. The King has to be a whole man. The *Tuatha Dé Danann* wouldn't let Nuada be King after he lost his arm."

"But that's an old story! I mean, people were different back then. I mean, they didn't vote like we do…"

"It was always going to come down to you or Pádraig. You're the smart one, so they would have picked you. But now…"

Ruairí felt a deep wave of misery and loneliness. "But Mister Geraghty is King now, and look at him! I mean…"

"He's not a regular King. He come from off the island, and he can write and all that, but he's only King because your Da isn't here."

"But it isn't – it isn't fair…" Sean stared uncomfortably at the floor. Ruairí found himself standing, fighting for air as the cottage seemed to close in on him. He ran out the door, hoping that his uncle had not seen his tears.

≈≈≈≈≈

He ran blindly along the path away from the cottage. It absolutely wasn't fair. Pádraig as King – he'd puff up like a rooster, all bluff and bravado. And he would make a bollocks of the land-shares. Pádraig couldn't remember what happened yesterday – how could he remember the agreements from last year? Could he even read?

Ruairí stopped running when the path turned down toward East Town. Two men were unloading baskets of fish from a *currach* on the dock, and he did not want them to see him red-faced and crying. He sat on the ground by the boxy iron winch that the island men would crank to drag the large boats onto the shore. He tried to collect his thoughts. Yes, he wanted to sail the South Seas, but somehow he'd thought that Toraigh would sit motionless like a hen on an egg until he returned. But now – did it even matter if he stayed?

He ran his fingers across the pebbly ground. He sensed the deep, immovable granite underneath the few inches of topsoil. Sure, the island would last forever, after he and Pádraig and Uncle Sean and Aunt Eithne and everyone else were long dead and buried. But he'd always known that. It was the people who bound him – the neighbours in East Town, the swarm of children at the schoolhouse, the women who collected the kelp, the farmers, the fishermen – the great *We* of Toraigh. They would have made him King.

He looked up. One of the men on the dock had noticed him sitting by the winch. It was Liam McClafferty, whose baby had died. By habit, Ruairí waved a greeting, an acknowledgement. Liam returned the wave, but he turned back to the fish-baskets. Ruairí knew that something had shifted. Something in Liam's regard for him was no longer there. Uncle Sean was right. He would not be King.

2 April 1884

Father Hayes did not enjoy approaching other people. He felt more at ease when they came to him, as most of them did – nervously, expecting to be scolded. After hearing thousands of confessions, he knew the rhythms of the exchange.

Bless me, Father, for I have sinned – I have committed the sin of – and their voices would drop to a mumble.

Louder! he would insist.

I have had impure thoughts, Father.

And did you take pleasure in these thoughts?

Oh, no, Father! I tried to put them out of my mind!

Very well, then. You will say one Pater Noster and ten Ave Marias...

Their relief would flood the confessional like the glow from a lamp. *Yes, Father. Thank you, Father.*

He felt particularly awkward about approaching the schoolmaster. He strode up the path toward the schoolhouse, his mind racing with words. *Now, see here, Geraghty...* No, that could come later. *Geraghty, you have influence...* No, that was nearly a confession of his own lack of influence. *Geraghty, you're an intelligent man. I appeal to you...*

"Father!" The schoolmaster popped up from behind a pile of turf. He was wearing a hat and working with a shovel.

"Geraghty!" he heard himself replying. "What are you at there?"

Geraghty smiled ruefully at a patch of dug-up earth. "I'm looking to put in a bed of potatoes this year, but I'd forgotten what it's like to dig in Toraigh soil. More rocks than soil, really."

"You ought to get your pupils to dig for you."

"Ah, they're needed in their homes. And on their boats." The schoolmaster leaned his shovel against the side of the stone building and wiped his hands on his trousers. "What can I do for you, Father?"

"There is a confidential matter I would like to discuss..." He dropped his voice and looked around pointedly.

"Then come in, Father." The schoolmaster wiped his feet on the grass and led the priest into the side door of the schoolhouse.

Father Hayes was taken aback by how small the schoolmaster seemed when they stood next to each other. The top of the schoolmaster's head barely reached the priest's elbow, but the little man moved with an assurance that made him seem larger. They entered the schoolhouse and walked up the stairs. The schoolmaster gestured for the priest to take a seat at the table while he hung a tea-kettle on the iron arm over the fireplace. Watching him take cups and spoons down from a shelf, Father Hayes realised that the schoolmaster's quarters were nearly as tidy as his own, without the help of a housekeeper.

Geraghty sat down in a chair not significantly smaller than the priest's. "Well, Father?"

"It's about Rory Mullan."

"Oh, God help us, yes. He has lost that eye."

"Yes, and they had to work to prevent any infection of the other eye."

"*Mmm* – to avoid what happened to poor Braille."

The two men glanced at each other, and Father Hayes realised that the schoolmaster might enjoy a fair amount of knowledge beyond the experience of most islanders. "Are you a Tory man, Geraghty?"

"No, not I," said the little man. "I was born in Sligo."

"And what brought you here?"

Geraghty twisted in his chair to reach the poker and stir the fire. "You can see for yourself, Father. In Sligo I was considered a curiosity, a freak of nature. My education counted for nothing in that city. Here I am – respected. I will always be considered a blow-in, but it is easier to live with that than to be dismissed as a mere oddity." He turned to face the priest. "How is it that you yourself came to Toraigh, Father?"

45

"By the order of the Bishop," Father Hayes said quickly, with a tone that did not invite further discussion. "I shall come to the point. I understand that Eithne Mullan sent for you when Rory was injured."

"That's right, Father."

"You must have some influence with her, then."

The schoolmaster smiled. "I'm not sure that anyone can influence Eithne..."

"Well, *you* can," the priest interrupted. "And I hope that you will agree with me that it is in the boy's best interest to seek more education."

"You'll get no quarrel from me there, Father."

"Then can I count on you to support me when I propose to send Rory Mullan to Maynooth?"

"To the seminary? Are you suggesting that he become a priest?"

"Exactly."

The schoolmaster busied himself pouring hot water into the teacups, not looking at Father Hayes. After a few seconds he said, "I wasn't aware that Ruairí had expressed an interest..."

"I have not yet spoken to him."

"Would this not be huge leap for the boy?"

Father Hayes admired how cleanly the schoolmaster had put him on the spot without stating his own position. He drew a deep breath and said, "There is much at stake. The people of Tory Island practice a form of belief which is dangerously close to heresy."

The schoolmaster looked genuinely surprised. "Seriously, Father?"

"Absolutely. I fear for their immortal souls."

"But – are they not following the instructions of Saint Colmcille himself?"

The priest rose from his chair and paced around the room. "Mister Geraghty, you are an intelligent man. Surely you can see that these people are practising a fanciful brand of Christianity."

The schoolmaster said nothing. Father Hayes said, "Do you believe this nonsense about Colmcille throwing his staff from the mainland to fly out here and land on Tory?"

"I'll confess that I take that story with a pinch of salt, Father. But it is part of a long tradition of folklore…"

"There is entirely too much folklore diluting the Faith!" said the priest. "For hundreds of years Ireland was cut off from Rome, and the people fell into error. Preposterous error! Some Irish priests drifted so far as to marry women and raise families!"

The schoolmaster seemed to be suppressing a smile. Father Hayes cleared his throat and said, "Tory Island is the last outpost of this – this debased blend of Christianity and paganism. It is my mission to change the hearts and minds of these people before it is too late."

The schoolmaster offered a mug of tea, and Father Hayes sat down. Both men sipped in silence until the priest said, "I am not unaware of how the people here perceive me, Mister Geraghty. I know that they see me as a stiff-necked nuisance who knows more about Rome than about Tory. I cannot persuade them of their errors by pretending to be one of them. But Rory is one of them."

"So you believe that if Ruairí becomes a priest, the islanders will be influenced by him…"

"That is my hope."

"Are you aware that Ruairí is already destined to become the Keeper of the Clay?"

"I certainly am aware!" the priest exclaimed, louder than he'd intended to. "That is a perfect example of the paganism of this island. Is that a suitable role in life for a young man like Rory – parcelling out so-called *holy clay* that is supposed to protect fishermen and repel *rats?*" Father Hayes paused, alarmed by the sarcasm in his own voice. "Can you imagine how this would sound if I wrote about it to Rome?"

Again the schoolmaster seemed to be on the verge of a smile. "I see no harm in it, Father."

"I fear that I have strayed from my point, Mister Geraghty. For many reasons – some of them quite fanciful – Rory Mullan enjoys the respect of the islanders. If he were to follow a priestly vocation, he could return here and lead the people back to the True Faith." Father Hayes looked intently at the schoolmaster. "Will you join with me in convincing Rory to take up this opportunity?"

The schoolmaster put down his mug and stared out the window. "I will need to think on this, Father."

"Surely you do not disagree, do you, Mister Geraghty?"

"You are asking me to become involved in a decision of great consequence for the boy and for the entire island. I will need to think seriously about it."

"Very well."

"And there is something that I want to ask you in return."

"What is that, Geraghty?"

The schoolmaster pulled a handwritten letter out of a drawer. "I am writing to the Society of Friends in London. They have been generous in providing supplies to Irish communities when food is needed. I am asking for help for Toraigh, and I would be grateful if you would also sign the letter."

The priest hesitated. "I will need to study this... Do you foresee hunger here on the island, Geraghty?"

"I know this much, Father. The herring are scarce this year. Many of the men are working on the mainland, or in Scotland, to feed their families. And an Assessor is coming to Toraigh to review our rents and taxes." The schoolmaster paused. "I fear that this coming winter may be a desperate one."

The priest stood up and looked around the room, wondering if the schoolmaster's predictions were accurate, and, if they were, why he had not been made aware of them. "I will read this letter carefully, Mister Geraghty."

"Thank you, Father. Your support would be significant."

He realised that it was time to leave, but Father Hayes was losing a battle with his curiosity. "I did not come here to press you about personal matters, Mister Geraghty, but – since you have not attended mass in the five years that I have been responsible for Tory, I have assumed that you dig with the other foot. Is that correct?"

"No, Father, I'm not a Protestant. I don't attend any church."

"You're a freethinker, then?"

The schoolmaster shook his head. "Labels make me uncomfortable, Father. I'm simply plagued with doubt."

The priest looked at the tiny man as a flood of objections raced through his mind. "I trust that you do not convey your doubts to your pupils."

"I keep them to myself. I have quite enough to teach without straying into religious controversies."

As slippery as a fish, thought Father Hayes. But the schoolmaster seemed to be offering a fair bargain – to encourage Ruairí Mullan toward Maynooth if he would sign the letter requesting relief supplies. The priest rose to his feet. "Thank you, Mister Geraghty. And thank you for the tea."

"You are welcome, Father. I share your concern about Ruairí. I appreciate the importance of what you're asking me."

The schoolmaster walked with Father Hayes to the door of the schoolhouse. The two men shook hands, and the schoolmaster watched the priest walk to the road while rain-clouds blew in from the west. The lighthouse was barely visible through the afternoon mist.

15 April 1884

The Assessor looked hopelessly unhappy. He walked with a limp, pausing every few steps to shake his left foot and catch his breath. His thighs rubbed together, making a whisking sound with each step. Although the evening was cool, his bald head glistened with sweat. He carried two heavy leather cases with straps and buckles. Sheets of paper peeked out from under the buckles, as though they'd been crammed into the cases in a hurry.

"Get me a chair!" he wheezed.

Around the classroom, the Toraigh men and women who leaned against the walls looked blankly at each other. Pointing to the teacher's desk at the front of the classroom, the schoolmaster said, "Would you like to sit up here, Mister Claridge?"

"I could use some help!"

The schoolmaster nodded at Ruairí, who sprang out of his chair and took the cases from the Assessor. They were as heavy as boxes of clay. The Assessor wobbled to the front of the room, mopping his forehead with a handkerchief. He reached inside his coat and pulled out a handful of steel-nib pens and coloured pencils. Ruairí placed the cases near his chair and waited for the thank-you that never came. The Assessor gripped the seat of his chair and squeezed until his knuckles turned white while he regained his breath. The schoolmaster nodded again, and Ruairí returned to his seat.

"The Land Act," the Assessor began, "requires you..." He stopped himself and began again. "Which of you are landowners?"

The Tory men and women looked at each other again. The schoolmaster translated the Assessor's question into Irish, and all of the hands in the room shot up.

The Assessor snorted and turned to the schoolmaster. "Did you translate that correctly?"

"You asked the landowners to identify themselves, did you not?"

"Yes, but the women are representing themselves as landowners. Their husbands can speak for them."

"But many of them own land in their own right, Mister Claridge."

"That's absurd!" The Assessor mopped his brow again. "I need a pitcher of water."

The schoolmaster nodded again at Ruairí, who stood up and walked through a doorway. Claridge's heavy breathing could be heard throughout the room. "There's a lad who can understand plain English clearly enough," he said.

"He can," said the schoolmaster. "He's one of the few who can."

They sat in silence while the Assessor huffed and puffed. He turned to the schoolmaster and said, "How can all of these women be landowners?"

"Most of them inherited it, I imagine."

"Don't take me for a fool, Geraghty. Women cannot inherit land."

"They can on Toraigh."

The Assessor shook his head. Ruairí placed an earthenware pitcher of water and a tin cup on the table in front of him. With shaking hands, the Assessor poured a cupful and gulped it.

The men and women in the classroom were growing bored, and some began to drift out the door. Speaking Irish, the schoolmaster urged them to stay. The Assessor rummaged in his leather case, pulled out a map, and placed it on the table. While the schoolmaster studied it, Ruairí looked over his shoulder.

The Assessor pointed at a crooked five-sided area on the map and turned to Ruairí. "Young man, can you tell me who owns this piece of property?"

Ruairí looked at the map and said in Irish *Who works this land?*

All the men and women rose from their seats and crowded toward the front of the room to see the map. Alarmed, the Assessor shouted, "Get back! Get back!"

In Irish, Ruairí said *He wants you to go back to where you were,* and everyone settled into their seats.

"This will never do!" Claridge spluttered. "Ask someone – that man! – ask him to come up here."

In Irish, Ruairí asked the man to come forward. He stood in front of the desk like a schoolboy expecting a rap on the knuckles.

"What is his name?" asked the Assessor.

"He's Anthony Whorisky, Sir. A farmer from East Town."

"Very good. Ask him which plot is his."

Whorisky and Ruairí turned the map around and studied it while the schoolmaster tried to conceal a grin. After some conversation in Irish, Ruairí pointed to a wedge-shaped area near the shore. "Mister Whorisky works this one," he said.

"Now we're getting somewhere," said the Assessor.

"And part of this one," added Ruairí, pointing to a square plot halfway across the island from the first one.

"Part of this one? Which part?"

Ruairí consulted with Whorisky and said, "From the shrine to the chicken coop."

The Assessor rubbed the bridge of his nose. "So the map is not correct? This plot is divided between two owners?"

"Oh, no. It's his sister's land."

"All of it?"

"No, just the part that he works. The rest belongs to his sister's husband."

"Dear God," muttered the Assessor. "And is this property registered?"

"It's the schoolmaster who keeps track of this. He sorts it all out at the yearly meeting."

"It must be an interesting occasion," said the Assessor, turning to the schoolmaster. "And how do you come by this privilege?"

"This responsibility came to me on a very sad occasion," said the schoolmaster. "Ruairí's father would have made these arrangements, because he was the King of Tory..."

"The King?"

"...but he drowned while fishing..."

"Mister Geraghty!" Everyone in the room sat stock-still as the Assessor exploded. "There cannot be a *King* on Tory Island! This is part of the British Empire, and we have a *Queen*, God save her!"

"Well, we call him a King," offered Ruairí, "but it's just a way of talking."

The Assessor poured another cup of water and drank it. Whorisky said something to Ruairí, who turned to the schoolmaster. "Can he sit down now?"

"I think that's up to Mister Claridge."

The Assessor said, "Yes – no, wait. Does this man own any other land?"

Ruairí and Whorisky spoke a few words, and Ruairí said, "No, not this year."

The Assessor stood up and leaned forward on the table. "And just exactly what is that supposed to mean?"

"Well, Sir," said Ruairí, "that's part of the meeting. There's some patches of land that's better than others, so next year Mister Whorisky gets a different patch. And then the year after that..."

"You're surely not serious..."

"No, it makes it fair, you see."

The Assessor sat down heavily in his chair and muttered something under his breath. The schoolmaster said, "I beg your pardon, Sir?"

"I said *This is madness.*" He turned to the schoolmaster. "Are you teaching these people the ideas of those godless French radicals?"

"Not at all, Mister Claridge. The islanders have divided their land this way since time immemorial."

"Well, I've heard quite enough." He rummaged in one of the leather cases at his feet and drew out an official-looking document. "Mister Geraghty, since you are the *King* of this island, be advised that taxes are owed to the government. They are normally apportioned to the population according to the size of their landholdings, but it appears that on Tory everyone seems to own everything. Or perhaps no one owns anything. I do not care *how* it is divided, or even if it *is* divided. I am leaving it entirely in your hands – *Your Majesty.*"

"I do not appreciate your sarcasm, Mister Claridge..."

"Well, I do not appreciate being made to appear a fool in front of your people. And by the bye, I hope you realise that rents are owing as well as taxes."

The Assessor stood up and looked at Ruairí. "I would very much appreciate it if you could bring my papers back to my lodgings. And arrange for a boat to return me to the mainland tomorrow morning."

"I will, Sir," said Ruairí.

"You seem like a decent young fellow, and I appreciate your efforts. But I hope to never see this godforsaken island again."

≈≈≈≈≈

A school of herring swam in the deep waters off the north shore of Toraigh. The herring moved like a swarm of insects with thousands of eyes, each flicking its tail to keep pace with the great *We* of the school. Waves of hunger rippled through the shimmering cluster, leading them from the cold depths into a warm surface current. A grey seal circled the mass of fish, eating the stragglers.

2 May 1884

Gubby watched Lieutenant Evans spin the ship's wheel to the left, turning the *Wasp* in a wide semi-circle to approach Port Doon. The deep-water port of Tory Island lay in a cove between granite cliffs where sea-birds wheeled in the air. The sea was calm in the shelter of the cliffs. "This wouldn't be possible under sail, would it, Sir?"

Without looking, Evans asked, "How long have you been standing there, Gubby?"

"A few minutes, Sir."

Evans cranked the handle on the brass engine-room telegraph, ringing the bell and moving the pointer to DEAD SLOW. "You might let a fellow officer know that you're there."

"You seemed busy, Sir."

Evans snorted. "Quite so, Gubby, but I need to know who's behind me as well as what's in front of me."

"Sorry, Sir."

On the deck, the men were uncoiling the ropes and lowering the cork fenders along the side of the ship to cushion its contact with the dock. Evans moved the telegraph handle to signal REVERSE and then STOP. The forward motion of the ship ceased, and the *Wasp* drifted sideways toward the pier. For all of its weight, the steam engine provided enormous power and manoeuvrability. Gubby admired Evans's touch with the controls.

A sailor with a rope in his hand jumped across the narrowing gap from the prow of the ship to the dock. He looped the line around a stone bollard that rose up from the flat surface. Evans signalled a brief REVERSE, and the *Wasp* snugged itself against the dock. Other sailors, halyards in hand, leaped to the dock and secured the centre and stern of the vessel. They shoved the gangplank across the gap between the ship and the dock, where it landed with a clank.

"Why don't the islanders come down to the pier?" Gubby asked. "They help with the docking in Westport."

"These Tory chaps obviously don't know why we're here," Evans grumbled. "If they did, they'd be welcoming us with a brass band."

O'Donnell's head and shoulders appeared at the top of the ladder from the deck. "Captain wants to see you, Mister Gubby."

Gubby said, "Right," and then hesitated, feeling that he needed to say something to Evans. "Well," he ventured, "I suppose I'd better go see what he wants."

As he started down the ladder, he was surprised to hear Evans say, "Give my regards to the Invisible Man."

Gubby followed O'Donnell through the swarm of men on deck who were shifting the cargo pallets toward the gangplank. He was cheered by Evans's jest – the Lieutenant seemed to be accepting him.

≈≈≈≈≈

O'Donnell opened the door to the Captain's quarters and Gubby stepped inside, hoping that he had not sweated through his uniform. Wooden shades masked the portholes, and his eyes were still adjusting to the shadowy light when the Captain said, "Oh, there you are, Gubby. Sit down. Say hello to Brother Andrews of the Society of Friends."

A heavy-set man in a black coat half-rose from his chair and shook Gubby's hand. "How do you do, Lieutenant."

"Very well, thank you. A pleasure to meet you, Sir."

"Gubby," the Captain said, "I want you to escort Brother Andrews today. It seems that he is on a mission of mercy."

"Do you fear an attack, Brother?"

Andrews and the Captain laughed, and Gubby wondered if he had said something foolish. "Not at all, Lieutenant," said

Andrews. "If they attack us, we will simply take our potatoes elsewhere."

"Potatoes, Brother?"

"Seed potatoes, actually."

"Gubby," said the Captain, "organise a party of twelve men and take the ammunition-wagons ashore. You and Brother Andrews will deliver the potatoes to the schoolhouse and obtain a receipt from the schoolmaster."

"Is there a map of the island, Sir?"

"Scarcely necessary, Gubby. There is only one road across the island, and it runs past the schoolhouse. If you find yourself at the lighthouse, you'll know that you've gone too far."

The Captain and Brother Andrews both laughed again, and Gubby wondered if they were codding him by assigning him to an absurd errand. Still, a mission was a mission...

"I'll make the arrangements immediately, Sir," he said. "And Brother Andrews – I'll see that you have a comfortable seat on a wagon."

"Actually, Lieutenant, since Tory Island is only three miles wide, I'd prefer to walk." He stood and patted his ample belly. "I believe I can use the exercise."

≈≈≈≈≈

As they climbed the steep slope from the Port Doon dock, Andrews and Gubby wheezed and sweated. The sailors who pushed the ammunition-wagons tried to conceal their smiles, but Gubby could sense their amusement. He could see their wobbling parade all too clearly from the men's point of view – twelve lean sailors in the peak of physical health, led by two chubby, faltering men, one in the blue uniform of a British naval officer, the other in a black coat with the flat hat of a Quaker.

Pausing for breath as the road flattened out, Gubby admired the craggy sea-cliffs. The island looked like it had been tilted, with cliffs on the north edge that dropped steeply into the water.

The southern side, a crazy-quilt of stone walls and green fields, ran downhill to become beaches that eased into the ocean. He could see the island men ploughing the fields with horses.

A dozen houses clustered at the foot of the slope. He could see another village near the centre of the island, about a mile away. A lighthouse was visible at the far western tip of Tory, a tall black cone-shaped building surrounded by a wall.

"That is the only place you'll hear proper English spoken on this island."

Gubby looked at Brother Andrew regaining his breath after the climb, wondering if he looked as red-faced and sweaty as the Quaker. "Do you mean the lighthouse?"

"Exactly. The rest of the islanders speak Gaelic, or Irish, or whatever they call it. Not even a proper alphabet."

Gubby pondered the Quaker's comment. "In Westport the people seem to manage in two languages."

"Yes, Westport is an international metropolis compared to Tory."

"Why did the Society of Friends decide to send potatoes here?"

"The simple answer is that the people need them to grow food. In fact, the situation is more complicated than that."

"In what way?"

"Well, let me ask you, Gubby – do you come from the landed gentry?"

"No, my father is a doctor."

"Then you rise in my esteem, Lieutenant. Most Englishmen who possess wealth and power have only inherited it, and they lack the education or good sense to use it properly. They are making an absolute wreck of this country of Ireland, not to mention the rest of the Empire."

Suspicion clouded Gubby's thoughts. "You are a Quaker, are you not? You're not one of the political radicals...?"

Andrews stopped and turned to face Gubby. "Hardly, Lieutenant." He waved his cane across the panorama of land and sea. "Do you see this beautiful island of Tory?"

"Yes, of course."

"It is owned – lock, stock, and barrel – by a businessman in Manchester. He has never set foot on this soil. If I am not mistaken, he has never left England. He bought Tory from another businessman twelve years ago. That man evicted one hundred islanders – banished them to the mainland – because he thought that Tory was too crowded for farming. Lieutenant, can you imagine someone coming into your home and telling you that you were required to move, bag and baggage, because they felt that your neighbourhood was too crowded?"

"Of course I wouldn't like it."

Andrews wiped his glasses. "You are too young to remember the Irish Famine, Lieutenant. It was forty years ago, and I scarcely remember it myself. But the simple fact is that our country – yours and mine – allowed millions of Irish peasants to starve to death. They lived on property that was owned by private citizens, and our government was more worried about the rights of the landlords than the lives of the peasants. Englishmen were actually shipping food *from* Ireland during the Famine. Are you familiar with any of this, Gubby?"

"I am vaguely aware of these things, Brother, but I do not seek to understand politics."

Andrews shook his head. "Men use politics to conceal their greed. Do you understand greed?"

As the wagons lurched over the heavily-rutted road, the wheels squeaked loudly and attracted attention. Women and children came to the doors of the small cottages to stare at the parade. The noonday sun highlighted the rich greens of the fields, punctuated by bright bursts of yellow gorse bushes. Hoping to change the subject, Gubby ventured, "This island would provide a fine subject for a landscape painter."

"It would, indeed," said Andrews. "But do you realise that we are walking across the site of a notorious massacre?"

"You're joking!"

"Not in the slightest. It was in the early 1600's, after English troops had established control of Ireland. Most of the Irish chieftains had fled the country, but a few Irishmen were still brave or foolhardy enough to resist the English conquerors. They attacked the garrison at Derry."

"I've never heard of this."

"History is written by the winners, Gubby. The English were better-organised and better-equipped than the Irish. Do you realise that Ireland is the last stronghold of Celts...? No matter. The Irish rebels were defeated, and some sixty of them fled to Tory Island. The English troops pursued them and slaughtered every single man, on the very ground that we're walking on."

Gubby looked at the unremarkable green fields and the dusty road. "Here?" he said. "Is there no memorial of this battle...?"

"It was a slaughter, my young friend. The memorial is in the place-names of the fields. One is called *The Hollow of the People's Breath*. Another is known as *The Remains of the Men*. In the Irish language, of course. I would venture that somewhere along this road we will find ourselves at *The Bank of the Massacre.*"

Looking at the sea-birds wheeling overhead, Gubby listened to the murmured banter of the sailors who were pushing the wagons. "It seems extraordinary, Brother Andrews – almost impossible – that men would slaughter each other in a place as fair as this."

The Quaker paused to look directly at Gubby. "Have you considered the implications of your commission, Lieutenant?"

"I – I don't understand your question, Sir."

Andrews removed his glasses and drew a piece of cloth from his pocket to wipe them. The sailors who were pushing the wagons paused and looked to Gubby, who gestured for them to continue along the road. The Quaker waited until they had passed before he spoke. "Did you see those women in the houses back yonder?"

"Yes, Sir."

"Do you realise, Lieutenant Gubby, that someday your Captain may issue orders to fire your ship's cannons at that settlement?"

"Surely not! For what purpose...?"

"That settlement might be accused of harbouring a hotbed of insurrection and treason. The orders to destroy it might come from the Admiralty."

"You must be having a jest at my expense, Brother Andrews. Surely no civilised country..."

"And if those orders are issued, and you do not obey them, Lieutenant, you will find yourself clapped in irons for insubordination. And if one of the men fails to obey, he will find himself imprisoned, or hanged."

Gubby tried to collect his thoughts, but he was unable to respond. Andrews continued, "You have sworn an oath to a military organisation, Mister Gubby, and military organisations require absolute obedience. Two hundred and fifty years ago you might have been assigned to slaughter those sixty Irish rebels." He replaced his glasses and put his handkerchief away. "Happily, we find ourselves on a more civilised mission today. Shall we continue escorting our potatoes to the schoolhouse?"

They walked together for several minutes without speaking until Gubby broke the silence. "Brother Andrews?"

"Yes?"

"Do you not find it ironic that your mission of mercy is being carried out by the military organisation that you condemn?"

Andrews broke into a wide grin. "Sometimes," he said, "in combating sin, one must join hands with the devil himself."

≈≈≈≈≈

The schoolmaster was the smallest man Gubby had ever seen. He tried not to stare while Brother Andrews produced copy after copy of many-paged documents for the schoolmaster to sign. *Had Andrews carried potatoes instead of paper,* Gubby thought, *the people of Tory would have been provided with another bushel of food.*

Although the schoolmaster was, Gubby guessed, no more than four feet tall, he had the air of an imposing person, someone to be reckoned with. His head was the same size as Andrews's head, and the schoolmaster had wavy black hair in contrast to the Quaker's stringy locks. His arms and legs were short, but his chest was thick as a barrel, and his posture was impressive.

Resisting an impulse to help the men unload the potatoes from the wagons, Gubby stood sweating in the May sunshine, drawing himself to full height. Children drifted out of the cottage-sized school building to gape at the sailors. They had dark hair like the schoolmaster, but they seemed taller and thinner than mainland Irish children. He wondered if they were descended from the Spanish sailors of the Armada.

A wiry red-haired boy with a brown eye-patch caught his attention. Unlike the other children who huddled in a giggling cluster, the boy wandered comfortably among the sailors, taking a close look at the wagons and pallets and potato-sacks without getting in anyone's way. He approached the schoolmaster and Brother Andrews, making his presence known without intruding on their conversation. Gubby felt a stab of jealousy – the boy moved with a graceful poise that he wished he could emulate.

The schoolmaster noticed the boy and said, "Ruairí, come and meet Brother Andrews."

The Quaker nodded gravely as he shook the boy's hand. "Very pleased to meet you."

"I'm pleased to meet you, Sir," the boy said with an odd, formal pronunciation. "Can I ask you a question?"

"You certainly may, my boy."

"Are you taking the spuds to the other islands, too?"

The Quaker looked surprised. "Why, no – they are all intended for here." He nodded an acknowledgement to the schoolmaster and added, "Thanks to the persistent efforts of your Mister Geraghty."

The boy turned to the schoolmaster and asked, "Sir, would it be all right if Eoghan and myself took a sack or two to Inishtrahull?"

"We can discuss that later, Ruairí," Geraghty said hurriedly. "Would you see about getting the others back to their lessons?"

The red-haired boy said, "Yes, Sir," and he began rounding up the straggling schoolchildren. Andrews leaned over to the schoolmaster. "What is the lad speaking of?"

"Inishtrahull," said the schoolmaster. "A desolate island north and east from here. A godforsaken rock in the sea."

"And are the inhabitants in need?"

"I can imagine that they must be." The schoolmaster seemed embarrassed. "They are certainly a deserving lot. I must confess that it did not occur to me..."

"...when you wrote to ask for help for Tory? Do not blame yourself, Mister Geraghty. None of us can be responsible for all of the ills of the world." He turned from the schoolmaster. "Gubby!"

"Yes, Sir?"

"I will take my leave of you now, Lieutenant," Brother Andrews announced, stuffing the signed documents back into his coat-pockets. "I am going to pay my respects to the local priest."

"Is that because..." Gubby hesitated, trying to frame the question that half-formed in his mind. *Did clergymen routinely make courtesy-calls on each other, or would the Quaker challenge the priest to a theological debate?*

Andrews seemed to read his mind. "Father Hayes also signed the letter that requested these food-supplies."

"Would you like us to accompany you, Sir?" asked Gubby.

"No, don't trouble yourself, Lieutenant." The Quaker broke into another wide grin. "But if the good Father locks me in his house to try to convert me, I trust that you'll rescue me by force of arms."

"Of course we will, Sir," said Gubby, with equal gravity. "Or at least we won't sail away without you."

"I'd appreciate that, Lieutenant. Farewell, then." The Quaker strolled off toward the cottages of West Town.

A stocky sailor approached Gubby. "That's all of the potatoes unloaded, Sir."

Gubby turned to the schoolmaster, feeling that some sort of courtesy was in order. "We – we must be getting back. "

"Thank you, Lieutenant. I wouldn't want your Captain to think that you'd deserted."

Gubby began to object before he saw the broad, friendly grin on the schoolmaster's face. "No indeed," he said, "although I daresay that it would be difficult to desert on this island. There appear to be precious few places to hide."

"You might be surprised, Lieutenant," said the schoolmaster. "You might be quite surprised."

Gubby walked back to the empty ammunition wagons where the sailors were idling in the sunshine. As he approached, they took positions at the sides of the wagons. He felt that he should say something, but the phrases that crossed his mind – *Well done – Back to the ship – Follow me* – seemed weak and unnecessary.

"Do we not get a fortnight of shore leave here, Sir?" ventured one of the men with a mock-innocent expression.

Gubby decided to share the jest. "No, the Tory women are too amorous. The Captain has decided to take us somewhere safe, like Calcutta."

The men chuckled and pushed the wagons onto the road. Walking ahead, Gubby felt a stab of loneliness – he would have enjoyed continuing the banter. Without Andrews, he was alone at the front of the column. But this was the price of command, he reminded himself, and he decided to exert a bit of authority by setting a brisk pace.

≈≈≈≈≈

He tore into the plate of cold roast beef and potatoes that the cook had set aside for him. He had nearly run to the Officers' Mess, half-dizzy with hunger after reporting to the Captain. Russell had dismissed him with an amused nod – *Well done, Gubby. I hope that the islanders have the good sense to plant those potatoes instead of eating them.* He shovelled in heaping forkfuls of food until the acidic craving diminished in his stomach, and he felt himself relax.

Were they codding him, indulging his boyish eagerness by assigning him frivolous tasks? He could take a different attitude, he realised – instead of accepting the potato-delivery mission with an enthusiastic *Yes, Sir!* he could have scoffed politely and acknowledged the assignment with an ironic phrase – *Whatever may arise in the line of duty, Captain.* Perhaps they would grow to respect him sooner if he stood more firmly on his own two feet.

"How you doing there, Gubby?"

Armstrong sat down across the table from Gubby with a mug of tea. Gubby felt a pang of worry – he had seen less of Armstrong than the other shipboard officers, and the Gunnery Officer seemed to wear a permanent scowl of disapproval. Armstrong kept to himself, tinkering with the mechanisms of the brass cannons and updating the inventory of munitions.

"I see that you deployed the wagons to carry potatoes onto the island," Armstrong said.

"All in the line of duty, of course."

"Did you detect any stiffness in the bearings?"

Surprised at being asked a serious question, Gubby looked Armstrong full in the face. "As a matter of fact, they squeaked quite loudly."

Armstrong nodded and exhaled loudly. "That confirms what I've been saying. The Admiralty has been buying its equipment from the lowest bidder, and those bearings do not meet the specifications. They are going to fail – and until that happens, they will produce enough noise to wake the dead."

"Can nothing be done about this?"

"I am sorely tempted to replace them, but that would require a press-fitting apparatus which is available only in England. And our Captain…" Armstrong looked Gubby in the eye. "These issues fall on deaf ears when I bring them to our Captain."

Thrilled to be taken into Armstrong's confidence, Gubby said, "Perhaps I can find an opportunity to mention the wheel-bearings to the Captain."

Armstrong nodded approvingly. "That can do no harm. Perhaps you will have better luck than the rest of us."

"Are there other improvements that need to be made on the ship?"

Armstrong laughed. "We could entertain ourselves with that conversation for weeks. Do you realise that we're floating around in an experiment?"

"An experiment?"

"Yes. This ship and her sisters are the first generation of gunboats to be built mostly from iron and propelled by steam."

"But the sails..."

"The sails are there for window-dressing. How often do you see them unfurled?"

"Well, not often..."

Armstrong sipped his tea. "The sails are the least of the problems. Have you noticed the skirting around the deck?"

"Do you mean the metal plates that keep everything from falling overboard?"

"Exactly. Wooden ships had railings, but we have this bloody metal skirting. Do you realise what is wrong with it?"

"I confess that I do not."

Armstrong looked at him for a moment before responding. "Master Gubby, is this your first posting on a ship of this size?"

"It is."

"Do you realise that in a storm we may well be swamped by high seas?"

"But has this not been taken into account...?"

Armstrong snorted with derision. "This boat has been designed around the requirements of the steam engine and boilers, with little regard for seaworthiness. The next time that you are on deck, take a look at the skirting plates and notice the size of the drain-scuttles."

"The slots at the bottom where the water runs off the deck?"

"Exactly. The scuttles are only an inch high."

"I'm afraid that I do not see the significance…"

"Those scuttles were designed for riverboats. If it rains on a riverboat, or if the cook spills a pail of water, it can easily run off. But if an ocean wave breaks over us, think of the deck as a giant dish – and then calculate the weight of the water that will be confined in that dish."

"But it is not a seamless dish. We could lift sections of the skirting…"

"That is exactly what our Captain said when he and I had this conversation. I told him that it would be impossible for anyone to lift the skirting under those circumstances."

"Then the skirting should be removed…"

Armstrong smiled. "And when I proposed that, he told me to mind my own business."

Gubby could imagine the *Wasp* tilting sideways with tons of water trapped on the deck. "Perhaps we should drill some drainage-holes in the skirting plates."

Armstrong grinned. "Perhaps you can suggest that to the Captain when you approach him on the subject of wheel-bearings."

The two men sat in silence as Gubby finished his food and Armstrong sipped his tea. Gubby felt a sense of inclusion, of belonging on the *Wasp* for the first time. He wondered if he might accompany Armstrong on his rounds as he calibrated the cannons and rotated the stocks of munitions.

"May I ask you something, Armstrong?"

"Yes, Gubby?"

"Am I being made a fool?"

"Why do you ask, Gubby?"

"This…" He groped for words. "This mission, this business of delivering potatoes, like a greengrocer…"

Armstrong took a long sip of tea. "We were all young officers once, you know. We have all had our share of…"

"…of fools' errands?"

"...of assignments which other officers might feel were, well, beneath their dignity." Armstrong smiled at the morose young Lieutenant. "Do not lose heart, Gubby. Perhaps your next mission will challenge your military skills."

I have enjoyed the company of Andrews on this mission. I have always imagined Quakers to be dour and unpleasant individuals, but Andrews shows a sunny disposition and a willingness to talk at length about nearly any subject. Some of his statements do alarm me, and I have cautioned him that his negative remarks about the military life may be taken as disloyalty to the Queen. But there is no malice in the man.

I have determined to keep this journal because I can no longer confide in anyone. My legs grow weaker by the day, and the mere act of standing can become painful. I am fortunate to have O'Donnell as my Commander's Aide. He fetches and carries everything that I ask without question. He accepts that I am afflicted with a temporary palsy, which a more experienced man might question.

I have heard that remarkable cures have been effected by the use of magnetism, and that a physician in Cardiff employs those techniques. But it is impossible to maintain discretion in England, where rumour-mongering seems to be inescapable. I would feel less exposed if such treatments could be had in another country. I will have O'Donnell collect whatever newspapers and journals he may find in Westport, although I doubt if this ignorant island traffics in any publications beyond almanacks and tide tables.

I must find a safe place to store this journal so that it does not come to the attention of prying eyes. Even the finest cypher can be broken.

4 May 1884

"I'll think about it, Father."

Ruairí hurried down the steps from the priest's house and turned quickly toward East Town. The wind chilled him, and he realised that he had been sweating in the house.

The moon was rising over the eastern cliffs, appearing large and waxy as it hovered close to the horizon. He followed the road past the straggling West Town cottages and turned onto a footpath that led down to the shore. The path led between two fields, one thick with half-grown barley and the other a tangle of potato plants. A corncrake rasped in the barley field, sounding close enough to touch.

The small inlet at the shore was only a notch between piles of boulders, scarcely large enough for a single *currach*. Eithne had led him to the inlet when he was barely able to walk, telling him the old stories. *And this is where Saint Colmcille first set foot on Toraigh. You can see his footprint on the rock over there. Sure, he must have been a big fellow!*

Ruairí sat on a boulder and listened to the gurgling waves slap against the rocks and sand. He could still see the delight in Eithne's eyes when she recited. She knew the stories by heart, and she loved to perform them with sweeping gestures. *And then the chieftain of the island come down, and he told Colmcille that he needed permission to set foot on the island, and that permission was going to cost him dear! But Colmcille, as smooth as you please, says, I am a poor man of God, and I have no money. But I will build a monastery on your island, and people will come here from all over the world.*

And the chieftain says, You have some right cheek, coming here and telling me you're going to build anything on my land. This island is mine from shore to cliff.

And Colmcille says, I don't need so much land, only what my cloak will cover. And he lays his cloak down on the ground, and it's old and threadbare, no bigger than a worn-out nappie, half-nothing. Surely, says Colmcille, you would not deny a Godly man the land under this cloak.

And the chieftain says, If that's all you want, you can have it. But if you build a monastery there I won't be dining with you, for there won't be enough room for a soup-pot and a piss-pot both.

So Colmcille thanks him kindly, and the chieftain laughs at him, but the next thing you know the cloak starts to grow. It spreads out like butter in a skillet. It grows right under their feet where they're standing, and it goes over the rocks of the shore and up the fields. And then over the road, and up towards the cliffs. And up along the road to Port Doon and Balor's Fort, and the other way over the lakes and fields and all the way out to where the lighthouse is now. It covers the whole island, and while it grows, it changes from an old raggy thing to a fine bearskin with a furry collar and a gold clasp. And after it reaches every corner of Toraigh, every nook and inlet and turf-stack and hole-in-the-ground, Colmcille reaches down and lifts it up. Quick as anything it shrinks back, but it's still a beautiful bearskin cloak that's fit for a powerful king, and he puts it over his own shoulders. Then he looks the chieftain right in the eye and says, Thank you, as saucy as you please.

And the chieftain starts roaring at him, You tricked me! And then he whistles, real loud, and his dog comes galloping across the fields. It's a hell-hound, for sure, as big as a horse, with red eyes and fangs as long as my fingers. And when it swings its tail, it splits a rock clean in two – that rock over there!

The chieftain whistles again and points at Colmcille, and the hound comes at him like he's going to tear his throat out. But Colmcille makes the Sign of the Cross, and the dog falls over – dead!

Ruairí half-remembered Eithne falling down onto the ground, mimicking the collapsing dog. Had she really done that?

He must have been very small, so she must have been fourteen or fifteen years younger, juicy, full of life. She seemed old and brittle now, although she sometimes surprised him with her strength.

So the chieftain sees that he can't match Colmcille's power, so he gets on his knees – he remembered Eithne rising to her knees to mimic the chieftain – *and he's the first on the island to convert.*

Ruairí remembered the joyful feeling of walking hand in hand with his aunt, picking wildflowers and sitting stock-still until the rabbits came peeking out of their holes. Those days seemed like a lost dream. Now it felt like a heavy cloak had been tied onto his shoulders – not a kingly robe like Colmcille's, but a cold, sodden blanket. *You are going to be a man soon, Rory,* the priest had said. *You have choices to make, and others are depending on you.*

He turned from the cove and headed back along the footpath to the East Town road. His aunt would be able to help him think clearly.

≈≈≈≈≈

Eithne sat at the table by the hearth. Heaps of yellow flower petals lay in piles on the table, between dishes of sunflower seeds and a bowl of reddish powder that Ruairí did not recognise. Eithne was grinding the seeds and petals in an earthenware pot, mixing a spoonful of the compound with a pinch of reddish powder, and wrapping each spoonful of the mixture in a paper square. A neat line of paper packets, each twisted and tied with thread, sat along the edge of the table.

"Hello, Aunt Eithne," he said.

She glanced up and smiled at him. "How are you keeping, Ruairí?"

"Oh, I'm fine."

They sat in silence for a few minutes while Eithne twisted the paper packets and looped white thread around them. When she finished the row, she said, "How did you get on with Father Hayes?"

He groped for words to express his murky feelings. "I don't exactly know, Aunt Eithne. He says…"

"He is grim, is he not?"

"Yes, it's something like that…"

"I know."

He looked at his aunt, at the fragile blue veins under the nearly-transparent skin on her forehead. "Were you listening outside his window, Aunt Eithne?"

"I can imagine what he said to you. But tell me yourself."

"He told me…" The words felt artificial in is throat, like reading out loud from a book in a schoolroom, but he continued. "He told me that we – all of us on Toraigh – are all in danger of going to hell."

Eithne smiled and scooped more petals and seeds into the pot. "He has told me that, too."

"Do you believe him, Aunt Eithne?"

She took an iron spoon and began crushing the contents of the pot into a sticky paste. "I've seen my mother in dreams," Eithne said. "She does not seem to be in a place of torment. But she seems quite sad, not like the angels who are supposed to be singing in heaven."

"Is that what we see in dreams? The other world?"

"That's not for me to say, Ruairí. Sometimes I dream of things that cannot happen in any world."

"Father Hayes seems quite certain."

"What did he say to you?"

"He said there is a college on the mainland where priests are trained. He says that I can go there for an education."

Without looking up, Eithne asked, "An education to become a priest?"

"Yes."

She put down the pot and the spoon. "And why does he tell you that we are all doomed to hell?"

Ruairí drew a deep breath. "He said that over the years the Irish people and the Toraigh people have drifted away from what he called the True Faith. He said that our stories about Saint Colmcille and other things have become fairy-tales."

"I see no harm in them."

"Do you worry about going to hell, Aunt Eithne?"

Eithne sat quietly for a moment. "That is the question, isn't it?" She reached into the bowl and picked out a sunflower seed. She said, "I've spent my life trying to keep things alive. When the babies are born, or when people are hurt, they could die. I know the island medicines, the ones that we can make ourselves. I don't know how they work, but most of them are made out of living things." She put the seed on the table in front of Ruairí. "It hurts me to see other people being hurt. I don't always know what to do, but sometimes I can help." She gestured at the paper packets. "Sometimes the medicines help ease the pain. But sometimes the only thing that stops the pain is death."

She stood up and walked to the doorway. Ruairí looked at his aunt as she stood silhouetted by the moon and the clouds, like a picture in a frame. "I'm old, Ruairí, and sometimes I am very tired. I don't know how much longer I am going to live."

"But sure, Aunt Eithne, you're not going to..."

"Wait, Ruairí. That's not what I'm meaning to say. Some day we will all know what happens after we die. But now, while I am here, I am going to make it my business to try to take care of life. I will leave it to Father Hayes to worry himself sick about what happens after."

Ruairí felt a surge of love, mixed with a dark memory of the priest's words. "Aunt Eithne?"

"Yes, Ruairí?"

"Father Hayes said... He said that if we are not doing the work of God, then we're doing the work of the devil."

Eithne laughed. "If I ever meet the devil, I'm going to take him by the hand and lead him over to Father Hayes's house. Then we'll hear some *craic.*"

Ruairí looked at the tiny tooth-shaped sunflower seed with its black stripes and hard shell. "So you would not want me to become a priest, Aunt Eithne?"

"Ruairí, I want you to choose for yourself. But make sure that you know exactly what you're choosing." She closed the half-door and turned to the fire. "Father Hayes isn't the only one on Toraigh who worries about you. Have you spoken with Mister Geraghty?"

"Only at school."

Eithne put sticks and turf into the fire. "Even if he is not a Toraigh man by birth, he can see very clearly." She turned to Ruairí and touched his hand. "Talk with him before you choose."

6 May 1884

"Mister Geraghty?"

Ruairí had never tried to enter the schoolhouse at night. A lamp was shining in the upstairs window, but there was no response when he knocked on the locked door. He walked around the building, avoiding the garden where potato-plants were beginning to sprout. His foot bumped against something, and a shovel fell with a scrape and a loud bang. He looked around self-consciously to see if he'd disturbed anyone, but there were no nearby houses. The schoolhouse, he realised, had been built on the outskirts of the town to muffle the noise of the children.

He circled the building without finding any trace of the schoolmaster. Standing at the front door, he dug in his pockets. He found a stub of a pencil, but nothing to write on. *And sure, what would I write if I had paper?* he asked himself. *Mister Geraghty, can I talk with you about my whole life?*

Aunt Eithne had been maddeningly vague when he had asked her for advice, pretending to be busy and forgetful. *Mister Geraghty is your man,* she kept saying. But he had not felt easy about going to the schoolmaster. For all that Mister Geraghty did, sorting the land and writing the necessary letters and documents, he lived a life that was separate from the world of Toraigh. He did not have the easy comradeship with the islanders that Ruairí felt in his bones, the sense of family roots that had intertwined for generations. He could never say, as Uncle Sean had once said about the Ó Mianáins and the Ó Dúgáins, *Our people have known their people for a thousand year'.*

And he had hesitated because he knew what the schoolmaster's advice was going to be. *Go and see the world!* he would say, as he had said so many times in the classroom. *The earth is growing smaller. A man can press a telegraph key in Ireland and his click will be heard in China. In the same instant!*

Not a month later, like a letter on a ship. And the man in the office in China can click back an answer. Immediately! The schoolmaster had posted a Morse Code chart on the wall, but Ruairí could not imagine the difference between the sounds of dots and dashes, or how anyone could sort out the clatter in his mind.

Sure there is no telegraph on Toraigh, Ruairí had said in class.

Oh, but there will be when they run a cable out from the mainland, the schoolmaster had said. *They'll do that when it becomes profitable.* And Ruairí had resisted the complicated and intimidating idea. A telegraph could click all day, but it could not catch fish or grow potatoes. Could dots and dashes feed a family?

He sat on the stone wall beside the schoolhouse. The beacon of the lighthouse seemed exceptionally bright in the moonless night. At the top of the tower, it looked like a single dazzling eye under a pointed crown. *Like Balor with his one eye,* he thought. *Like me.*

He was surprised to see the dim shapes of three men walking across the field. Two tall men and a short one – clearly the schoolmaster. He called out *Mister Geraghty!* and they stopped. The three shapes huddled in a brief conversation, and the two tall men turned away, walking back toward the north cliffs. The short figure of the schoolmaster continued toward the schoolhouse, and Ruairí could hear the scuff of his boots as he approached.

"What brings you out at this unearthly hour, Ruairí?" the schoolmaster puffed as he climbed over the stone wall.

"I was hoping to have a word with you, Mister Geraghty."

"I wish that you'd let me know beforehand. I was not expecting you."

"Have I interrupted something, Sir?"

The schoolmaster looked across the field. The figures of the two tall men had disappeared into the shadows. "There are more things in heaven and earth, Ruairí, than are dreamt of in your philosophy," he said.

"Sorry, Sir?"

"Shakespeare," said the schoolmaster. "Sometimes useful for obfuscation. Come in."

Geraghty unlocked the schoolhouse door and led Ruairí up the stairs to his quarters. The schoolmaster hung up his jacket, and Ruairí saw that his boots were streaked with mud. They sat at the small table. The schoolmaster broke open a pack of biscuits, but he did not offer to make tea. There was no fire in the hearth.

"So what is your concern, Ruairí?"

Ruairí scanned the schoolmaster's face. He seemed tired and worried. "Perhaps I should come back another day, Sir…"

"No, no. Carry on."

"Well, a few days ago I spoke with Father Hayes…"

"Ah! Go on."

"…and he thinks I should go to a school in Maynooth."

"To become a priest?"

"Yes."

"And how do you feel about that – that career?"

Ruairí shook his head. "I don't know how I feel, Sir. Or what to think. That's why I've come to you."

The schoolmaster took a biscuit from the pack and bit off a corner. "I'll not say a bad word about Father Hayes," he said quietly, and then he looked directly at Ruairí. "Toraigh is a very small island, and we cannot afford to have strife between himself and myself."

"Yes, Sir."

"So you will promise to keep our conversation in absolute confidence?"

"I will, Sir."

"Do you remember the names of the planets that revolve around the sun?"

Ruairí hesitated, offended by the school-ish question. "I think I do, Sir, but…"

Geraghty waved his hand as if to dispel his words like smoke in the air. "Forgive me, Ruairí. It is an old teacher's habit to answer a question with another question. But do you remember that the earth goes around the sun?"

"Yes, but…"

"Do you realise that only a few years ago you could have been burned at the stake for saying that?"

"You must be joking, Sir."

"Not in the slightest. And you could have been tortured into swearing that the sun goes around the earth."

His mind whirling, Ruairí said, "It does appear that the sun moves… But who would torture someone over – over such a thing?"

"I'm afraid that it was the priests in Father Hayes's church who did the torturing."

"But why…"

"They had taught that our earth was the centre of the universe, and they thought it would undermine people's faith to think otherwise." The schoolmaster took a deep breath. "I believe that they had other motives, but that is only speculation."

"Was this during the Dark Ages?"

"I'm afraid it was more recent than that – only three hundred years ago." The schoolmaster sighed again. "But torture was not the exclusive province of Father Hayes's church. The Swiss and American Protestants have inflicted their share of pain."

"Sure, this must have happened when – before we knew about things? When people were ignorant and afraid?"

"Let me show you something." The schoolmaster rummaged in a wooden chest and pulled out a book. Ruairí read the title: *On the Origin of Species.* "This was published only twenty-five years ago," said the schoolmaster. "It describes how life adapts to changing circumstances. Does that sound reasonable?"

"Sure, like we grow crops in the summer and fish for the rest of the year?"

"Yes, but think about bigger changes. What if a plague came over Toraigh and killed everyone except people with red hair?"

"Then it would be just me and Peggy Doohan and a few others left."

"And if you and Peggy Doohan had children…"

Ruairí blushed. "Sure, they'd all have the red hair."

"Yes – it's more complicated than that, but you've got the basic idea. Now, does that say anything about whether there's a God in Heaven or not?"

Ruairí hesitated, wondering if the schoolmaster was codding him. "I thought we were just talking about things we can see."

"We are. But there are a remarkable number of people – in Father Hayes's church and in others – who would like to burn every copy of this book. They want to think that the Good Lord is organising everything for a purpose, and if all of the people on Toraigh end up with red hair, it's because God made a decision and not because a plague came along and killed off everyone else."

"Well, I can see how they could argue…"

"Ruairí," said the schoolmaster, "you can see both sides of the question. If you go to school as Father Hayes suggests, you'll be told that there is only *one right answer*. And that you'll have to teach other people that there is only *one right answer*. Could you do that?"

Through a small window, Ruairí could see a sliver of moon in the sky. "No, Mister Geraghty, I don't think I could."

"Then your calling may be elsewhere."

"But Sir, that's what I am so confused about. I don't know what my calling is."

"I'd be very surprised if you did know," said the schoolmaster.

"Did you know when you were my age?"

"When I was fifteen, I was so desperately lonely that I gave no thought to the shape of my life. It took another fifteen years for me to feel the ground under my feet." He smiled to himself. "That ground happens to be Toraigh Island."

"You were lonely? At fifteen?"

"I was not like you, Ruairí. I was not born into a family of clans. I was a misshapen…"

He stopped talking, and Ruairí felt dizzy at the glimpse of the schoolmaster's physical limits and his un-befriended life. They sat in silence until the schoolmaster said, "You came here tonight to talk about your future, not my past. I would like to return to that subject."

"Yes, Sir."

"Like Father Hayes, I hope that you will choose to get an education. But I suggest that you take up a field of study which leads to broader opportunities."

"Do you think I could become a schoolmaster?"

"Oh, dear God… No, Ruairí, let us start with a different idea. Have you ever looked inside a clock?"

"Yes, I have. One time I took the schoolroom clock down from the wall and opened the back, but…"

"But what?"

"When I saw all of the wheels and springs inside, I closed it and put it back."

"And why did you do that?"

"Because it all looked like it would be easy to break, and if I broke it, I couldn't fix it."

"That was sensible, Ruairí. But you had the curiosity to take it down, and then the good sense not to toy with it. But most importantly, you've seen what practical men can accomplish."

"Are you suggesting that I become a clock-maker?"

"No, not exactly. My point is that clocks have been designed by a new breed of man. Not by philosophers and theologians, but by practical men who value what they see. The kind of men who have explored the globe, who have printed books, who have built…"

"…the lighthouse?"

"Exactly!

Ruairí imagined a panorama of men constructing bridges, sailing the oceans, building cities. "Then what do I need to learn?"

"I know of an opportunity that I would find enjoyable if I were your age. The Admiralty is organising a cartography school in Westport..."

"Cartography?"

"Map-making. They are seeking to employ bright young lads, and... Ruairí?"

"Yes, Sir?"

"You look suddenly downcast. Does this idea not appeal to you?"

Ruairí groped for words. "Drawing maps on paper... It wouldn't be like building something, would it?"

"No, but if you seek to find work in the construction of buildings, I'm afraid that you'll find yourself carrying a hod of bricks. Englishmen see themselves as the architects and foremen, and they see us as labourers. But map-making is a skilled trade – one that will always provide a sound wage. And..."

The schoolmaster interrupted himself, but Ruairí could imagine the words he'd suppressed. "Mister Geraghty, do you mean to say that it would be a good trade for a one-eyed Irish boy?"

"There are limits in life, Ruairí. Some we're born with, and others are imposed on us by..." He paused and reconsidered what he was going to say. "No matter. As a mapmaker you can learn a great deal, and I daresay that it will lead to other opportunities. I can write a letter of recommendation for you, if you wish."

Ruairí tried to imagine what life in Westport might be like. He was not entirely sure where Westport was, and he had a vague impression of cargo ships and dark warehouses. It would not be like life on Toraigh – no web of stories to link everyone, no families that had known each other for a thousand years...

"I'll have to think about this, Mister Geraghty."

"As you should. But if you have any interest at all, please tell me before the first of June. I'll need to write by then."

"What happens on the first of June?"

"Nothing happens then, except that some officious fellow in the Admiralty has decreed that all applications must be submitted by then. The world on the mainland runs very differently from the world on Toraigh – as you'll see." The schoolmaster yawned. "I need to get some sleep, Ruairí. We can talk of this more on another day."

Ruairí thanked the schoolmaster and walked down the stairs. As he heard Mister Geraghty locking the door behind him, he saw the early sprouts in the schoolmaster's potato patch. He wondered what would happen if someone in the Admiralty decreed that the potatoes must be ready to harvest by the first of June. He walked home in the moonlight, wondering what combination of skill and learning he'd need to draw a map.

23 May 1884

Liam McClafferty nursed his pint until he could not stand the taste of the warm spitty dregs. He did not want to go home.

His baby boy had been in the ground for two months, but his wife was still out of her mind with grief. Sitting beside the unlit hearth, Grainné would cry for hours, pausing only to curse him for making her pregnant in the first place. He cooked the meals and tried to reassure the children that their mother was only sad because the baby had died, but they were all wearing thin under the constant assault of her bitter tears. *Is Ma away with the fairies?* his daughter had asked, but he could give her no answer. After the children were in their beds, he would leave his wife in her shell of misery and walk to the pub.

He sat alone. The other men sensed his need for quiet, and they did not encourage him to pass remarks about the fishing or the barley crop. He could hear them talking about who might become King, and he was briefly tempted to join in the conversation, but he could not summon the effort. He nodded instead to Peadar, who pulled another pint and sat it in front of him without comment.

Eamonn, he thought. If the boy had lived, his name would have been *Eamonn*. He felt a twinge of sympathy for his wife's bottomless anguish until he remembered her harsh words. *Sure you just plow me like a bull, Liam. I might as well be a dirty old cow for all you care.*

He took a sip of his fresh pint. Grainné should be in the bed soon, and if she wasn't, he'd be able to fall asleep regardless of what vile words she might spew at him. He drank slowly.

≈≈≈≈≈

The moon cast sharp shadows as he walked along the road to his cottage. He held up his hands and wiggled his fingers. The shadows of his fingers looked elongated and menacing, like the tentacles of a stinging jellyfish. He half-laughed at himself, a grown man acting like a child with shadow-puppets. If his wife could see him, she'd give out scorn for hours.

He tried not to look in the fields. On bright moonlit nights *She* would be there, watching. *She* had never come after him, but *She* didn't need to – his legs felt weak and watery when he only thought about her.

He glanced toward the north shore of the island, where the fields ran up to the cliff-edges. On a foggy October night when he was a boy, his father had told him that was where *She* lived. *She* was a half-human thing who would bite off his nose and ears, his father had said, and fear had washed over him like a cold tide when he saw a tall skin-and-bones shape in the field. When he went back the next morning, he found a cross of crude sticks with ragged clothing and a clump of seaweed-hair tied onto it, but he could not bring himself to believe that the homespun scarecrow was the same greedy creature that his father had pointed out in the darkness. He had seen something more, something worse.

And that had been – how long? – twenty years ago? But the black-clad figure never faded from his imagination. He had taught himself to keep his eyes on the road in front of his feet, not looking into the fields. If he did not look at her, perhaps *She* would not come after him.

≈≈≈≈≈

He was relieved to see the light in his cottage window ahead. The small mis-matched windowpanes were too grimy to see through, but they glowed with the light from inside. Grainné must have left the lamp on – or had she forgotten to turn it out when she crawled into bed? Was she still awake, working up a huge ball of wrath? He hesitated, and then hurried toward the door – his door, a haven away from night-spirits and prowling witches.

Inside the cottage, he closed the door and lowered the latch quietly into place. Grainné lay asleep on their bed by the hearth, whimpering quietly in the grip of a dream. Enormously relieved, he turned to the table and blew out the oil-lamp.

But *She* was at the window, looking in, her head and ragged hair silhouetted against the moonlight. He could not see her eyes, but he could feel them, feel their black, gnawing hunger. *She* turned slowly from the window and moved toward the door. He could hear the scratching of her claw-fingers across the wood of the door and then along the stone wall of the house.

He choked out *Go away!* and Grainné sat bolt upright in bed. *What are you saying, Liam?*

Did you see her?

See what?

Her! he shouted. He flung the door open and looked outside. He thought he could see the tail of a black dress disappearing behind the corner of his house. Shouting *God damn you!* he ran to the corner and stared into the darkness. A small shape, the size of a cat, darted away from his house and disappeared into the shadows of the field.

25 May 1884

The lifeboat rocked in the Atlantic swells, and Gubby pulled his coat tighter as the salt water sprayed over the stern. As they rowed away from the *Wasp*, he could barely see the darkened vessel in the pre-dawn mist. The glow of the lighthouse reflected off the clouds, but the ship lay in the shadow of the cliffs on the north side of the island.

"Take care as you approach the inlet," Evans had cautioned. "If you draw too close to the cliffs, the waves will push the boat against them. And beware of the tall sea-stack to the left of the inlet. The waves swirl around it, and the water between the stack and the cliff is constantly churned into a boil. Head into the calmer water to the right side of the stack, and you'll find it dead easy to row from there into the inlet."

Gubby sat in the stern of the lifeboat, manning the tiller while eight sailors rowed in a heavy rhythm. Three policemen sat in the front of the boat, looking anxiously at the churning water ahead. He looked for the sea-stack, hoping that the ceaseless pounding of wind and waves had not deflected the boat off-course.

The mist thinned, and the stack rose up out of the sea like a pillar of granite. High overhead it leaned into the island, forming a dramatic arch. They had drifted, but not far. Gubby leaned hard on the tiller, remembering to *Tiller Toward Trouble*. For once his weight worked to his advantage, and the lifeboat swung to the right.

Without being instructed, the men on the port side rowed harder, helping to adjust the course. One of the policemen gestured toward the right side of the stack, and Gubby could see the opening in the cliffs. He pulled the rudder back to a straighter course, feeling the interplay of waves, wind, and oars.

The lifeboat moved forward into the calmer waters at the mouth of the inlet.

Gubby felt the crunch of the keel on the sandy bottom, and he signalled the men to ship the oars. Two of the sailors jumped out and waded forward, pulling the lifeboat with a rope. The boat listed sideways, and the policemen scrambled out onto the narrow beach.

Leaving two men to watch the boat, Gubby and the other sailors followed the policemen along a path that led up from the water at a steep angle. The Chief Constable held a finger to his lips for silence. The path met another footpath halfway up the incline, and the Constable pointed in the direction of the side-path. It ran to the mouth of a small cave in the rocks. Smoke drifted out of the cave entrance, mingling with the mist from the sea.

The Constables dug in their pockets for matches and lit three kerosene lanterns, casting a harsh light over the cliff face and the faces of the sailors on the path. The Chief Constable shouted "Police!" and stepped into the entrance to the cave.

Dense smoke filled the air in the cave, obscuring a glowing turf fire on the floor. Coughing loudly, the three Constables stepped into the smoke and kicked at the fire. A boot clanged against metal, and a few seconds later there was a loud pop of breaking glass. "Get back!" the Chief Constable shouted, and the sailors retreated to the path outside the cave.

The Chief Constable emerged, spluttering and shouting, "Get some water up here!" Gubby nodded to two sailors, and they hurried down the path. The Constable wiped his eyes with a large soiled handkerchief, muttering *Irish bastards*. The policemen conferred angrily among themselves while the remaining sailors, relieved and giddy, tried to conceal their smiles.

The two sailors came back with canvas buckets of seawater. The Chief Constable ordered them to douse the fire, and they stepped into the mouth of the cave. A cloud of steam and smoke billowed out as the fire died with a loud hiss.

As the air cleared, the Constables led the sailors back into the cave. The fire still smouldered under an old copper tank. Short lengths of corroded pipe lay scattered on the floor, and a corked bottle of clear liquid sat next to the broken pieces of another bottle.

The Chief Constable snatched up the bottle and turned angrily to the sailors. He shouted, "Collect this lot and fetch it back to the boat!" and Gubby nodded another confirmation to the men. Two sailors pushed gingerly at the still-hot copper tank while others picked up the loose pipes and fittings from the floor. As they carried the pieces back down the path to the lifeboat, Gubby overheard the Chief Constable grumbling to the other police officers. *What kind of fools do they take us for? I smell a rat.*

≈≈≈≈≈

"Well, Gubby, how did the mission go?"

The Captain's quarters felt warm and cheerful after the cold, rainy hour in the lifeboat returning to the *Wasp*. Gubby and the Chief Constable stood before the mahogany desk where the Captain sat, looking crisp and alert in full uniform at four o'clock in the morning.

Gubby had given some thought to his answers. "The men did well, Sir. Lieutenant Evans's directions were accurate, and there was no problem with the landing. We assisted the Constables in their duties, and we brought the evidence back to the ship."

The Captain nodded. "Did you encounter any resistance?"

"No, Sir. The islanders – that is, the perpetrators were nowhere to be found."

The captain turned to the Chief Constable. "And are you satisfied with the support that the crew provided?"

The Chief Constable scowled and said, "Your men were quite satisfactory, Captain."

"Very well. Thank you, Gubby. You may go."

Gubby looked at the Captain and the Constable, and it seemed clear that they were going to continue to talk. "If I may, Sir," said Gubby, "I should very much like to hear the Constable's thoughts on the night's events."

"I have no objection. What do you say, Constable?"

The Chief Constable looked at the floor. Gubby felt a cold wave of worry, and he wondered if he had blundered into some embarrassing private matter. He was about to excuse himself when the Constable blurted out, "It was a bloody balls-up, Captain."

The Captain snapped to attention, glaring at Gubby. "How was the raid a balls-up?"

The Constable growled, "It was a sham. That wasn't a still. That bloody tank hasn't been used to make *poitín* for years, if it ever was. Some bastards put those pieces in that cave, and they lit a fire, and I'll wager that they were sitting up on those cliffs laughing at us! Who the bloody hell do they think we are? That ruse wouldn't fool a child!"

Gubby felt a hot flush on the back of his neck. The Captain said, "You suspect that the lifeboat was seen, then?"

"No! That – that fraud was planned long before today. There is an informer on the island, but his reliability..." The Chief Constable's voice trailed off in disgust.

The Captain shook his head. "Well, there you have it, Gubby. That will be all."

"Thank you, Sir." Gubby fled the cabin, immensely relieved and embarrassed at the same time. His cheerful report of the success of the mission must have sounded ridiculous to the Constable and the Captain alike. He felt like a clumsy ten-year-old child, barely tolerated in the company of angry adults. Would the world ever feel solid under his feet?

26 May 1884

"Uncle Sean, have you lived away from Toraigh?"

"Oh, I have, boy!" Sean spat out his words with a bitter edge, and Ruairí wondered what festering wound he might have touched.

"Father Hayes spoke to me about going to a school for priests."

Sean chuckled. "I'll wager that my sister had some words about that!"

"But what do you think, Uncle Sean?"

"Father Hayes is different. When old Father Kerrigan was here, he brought everyone out to bless the grave where the clay comes from. Father Hayes has done aught of that."

"He doesn't believe in the clay?"

"I don't know what your man thinks. He won't trouble himself to speak to me."

"He told me that we had made Colmcille's life into fairy-stories."

"No!" Sean looked deeply shocked.

"He said that we're the last of something here on Toraigh."

"The last of what?"

Ruairí groped for words. "He said that the Church on the mainland is different, and that they're better for it, and he said that we're clinging to the Old Ways…"

"He said that, did he?" Sean spat on the floor. "I'll tell you something about the mainland. Do you know how your father died?"

"He was out fishing, and he drowned, no? Him and Uncle Daniel?"

"Eithne never told you the end of it?"

"I don't know…"

"They was out setting lobster-pots, like you and Eoghan and every other Toraigh man that ever was. And nobody knows exactly what happened to them, if they ran up on a rock, or if something came up out of the water and tipped them over. It don't matter.

"Daniel must have drowned right away, because his body washed up here on the island, down by the lighthouse. But your father – he must have hung onto something. Maybe part of the *currach*. He hung on, and the tide carried him across, over to the Bloody Foreland.

"He had a strong grip, your father did, like you yourself. He hung on, and it must have been in the middle of the night that he drifted up against a rock. So he climbed onto that rock and let go of the *currach*. And then the morning come."

Sean breathed loudly through his nose. "We heard about it later. Some mainland people come down on the beach, and they seen your father out on the rock. He was waving to get their attention, and they seen him. And do you know what those bastards did?"

"What, Uncle Sean?"

"Nothing! Nothing at all is what they did. They seen your father out there, half-dead and barely hanging on, and they did feck-all to save him!"

Sean spat on the floor again. "We didn't know nothing about it at the time. Your Da kept waving and trying to get them to help him, but then the tide come in, and it lifted him right off those rocks. He was wore out, and he couldn't swim. His body come up on the shore with the tide."

"But why wouldn't they help him? Didn't they have a boat, or..."

"Over there they think it's a curse if you save a drowning man. They think if you save your man, you cheat the sea, and the sea gets you."

"You mean like when Eoghan pulled me out of the water...?"

"You weren't drowning then, I don't suppose. And you weren't wrecked... But that don't matter. What I'm telling you is, those people over on the mainland, the ones that you say Father Hayes thinks so much of – they let your father die out there on that rock. A Toraigh man wouldn't do that."

They sat without speaking for a long time. Ruairí thought of the stories that he'd heard about his father – his rich voice, his energy, the jokes he loved to tell in the pub. He did not remember his father – he'd been only a year old, and Eoghan hadn't yet been born, when Brendan Mullan died. He was lost in a reverie when Uncle Sean surprised him by speaking again.

"I'll tell you another thing about the mainland. That's where you're going, isn't it, Ruairí?"

"I'm thinking I might..."

"You have to watch out for those women! You have to watch yourself!"

"What do you mean, Uncle Sean? What do I have to watch for?"

"I don't mean all the women! I mean the ones down by the docks. The doxies. The hoors."

Surprised by the outburst, Ruairí sat without speaking. Sean took a pipe out of his pocket, rummaged for tobacco and matches, and made a long procedure out of lighting the pipe. Sensing that his uncle was calming down, Ruairí finally said, "I don't know what you're talking about."

Sean puffed on the pipe a few times before speaking again. "If you go off the island," he said, "there's some women you need to stay away from. They sell their bodies for sex, and they do it with as many men as has money. Sailors off the ships. Lonely men. Do you know what I'm talking about, Ruairí?"

"I – I think so..."

"The Good Lord give us a powerful urge to do what it takes to make babies, but it can get us into trouble." Sean puffed furiously on his pipe. "A lot of them doxies has the pox, and the men that does it with them gets it, too."

"The pox? Smallpox?"

"No. They can cure the smallpox. There isn't a cure for this kind of pox."

"What happens if somebody gets the pox?"

"After a while they can't walk right. Some of them goes blind, and some goes daft. But it don't happen right away. And it's not the same for everyone."

"How can you tell if they've got it?"

"You can't. Not by just looking, you can't."

"So, if there isn't a cure..."

"Then a person who's got it, if they got any conscience, they stay away from other people. They keep it to theirselves and take it with them when they die. Mostly they live alone."

Ruairí stared at the man who sat across the table from him, the man he had always known but, he realised, had not known at all. Before he could bring himself to ask, his uncle interrupted his thoughts. "Times was bad when I was your age, Ruairí. There wasn't any jobs in Ireland, or nothing to eat. So I went over to England. They needed stevedores, and I could lift and carry as good as the next one, so I got work. But I got lonely one night, and I had too many pints. I was down by the docks, and there was this girl. She wasn't any older than you are now, I don't think. She had a sweet voice, and nobody hadn't talked to me for days, and..."

"And what, Uncle Sean?"

"And – and I felt sorry for her. One thing led to another..."

They sat in silence for a while. Ruairí asked, "Does anybody know?"

"They all know, on the island. And your aunt makes me some kind of powder that I take. That's saved me from the worst of it."

Sean put down his pipe. "It's a good thing that I had a brother, and he had your father for a son, or I'd be the last Mullan man. The last Keeper of the Clay."

Ruairí thought of his uncle's solitary life of closed doors and quiet, lonely routines. But the islanders still came to him to mind the cattle and parcel out the clay. He wasn't completely alone.

Had he wanted a family? Ruairí was certain that he had. "I think you'd have been a good father, Uncle Sean."

The old man turned his head away. "Go home, Ruairí. I can't tell you what to do, but watch yourself. Whatever you do, watch yourself."

27 May 1884

The brass cannons gleamed in the sunlight when Armstrong removed the canvas shrouds. Gubby followed the Gunnery Officer as he circled the deck, inspecting each of the four cannons and making notes in a leather-bound journal. He loosened the catches and swivelled each cannon in a full circle. He tilted the barrels up and down through their full firing ranges before securing them back into their straight-ahead dead-level positions. To Gubby, the posture of each cannon looked like a precise, muscular salute.

He followed Armstrong down into the munitions locker. He admired the spotless precision of the room – the snug fit of the ammunition-cases into the steel shelves, the purposeful safety brackets that held them in place, the unambiguous log-books that tracked the age and disposition of every shell. Precision, he realised, would be absolutely necessary in dealing with munitions – it would be folly if unexploded shells were permitted to roll about loose.

"These are the armour-piercing shells," Armstrong was saying, pointing to a wooden case on a tall rack. "They detonate a few seconds after impact, not on impact."

"So that they explode on the inside, and not on the outside?"

"You have it, Gubby. Now, these down below are anti-personnel ordnance. These on this side are the concussion devices, and those over there produce shrapnel. They detonate without impact. Do you see the implications for the trajectory?"

"Well – I suppose you'd want them to be as far away as possible…"

"Exactly. Shallow arc, nothing over thirty degrees elevation."

Feeling a glow of pride, Gubby watched from the doorway as Armstrong made notes in the logbooks. It had not occurred to him to apply for Gunnery-Officer training, but he felt that he could grasp the principles quickly. He would need to shed some weight, he thought ruefully, to fit more comfortably into the narrow munitions room. Perhaps this was the motivation that he'd been waiting for.

"Of course," Armstrong said, "you realise that all of this is bollocks."

Surprised, Gubby asked, "How is that, Sir?"

Armstrong wrinkled his nose. "We are patrolling the shores of Great Britain," he said. "There are no strategic targets. And if a foreign warship was dispatched to invade Ireland, it would blow the *Wasp* out of the water before it came within the range of our popguns."

"But do these have no purpose whatsoever?"

The Gunnery Officer looked amused. "If the Admiralty had its way, we would be sailing up the Nile to reinforce Gordon at Khartoum. But we are hamstrung by politicians, and so we find ourselves transporting policemen and civil servants around Ireland."

"It does seem rather a waste..."

"We might fire a blank charge to salute the Queen's birthday. And, I imagine, we might need to discharge shrapnel if a civil disturbance arises. Do you remember Napoleon's *whiff of grapeshot?*"

"He fired into the mob to end the Reign of Terror, did he not?"

"Not exactly. He was on the side of the revolutionaries, firing at the Royalists who were attempting a counter-revolution."

Gubby's face darkened, and Armstrong smiled at the Sub-Lieutenant's distress. "History is a nightmare, Gubby, but we are spared its confusions. Her Majesty's Navy is clearly on the right side of things."

"Yes..." Gubby looked into an open crate of anti-personnel shells. A criss-cross pattern was moulded into the explosive head of the device, creating a jacket of small metal rectangles that would fly apart when it detonated. Each piece would become a red-hot spinning projectile.

"Armstrong," he heard himself asking, "do you remember the day that we docked on Tory Island?"

"I certainly do."

"If we had received orders to fire onto the island – into East Town, for example…"

"Well, it wouldn't have done to fire from the inlet." Armstrong seemed to shift into a different mode of speaking, looking at a point over Gubby's head. "That would have meant firing up from the dock and over the hill. The trajectory would have been too high, too much like firing straight up into the air."

"But what I'm asking…"

"We'd have needed to sail out of there and proceed to the south of the island. It would have been prudent to lie at least two hundred yards offshore, out of rifle range. Then it would have been a straightforward matter."

"Would you have fired a warning shot?"

"That would depend…" Armstrong stopped and looked at Gubby. "You were talking to the Quaker, weren't you?"

Gubby felt a profound sense of emptiness. "I was."

Armstrong took a deep breath and drew further back into himself. "I would suggest that in the future you avoid such conversations."

Feeling the ground slipping out from under his feet, Gubby ventured, "I was only asking theoretically…"

Silence filled the small room like fog. Armstrong finally said, "The Navy has been good to me." He spoke in a formal tone, as though he were making a speech. "My father was a blacksmith, and he had a difficult time feeding us with his earnings. Now I have a family in Herefordshire, and a small holding there."

"I did not mean to suggest…"

"When I trained in gunnery, we were advised to remember three words: FIRE AND FORGET." Armstrong placed the logbook firmly in its slot and nodded toward the door. "We're done here," he announced.

Gubby stepped into the passageway and watched Armstrong secure the door. The Gunnery Officer looked up and locked eyes with him. "Whatever virtues the Quakers may have, they are demoralising. And it did not appear that your friend had ever missed a meal."

≈≈≈≈≈

"Do you have anything to eat?"

Gubby stood in the doorway to the galley, half-in and half-out. The cook looked up from the account-book that was spread out over a steel table. Two sailors who were scrubbing pots and pans glanced at him and turned back to their work. He knew how he must appear in their eyes – nervous, nearly trembling, begging for food an hour after the midday meal. But the craving in his stomach overwhelmed his impulse to flee.

The cook closed the account-book and looked at him with some sympathy. "I believe that there may be some meat and cheese left over," he said. "Shall I send it to the Officer's Mess?"

"I'd be very grateful if you would."

Gubby retreated down the passageway in relief. *Why is it not like this for everyone?* he wondered. Other men seemed to be able to work for hours, even days, without eating, but his appetite always flared into an acidic craving that drained his energy and made it impossible for him to concentrate. The longer that he put off eating, the more his hands twitched. The pressure of his appetite had ruined his many attempts to grow thinner, to shed the belly-fat that everyone seemed to look at. *What is wrong with me?*

Nearly in tears, he entered the Officer's Mess and was relieved to find that the table was vacant. He could not face Armstrong again – not yet. Could he face anyone? Could he manage at least one encounter which did not leave him feeling like a child, a dunce?

He heard footsteps in the passageway and tried to compose himself, not wanting one of the men to see him in such despair.

But it was the cook himself who carried the tray into the Mess. Gubby saw with a flash of giddy relief that the cook was nearly as fat as himself, and that he also needed to turn sideways to squeeze through the hatch.

The plate on the tray was stacked with slices of ham, cheese, and bread, and the mug of tea smelled delicious. "Would you care for some mustard or chutney?" the cook asked.

"No, no thank you – this will be grand." With trembling hands, Gubby picked up a slice of cheese and popped it into his mouth.

The cook turned to leave, but hesitated. "Are you quite well, Sir?"

"Yes, thank you – I'm sorry to have troubled you…"

"Was today's meal unsatisfactory? If you did not care for it, I could have provided…"

"No, not at all! I mean, I was not dissatisfied…" Trying to remember the noon meal, Gubby began to feel a wave of desperation washing over him. What had been served? He looked into the sympathetic eyes of the cook, and he turned away as tears welled up in his own.

"You're having a difficult time, aren't you, Sir?" the cook was saying.

He wanted more than anything to blurt out a *Yes!,* but pride gripped his throat like a hard fist. He heard himself saying, "There is a great deal to learn… I want so very much…"

"The Navy may not provide a career for everyone," the cook said.

Gubby's stomach surged again, and he ate a bite of ham. The very act of chewing and swallowing seemed to help him relax, but he felt embarrassed by the power of his need. He could not bring himself to look at the cook.

"May I ask you something, Sir?" the cook was saying.

"Of course, ah… What is your name, cook?"

"It's Hatton, Sir."

"Yes, Hatton?" He felt odd speaking formally to the fatherly man.

"There was apple tart and cream at the noon meal here in the Mess. Did you have any of that, Sir?"

Gubby said, "I did," but he did not add that he had eaten two helpings. "Why do you ask?"

"Our Navy pastries are made with a great deal of sugar, Sir. It makes them more palatable, and most of the men who eat them feel energetic afterward. But I have seen that it wearies some men. It makes it difficult for them to perform their duties."

Gubby was stunned. "Surely you don't mean that sweets... But I've always found them rather bracing!"

The cook hesitated, choosing his words. "Most of us find sweets to be bracing, as you say. But for some there follows a lassitude, an unsteadiness of nerves. It has nothing to do with character and everything to do with digestion."

"Are you saying that if one does not eat sweets...?"

"Some men find themselves more steady with another bowl of soup rather than sweets."

Gubby studied the cook for the first time. Hatton was nearly bald, and the fringe of hair around his temples was grey. Gubby realised that he might be the oldest man on the *Wasp*. "Are you quite certain, Hatton?"

"I am a cook, Lieutenant, not a doctor. I can only tell you what I've seen."

Gubby looked at the food and realised that his craving had already diminished. He looked back at the cook. "Thank you, Hatton. Your – your advice means a great deal to me."

"Hatton!"

Both men snapped around to find the Captain standing at the door. Gubby jumped to his feet.

"Have you taken it upon yourself to serve the Officers' Mess personally?"

Before Hatton could speak, Gubby interrupted. "I asked Hatton for – for some food, Sir."

"Was our noonday meal not sufficient for you, Gubby?"

Gubby could think of nothing to say. Hatton said *Excuse me, Sir* to the Captain and squeezed out through the door. The

Captain stepped into the Mess-room, closed the door, and sat at the table. Gubby looked at the ham and cheese on the plate, his stomach churning again.

The Captain surprised him by taking off his hat and sitting back in his chair like a man contemplating an interesting situation. He drummed his fingers on the tabletop. "How long have you been with us, Gubby?"

"Two months, Sir."

"And you trained in the Midshipman's School, yes?"

"I did, Sir."

The Captain looked around the small Mess room. "I have not spent a great deal of time with you, Gubby. Perhaps I should."

"I would welcome that, Sir."

"There are some points of navigation that you might find valuable... Evans is acquainting you with our practices, is he not?"

"To the extent... I mean, Lieutenant Evans is a busy man, and..."

The Captain said *Hmmm* and drummed his fingers again. "I fear that we have somewhat neglected you, Gubby. That is going to change."

Gubby felt a wave of relief and joy, and his craving seemed to evaporate. His struggles were not entirely his own making. He looked at the Captain, wondering if he could say *Thank you, Sir* without a quaver in his voice.

"But there is another issue at play here." The Captain looked Gubby in the eye. "You are too familiar with the men."

"Sir?"

"We officers must keep our own counsel, Gubby. It is unseemly for us to be – to be fraternising with the crew."

"I did not realise that I..."

"In wartime, fraternising with the enemy is a crime. In peacetime, fraternising with the crew... It creates problems, Gubby. It undermines discipline."

"Yes, Sir. I did not realise..." Gubby let the sentence drop as he saw a flicker of pain across the Captain's face.

The Captain stood up abruptly, and Gubby rose as well. "Tomorrow," the Captain said, "O'Donnell will notify you about a schedule of training. You do not have a sextant of your own, do you?"

"No, Sir..." The Captain grimaced again. Gubby said, "Is there anything..."

"As you were, Gubby!" the Captain snapped as he strode out of the Mess. Gubby listened to his footsteps as the Captain moved down the passageway, and he heard a door open and close. He sat down and wrapped pieces of the ham and cheese in bread. He wondered what was bothering the Captain, but his mind drifted what the Captain had said. *We have been neglecting you... There are some points of navigation...* He took a deep breath and relaxed for the first time in days. Perhaps things were truly going to change.

2 June 1884

The schoolmaster looked forward to his Monday-evening chess games at the lighthouse. He found himself hurrying along the road toward the west end of the island, warmed by the late-evening midsummer sunshine. The light would linger until nearly midnight, when the sun dipped briefly below the horizon for a few brief hours before rising again. If he lived further north, he knew, the sun wouldn't dip below the horizon at all.

In the Sligo library, he had walked around the huge globe in the reading room, admiring the mechanics of the solar system. The slight tilt in the axis of the earth created summers and winters, frozen poles and temperate zones where people could live. It disturbed and depressed him to think that a church – Father Hayes's church – had fought so viciously against the emerging discovery that the earth was not the centre of the universe. What difference did it make? It was still a magnificent, awe-inspiring world.

Tory Island, for example – *Oileán Toraigh,* a small place, and a demanding one, where two hundred people could find food and raise families if they worked hard enough. But they had to know the island – its slanting fields, its unforgiving cliffs, the moods of its winds and tides. To the schoolmaster, the island and the islanders seemed to be the body and fingers of a living organism.

The stone-and-earth walls along the road were riddled with rabbit-holes. Nibbling grass in the fields, the rabbits snapped into alert poses as the schoolmaster approached, and then dashed into their warrens with comic urgency. *No natural enemies,* he thought. *At least not many.* They were a nuisance for the islanders who tried to plant vegetable gardens, but somehow a balance was struck, and the rabbits generally minded their own business and kept away from the cottages.

Natural enemies...natural selection... The schoolmaster reminded himself to keep his copy of *On the Origin of Species* out of sight. Again it depressed him to think that many churches were fighting tooth and nail to deny something that was manifestly true, and which wouldn't influence most people's beliefs one way or the other. Still, he thought, it would be prudent to place Darwin's book in a drawer, and not out on a shelf.

The tall cone of the lighthouse looked impressive at close range. The black tower on Tory, he knew, was the first glimpse of Europe that a passenger from America would see. The lighthouse tower stood in the middle of a large square compound surrounded by a high wall. The compound seemed like a land-based ship – highly-organised, trim, and completely self-sufficient.

Entering the gate, he was surprised to find the Keeper chatting with the priest in front of the residential quarters. They waved greetings as he approached. "Geraghty!" boomed the Keeper. "You know Father Hayes..."

"Of course..." They shook hands.

"And I know that you and Corish are looking forward to your chess game," said the priest. "I'll bid you both good evening." He walked out through the gate with long strides.

"I didn't know that you were a religious man, Edward," said the schoolmaster.

"Ah, not very," said Corish. "But there's an old link. The first lighthouse-keepers were monks, you know. They liked living out on the rocks and islands, so Henry the Eighth gave them food if they'd keep some fires burning."

Corish led the schoolmaster into the residence where the chess table and two pint mugs were sitting. As he uncorked the stout bottles, the Keeper said, "I have some news to share this evening, Peter."

"Yes?"

"It's a bit of a balls-up, actually. Which is why I was speaking with Father Hayes. Perhaps..." He thought for a minute while he set out the bottles. "Yes, I will confide in you as well, if I may."

"Of course."

"You know that I have two assistants here – Varney and O'Brien? I've just learned that O'Brien is being shifted to Waterford, and his replacement will arrive in July."

"Does this pose a problem?"

"Hopefully not. But the man they are sending... Let's say that he has had a chequered career."

"In what respect?"

Corish held up his mug of stout. "In this respect, unfortunately. This man Quinn has been a devil for the bottle."

The schoolmaster raised his eyebrows. "And the Lighthouse Service knows about this, no?"

"They do. Now, I am assured by the powers-that-be that Quinn has put all of that behind him. Nevertheless, I want to make sure that he is not left entirely on his own on Tory. When he arrives, I will introduce him to Father Hayes, who has agreed to look in on him from time to time."

"That's very sensible, Edward. But you'll be here to work with him..."

"Ah, that's my other piece of news. I'm being reassigned to Dun Laoghaire. In September."

The schoolmaster put down his glass. "I'm truly sorry to hear that, Edward. I'll miss – I'll miss our games."

The two men sat in silence for a moment. The schoolmaster said, "If it would help, I could look in on Quinn myself."

"Thank you, Peter. I'd appreciate that very much."

"And what of Varney?" asked the schoolmaster. "You've mentioned this Varney fellow, but I never see him."

"Varney?" Corish smiled to himself. "He's too busy preparing himself to become the next Lighthouse Elder to take notice of Quinn. Or of anyone else."

"An ambitious yob, is he?"

"Oh, I shouldn't speak ill of him," said Corish, putting down his pipe. "He's completely reliable, and he makes no mistakes that I can see. It's just that..."

"That what?"

"It's just that there's usually a comradeship on the Lights. Most of us are a dogged breed, and we've found our niche in life. We get on well, and we don't worry about the future because we're – we're needed. It's a comfort to know that. But Varney seems to be thinking about the future instead of enjoying his life. Does that make sense, Geraghty?"

The schoolmaster shrugged. "It makes me wonder if you don't care for the man."

"I don't mind him, really. I've worked with all kinds of fellows. But he is a bit of a cold fish... Oh, damn!"

"Now I know you really don't like your man Varney."

"No, that's not it." The Keeper looked exasperated. "I forgot to ask Father Hayes about a warehouse boy."

"A warehouse boy?"

"Yes. This place is designed for three Keepers and a warehouse boy – some young bloke to help us old feckers with the heavy lifting. O'Brien was doing all of that work, but now that he's leaving..."

The schoolmaster smiled. "I know the perfect fellow for you."

4 June 1884

Evans handed the sextant to Gubby. The shining brass instrument felt solid and purposeful in his hands. "When you shoot the sun from here, there is very little error to take into account. We're nearly sitting on the Prime Meridian."

Gubby peered through the telescope of the sextant. He could see the horizon through the half-mirror. He squeezed the clamp to release its grip and began to slide the index-bar through its arc.

"Whatever you do, remember to use the optical filters when you shoot the sun, even here in cloudy old Ireland. I cannot tell you how many officers are half-blind in one eye from peering at the sun without a filter."

Gubby took the instrument away from his eye. "I will remember, Sir."

Elated by the brotherly attitude that Evans was displaying to him, Gubby paid rapt attention to the senior officer's instructions. They had reviewed the fundamentals that he had learned in Midshipman's School, and Evans had chuckled at Gubby's stories of his training. "I'll wager that those instructors haven't set foot on a ship for twenty years. It wouldn't surprise me if they taught you to use an astrolabe."

"They were an elderly lot," Gubby agreed.

"Navigation has become a fine science. With a sextant and a proper marine chronometer, you can determine your position within two hundred yards anywhere on the face of the earth. Of course, it's still a fine idea to look 'round from time to time."

"And the compass?"

"I would not stake my reputation on a compass-reading, Gubby. They are somewhat error-prone…"

O'Donnell's head appeared as he climbed the ladder to the bridge. "Lieutenant Evans?"

"Yes, O'Donnell?"

"Captain says that he wants to take her over to Clare Island. To evaluate the docking facilities."

Evans shot a quizzical glance at Gubby, but he said, "Very well. Tell him we'll be underway within the hour."

"Yes, Sir!" O'Donnell scrambled back down the ladder and hurried across the deck.

Gubby watched Evans shake his head. "Is that not Clare over there?" he asked, pointing to the large whale-shaped island across Clew Bay.

"Yes, Gubby, that is Clare. That is where our Captain wants us to go. For reasons, I'm sure, best known to himself."

"That can be only – perhaps twenty miles away?"

"Twenty or less. If we did not have a direct command to proceed in the *Wasp*, we might simply paddle over in a lifeboat."

Gubby delighted in sharing Evans's cynicism. "And how can I assist in this vital mission, Sir?"

Evans thought for a moment. "Keep watch at the prow, Gubby. I don't want to ram any Clare fishing-boats if we can avoid it."

≈≈≈≈≈

Gubby was surprised at the length of time that it took for the *Wasp* to leave the Westport docks. It took a full hour to stoke the boilers and develop enough steam-pressure to set out for Clare Island. He tried to think through the military consequences. If we were attacked... As he watched the men preparing the ship, he remembered what Armstrong had said about their ineffective small-bore cannons. The *Wasp*, he realised, was truly a glorified river-boat – a tiny afterthought of the mighty British Navy, well suited to delivering potatoes and raiding halfpenny *poitín* distilleries. He wondered briefly why he had been assigned to the *Wasp* – if he had somehow failed to impress his superiors, and if this backwater posting was a sign of their low regard for him.

But no, he swore, he would not demoralise himself in this way. Surely every officer had done his term in routine service, and in peacetime he could build a career as surely off the coast of Ireland as on a dry-docked warship. Feeling a burst of energy, he strode around the deck. The cook's advice seemed to be producing results – by avoiding sugary desserts, he had felt more steady and less tense.

As the men were retrieving the mooring-lines from the dock, Gubby returned to the bridge, where Evans was at the wheel. "Sir?"

"Yes, Gubby?"

"Can you advise me about what to watch for?"

Evans smiled and cocked his head. "There's little to worry about in Clew Bay. Most of the underwater hazards are marked, and Grace O'Malley likely pulled the others out with her bare hands."

"Who, Sir?"

"You haven't heard of the Irish Pirate Queen, Gubby? She was a ballsy old girl. Sailed up the Thames to parley eye-to-eye with Queen Elizabeth, she did. Not like our current crop of Parliamentary toadies."

"She must have had some nerve."

Evans grinned. "They say she ran a line from her ship right through her bedroom window, and she held onto that rope while she slept. Tough as old shoe-leather, she was. Not your blushing bride."

A lewd speculation sprang to Gubby's mind, but he didn't feel sure enough to share it with Evans. "Sir – when I'm on the watch, what should I be looking for?"

Evans shrugged, as though a moment for a good joke had passed. "Just keep an eye out for submerged rocks. There's not much else that can cause us any harm."

Gubby thought for a moment. "Sir? Forgive me if I seem ignorant, but how does one detect a submerged rock?"

To his relief, Evans said, "Fair question, Gubby. If it's near enough to the surface to threaten harm, there's usually a disturbance. An upswelling, or a boil. Sing out if you see anything."

With a bounce of enthusiasm, Gubby climbed down the ladder to the deck and strode to the foredeck as the *Wasp* picked up speed. The men who were working on deck stepped back to let him pass. He breathed a deep lungful of fresh sea-air. Things were going wonderfully well.

≈≈≈≈≈

The *Wasp* passed through the cluster of small islands that sheltered Westport Quay. Gubby admired Evans's touch with the ship, confidently threading through the maze of painted buoys that warned of sunken rocks and indicated the navigable channels. Despite Evans's gruff voice and cynical manner, Gubby felt a warmth from the man that he had not felt from Armstrong or the Captain.

The Captain had kept his promise to teach the fine points of navigation, but Gubby's initial enthusiasm had sunk to dismay as Russell attempted to instruct him in a complex longitude calculation called "lunar distance." Taking the sightings of the sun and the moon had been straightforward enough, but the lunar formula involved multi-factor equations and repeated references to a book of cosines and secants. Gubby, who had always struggled with mathematics, felt increasingly depressed as he tried to concentrate on the columns of figures and the complex arithmetic.

The Captain led him through the lunar exercises for several days, and Gubby felt a growing irritation radiating from the man. Then, without explanation, the Captain announced that he was turning Gubby's training over to Lieutenant Evans. Gubby and the Captain sat for a long moment at the chart-strewn table in the Captain's quarters, and the fat lieutenant had wondered if he should apologise or confess his confusion about the lessons. But he had said nothing, working in silence as the Captain clenched his teeth and nodded his head in a slow, steady rhythm.

Evans had probed him about the navigation lessons, as Gubby feared he would. "What did our Captain emphasise to you, Gubby?"

"He's keen on precision, Sir."

"In what respect?"

"Well, he pressed me to double-check each calculation when we were working lunars..."

Evans laughed. "Lunars! I wondered if he would try to indoctrinate you in his favourite pastime."

"*Pastime*, Sir?"

"No one in the British Navy has made those calculations since the last century. Oh, it was useful before our clocks were made accurate, all right, but now it's an obsolete skill. Our Captain prides himself on that sort of Ancient Mariner lore." Evans clapped Gubby on the shoulder. "I'll show you how to steer a modern ship."

≈≈≈≈≈

Sweating in the mid-afternoon sun, Gubby squeezed himself into the foredeck shelter as the *Wasp* cleared the near-shore islands. The cool westerly breeze felt refreshing. Clare Island looked like a painting of a whale-shaped landmass under fleecy white clouds. The steam engines made the deck buzz pleasantly.

The Chief Petty Officer knocked on the bulkhead. "Excuse me, Sir."

"Yes, Carlisle?"

"Shall I take the watch, Sir?"

"No, that won't be necessary, Carlisle. I'm taking it myself."

"Very well, Sir."

The *Wasp* picked up speed, and a salt spray blew across the prow as the ship cut through the choppy waves. How, Gubby wondered, would the *Wasp* have managed under sail in the confines of Clew Bay? Would the men be constantly scrambling to set and re-set the sails as they tacked into the wind? Would there have been a tug? Or would they have simply dropped anchor off-shore and rowed to Westport Quay?

A shape, a bulge, appeared in the water in front of the ship. It disappeared as a wave rolled over it and then reappeared in the trough, creating a v-shaped ripple on the surface.

"Hard a-port!" Gubby shouted.

He looked toward the bridge. Evans did not seem to hear him. Gubby leaned toward the voice-tube and shouted "Hard a-port!" again. One of the sailors on the deck repeated his call.

Evans cocked his head quizzically but spun the wheel. The Wasp veered to the left, and the ship began to roll as the incoming waves smacked against her side.

The v-shaped ripples reappeared in the trough between the waves. A brown face with large curious eyes appeared from under the water. The seal took a long look at the ship and then slipped back under the surface, disappearing from sight.

The men on the deck guffawed, and Gubby felt a hot flush in the back of his neck. *An upswelling, a boil...* For God's sake, that was what it looked like! What if it had been a rock? What if he hadn't called out?

Tears welled up in his eyes. Why did every lesson have to be a public humiliation?

≈≈≈≈≈

He remained in the foredeck shelter as the *Wasp* nosed into the cove that surrounded the Clare Island harbour. O'Donnell emerged from the Captain's quarters, crossed the deck and conferred with Evans. Gubby envied O'Donnell's ability to scamper up and down the bridge-ladder without apparent effort. *If only I were thinner,* he thought, and he sank into a familiar self-absorbed fog.

Evans barked an order, and one of the men took a spool of cable from a metal cabinet at the side of the bridge. The sailor moved to the prow of the ship, next to the shelter. Gubby watched as the man clipped a lead weight to the end of the cable and tossed it into the water. As it unreeled from the spool, he saw that the cable was fitted with smaller weights at regular intervals, like beads on a long string. The sailor called out *Six fathom,* and another sailor held up six fingers to relay the measurement to the bridge.

Steadily, the *Wasp* edged toward a docking pier. The ruins of a tall square castle stood near the water. It looked close enough, Gubby thought, to stretch a line from the ship to one of the castle windows. The bantering conversation about Grace O'Malley seemed like a distant memory, and he wondered if he would ever enjoy an easy comradeship with Evans. *Not soon,* he thought, *if I cannot distinguish a rock from a seal.*

Several sailors held the cork fenders over the side as Evans eased the *Wasp* up to the dock. As the ship bumped gently against the stone structure, the sailor with the cable called out *Four fathom!*

On the bridge, Evans said something to O'Donnell, who scrambled down the ladder and back to the Captain's quarters. Gubby looked away to avoid catching Evans's eye. He could feel the increased hum of the deck as the screws began to turn, and the *Wasp* eased away from the dock. He tried to concentrate on the water ahead of the prow, but his mind kept drifting. *Evans got us into this harbour without incident,* he told himself. *Surely he can get us back out.*

He realised that Carlisle was standing at the rail near the prow, watching as the ship pulled out of the cove and into the open water. He felt another hot flush building in the back of his neck. Did Evans consider him to be so incompetent that he'd ordered Carlisle to stand watch as well?

"Carlisle!" he heard himself shouting.

"Yes, Sir!"

"What are you doing here?"

"Am I bothering you, Sir?"

"No! What I mean is..." He floundered, feeling lost. "No one has ordered you to the prow, have they?"

"Not at all, Sir. Sorry if I've interfered, Sir." Carlisle stepped back from the rail and started to move away. Feeling a hot flush of shame, Gubby fought with an impulse to apologise. As he groped for words, he could hear the Captain's voice: *You are too familiar with the men.* He watched Carlisle's back as the Petty Officer crossed the deck and disappeared down the stairwell behind the bridge.

The *Wasp* turned and began a slow circle around Clare Island. Miserable, Gubby leaned against the wall of the shelter. The enclosure felt like a jail, a display-cage for unpracticed officers and their conspicuous errors. His stomach clenched as he imagined his father and brothers standing with Evans on the bridge, laughing or embarrassed. He could almost see himself through their eyes, his pudgy frame sagging in a dejected slump. He took a deep breath and drew himself up. At least he could stand on his own two feet.

≈≈≈≈≈

The ship rounded the north coast of the island, and the lighthouse came into view. The red-striped tower sat at the top of a craggy cliff, bright and purposeful in the August sunshine. Gubby looked at the tower with a pang of envy. There, he thought, would be a blessedly-simple life. He could imagine a lighthouse-keeper making his rounds with clock-like regularity, following a schedule, outfitted with a generous trove of supplies – a warehouse of fuel-oil, a well-stocked larder in the kitchen...

A brown shape flickered in the water at the edge of his vision. He craned to look at the spot where it had been, but the sun-sparkle on the waves made it difficult to see. He felt himself taking an involuntary breath to call out, but he resisted – *not another damned seal, not twice in one day.* He could see no boils, no upswellings – for all he knew, it could have been a floating strand of seaweed.

He was looking back at the lighthouse, recapturing his reverie when he felt a thump underfoot. The deck stopped vibrating as the engines went quiet, and he could hear the sound of the bell as Evans pushed the handle of the engine-room telegraph back and forth. The men peered over the sides of the ship, and Gubby could hear the sound of the waves slapping against the side.

"It's a net!" someone shouted from the stern. "It's a fecking fish-net!"

As Gubby squeezed out of the shelter, he could see Evans hurrying down the bridge-ladder and running across the deck. The cluster of men who were crowding around the stern parted to let Evans peer over the skirting.

"Bloody hell!" the Lieutenant shouted. "Lower the anchor!"

As the anchor-chain unspooled and clanked, Gubby worked his way to the stern. The water was thick with brown strands that looked like the severed tentacles of an octopus. Looking more closely, he saw netting, rope, and cork floats.

Evans was suddenly at his side. "You didn't see this, did you?"

"No, Sir, I didn't."

The Lieutenant glared at him for a second before he turned away. "Drury! Cobb! Strip down and get your knives!"

O'Donnell pushed his way through the crowd. "Captain wants to know what's going on, Sir!"

"Tell him..." Evans stopped and spat over the rail. "Tell him that the propeller has been fouled with a fishing net. It's being cleared."

O'Donnell hurried away while the two sailors dropped their shoes and shirts on the deck. One jumped overboard and disappeared briefly under the water. He re-emerged in the middle of the tangled net-ropes. "It's not bad, Sir!" he shouted. "She's wrapped around the shaft, all right, but she seized up quick."

"Right. You know what to do, Cobb." Evans looked at the other sailor. "Drury?"

"Aye aye, Sir." Drury jumped into the water beside Cobb. Like seals, they began diving under the surface to cut away the tangle with their knives.

"Carlisle!" said Evans. "Assign someone to stand by and pull that bloody mess out of the water. I don't want to do this twice. Gubby?"

"Yes, Sir?"

"Come with me."

≈≈≈≈≈

The Captain's quarters seemed exceptionally dark as they stepped in from the midday sunshine. Russell was seated at his desk, and O'Donnell could be heard moving about in the adjoining room.

Gubby was surprised when the Captain spoke in a mild tone. "So we're becalmed, are we?"

"Yes, Sir. For an hour or two, at least."

"And who was standing the forward watch?"

"I was, Sir," said Gubby.

"And you saw nothing?"

"I – no, Sir."

"Are fishing nets not fitted out with coloured floats, for identification?"

Feeling a flutter of panic, Gubby searched for words to describe the brown flicker he had glimpsed, but Evans interrupted him. "There are no markings on the net, Sir. This is Ireland."

"So it is, Evans. So it is." The Captain toyed with a pencil on his desk. "Is it possible that this was done deliberately? Perhaps by an agitator for what they call *Home Rule?*"

"Who can say, Sir?" Evans thought for a moment. "Our circuit of the island was not planned, or announced."

"No, indeed." The Captain seemed lost in thought. "The weather is fair, and we still have several hours of daylight..."

"The men should be able to clear the prop in an hour or two," added Evans, picking up the thread. "Unless some damage has been done to the engine, we should dock by nightfall..."

"And so we should... Gubby!"

"Yes, Sir?"

The Captain held his gaze for a long moment. "Tell Carlisle to take the watch for the return trip."

10 June 1884

"Why did you ask me to come along, Mister Geraghty?"

The sail of the schoolmaster's boat hummed in the brisk westerly wind, and it felt like they were flying over the water. A flock of gulls had followed them from the Toraigh harbour, but they dropped back as the island receded in the wake of the sailboat. The schoolmaster seemed to be enjoying himself, leaning against the tiller and keeping an eye on the mainland coastline. "Well, Ruairí, it was your idea to take some potatoes to Inishtrahull, wasn't it?"

"Yes, but I only thought that Eoghan and I might..."

The schoolmaster grinned. "Have you been to Inishtrahull before?"

"No, but Uncle Sean told me about it. He says that people are near-starving over there."

The schoolmaster looked out at the horizon. "They're not the only people in Ireland who are starving."

"I suppose it just seems – well, since they're so close to us..."

"I'm not debating with you, Ruairí. It's a fine idea to share the potatoes. But it's farther away than you think."

"Eoghan and I can cover a lot of distance when we row."

The schoolmaster grinned. "Inishtrahull is forty-five miles from Toraigh. That's a lot of rowing, even for you and Eoghan."

They skimmed along in companionable silence for a few minutes before the schoolmaster spoke again. "I asked you to come along for a couple of reasons. Do you remember the last time you were in this boat?"

"Was that the night you took me to the doctor? For my eye?"

"That's exactly it. And every time I get on board I remember that night, and I cannot get rid of the feeling that – that something of that night is still on this boat." He looked at Ruairí and then looked back out over the water. "This goes against everything I've ever taught and believed, but I cannot shake the feeling that some of your pain, and my worry, are still sticking to this boat like pitch. Does that sound mad?"

"Aunt Eithne says things like that happen all the time. She says that's why people see ghosts."

The schoolmaster laughed. "Eithne – of course! I should have told her about this. In any case, my own form of – let's call it an exorcism – is to bring you along to Inishtrahull to let the boat know that you're all right."

Ruairí looked at the small, serious man at the tiller, realising how much he was going to miss him. "I think it's a good idea, Mister Geraghty. As long as we don't sink."

"Don't say that, Ruairí! Now I'll worry until we get back!"

≈≈≈≈≈

The mountains of the Irish mainland slid past slowly as they sailed eastward. Ruairí could see an occasional fishing-boat hugging the shore. The schoolmaster had said they would follow the coastline to Inishtrahull, sailing about seven miles from the land. Ruairí's eye watered in the wind, blurring his vision. Wiping his cheek with his sleeve, he felt a pang of loss – he couldn't tell whether the coastline was seven miles away, or one mile, or ten. At least, he consoled himself, he could still read – something that most people couldn't do with two eyes – and he hoped that his vision wouldn't interfere with his assignments at the map-school.

"Do you know anyone in Westport, Mister Geraghty?"

"No, I don't. Most people I know are from Sligo. Or I should say *Most people I knew*. I haven't lived there for a long time."

"Why did you come to Toraigh, Sir?"

The schoolmaster was silent for a few seconds before answering. "I tell most people a story that they accept. I tell them that I was treated as a freak of nature in Sligo, and that I came to Toraigh to get away from all that. That's partly true, but it's not the whole truth."

They sailed along in silence, and Ruairí made no effort to ask questions. The schoolmaster seemed to be sorting out a memory – how much to tell, how much to withhold. He said, "My brother..." and then stopped without explanation. Ruairí trailed his hand in the water and waited.

"Life on the mainland is different from life on Toraigh," the schoolmaster finally said. "I don't know how much I should explain to you."

"Sure, we're in no hurry," said Ruairí.

The schoolmaster stared at the horizon until he seemed to come to a decision. "My brother is in Mountjoy Prison in Dublin," he said. "And I came within a hairsbreadth of being locked in there myself."

"Why would they do that to you, Mister Geraghty?"

"Frankie – that's my brother – he and I were close. He was only a year or two younger than me, but he was big – bigger than most everybody else. Our Da used to say that what was left over from me went into Frankie. I didn't like it when he said that, but that was his kind of joke."

Ruairí could hear a change of tone in the schoolmaster's voice, less of a formal teacher and more of a reminiscing man. "Frankie was real protective of me. There were plenty of boys that would make fun of me, or push me around. I could handle just about anybody one-at-a-time, but they'd gang up on me. And that's when Frankie would come in. He'd grab the biggest one and twist his arm behind his back and make him tell the others to quit. He must have done that a hundred times.

"And then afterwards, after he'd chased them all away, he'd come back to me and say, *What are we gonna do, Petey?* He'd act like nothing had happened, and he'd ask me to organise a game, or a joke, or something." The schoolmaster stared across the water. "He saved me, but he looked up to me."

"He sounds like Eoghan," said Ruairí.

"He's a lot like Eoghan. We were close, like you and him."

They sailed past a lobster-trap buoy, and Ruairí wondered who had dropped it so far out at sea. It had to be a mainlander – they were too far from Toraigh.

"Then I went off to the teacher-training college in Dublin," the schoolmaster continued. "I wanted to go, but the hardest part was leaving Frankie. I remember him standing there in the rain at the railway station, staring at me from the platform, getting wet as a rat and not even noticing it. I almost got off the train. I didn't, but sometimes I wish I had.

"It was a couple of months later that he wrote to me. I knew it was from him right away because of his big clumsy printing. He wrote *Helo Petey. Rite me and tell me how we made gunpowder.*"

"You made gunpowder?"

"It was something we did for fun. I'd read about Chinese fireworks, and Frankie had got excited about how we could make a rocket, so I found the recipe for gunpowder. We both knew the horse-doctor – he'd pay us a shilling sometimes when he needed help to hold down an animal – so we pinched some sulphur and saltpetre from his store-room. Then we ground up some charcoal and mixed it all together."

"Did it work?"

The schoolmaster grinned. "Well, it did and it didn't. We made a paper tube and put the gunpowder into it. And we tied a stick onto it, like we saw in the Chinese pictures. But we didn't know how long to make the stick. So when we lit it it took off with a whoosh, but instead of going up in the air it flew around in a circle. Then it came down on the roof of our house and set fire to the thatch. My Da put it out, and then he paddled both of us."

Ruairí laughed. "How old were you, Mister Geraghty?"

"I must have been about thirteen."

They sailed along in silence for a few minutes before the schoolmaster spoke again. "Anyway, I was so glad to hear from Frankie that I sent him a long letter, and in it I wrote out the gunpowder recipe. I should have known better. The next thing I knew, the police came to the school and told me that Frankie had been arrested. He had fallen in with some blokes who..." He looked at Ruairí, weighing his words. "Do you know about the drive for Home Rule? About Parnell?"

"No, not really..."

The schoolmaster looked grim. "There are many people who think that the English government has no right to rule over Ireland. Or even be here." His voice rose. "They conquered us with their armies, but then they turned Ireland into a playground for their aristocrats. For an Englishman, having an estate in Ireland is like having a small country house for occasional hunting-parties. A luxury, a place for retreats and entertainment. Can you imagine living such a life, Ruairí?"

"Sure, no one on Toraigh has two houses..."

"Most of the people in the world don't have two houses. Most of the people in the world are lucky if they have a roof over their heads." The schoolmaster shifted his weight against the tiller. "Many Irish people believe that the English should go home and leave us to take care of ourselves, to run our own country. Some are trying to convince the English through laws and voting and politics. Others are taking a more direct approach."

"What kind of approach?"

"Guns. And bombs."

The schoolmaster seemed to withdraw into himself. Ruairí listened to the thrumming of the wind in the canvas sail.

"Frankie fell in with some blokes who were on the fringe of all this," the schoolmaster finally said. "One fellow was a farm-boy from a family who'd been evicted. Another was a local drunk who had been rejected by the Fenians because he wasn't reliable. If I'd been at home, I would have warned Frankie away from those two yobs, but I wasn't...

Geraghty took a deep breath. "They concocted a scheme to blow up the Army barracks in Ballyshannon. It made no sense at all – it would have taken a massive bomb to damage the barracks building, and they would likely have killed a hundred innocent people. In any event, it never happened. They were caught after they broke into the horse-doctor's storehouse, and Frankie, bless his ignorant heart, lost his nerve and told the police about their plan."

The schoolmaster looked directly at Ruairí. "They searched his room and found my letter. They kept me locked away for days, questioning me again and again. Finally they let me go. It is a miracle, Ruairí, that I am not whiling away my life in Mountjoy. Frankie may have convinced them that I had nothing to do with their scheme. Or perhaps they thought that they could use me."

"How could they use you, Mister Geraghty?"

"There are some things I'd rather not tell you about, Ruairí. I'll just say this – as long as they have Frankie in custody, they know I can be forced into cooperating with them. So when I graduated from the teacher-training school, I was determined to get as far away from Dublin and Sligo as possible. And that's how I came to Toraigh."

An island appeared on the horizon, breaking the straight line where the sea met the sky. The schoolmaster adjusted the tiller and drew a deep breath. "Ruairí, I have very little doubt that someone, somewhere, will ask you to join the fight against England. The best advice that I can offer you is not to let yourself be pressured into anything. I fear that there can be no success without force, but I would grieve if you lost your life or freedom in some mad, near-sighted scheme that would accomplish nothing. Whatever you do, think before you choose."

≈≈≈≈≈

Inishtrahull was even smaller than Toraigh. The schoolmaster steered toward the north side of the island, skirting the rocks that protected Inishtrahull like sentries. Ruairí looked for cottages along the shore, but he was distracted by a slate-grey triangle that appeared among the waves between the rocks. Old and leathery, it slid along the surface. If basking sharks cruised the waters around the island, he knew, the fishing would be good.

124

The schoolmaster said, "This is the northernmost landfall in Ireland," as he heeled the boat around to turn into Port Mor inlet.

"That looks like another island up there," said Ruairí, pointing north.

"That's Tor Mor. It's just a rock. No one lives there, except the birds."

The schoolmaster released the sail, and Ruairí lifted the oars into the oarlocks to row the boat into the small inlet. The landing-dock sat at the base of a lighthouse tower, and a handful of children in ragged clothes waved from the dock. A tall girl gestured to them to toss her the landing-line, and the schoolmaster threw the coiled line in her direction. She did not try to catch the rope, but she scrambled to pick it up as soon as it landed on the dock. She looped it around a bollard with a flourish, and two other children helped her pull on the line to bring in the boat.

"Thank you!" the schoolmaster shouted. "What's your name?"

The girl shouted back in heavily-accented Irish. The schoolmaster turned to Ruairí. "Can you understand her? I can't make out what she's saying."

"She says her name is Tara. She wants to know who we are."

"Can you tell her?"

"I'll try." Ruairí turned to the dock. *Tara?*

Yes?

We sailed from Oileán Toraigh. We're friends.

The girl smiled. "I can talk a little English. Why did you come here?

"We've brought potatoes."

"For the lighthouse-keeper?"

"No, for the families."

"Really? Can I have one?"

"They're for planting, not for eating."

Tara looked disappointed. In Irish, Ruairí said, *You can have one to eat.*

The other children began shouting and waving. *Can we have potatoes, too?*

"What's going on?" asked the schoolmaster.

"I think I made a mistake. I told the girl she could have a potato..."

"...and now they all want one? First lesson in charity, Ruairí – be careful about what you promise."

Ruairí felt embarrassed. "What should I do now?"

The schoolmaster looked at the gaggle of children the dock. "Give the girl three potatoes and let her distribute them."

Ruairí lifted the rough-woven bag of potatoes from the bottom of the boat. Pale sprouts poked through the loosely-woven fabric, and the bag was wet with bilge-water. "Tara," he said, "do you have a knife?"

Tara said something to the children on the dock, and one of the boys produced a pocket-knife. Ruairí handed her three fat potatoes which she passed along to the boy. She said, "Do you have any books?"

The schoolmaster looked pained. Ruairí said to the girl, "Books? Don't you have any books?"

"There's some at the lighthouse, but I've read all of 'em."

"I'm afraid all we've brought is potatoes," said the schoolmaster.

"What do you want for them?"

"Nothing. The Quakers sent them to Toraigh, and we had some extra."

The girl looked into the boat, twisting her head sideways. Ruairí saw that her eyes were severely crossed. After a moment she said, "Are you taking them to the lighthouse?"

The schoolmaster hesitated. "Is there a schoolmaster on the island?"

"The lighthouse-keeper teaches us when he can."

The schoolmaster turned toward Ruairí. "This is going to be more complicated than I thought. I should have a word with the lighthouse-keeper before we do anything." He turned back to the girl. "Can you tell me where to find the Keeper?"

She smiled and nodded toward the lighthouse tower that loomed behind her. "He might be over there."

The schoolmaster shook his head. "It must be my day for foolish questions. Ruairí, do you want to come with me?"

Tara quickly said, "I can show you around the island."

"I'd like that," said Ruairí. "How long will you be, Mister Geraghty?"

"It don't matter," said Tara. "All he has to do is holler, and somebody will hear him. And they'll tell us."

"This isn't a very big island, is it?"

"No, it isn't. Not at all."

≈≈≈≈≈

The schoolmaster climbed out of the sailboat, stretched his legs, and started up the road toward the lighthouse. The children on the dock giggled at him, but Tara said something that Ruairí couldn't hear, and they ran away. One heavyset boy stayed behind, playing with pebbles. He had a round, moony face, and Ruairí thought that he could see the stubble of a beard on the boy's chin. "Who's this?" he asked.

"That's Feargal. He's my brother."

Ruairí looked closely at Feargal, who was rubbing a pinch of dirt between his fingers. There was a boy on Toraigh who looked like him, a sweet-natured, slow boy who didn't go to school. "Can he talk?"

"He don't say much. Da says he's a changeling."

"Do you have to watch him?"

Tara shook her head. "I think he watches me. One time one of the Muldoon boys pushed me down, and Feargal broke his arm. Come on, I said I'd show you around."

Ruairí followed Tara as she scrambled up the path from the dock and turned away from the lighthouse toward a small hill. Feargal followed them, crooning softly to himself. Low stone walls bordered the path, with buttercups and grasses growing between the stones. A handful of sheep looked up as they passed, returning quickly to their nervous grazing.

"This is it," Tara announced as they reached the top of the hill. Ruairí looked around and saw everything – absolutely everything – on Inishtrahull. It was like Toraigh in miniature – green fields running to the edges of steep granite cliffs, a few beaches, and a cove. The lighthouse stood like a tall tower in the middle of the island, taller than the hill where they stood. To the north he could see the bird-stained rock of Tor Mor, and beyond, in every direction, the sea.

A few cottages were scattered across the island. "How many people live here?" asked Ruairí.

"There's just six families," said Tara. "There's mostly the McGonagles and the McLaughlins. I'm a McLaughlin. And there's old Mister Houton. He lives by himself out in a hut. There's about forty of us, I suppose."

Ruairí looked around at the rocky fields and the thin, hungry sheep. "How does everybody get enough to eat?"

"My Da's a fisherman."

"Does he catch enough to feed you?"

"He says it used to be better before the dog-fish came. They eat all the bait. But he can still catch fish."

"What about in the winter...?"

Tara looked down. "The lighthouse-keeper gives us some of his stores. Our Da don't like to take them, but Feargal cries when he's hungry."

Ruairí looked at Feargal, who was scraping moss off the stone wall with a stick. "Don't you get hungry, too?"

Tara looked at Ruairí, started to say something, and then seemed to change her mind. "What happened to your eye?" she asked.

"A bird poked it out. It was an accident."

"I bet that hurt."

"It hurt worse than anything." He looked at Tara for a moment, emboldened by her frankness. "What about your eyes?"

"They always been like this."

"Do you see two of everything?"

"No, I can only see out of the one." She put her hand over her right eye. "Well, that ain't exactly true. I can see out of the other one, but it's all smeary."

"Is that why you didn't catch the rope from the boat?"

"Yeah, I can't always tell how far away a thing is."

"It's the same for me."

"My Da says that one eye is good enough for cooking and changing nappies. What are you going to do?"

"I'm going to a map-school on the mainland. It's up somewhere called Westport."

Tara thought for a moment. "They let you draw maps, with just one eye?"

"Mister Geraghty tells me that it won't make any difference."

"Would they let girls into a map-school?"

Ruairí looked at her, sensing her restlessness, her dreams. "I don't know. How old are you, anyway?"

"I'm twelve."

"I think you have to be sixteen or something to go there."

"I could probably go when I'm fifteen. I'm tall for my age." Tara looked out to sea. "There's lots of maps at the lighthouse. They're beautiful."

Feargal made a whining sound, and they both turned to look at him. He had stuck his finger between two rocks in the wall, and he was pulling unconvincingly, pretending it was stuck. Ruairí reached over to help him, but Tara put her hand on his arm to restrain him. "He wants me to do it," she said quietly. Then she began talking to her brother in a cooing tone. *Is your finger stuck in there? Here, let me help you...*

She took her brother's hand, and Feargal abandoned the pantomime of being stuck. Tara glanced at Ruairí, and he understood. "Does he always do something like this...?"

"Every time I talk about other places. Even if I just think about them..."

"Hey, Ruairí!" They turned to see the schoolmaster waving from the door of the lighthouse, standing beside another man. As they waved back at the two men – one half the height of the other – Ruairí felt a surprising surge, like an up-rush of air. He felt like he was looking down on Inishtrahull, seeing the entire boxy island – the lighthouse, the two men, the cottages and the fields, even himself and Tara and Feargal waving from the hilltop – seeing it the way a falcon would see it, hovering and swooping in the wind.

Then the wind seemed to pick up speed, and he soared higher. He could see across the water to the mainland, with the deep notch of a bay that thrust for miles into the land between the coastal mountains. Toraigh looked like a dot, a tiny speck, on the horizon. He turned to see the sea-islands and the shoreline of Scotland far across the water to the north-east. He rose higher – what would stop him from soaring to the sun? Thrilled and dizzy, he closed his eye – and then he was back on the ground again, his blood pounding in his ears.

"...come to meet Mister Rafferty," the schoolmaster was shouting.

Shaking, he said to Tara, "Did I...?"

"Did you what?"

"Have I been...?" He hesitated. Would she would think he was daft if he asked *Have I been flying?* He said, "Have I been here?"

Tara smiled and said, "Where else would you be?"

≈≈≈≈≈

Ruairí sat in the sailboat, trying to sort out the blur that the day had become. He remembered shaking hands with the lighthouse-keeper, but his mind had been miles away. He could not forget how vast the ocean seemed from high above, so high that the curling waves and breakers looked like tiny white shadows – which made no sense. The schoolmaster had steered him back to the dock like an indulgent uncle who'd found his nephew be-fogged in a pub. The sack of potatoes had vanished from the bottom of the boat, but Ruairí had no idea who took them, or when they changed hands.

And where had Tara and Feargal gone? He started to climb out of the boat, but the schoolmaster said, "Where are you going?"

"I – I never said good-bye to Tara. I don't know where she is..."

"Ruairí," the schoolmaster said, "we need to leave now. I want to be sure that we can get back to Toraigh by dark. Do you feel well?"

"I'm – I was..." Ruairí heard himself stammering, trying to say something that didn't sound ridiculous. It was impossible to explain. He saw the schoolmaster looking at him with worry. Finally he said, "Do you ever feel dizzy?"

The small man shook his head. "I've heard of this," he said. "Sometimes sailors find themselves staggering around when they're on land. I'm told that it happens to some mainlanders when they visit islands. But it's never happened to me."

Ruairí leaned back in the prow of the sailboat as the schoolmaster loosened the moorings and pushed away from the dock. The westerly breeze pushed them to the mouth of the harbour, and the schoolmaster began turning the boat around and setting up the sails to tack into the wind. Ruairí said, "Can I do something to help, Mister Geraghty?"

"No, I'll feel better if you stay where you are, Ruairí. Just keep a lookout for rocks until we clear the island."

As the boat tacked north-west toward Tor Mor, Ruairí looked back at the island and saw two small figures waving from the beach. He waved back, and they jumped up and down wildly. The schoolmaster looked back at the island and said, "I think you made some friends today."

Ruairí felt his head clearing in the brisk breeze. "Mister Geraghty, do you know if they take girls in the map-school?"

The schoolmaster frowned. "I doubt it, Ruairí. It's rare to find a woman in the professions, except – well, it's just rare."

"Would you mind if I asked at the school?"

"Not at all. In fact, I hope that you will ask a million questions. You'll need to."

Ruairí felt a surge of gratitude toward the tiny man. "I wish you were going to be there in Westport, Mister Geraghty."

"You'll be fine on your own, Ruairí. I have confidence in you, and I know you won't let me down."

The schoolmaster adjusted the sails. He began tacking toward the south-west, and Ruairí watched the island as it fell behind them. He had already lost sight of Tara and Feargal. He turned around to look ahead at the expanse of ocean that they would need to cross to return to Toraigh. He felt exhausted, and profoundly glad that the schoolmaster was able to sail the boat on his own.

Whatever had happened to him in those heady moments on the island, he knew that it was not entirely a figment of his imagination. But he decided not to confide in the schoolmaster – Mister Geraghty was a practical, earthbound man. And then he laughed, realising that he knew the perfect person to confide in about strange and inexplicable things, and how happy she would be when he arrived home to tell her.

1 July 1884

The note from Corish was terse: *Quinn here.* Father Hayes felt mildly offended until he reasoned that the lighthouse-keeper, who sent most of his messages by telegraph or semaphore, would have trained himself to use a minimum of words.

Eoghan Mullan had brought the note, and the priest asked him to tell Corish that he would stop by later in the day. Eoghan ran from the priest's door with a galloping stride. Father Hayes wondered for the thousandth time how things came to be decided on Tory Island. How had Eithne's nephew been chosen to do the heavy work at the lighthouse? There were other boys who could have done as well, if not better – were they considered? And why had he himself not been consulted in the choice?

The priest returned to his desk and read for the third time the letter he had received from the Bishop.

Father Hayes:

It has been brought to our attention that your name has appeared as a co-signatory on an application to the Society of Friends in London, requesting a donation of potatoes to the Tory parish.

I admonish you to avoid involving yourself in such matters. Discussions of great significance are taking place in London concerning Home Rule for Ireland. Powerful forces are working to establish an Irish Nation built around the wise leadership of our Holy Mother Church.

Our opponents seek to paint us as a backward race, unable to manage our own affairs. Your signature as a representative of the Church on a letter appealing for food and assistance from a Protestant denomination only reinforces those who oppose us.

Your mission on Tory Island is spiritual, not political. I warn you that any future actions which undercut our purposes will be dealt with severely.

He could imagine the Bishop's face as he dictated the letter, red and beefy and full of righteous indignation. He had started to compose several replies, and his most recent draft was lying on his desk next to the Bishop's letter:

Your Excellency,
With all due respect to your admonition, I wish to advise you of the circumstances surrounding my actions. There is a young man on Tory Island whom I have been attempting to persuade to take Holy Orders. He is greatly influenced by the local schoolmaster. I had established an understanding that he would urge the Mullan boy to enrol at Maynooth if I were to endorse…

He wadded up the half-written letter and tossed it into the hearth. He could imagine the Bishop's next question: And where exactly is this young man today?

The priest looked out the window at the clouds that were blowing in over the western end of the island. Had the schoolmaster played him for a fool? What exactly had Geraghty said to Rory Mullan? Was it true that the boy had chosen to apprentice himself to a map-maker in Westport?

On the other hand, he realised, there would have been risks if Rory had enrolled at Maynooth under his endorsement. His thinking would have been confused – even corrupted – by Eithne's lifelong influence. If Rory had spread doubt and disbelief at the school, it would not have reflected well on the priest who recommended him.

Still, he thought, the boy is only sixteen. He might grow weary of copy-desks and ink-blotters, and he might change his mind. Sixteen-year-old boys were probably impulsive in their decisions…

And what do I know of sixteen-year-old boys, beyond my own life? Father Hayes bit his lip as a wave of doubt swept over him. What do I know of anyone's life?

The clouds on the horizon were rolling northward, framing the lighthouse with a dramatic backdrop. It would be sensible, he thought, to visit Corish and Quinn now, before the rain.

≈≈≈≈≈

The priest was about to knock on Corish's door when a woman opened the door to the adjoining house. She was stout and dark-haired, no longer young, with a self-possessed air. Before he could speak, she said, "You must be Father Hayes. I'm very pleased to meet you. My name is Mary Quinn."

"How do you do, Mrs. Quinn." He saw that she looked at him with the air of a parishioner. Mrs. Quinn would be coming to Mass.

"Will you please come in?" She opened the door, and he stepped into a room half-filled with shipping crates and steamer-trunks. "We've just today arrived, and everything is higgledy-piggledy. Will you have a cup of tea?"

"That would be grand, thank you."

He stood in the sitting-room while Mary Quinn fussed with cups and tea-kettles in the kitchen. From her chatter he gathered that her husband was on a tour of the lighthouse with Corish, being introduced to the buildings and the procedures. He also gathered that the Quinns had two daughters who were exploring the lighthouse compound on their own.

He looked around the sitting room with its bare walls and uncurtained windows. The Quinn family trunks were overflowing with china dishes and lace doilies and knick-knacks that would soften the room's hard corners, its boxy indifference. It occurred to him that a lighthouse-keeper's life was not so different from his own – moving from place to place, living in furnished rooms that he could occupy but not possess. But while the Quinns had lorry-loads of boxes and furniture, he had only his suitcase.

Mary Quinn was still talking as she carried a tray of tea-paraphernalia and biscuits into the sitting room. "...and sure, it was in the rectory all along. Of course, we wouldn't dare tell Father O'Malley to his face, so we snuck it out and then Sister Bernadette pretended that she'd found it behind a gravestone in the churchyard..."

Father Hayes had lost the thread of her conversation, but he knew that she had been chattering only to fill the silence. "So you've moved from parish to parish, then?"

"Haven't we, though, Father? My mother warned me about the life on the Lights when Paddy and I were to be married. But of course I took no notice."

"It's not an easy life, no?"

Mary Quinn put down her teacup, and Father Hayes wondered if he had moved too quickly by asking a question that could bring forth a painful answer. She said, "You must know yourself, Father, that we don't always realise what we're bringing onto ourselves."

"Yes..."

She raised her head like someone who had made a decision. "With the Lights, we've moved every three or four years. We've lived in places where the lighthouses were on the shore, and we all lived together. But other times we've been posted in places where the lighthouses were out on the rocks, and Paddy would be working away out there for weeks at a time. They'd try to keep a regular schedule, so we'd know when he was coming home, but the weather... When the sea was rough, he could be out there for an extra week. Sometimes two extra weeks, in the winter..."

"It must have been difficult for you, and for the children..."

She smiled and looked into the middle distance. "There were times when I wondered if they'd ever know him at all. He was like a sailor, coming home and taking over everything, and then going away again and leaving us on our own."

Father Hayes said nothing. He knew the reputations of some Keepers who swung wildly away from their monastic disciplines when they came ashore, drinking heavily and picking quarrels with their neighbours and families. And Quinn, according to Corish, had a fondness for the bottle.

Mary Quinn interrupted his thoughts as though she were reading them. "I'm pleased that we're assigned here, where we can all live together. Paddy... He's – well, I'm happier, for a certainty."

The priest suddenly realised that she was speaking with a familiar accent. "And where are you from, Mary?"

"Well, Paddy was on Tuskar for several years, and the children and I lived on the shore. But before that..."

"No, I mean you yourself."

"Where was I born? I'm from Cork, Father. Like yourself, if I'm not mistaken."

Jolted, the priest felt a stiffening in his chest. Of course – although her accent was blurred by years of living here and there, she was from his own home county. *And could she possibly know...?*

Better to ask now than to wonder, he thought. "And how many years has it been since you lived in Cork?"

"Now, let me see – this is 1884, and we were married in 1866, so it has been – goodness, almost twenty years!"

There was a sound of footsteps in the front hall, and Corish came striding in through the open door to the sitting-room. "Oh, there you are, Father! Quinn, meet Father Hayes." The priest found himself standing and shaking hands with a thin, intense man who appeared at the doorway behind the Keeper. Paddy Quinn looked uncomfortable and irritated at finding a priest as well as his own supervisor in his new quarters.

Father Hayes found himself saying, "Your wife was telling me that you have moved here from the Tuskar."

"That's right, Father. Mary, where are the girls?"

"They're outside, dear. Father, will you have another cup..."

"No, thank you, I really must be going..."

Corish raised an eyebrow. "But Father, won't you stay and – and get acquainted with the Quinns? I mean, they're new to Tory Island..."

The priest could see Quinn's face darken as Corish tried to engineer the situation. "Yes, I've been making Mrs. Quinn's acquaintance, but... I'm afraid that it's threatening to rain."

Corish looked exasperated, as if to say *Aren't you going to stay long enough to size up this fellow?* But the priest felt claustrophobic in the now-crowded sitting room, and he wanted to leave. He said, "I'll stop back after you've had more time to settle in."

"You're always welcome, Father," Quinn said unenthusiastically.

Mary Quinn walked to the door with the priest, saying something about how grateful she was for his visit, and urging him to return as soon as possible. They met two girls in their early teens walking up the pathway. In what seemed like a single breath Mary Quinn said *Oh, here are my daughters*, introduced them to the priest, and shooed them inside. Father Hayes found himself hurrying away from the stifling house in relief. He was outside the lighthouse compound gate before he realised that he'd forgotten to tell them the schedule for Sunday Mass.

≈≈≈≈≈

It was unlikely that they knew, he tried to convince himself. If they had married in 1866, and if Quinn was working on the Lights, they would likely have been posted to a lighthouse on another part of the coast. But gossip was like quicksilver and would flow through any channels. Did she know? Did they both know?

A scattering of cold raindrops fell around him as he hurried back along the road toward West Town. He could clearly see himself, a gaunt man in a black skirt-like cassock, striding in haste to reach shelter before the rain would come pelting down. A forbidding figure, head bent – the islanders would wonder if he was hurrying to someone's deathbed to perform the Last Rites. He could imagine them soothing their frightened children – *No, he's not coming to our house.*

It must have been a mistake, he'd often reflected. He'd never heard of another newly-ordained priest being posted directly back to his own home parish. It made sense to begin somewhere else. In a different parish, a young priest would enjoy a certain glow of respect, fresh from Maynooth and brimming with ideas and energy. The respect of the parishioners would build his confidence, and he would settle into his role with the support of the whole community. But in Cork, Michael Hayes had been thrust among the still-young faces of the boys he'd played football with, and the girls who had mocked his shy ways when they had been in school together. Even the old priest seemed to treat him like a schoolboy. He had always felt awkward, on the edge of things – and now his priestly vestments, and his duties, made him feel that he was even more of an outsider.

In the lonely nights in the rectory, he had discovered that whiskey could ease his sadness. At first it was only a nightcap, a single glass to help relax his jittery body and help him sleep. There seemed to be no harm in it, and didn't the Good Lord perform his first miracle by making wine for the marriage feast at Cana? He found himself looking forward to his bedtime glass of *uisce beatha.*

Then the lapses had begun. *Father? Did you hear what he said, Father?* He had sat at the bedside of a consumptive farmer, a skeletal man whose skin barely concealed the bones of his face. From his boyhood he remembered the old man, an unapproachable tyrant who seemed to take pleasure at beating his animals with a cane. The stench of the farmer's breath made his stomach turn. He'd tried to find a prayer of consolation in his breviary, but he became desperately afraid that he would grow sick in the airless room.

His trembling hands embarrassed him as he tried to leaf through the pages of his leather-bound book, and he was alarmed to feel a tug at the sleeve of his cassock. The farmer's bitter-faced wife was trying to get his attention, and he wondered how long he had been thumbing through the pages without reading a word.

"Did you hear him, Father?" she asked.

He gasped for breath. "What is it?"

"He's asking you if there's going to be a Resurrection."

He looked at the toothless old man with the strings of phlegm glistening on his unshaved chin. He started to say *Of course there will be,* but his throat was too swollen to speak. Rising from his chair, he walked unsteadily toward the door.

"You're not leaving, are you, Father?" the old woman demanded.

He managed to croak, "I'm going to bring Father Clancy." He fled down the stairs and away from the house of death. Half-running back into town, he gulped huge lungfuls of air. He hurried into the rectory, mounted the stairs to his room, and fumbled the cork out of the whiskey bottle in his wardrobe drawer. As it burned its way down his throat, he could feel his muscles unclenching and his breath slowing down. It crossed his mind that Father Clancy might be able to smell the liquor on his breath. He would need to stand outside the doorway to the old priest's study – and then he realised that he didn't care. He took another deep swallow.

≈≈≈≈≈

The whiskey was always *there*, he had discovered, coiling comfortably around him the way that he imagined the Serpent had coiled itself around the tree in Eden. When he felt discouraged at the prospect of hearing confessions, or unhappy with the necessity of visiting the sick, the whiskey was always there to make his life less painful. Eventually he realised that he didn't need to wait for the pain to appear – it was a comfort to take a small glass in the morning, like greeting an old friend who would be his companion for the day.

He was surprised at how easy it became to keep the senior priest at arm's length. He saw with sudden clarity that Father Clancy was himself an old man, putting in his last years as a parish priest, more concerned with keeping the peace than with addressing his parishioners' woes. Michael Hayes began to distract Father Clancy's attention with a litany of small, annoying matters. *Did you know there's a leak in the rectory roof? Did Mrs. Halloran tell you about the problems her daughter is having with her husband?* He enjoyed a thrilling sense of control. What did it matter if he had no friends, or if he was leading a life that he never really chose? His new-found power had its own satisfactions.

The Bishop's visit was a surprise. Father Clancy had not forewarned him, and he made no attempt to explain why the Bishop would choose to spend a week in Cork. He kept himself busy by fussing over every detail of the parish, even polishing the hinges and tightening the screws of the antique cabinets in the baptistery. He was certain that the Bishop would return to Dublin fully impressed that everything was under control. The Bishop and Father Clancy spent the days conferring behind closed doors, and he felt sure that the Bishop was advising the old priest to retire.

On Wednesday night he could not find the bottle in his room. At first he blamed himself – had he left it sitting out for the housekeeper to see? He was fairly certain that he had returned it to the back of the wardrobe drawer, but it was not there. Could he have kicked it under the bed? As he explored every cranny of his room, he began to feel a cold sweat and a tightening in his chest.

His mind began racing with suspicions. That meddling Mrs. Halloran had looked at him oddly – was she getting above her housekeeping duties and trying to interfere with his personal life? His teeth clenched. He needed a glass to steady his nerves, to think matters through. But it was far too late to buy a bottle, and the pubs were closed.

His room felt small and barren, like a cell. He needed to get out. He needed to walk, to run, to burn away the hungry energy that gripped him from the inside. Father Clancy and the Bishop were surely asleep – he could pass through the rectory and out the front door without a sound. And then he would... What?

He knew what he would do. Without permitting the thought to take shape in his mind, he knew.

≈≈≈≈≈

A doorway at the side of the church led directly into the sacristy. He closed the door and waited until his eyes became accustomed to the darkness. He had not seen anyone on the street, but he did not want to attract attention by lighting a candle.

The sacristy was full of closets and cupboards, of small confined spaces. Ceremonial vestments hung on pegs in the tall wardrobes. Long candles were stored in a deep chest that looked like a child's coffin. A cabinet with narrow glass windows held the chalices and altar furnishings. The wine was stored in a cupboard with a solid oak door.

It is only wine, he kept telling himself. *It has not been blessed.*

The cupboard was locked, and he did not have the key. He moved from the sacristy through the cavernous empty church, not looking at the dark latticework of the stained-glass windows. He found his small toolbox in the back of the cabinet in the baptistery and he returned, trembling, through the nave.

The screws in the hinges of the wine cabinet were crusted over with layers of congealed varnish. His fingers shook as he scratched at the slots with the screwdriver. Hungry and exhausted, he heard the bell of the town clock strike two.

The groaning screws yielded as he twisted them out of the oak. As he loosened the second hinge, the cabinet door tilted out far enough for him to reach inside. He was groping for a wine-bottle through the half-open door when he heard the footsteps behind him.

A policeman was standing in the doorway, with the Bishop and Father Clancy looking over his shoulders. *What in God's name are you doing, Father Hayes?*

Book Two

In early morning twilight, raw and chill,
Damp vapour brooding on the barren hill,
Through miles of mire in steady grave array
Threescore well-arm'd police pursue their way;
Each tall and bearded man a rifle swings,
And under each greatcoat a bayonet clings...

A hamlet clustering on its hill is seen,
A score of petty homesteads, dark and mean;
Poor always, not despairing until now;
Long used, as well as poverty knows how,
With life's oppressive trifles to contend.
This day will bring its history to an end.

– The Eviction, from *Laurence Bloomfield in Ireland,*
a verse novel (1864) by William Allingham

5 July 1884

In the map-room, everything fit together perfectly. The broad drafting tables, the tall chairs, the map-chests with dozens of wide, flat drawers – all were carved from waxy mahogany with shining brass fittings. Pens and compasses, straight-edges and french curves were stored in velvet-lined cases – brass-and-mahogany cases for the tools that stayed in the map-room, leather cases for the tools that were taken out by the surveyors. Coloured inks were stored in tall ceramic bottles until they were poured out into thick glass inkwells. *It must be like this on a ship,* Ruairí reflected – *not an inch of wasted space anywhere.*

Ruairí pinned a fresh sheet of thin paper over the map of Donegal Bay on his drafting table. *Four more copies*, he thought, *and I will move on to – what?* The six copies that he had completed yesterday were lying in a drawer of the map-chest, under the brass hygrometer that measured the moisture in the atmosphere inside the chest. Ruairí was fascinated with the instrument, especially the pen-nib that drew a scratchy up-and-down line on a roll of paper that was pulled under the nib by a slow clockwork. The others in the map-room took no notice of the hygrometer beyond checking once each day to make sure that the air in the chest was neither too damp nor too dry. Ruairí wondered who had designed it, and how such a device might work.

"Aye, Rory!" Simmons beckoned from his drafting-table across the room. "Here's something you'll want to see."

Ruairí threaded his way between the desks where a dozen draughtsmen and apprentices were copying maps. Some of them eyed him with a hint of hostility. In the weeks since he had been brought into the Westport school, he had grasped the essentials of map-drafting quickly, and he had an instinct for the tricks of the trade – pinning the papers firmly, using the coloured inks sparingly, starting at the top of the page to avoid smearing lower areas with his sleeves. Simmons, the supervisor, had taken a liking to him as well. Sensing the grumbling of the other copyists, Ruairí had made a point of not out-pacing them, even when he knew he could.

Simmons's table was a jumble of maps and notes and work-records. He had cleared a space in the centre and pinned up a surveyor's rough sketch of an island. It was shaped like a shallow W, with jagged edges along the top.

"So what do you think?" asked Simmons. "Would you want to live there?"

One of the draughtsmen coughed loudly, and Ruairí hesitated to make a smart answer. "Where is it?" he asked. "Australia?"

"Closer to home, my boy."

"Around here?"

Simmons couldn't contain himself. "It's Tory, don't you know?"

"It is?" Embarrassed, he craned his neck to try to look at the map from different angles. "I didn't see it, but now I do. And the mainland is down this way..." He pointed to the lower edge of the paper. "I had it pictured in my head that the mainland was up and we was down."

"Ah, that would be heresy, boy."

"I see it, now." Ruairí pointed at the details on the map. "There's *An Baile Thoir*, and *An Baile Thiar...*"

"More heresy," said Simmons, relishing the role of schoolmaster. "That's East Town and West Town now."

"Sure, but you'll never get my Aunt Eithne to call them that."

Two of the draughtsmen had stopped working and were staring pointedly at them. Simmons put a formal tone into his voice and said, "I want you on the detailing of this map, Mullan. You can put in the old names along with the new ones." He pulled two pins and lifted the sketch from his drawing-board. "You can admire this while you're copying the Bay."

≈≈≈≈≈

While the other draughtsmen and apprentices left the building to eat their midday meals, Ruairí stayed at his board with his bread and a jar of cold soup. He pinned the map of Toraigh Island at the top of the board and admired its contours. On the schoolmaster's globe, the sliver of paint that represented his island had looked like a scrap of eggshell in the ocean.

He remembered the way that Simmons had pronounced the name. *Torry.* It sounded flat and hard, like *Colchester* or *Newcastle.* He'd put the real name of the island on the map, if he knew how to spell it. Toraigh? Tor Rí?

"What's that?" Harris was standing behind him, looking over his shoulder at the map. Ruairí didn't mind Harris; of all the apprentices, he was the friendliest.

"That's where I come from. Up off the Donegal coast."

"Them's wee bloody islands up there," said Harris. "'How big is it?"

"It's about three miles east-to-west. Not quite a mile north-to-south, but it depends on where you measure from. If you start with Balor's Army..."

"Start with what?"

"It's sea-stacks. Like a row of teeth."

Harris rolled his eyes. "I don't know what you're fecking talking about."

"They're on the far end of the island." Harris still looked blank. "We went out with a rope one day. It was a hundred feet long." Ruairí felt a warm surge of memory, recalling the sunny, interesting day. "The schoolmaster took us down by the lighthouse, and we measured across until we come to the other side..."

"Is that what they teach you, up in the islands?"

"What did they teach at your school? How to sit on your arse and do sums?"

Harris sized up Ruairí before he spoke. "I got no quarrel with you, mate. Some of the others gives out about you, but I don't.

Your copies is better than anybody's. It just – well, it sounds comical to me, living in a place you could measure with a rope."

"So where do you come from, Harris?"

"Belfast." He looked down at the map of the island on Ruairí's desk. "You could drop that whole island inside Belfast. What's the coordinates up there, anyway?"

"Now I don't know what you're talking about."

"You serious? You're in map-school, and you don't..."

"I know what shit smells like."

They glared at each other. Harris started to walk toward the door, but Ruairí said, "Wait a minute..."

"Wait for what?"

"Come 'ere, Harris. I know I come from the arse-end of nowhere. All I know is how to ask questions. What's a coordinate?"

Harris paused and turned to the shelves at the back of the copy-room. He lifted a leather-bound book and opened it to look at the date. "Here," he said, bringing it to Ruairí's desk. "There's a lot more in here than you need, but it'll get you started."

Ruairí read the name on the spine. *Bowditch's Practical Navigator, 1880.* "Thanks, mate."

"Don't thank me till you read it. It's all numbers. I'm off for some fresh air. I'd get some too if I was you."

Ruairí sat listening to Harris's footsteps as he opened the book on his lap. He'd heard footsteps on the stairs every day, but he'd never counted them before. Fourteen.

≈≈≈≈≈

FROM THE PRIVATE JOURNAL
OF JOHN H. RUSSELL, CAPTAIN
HMS WASP
5 July 1884

Without discipline there can be no Navy. The codes are as old as time. Discipline, obedience, swift justice. We are not here to win each other's affections. We are here to establish order. And the first principle of order is self-discipline.

I have known these truths all of my life. I needed no one to teach them to me. I did not need to be instructed, or reprimanded, or punished. I perceived a Divine Hand behind the principles of order, a Presence which would reward those who obey and punish those who do not.

But even now I find it difficult to accept that the penalties for disobedience are so great. I can accept that the Good Lord is a severe taskmaster, not disposed to indulge the whims of His servants. And I do not dispute that I have strayed from the Paths of Righteousness. Yet I am crushed by the magnitude of the retribution for my sins.

One moment of weakness. The woman who tempted me seemed young and fresh before I knew her, then bitter and agéd afterward. I cursed myself for selling my soul for an illusion, even before the symptoms began to manifest.

Now I can seldom walk without dragging my feet. As I perceive myself in the mirror, I am a wretched sight, a pitiful figure who could not inspire respect in the lowliest or most compliant soul. I find it painful to perform the simplest tasks – to rise, to bathe, to dress myself. My legs are losing the power to move.

Light, any light, causes pain to my eyes. I can scarcely see what I am writing, and yet I cannot bear to open the cabin shutters.

And, pray God no one deciphers this, I am beginning to soil myself at night. I have taken to wearing two layers of underclothing beneath my night-shirt to absorb the urine. I soak my undergarments in my basin to disguise the odour, and sometimes cast them out the porthole at night when we are at sea. What O'Donnell must think I cannot imagine.

I cannot sustain this misery, this humiliation. My own body is a stranger to me. I will resign my commission when we return to Southampton. If I permit myself to live that long.

Gubby has become my nemesis, my bête noire. He avoids me, and will not meet my eyes. How dare he remain aloof? When he speaks, I hear the voices of the landlords and bankers who hounded my father into an early grave. Of course, he did bring ruin upon himself. He was a cold man. What must have possessed him to leave the farm and attempt to feed us on the meagre profits of a pub? His was a joyless place, patronised only by sots and derelicts. Why did my father aspire to provide hospitality to others when he wanted only to dwell in solitude? He must have seen the pub as a path to riches. Or perhaps it was my mother's influence – I shall never know.

It was my mother who first told me about Cook. I was thrilled by the prospect that a farm-labourer's son could rise to wealth and prominence in the Navy, unrestricted by the limitations of his birthright. Like Cook, I had an aptitude for mathematics, and I applied myself. I even worked out the exact latitude and longitude of our bleak home.

When I think of Cook and his days of triumph, I wonder if he benefited from a coincidence of opportunity. He lived when civilised men were first discovering the contours of the world – Newfoundland, Australia, New Zealand, the Antipodes. Who could not make a name for himself in those days, if he were bold enough? I have inherited a world which is completely charted and claimed. If I happened upon an overlooked spit of land and claimed it for the Queen, what reception would I receive in London? Would I be rewarded for enriching the Empire, or would I be dismissed as a nuisance for the map-makers?

But was it only circumstance that enabled Cook to rise? His legend is one of command – he could stir men's spirits, seize opportunities, inspire crews and officers alike. Even his signature flows with confidence, with elegance. What would he have made of an ungainly iron vessel like the Wasp, more like the colliers and merchant-ships that he sailed in his youth?

It is a pedestrian age in which I find myself. When I think of Cook's day, who would not be inspired by the elegance of commanders, by the splendid uniforms? How did that all slip away? My own uniform looks more like a butcher's-coat, a utilitarian garment to repel the rain.

Gubby looks ridiculous in his uniform, like an overweight child playing in his father's wardrobe. By God, it infuriates me! With the advantages of his birth, Gubby can rise in the Navy if he makes the slightest effort. Not as commander, certainly – he lacks the presence, the determination to inspire other men. But his fat rump would be well-suited for an overstuffed chair in Southampton, or Whitehall.

It falls to me, as Gubby's superior, to challenge him with assignments which will test his mettle. If he succeeds, it will reflect well on me, and if he fails, the blame will be his alone. If we were commissioned to portage up the Nile and reinforce Gordon at Khartoum, there would be opportunity for all of us to make our names, and rise. But even in these backwaters of the Empire, this godforsaken coastline of shoals and tenant farmers and petty criminals, there must be challenges and opportunities. I will make it my business to watch for them.

7 July 1884

The other copyists left the map-room at six o'clock, stretching to relieve exaggerated aches and pains, challenging each other to foot-races as they headed to the nearest pub. Ruairí sat at his desk, his head swimming. Simmons, he knew, would putter about in his office for some time. The others might think that he was sucking up, currying favour by staying behind, but he nearly laughed at the idea. He had more important things to think about.

In its first few pages, *Bowditch's Practical Navigator* had sent his imagination soaring. The world became a spider-work of curves and circles, suspended like a shining ball in space. Over the oceans and terrain of the earth, over the valleys and ridges and ragged beaches, a grid of silver lines formed a perfect sphere. The lines ran from pole to pole, from top to bottom like a silver ring spinning on its side. Those lines crossed other lines, concentric circles that started with a broad line at the equator and stacked up, nesting on top of each other, each smaller and smaller until at the North Pole all of the rings converged into a single brilliant point.

And the numbers – every line had a number, and the points where those lines crossed had two numbers, one for each ring. Those numbers could be divided in twos, or tens, or thousands. The corner of his desk was the intersection of two lines, one from pole to pole, one parallel to the equator – each corner of his desk, each corner of every desk, and the spaces between the desk – every point on the face of the earth...

"Mullan!"

"Yes, Mister Simmons?"

"I'm going to leave now, and I must lock the room."

Simmons was standing by the door with a key in hand, and Ruairí wondered how long he had been sitting in his reverie. "Very well, Mister Simmons. I'll leave too."

Ruairí opened a drawer and put away the loose papers and pens from his desktop. Simmons seemed to be smiling, half-amused. "May I ask what keeps you here this evening, Rory?"

"I'm sorry if I've delayed you, Sir..."

"No, I don't mean to suggest that at all. But I've been watching you out of the corner of my eye, and you seem to be – well, lost in thought, to say the least."

Ruairí blushed. "You must think me a fool, Sir..."

"Absolutely not. But I am curious to know what you may be thinking about."

"It's – it's this business of longitude and latitude, Sir. It's..."

"It is quite stunning, isn't it?" Simmons rubbed the back of his neck. "I have worked with it for so many years that I have half-forgotten the wonder of it."

Relieved, Ruairí said, "To know exactly where everything is... And where ships are when they sail..."

"Yes," said Simmons, "although in practice you'll find that there is no such thing as complete certainty."

Ruairí stepped through the office door and waited while Simmons locked it behind them. As they walked down the stairs together, Ruairí said, "My schoolmaster used to talk about human frailty – is that what you mean?"

"That is most certainly true, but there are other complications, too. It would have been most helpful if the Good Lord had placed Magnetic North at the North Pole."

"Sure, but isn't it very close?"

"There are a few places on the earth where a compass will point toward True North, but generally there is a measurable error. It the South Seas, the error is significant. That is one of the reasons why the mutineers from the *Bounty* were not easily found – Pitcairn Island was mis-charted on the Admiralty maps." Simmons closed and locked the outside door. "Even here in the

British Isles, there is a variance of nearly fifteen degrees between True North and Magnetic North."

"Is that a significant error, Sir?"

"It can be, especially if it combines with calibration errors in the instruments or the chronometer." Simmons put on his hat. "It will always be important for a navigator to look across the water as well as at his compass. Good evening to you, Mullan."

"Good evening, Sir." He walked to his lodgings, wondering what Aunt Eithne would think of his new world of instruments and numbers, his shining vision of longitude and latitude. She would be pleased, he thought, that the compasses would never be quite right.

≈≈≈≈≈

A brilliant red-and-yellow sunset reflected blindingly off the surface of Clew Bay, turning the islands into black silhouettes. From the map-school building he walked along the docks toward the end of the quay. He had studied the map of the bay, trying to work out what he could see from the quay – which outlines were islands, and which were mainland. He had given up trying to sort out the small islands that clustered near the harbour like turf-sods in the bottom of a sack. One island for each day of the year, the locals said. The most-detailed maps were inconsistent, and Ruairí guessed that the surveyors, or the copyists, had probably grown lazy and sketched a scatter of island-shapes from pure imagination.

A black cat with white feet was sunning itself on one of the bollards. Thick ropes around the wooden upright secured an English gunboat to the dock, and the sailors were lounging on the deck. Ruairí let the cat smell his finger and then rubbed the shiny black fur behind its ears. One of the men took a pipe out of his mouth and said, "I think you've got a mate there."

Ruairí nodded. "He's a fine-looking cat."

"Is it an 'e or a she? Everybody here's afraid to look."

"I suppose as long as the other cats know..."

The man with the pipe nodded and chuckled. Ruairí walked on, happy for a hint of the old camaraderie that he used to feel on Toraigh. The ship was a long vessel, with white metal skirting-panels around the deck. Tall wooden masts creaked slowly back and forth as the swells of the bay rocked the ship. Neat coils of rope lay on the deck. The sailor tapped his pipe on a railing, making a loud metallic clang. Ruairí thought of Uncle Sean's cowhide-and-pitch *currachs* and wondered, not for the first time, how metal ships managed to float.

A man in an officer's uniform stood at the prow of the ship, studying the sunset. The man was fat, with a thick roll of flesh bulging over his collar. Ruairí paused and walked back to where the sailors were lounging on the deck. "Excuse me?"

"What is it, mate?"

"Has this boat ever been to Toraigh?"

The men chuckled, and the man with the pipe said, "Don't let the Captain hear you callin' her a *boat*, boy. He'll have you flogged."

"Well, I hope he didn't hear me."

"He didn't. Where did you say?"

"Toraigh."

The sailors looked at each other, and one said, "You mean Tory Island, don't ye?"

Deciding not to quibble about pronunciation, Ruairí said, "That's right."

"We shipped a load of potatoes up there – in May, was it? Wasn't you at the schoolhouse up there?"

"I was."

"Yea, I remember you. I was on the detail that wheeled them sacks of spuds over to the schoolhouse."

"You remember me?"

"I don't see that many lads your age with an eye-patch."

The fat boyish officer walked stiffly along the rail on the far side of the ship, and the men lapsed into uncomfortable silence. It was the same officer who'd been talking with the schoolmaster on Toraigh, along with the red-faced Englishman who wore the strange hat.

Ruairí nodded to the sailors and walked along the dock. At the prow of the ship, near the spot where the officer had been standing, the black cat with the white feet lay curled on a coil of rope. It regarded Ruairí briefly, yawned, and closed its eyes.

≈≈≈≈≈

One of the wicks had clogged. Quinn made a note of its location, and the exact time that he'd noticed it. Rings of brass pipes and wicks stood like a multi-tiered wedding cake in the centre of the lantern room, creating a tall, steady light. The clogged wick sat in the third level of the rings. It would be impossible to deal with it until the morning watch, but he knew that Corish would see his note and unclog it after the light was extinguished.

Quinn loved the machinery of the lighthouse – the beacons, the pumps, the ventilators, and the lenses. He had cleaned oil-pumps so many times that he could nearly reassemble them with his eyes shut. The carefully-machined parts slipped together with satisfying clicks when people treated them with respect, but they would jam and deform if anyone tried to force them. It took a special breed of people to work with machinery, he told himself, and he was one of them.

He was less enthusiastic about the human machinery of schedules and information that kept the lighthouses working. Unlike pump-and-engine components, people were... He broke off his thoughts and looked out the window at the sunset reflecting on the sea-swells. People were – what? Erratic? Unpredictable? It bothered him that others sometimes seemed to have a language that he did not know, an understanding of each other that he did not share. His wife would astonish him with information she'd picked up from conversations that he'd ignored, thinking them to be dull or unnecessary. Sometimes he made efforts to pay closer attention, but he found it hard to concentrate.

Through the spotless windows he could see the lights of a ship on the northern horizon, sailing toward Belfast or Liverpool. Quinn noted the sighting in the log. The Tory Island lighthouse, he knew, was the first light that most ships would see after leaving America or Canada. He had been surprised to see that the Tory light had not yet been converted to a rotating beacon. The North Atlantic passage could be stormy and treacherous. On a dark night, how would a ship know if the first light she sighted was Tory or Inishtrahull – or even Aranmore, twenty miles south? If she mistook Aranmore for Tory, she'd be heading straight for the rocks off the Bloody Foreland.

How to make each lighthouse appear unique, unmistakeable? It was the kind of problem he liked to think about. Some lighthouses, he knew, were being equipped with rotating lenses that sent tightly-focused beams streaming out like spokes from a wheel. A large-scale clockwork turned the lenses in a slow circle as they floated in a bath of mercury. He had worked with a rotating installation on the Tuskar lighthouse, and he had touched and learned every detail of the mechanism. There was also the challenge of working out a code of flashes and intervals that would identify each light unmistakably...

"Paddy?"

"Mary?" His wife had appeared at the top of the stairs to the lantern room, holding a mug of tea. "Is that for me?"

She smiled. "If it was just for me, I wouldn't have carried it all the way up here. Do you have a minute to talk?"

He looked at the clock. "It's fifteen minutes before the next oil-barrel."

Mary Quinn stepped onto the platform that ran around the windows of the lantern-room. She handed the mug to her husband, who accepted it with a nod. They stood together, admiring the reddish-orange sheen of the dwindling sunset. "It'll be a clear night tonight, thank God," she said.

"Aye, it will."

"Paddy," she said, "there's something that I want to ask you."

"Yes, Mary?"

"There's going to be a *céilí* in the town on Saturday night. The girls would like to go."

"You'll be going with them, will you?"

"No, I'm thinking that they're old enough to go on their own. If you agree."

Quinn imagined a noisy room full of drunken louts ogling his daughters and asking them to dance. "They're too young, Mary..."

"They aren't so young any more, Paddy. And it would be a way for them to meet some girls from the town."

"But they'll be coming home in the dark, and it won't be safe..."

"Oh, we'll tell them to be back by sunset."

He heard the whirr of the oil-pump in the room below. He had not gone out to *céilís* in his teens, and he felt an emptiness inside himself. "Ah, you decide, Mary. I don't know..."

"So you don't object, then?"

"Not if you think they'll be all right."

They watched a distant ship scudding along the horizon, headed for Labrador or Boston. His wife said, "You know, Paddy, when we're sitting at tea, and we're all together as a family..."

"What?"

"...perhaps you could talk with the girls more?"

"Don't we all talk together?"

Embarrassed, Mary Quinn squinted her eyes. "Well, of course we do. But I seem to do most of the talking, at the table..."

As his wife's voice trailed off, Quinn struggled to think of what to say. "I know you're a grand talker, Mary, and sometimes I think I must not be good company for you..."

"No," she said, "it's not that. I know how you are. But the girls – they think you don't like them."

"Why?"

"You see, they're turning into young ladies..."

"They're growing up, all right..."

"...and it's nice for them if their Da takes an interest in them."

He hesitated. "Do you mean asking them about how they're getting on in school?"

Mary Quinn smiled and shook her head. "That would be a start. Here, give me a sip of your tea." He handed the mug to her. "I know you're a good man at heart. I'm just asking you to try to think about the girls, and make an effort. They're only young once."

He looked at the floor, feeling small. "All right, Mary. I'll try."

She handed back the mug. "Good night, Paddy. You'll come in after midnight, then?"

"I'll try not to wake you..."

"I don't mind if you do. Good night."

Quinn waited until he heard her footsteps reach the ground floor of the tower before he moved from the lantern room to fill the oil-pump. He felt shaken inside, as though he'd been scolded. He tried to remember the last time he had talked with his daughters, and what they might have talked about. Was he failing at something? He couldn't imagine that they would take an interest in his world of gears and bearings and stabilisers. What might his daughters be interested in?

As he topped up the oil tank, he listened to the steady rhythm of the pump. The mechanism was running smoothly, but he knew that it should be overhauled and cleaned before September, when the nights would grow longer. He wished that he understood other people half as well.

≈≈≈≈≈

From the end of the Westport quay Ruairí could see the outline of Clare Island. Someone had said that it looked like a whale, but he could not stretch his imagination that far. He remembered the day that the schoolmaster had looked at the clouds over Toraigh and muttered, half to himself, *Very like a whale.* When Ruairí asked why he said that, the schoolmaster chuckled and said, *It's a long story, and difficult to explain.*

Thinking of the schoolmaster made him feel a stab of loneliness. On Toraigh, Eoghan would have finished Eithne's chores and would be heading for the football pitch. Unless he has to spend the evenings at the lighthouse now... He wondered how his brother would be feeling, tied to the slow-but-endless schedule of hauling barrels of oil up the steps of the tall tower.

He knew no one in Westport. Harris spoke to him from time to time, but his loyalties were with the other copyists – some English lads, some Scots. At lunchtime they kicked a football on the green near the map-school, but Ruairí knew better than to try to join in. He couldn't judge how fast the ball was coming until it hit him in the nose.

He had tried to write to the schoolmaster, but he had found himself sitting at a table and staring into space, overcome with memories and homesickness. He remembered the evenings when Mister Geraghty had sat at Eithne's table, prompting her to tell the old stories of Balor and the Formorians and the Tuatha Dé Danann. Tears welled up and stung the raw muscles of his missing eye. He missed Eithne terribly. He felt flashes of companionship with Simmons, who sometimes reminded him of the schoolmaster. But there was no one in Westport who felt the sunsets and the tides, the great wheel of the earth turning, as Eithne did. What if he never saw her again? The thought squeezed him like a cold fist.

He felt the ground tremble as a low steady sound grew louder behind him. A plume of white smoke emerged from the low hills near the town, and a freight-train rumbled along the tracks toward the tall stone building on the quay. The trains, he knew, carried barley from the fertile midlands, and he marvelled at the vast quantities of grain that they disgorged. Each freight-car carried more than an entire year's harvest on Toraigh. It struck him that he could write to the schoolmaster about the railway and the grain. The content of his letter would make no difference – it was the writing that was important. He would write to Eithne, too.

Heartened, he walked back along the quay. The sun was setting, and he cast a long shadow on the stone walkway, a figure with huge feet and elongated legs and a tiny head. His stomach grumbled. The men who'd been lounging on the deck of the

Wasp were nowhere to be seen. He began to compose the letters in his mind. *Mister Geraghty, thank you for encouraging me to come here. Westport is a busy town. There is a grain elevator by the harbour, and the quay is long enough for a dozen boats.* The conversation with the sailor came back to him – were they boats or ships? Would the schoolmaster care? *A gunboat is tied up here too, the same one that brought us the potatoes last May...*

The road forked at the end of the quay, near the map-school building. His empty stomach urged him to hurry to his room in Westport where he kept his bread and cheese and pickle to make ploughman's sandwiches, but a line of horse-drawn carriages from the town distracted his attention. The carriages made sharp right turns and clattered through a stone archway next to a gate-house. Two men in long-tailed coats nodded in greeting to each coach. Ruairí caught glimpses of women wearing elaborate hats in the carriages, while well-groomed men glared at him from the passing windows. Some of the men wore black coats, and others wore military uniforms.

The last carriage in the procession rolled under the arch, and the two men swung the gates shut and stepped into the gate-house. Curious, Ruairí walked to the doorway.

One of the men was sitting in a chair, scratching his leg inside a high boot. The taller man, shoving sticks into a weak fire, looked over at him. "What the feck to you want?"

"Sure, I was just wondering what..."

"None of your business. It ain't any of his business, is it, Willie?"

The second man looked Ruairí up and down with deliberate slowness. "Looks like a fecking culchie come to town, he does. I'll bet he still got pig-shit on his shoes."

Ruairí stifled a hot wave of rage. "Look, mate, I only just saw the carriages..."

"I ain't your feckin' mate. You're Irish, and I ain't. Am I, Freddie?"

Freddie took a step toward Ruairí. "No feckin' Irish here. Not tonight, and not tomorrow, neither."

Willie stood up and pushed his foot firmly back into his boot. "You'd like to go up there to the Manor House and help yourself to the silver, wouldn't you? Maybe stuff a few sausages in your pockets?"

Ruairí felt his legs tensing, itching to kick. "Is that what you piss-arses do on your day off?"

Willie spit on the floor. "I'll show you what I fecking do on my day off..."

A carriage rattled up to the gate-house, and Ruairí stepped away from the doorway. The guards hurried out and swung the gates open. Ruairí walked down the road at a tense, deliberate pace, fighting a deep impulse to run back and fight. He'd likely take a bruising from the two men, but he knew he could make them sorry they'd tried.

He heard the gate clang shut as he turned the corner near the map-school building. He paused, thinking of what Simmons would say if he came to his desk with bruises and cuts. *And if the schoolmaster found out...* He turned onto the road toward town, wondering how Mister Geraghty had contended with the hateful bastards who must have bullied him.

"Lovely night, sailor."

He flinched and snapped upright, trying to see where the girlish voice had come from. He was passing an alley between two warehouses, and the narrow brick walkway was strewn with barrels and crates. Peering into the gloomy passage, he could see the dim shape of a young woman waving a handkerchief at him.

"Come on back here. I won't bite, you know."

Hesitating, he realised that it would be a good idea to step away from the main road in case the gate-house guards decided to come looking for him. He wound his way around piles of wooden slats and packing material, stepping over puddles of stagnant water. Broken glass crunched under his shoes.

The girl sat on a crate in a half-cleared spot behind a Bristol barrel. She rocked back and forth with her knees spread apart under a long skirt. She had pulled her blouse to one side, exposing her shoulder. In the gloomy light of the alley, he couldn't see her face well.

"Are you off the grain-ship?" she asked.

"No, I'm not a sailor at all."

"You're Irish!" she said. "I thought you was one of those English boys. Step over here."

Ruairí started to move before he hesitated. "Who are you?"

"I'm Rosie. You know – *The Last Rose of Summer*. What's your name?"

"Ruairí," he said. "What are you doing back here?"

"What do you think I'm doing back here, Ruairí?"

He was surprised that she pronounced his name well – not like the islanders, but still like the old language. "You're Irish too, aren't you?"

"I'm not fecking English, that's for sure. So what do you want?"

"What do I want?"

"You're just a boy, aren't you?" She stood up from the chair and moved closer to him. She walked with a limp. "Sure, you're not even seventeen."

"I'm sixteen, that's right."

She ran her hand up and down his arm, and he felt a surge of longing. "And you're not from around here, are you? Where are you from?"

"I – I'm from Toraigh."

She shook her head. "Where's that?"

"It's north from here – out in the ocean..."

"You're a long way from home, aren't you?" She moved closer, and he could feel the warmth of her body. "I'll bet you get lonely, a long way from home."

A wail rose up from behind a pile of crates, and the girl said, "Oh, damn! Just a minute." She turned away from Ruairí and bent over a box in the darkness.

"You've got a babby in there," he heard himself saying.

"Just a minute!" She fussed with the shape in the box, crooning softly.

"It's cold back here..."

"I know it's cold! When we get our business done, I'll take him inside."

His surge of desire ebbed away as he watched the girl bending awkwardly over the box in the dark. She looked like an old crone fussing over a fish. "I'm sorry," he said. "I don't... I can't..."

She looked up at him. "Would you have sixpence for the babby?"

He hesitated, wondering if the whole situation was some kind of ruse. She said, "He's cryin' because he hasn't et all day."

Ruairí groped in his pockets. "Here," he said, "here's sixpence. Get him something."

She stood up and walked to him, taking the coin from his hand. "You're a nice lad," she said. "You come back and I'll do you."

His heart hammered in his chest. "No," he said, "I – I promised my uncle..."

The baby started to cry again. She looked at him and put the coin in her pocket. She said, "All right, then," and turned back to the box, making cooing sounds. Ruairí walked like a wounded man through the labyrinth of the alley and back onto the Westport road.

10 September 1884

Lying in his bunk, Gubby could hear the men writing at the mess tables - the shuffling of their papers, the scratching of their pens. The cloth curtain that separated his quarters from the mess barely covered the opening, and he could catch glimpses of the men on the other side. Not that they bothered him – most of the sailors avoided him, speaking only when spoken to. But it made no sense to warn officers about fraternising with the men, and then assign quarters which were separated from them by only a thin cloth. Evans and Armstrong had private cabins with proper doors, and the Captain had a two-room suite. Were all junior officers assigned to such exposed quarters?

He should, he reflected, write to his father more often. At the Midshipman's School, he had made it a point to write weekly, cheerfully reporting on his courses and examinations. During the year when he sailed with the young Royals, he had posted enthusiastic letters in every port, knowing that the mere arrival of correspondence from Cape Town and Melbourne would create a stir. He had restrained himself from writing about the Princes – their condescending attitudes, their unwillingness to lift a finger for themselves – worrying that critical comments, even in the context of family letters, might re-emerge on some awkward day to sabotage his career. But since his assignment to the *Wasp*, he had scarcely written at all. What could he write? *Father, I am without companions, and I fear that I may not be suited for a military career?* He could imagine his father throwing such a letter into the fire.

But he also realised that a protracted silence might lead his father to draw conclusions, or to make inquiries. He sat up in his bunk and opened his sea-chest. As he lifted paper and envelopes from under the jumble of clothing in the chest, his pen fell onto the deck and rolled under the curtain into the mess area. Trying to avoid looking at the men at the tables, he pulled the curtain aside and stooped to retrieve the pen when he heard O'Donnell's boots clanging in the passageway.

"Mister Gubby?"

"Yes, O'Donnell?"

"Captain wants to see you in his cabin, Sir."

He felt a flush of embarrassment, wondering if O'Donnell had seen him groping around for the pen. "Please tell him I'll be right there."

"Aye aye, Sir!" O'Donnell clattered back up the stairs, and Gubby closed the curtain while he pulled on his boots and tucked in his shirt. Why would the Captain want to see him? A dozen possibilities raced through his mind, from reprimands to reassignments. At least, he thought as he heaved his bulk up the stairs, he might have something to write to his father about.

≈≈≈≈≈

A telegram lay on the Captain's desk, but the light in the cabin was so dim that Gubby could not make out the wording. The Captain had pushed his chair away from the desk, turning sideways and staring into space. He acknowledged Gubby's arrival by pointing to one of the chairs in front of the desk. Squeezing between the arms of the chair, Gubby felt a trickle of sweat run down his back while his stomach clenched with apprehension. *What now?*

When the Captain spoke, his voice seemed far away. "I am stunned, Mister Gubby..." His voice trailed off into silence.

"Have I – is anything wrong, Sir?"

The Captain turned abruptly, as though he had just realised that another person was with him. "What is wrong, Mister Gubby, is an interesting philosophical question."

"I'm afraid that I'm not following, Sir..."

"Why did you join the Royal Navy, Mister Gubby?"

Feeling a deep sense of dread, Gubby struggled to find words that would not betray his fear. "I suppose it was because I always wanted to be part of something meaningful..."

"I joined the Navy to serve England," the Captain interrupted. "To battle her enemies. And to seek an honourable career." He glared at Gubby across the desk. Baffled and frightened, Gubby tried to meet his gaze.

"Some weeks ago I received orders to confirm access to the Clare Island docks," the Captain continued. "Now this."

He picked up the telegram and handed it to Gubby. Strips of paper ribbon from a teletype printer were pasted to a yellow page, and he struggled to read the faintly-inked words. ESCORT WESTPORT SHERIFF PROPERTY RECOVERY CLARE ISLAND ESTABLISH SCHEDULE CONFIRM DARLINGTON

Gubby read the message twice, trying to understand the blurred lines of words. "Is this from Admiral Darlington?"

"None other."

"Sir, I don't – what is SHERIFF PROPERTY RECOVERY?"

The Captain exhaled loudly before he spoke. "It seems that Her Majesty's Navy is being pressed into the service of the merchant classes." Still not understanding, Gubby hesitated to speak. "This means that we are to collect rents, Mister Gubby. And failing that, we are to perform evictions. How do you feel about that?"

Shadows flickered across the porthole, and Gubby could hear the cries of sea-birds feeding on the scraps which the cook tossed into the bay. He struggled to find something to say. "Perhaps there are extraordinary circumstances, Sir," he ventured. "A fraud of some magnitude..."

"This is Ireland, Mister Gubby. Nothing is of any magnitude."

Gubby felt a jolt of recognition, and he wondered if Captain Russell shared his unhappy suspicions about being posted to the gloomy Atlantic coast. The Captain interrupted his thoughts. "In times of conflict, Gubby, we are indispensable. When they are frightened, they want their Navy and their Army. They cannot do enough for us. In peacetime we are an expense – a nuisance –

and we are to perform their dogsbody errands. It is no wonder that Gordon stirs the pot into crisis in Khartoum. By God, he maintains their attention."

Gubby sat miserably, fearing to say a word. The Captain seemed to pull himself out of his reverie, turning to face him squarely across the table. "I have been seeking an opportunity to challenge you, Mister Gubby. I thought that circumstances might offer us a raid, or an insurrection. Mediterranean pirates have ventured into these waters, more recently than you might think. But instead..." He gestured at the telegram in Gubby's hands. "Instead, we have this."

The Captain sat upright and stared without blinking – a posture, Gubby knew, that signalled formal orders. "You will contact the Sheriff's office and arrange to escort the Sheriff to Clare. Select eight men for the detail. Set a schedule and report back to me. You will be establishing precedent, Mister Gubby. Whatever this may involve, I want it done properly."

Gubby said, "Yes, Sir," realising that he had risen to his feet.

"And one other thing."

"Yes, Sir?"

The Captain handed him the telegram. "Include someone in the detail who speaks Irish. It may well be the only tongue that the islanders understand. That is all."

Gubby found himself on deck, blinking in the sunlight and holding the telegram in his trembling hands. A group of sailors who were mopping the deck-plates glanced at him, but avoided meeting his eye. He walked over to them. "Drury?"

"Yes, Sir?"

"Hurry into Westport and fetch a rig. I will need it for an hour or longer."

"Aye aye, Sir!" Drury handed his mop to one of the other sailors and hurried down the gangplank. Gubby watched as Drury ran along the quay toward the town. The other sailors looked up at him quizzically, but he ignored their eyes and strode back to his quarters. He had a mission.

12 September 1885

"So you've drawn the short straw, have you?"

Evans eased himself into the chair across the table in the Officers' Mess. Looking up from his rashers and eggs, Gubby was surprised to see that Evans was wearing his Dress Whites. "Are you going ashore, Sir?"

"I am indeed. The Navy owes me a good deal of leave, and I am choosing to collect some of it. Tea only, Steward."

Gubby waited until the sailor had left the Mess before leaning across the table to Evans. "Will you not be taking the *Wasp* out to Clare, then?"

"I'm leaving her in your capable hands, Gubby."

Gubby pushed his plate to the side, nauseated by the streaks of congealing yolk. "This is going to be a rather difficult day, Sir. I had hoped..."

"Hmmm." Evans waited until the Steward placed his tea mug on the table and again stepped out of the Mess. "You'll have smooth sailing on Clew Bay. And the Captain and Armstrong will be on hand if you need them."

"Yes, but..." Gubby declined to finish his thought, realising how much he had grown to depend on Evans's gruff humour and calm.

"Have you found your Irish-speaking sailor yet?" Evans asked.

"No, in fact, I intend to ask the Sheriff if he has someone. The men seem reluctant..."

"O'Donnell is your man."

"O'Donnell? The Commander's Servant?"

"I have heard him rattle on in what I take to be Irish. He should suffice." Evans stood up. "I wish you success in this enterprise, my young friend." He started toward the door.

"Have you ever taken part in an eviction, Sir?"

Evans paused and looked down at the deck before he spoke. "Not in this part of the world, Gubby." He took a step toward the door but paused again. "Thankfully, my battles have been farther afield. The best of luck to you."

≈≈≈≈≈

Hesitating before he knocked on the Captain's door, Gubby heard a groan from inside the cabin. He looked around the deck. Evans and Armstrong were speaking to each other near the gangplank. Prescott was standing guard. The other men who usually performed morning duties on the deck were nowhere in sight. Consulting his pocket-watch, Gubby saw that it was 0850, and the Sheriff was due to arrive at 0900. He knocked on the cabin door, and a voice said, "Come in!"

The Captain was sitting at his desk, and it seemed to Gubby that his posture was unusually rigid. Squinting his eyes, the Captain said, "Close the door. What do you want?"

"Sir, I need to request O'Donnell's participation in today's detail."

"O'Donnell? What for?"

"He seems to be the only man on board who speaks Irish, Sir."

"Bollocks!" The Captain spat out the word. "Do you believe that, Gubby? Can you not tell when the men are lying to you?"

"It was Lieutenant Evans's suggestion, Sir."

"Evans!" The Captain turned aside and wiped his mouth with a napkin. "Evans is on leave."

"I spoke with him at breakfast, Sir, and..."

"Evans seems to wield great influence, does he not?"

Gubby found himself on the verge of saying *Could you not order him back, Sir?* but he feared what the Captain might say. Fighting panic, he groped for a response. "Sir, was it not yourself who advised me to find an Irish-speaking man for the detail?"

"Of course it was, Gubby. Don't you think I remember that?" He turned sharply sideways in his chair. "O'Donnell!"

"Yes, Sir!" O'Donnell appeared at the interior door of the Captain's suite.

"Lieutenant Gubby needs your participation in today's detail on Clare!"

"Aye aye, Sir. But I thought that you had asked me to go into town..."

"You will accompany Lieutenant Gubby today. That is all."

Gubby heard the sounds of footfalls on the gangplank. He looked at the Captain, who seemed to be gritting his teeth. "Is there anything else, Gubby?"

"No, Sir..."

"Then I suggest that you greet the Sheriff. Take O'Donnell with you. That is all."

≈≈≈≈≈

Blinking in the morning sunlight, Gubby crossed the deck to the gangplank. A short, pudgy man with a red face stood impatiently by the sailor who was standing guard. Two muscular-looking men stood on the gangplank. Four thick poles and a coil of greasy rope lay on the dock beside a wagon. The men on the gangplank wore military coats without insignia.

Gubby approached the short irritated-looking man. "Sub-Lieutenant Gubby at your service, Sir..."

"Name's Pitt," the man said, not offering his hand. "Sheriff. Where is your Captain?"

"Captain Russell has assigned me to accompany you..."

"I will speak to your Captain."

"Shall I take him to the Captain's quarters, Sir?" asked O'Donnell.

"Right, O'Donnell." Gubby stifled an impulse to say *Thank you.*

The Sheriff started to follow O'Donnell and then turned to Gubby. "Have your men bring the ram aboard." He walked across the deck to the door of the Captain's cabin.

The Sheriff's men stepped onto the deck of the ship, staring at Gubby with a directness that bordered on insolence. Gubby said, "Right. Prescott?"

"Yes, Sir?"

"Go below and tell Drury to have the detail report here. I'll mind the watch."

"Aye aye, Sir." Prescott hurried to the stairs.

In the silence that followed, Gubby could hear the waves lapping at the dock and the scrape of the gangplank as the ship shifted in the water. A gull landed on the mast. One of the deputies leaned over the skirting and spat into the water. Irritated at the man's attitude, Gubby said, "Where is the ram?"

"That lot, there," the other deputy said, nodding at the poles and rope on the dock, but making no movement in that direction.

Footsteps rang on the metal stairs, and Prescott returned with Drury and the other sailors in the work-party. "Bring that material on deck," said Gubby. "Stow it by the skirting."

"Aye aye, Sir."

The door to the Captain's cabin opened, and Gubby saw O'Donnell and the Sheriff coming out. He felt relieved that O'Donnell would be part of the detail. The Sheriff gestured to the deputies, and they huddled in conversation on the deck.

"Well, O'Donnell," said Gubby, "is our guest satisfied with the arrangements?"

"Yes, Sir. Captain says we'd better get going, Sir."

"Right." He turned to the sailors. "Take up the gangplank, men. We're bound for Clare."

≈≈≈≈≈

In the bright September sunshine, the *Wasp* moved effortlessly through the waters of Clew Bay. Relaxing at the wheel, Gubby hummed a half-forgotten tune. In his weeks of training with Evans, he had taken the ship around the bay, up along the Achill coast, and out into the open sea. They had circled Clare Island and had brought the ship alongside the dock. Manning the ship was, Gubby realised, a matter of foresight – thinking ahead of the moment, seeing opportunities and obstacles, moving with deliberation. *Imagine the worst possible events that can happen,* Evans had advised. *Do not dwell on them, but take care that they do not develop.*

The ship seemed exceptionally responsive in the calm waters. Gubby avoided the cluster of rocks on the south shore of the bay and kept to the centre of the channel. From the wheel he could see the Sheriff and the two deputies hunkering down, damp and uncomfortable in the spray and the breezes. He thought of sending O'Donnell to invite them below for tea and a dry room to sit in, but he decided against it. If they had shown more respect, he would have been more gracious.

Carlisle, he noticed, was standing watch in the foredeck shelter. It struck him with a nearly-physical impact that he had made no inquiries or arrangements about the general running of the ship – who was on watch, who was manning the engine-room. He was piloting a vessel that carried fifty-six men – now fifty-nine – but he had not made even the most general inquiries about how the complex organism that was the *Wasp* would function while he was at the wheel. He felt dismayed at his own short-sightedness, his lack of vision.

"O'Donnell!"

"Yes, Sir."

"Would you ask Armstrong to come here?"

"Aye aye, Sir."

He heard the quick clangs of O'Donnell's boots on the ladder. The Sheriff and the deputies looked up briefly and then turned away. A moment later he heard heavier footfalls as Armstrong climbed up to the bridge.

"You asked to see me, Gubby?"

"I did, Sir."

"What do you want?"

Gubby drew a deep breath. "I was wondering, Sir – did you oversee today's assignments and details?"

"Evans did, although we conferred about it since he was planning to take leave. Except, of course, for the detail which you are overseeing."

Armstrong's air of solid competence made Gubby feel empty and foolish. "I am wondering, Sir, if I have overlooked something – if I have neglected to confer with you..." His voice trailed off, unable to complete his thought.

"I have taken the liberty, Gubby, of issuing side-arms to the men in your detail. I trust that you have no objection."

"Not at all, Sir! I truly appreciate... I mean, I wish that I had requested..."

From the corner of his eye, he could see Armstrong grinning. "Quite so, Gubby," he said, "we have been watching your back. Our Captain has seen fit to assign a demanding detail to you, and at the same time he isolates himself from providing assistance. But you, Mister Gubby, you isolate yourself as well."

"It was not my intention..."

"Do not berate yourself, Gubby. I am glad you have broken the ice on this subject." Armstrong stepped forward and leaned on the rail. "If you ever quote what I am about to say, I will swear that you are a liar. Do you understand?"

"Yes, Sir."

"We tell each other the stories about Cook, and Drake, and Raleigh to inspire ourselves. But for every captain who can build confidence in his crew with courage and vision, there are fifty others who might as well be shopkeepers or pig-farmers. Do you follow?"

"I think I do."

"And they lurch about, like unsecured cannonballs on deck. They seek ways of reassuring themselves that they are fit for command, and they grasp at half-formed ideas. At the same time, they are given orders by others who lurch about, issuing orders from armchairs in well-warmed rooms far from the sea."

Armstrong turned to look Gubby full in the face. "Then there are men like us – you and Evans and myself. It falls to us to implement the orders of our so-called betters. Sometimes we perform distasteful duties. Sometimes we risk the blood and sanity of the men. And sometimes we simply sit in the background, keeping the engines running and the assigning the rotations of the watch.

Armstrong paused and drew a deep breath. "What is vital, Gubby, is that we communicate with each other. For example, when you were assigned this detail..."

"I should have reviewed it with you and Evans, then," Gubby interrupted.

"It would have done no harm. As it was, we deduced your assignment and recognised that you were keeping it to yourself. We also realised that a jaunt to Clare Island would require nothing special on anyone's part, except perhaps to stand extra men on watch while we tie up at the harbour. However..."

"However, I have neglected to..."

"No, Gubby. I would not accuse you of neglect. But you have kept rather to yourself since being assigned to the *Wasp*. You could do worse than to share your thoughts with Evans and me."

Gubby felt a hot ball of shame in the back of his neck as tears welled up in his eyes. Armstrong said, "Do you now understand why I will swear that you are deluded, and a liar, if you ever attempt to quote me on these matters?"

"I do, Sir."

"Then I will leave you for now. When you dock at Clare, I am going to supervise the men personally as they lower the cork fenders. We don't want to scratch her new paint, do we?"

≈≈≈≈≈

On the Clare Island dock, the Sheriff pulled a map from his coat-pocket and examined it. Gubby stood closer to the sailors than to the Sheriff, wanting to distance himself from the self-important little man. At the other end of the dock, two Irish fishermen loaded nets and floats into a *currach*, averting their eyes when Gubby looked at them. Crows fluttered around the ruins of the square castle at the edge of the cove. A dirty shoeless child stared from the doorway of a nearby cottage until a woman's hand reached out to pull it inside and shut the door.

"This way," said the Sheriff, and he started toward the road at the end of the dock, followed by his two deputies. Gubby nodded at the men in the detail. The sailors picked up the four logs, and O'Donnell threw the coil of rope over his shoulder. Gubby began to foresee the letter that he would write – *We follow'd the Sheriff and his two Associates, making a sorry spectacle of a parade.* The Sheriff walked briskly, but Gubby made no attempt to match his speed. *At the very least,* he thought, *we will keep our own pace.*

They followed the road from the end of the dock past a cluster of stone cottages and along a tree-shaded lane. Cultivated fields bordered both sides of the lane, and cattle and sheep grazed on stony hillsides. At one lane the Sheriff paused, consulted his map, and continued walking.

"Mister Gubby?"

It was O'Donnell, walking awkwardly with his coil of rope. "What is it, O'Donnell?"

"Did you see this, Sir?"

"What are you talking about?"

"This, Sir." O'Donnell held up an end of the rope that was tied in a slip-knot. "It's a noose, Sir. Are we going to...?"

Gubby stopped and stared at the well-worn rope with its hangman's knot. "No! The Captain said nothing..." His mind whirled at the ugly possibility. "No, I saw the orders. Our mission is property retrieval."

"But, Sir..."

"Yes?"

"Where is everyone?"

Gubby looked back along the road past the sailors. No other people, no islanders, were on the road. He said, "I imagine that they are minding their own business," but his voice sounded hollow to himself.

"This is one!" the Sheriff shouted. He had stopped beside a gate. A broken fence surrounded a small cottage with a roof that needed new thatching. A pig was rooting in the yard, and smoke curled out of the chimney.

The Sheriff and his men pushed the gate open, walked to the cottage, and knocked loudly on the door. Gubby and the men stood at the gate, unsure of what to do. A deputy walked back to O'Donnell and said, "Get up there."

O'Donnell looked at Gubby, who nodded. He started to slip the rope from his shoulder, but the deputy said, "You'll need that."

As O'Donnell made his way toward the cottage, a woman opened the door. She held a baby in the crook of her arm, and she had a wooden spoon in her other hand. In a loud, declaiming voice, the Sheriff said, "You are a tenant on the property of Mister George Coombs!"

The woman looked blankly at the Sheriff and at the men standing behind him. O'Donnell stopped, unsure of what to do. In his public-announcement voice, the Sheriff said, "Your rent is two years in arrears!"

The woman started speaking in a language that Gubby did not recognise. It sounded like she was asking a question, but the Sheriff turned to O'Donnell and shouted, "Get up here! Tell her to pay the rent or get out!"

O'Donnell said, "I don't know how to say that, Sir."

"Yes you do, you little Irish bastard!"

"No, honestly, Sir, I don't know who thought I could speak Irish..."

The woman closed the door. The Sheriff spun around and hammered on the door with his fist, and inside the woman began screaming. The Sheriff shouted, "Bring that ram over here!"

The sailors looked at each other. One of the deputies gestured and pointed at the logs. "Bring those over here. By the door." The men looked at Gubby, who nodded again.

Following the deputy, the sailors carried the logs to the cottage door. While the deputies barked orders, they stood three of the logs on end, leaning the tops together to form a crude tripod. One deputy took the rope from O'Donnell and lashed the tops of the logs together, leaving the noose-end of the rope hanging down in the centre of the structure. The deputies lifted the fourth log and slipped it through the noose so that it hung by its middle. They swung the log back and forth and then nodded to the Sheriff.

With a beet-red face and bulging eyes, the Sheriff shouted, "You will pay your rent immediately or you will vacate this property!" The woman in the house kept screaming, but she did not come out. The deputies swung the log back, and O'Donnell shouted, "Get away from the door!"

The deputies swung the log forward, smashing the door and door-frame off the walls and into the house. The woman screamed louder, and a little boy ran out of the house with a fork in his hand. He ran at one of the deputies, but the other one tripped him. The big men closed in on him, and Gubby could hear a howl of pain.

With the baby in her arms, the woman ran out of the house to where her son lay sobbing on the ground. Another child, a small girl, was with her. Gubby realised that the Sheriff was now shouting at him. "Take everything out of this house!"

"Take it – where?"

"Off the property! Now!"

The sailors were standing in a clumsy knot beside the house, looking at him with desolated eyes. The Sheriff was still shouting, "Are you going to cooperate, Lieutenant, or do I need to report this..."

His stomach churning, he nodded to the men. They entered the house, shaking their heads. The first man emerged with two wooden stools, the next with a small handmade table, and the next with a straw mattress. One of the deputies pointed to the gate where Gubby was standing, and the sailors began to pile the possessions on the lane beside him.

O'Donnell stood like a statue beside the broken door. One of the men handed him a soup-pot and said, *C'mon, mate.* He carried it to the lane and placed it on the small pile, avoiding Gubby's eyes.

Wailing and huddling with her children in the yard, the woman stretched her hand out toward Gubby. He turned his head away in misery, ashamed at his impotence. He forced himself to look back at the woman, but she had twisted herself down into a ball of pain, her hands clasped in prayer.

The house was empty in minutes. One of the deputies looked at the pig that was still rooting near a gorse-bush. He shot an inquiring glance at the Sheriff, who waved his hand dismissively and gestured with his head toward the cottage. The deputy stepped through the door and shouted *Everybody out* to the men who were still inside.

Following directions from the other deputy, the sailors dismantled the ram and carried the logs and rope back to the gate. They looked back to see the first deputy leaving the house, ducking his head. Smoke was beginning to emerge from the thatching, and flames could be seen through the hole where the door had been.

The woman and the children wailed. Gubby feared that the Sheriff would order him to remove them physically from the property, but the red-faced little man drew the map from his pocket again. "That is *one*, Lieutenant," he said in a surprisingly-calm voice. "There are three more to be done today. Follow me."

≈≈≈≈≈

A knot of island men trailed behind them as they walked away from the last house. *English bastards!* someone shouted, but the sailors stopped in their tracks and turned to face them. The other island men did not take it up. Some of them carried sticks. Unaccustomed to wearing side-arms, the sailors kept adjusting their belts and holsters. With a sinking heart, Gubby prayed that the islanders would keep their distance.

The day had become a blur in his mind – the screaming of women, the angry shouts of men, the small, scattered piles of possessions on the muddy lanes. The four eviction properties were scattered across the length of the island, and they had doubled back twice as the Sheriff studied and re-studied his map. None of the tenants seemed to understand a word of English, and Gubby wondered how the Sheriff could be sure of the locations.

As the day wore on, Gubby's stomach began to churn. He had not thought to bring food, and the sheer misery of the work began to twist his insides. Nodding in assent to every instruction from the Sheriff, he had said almost nothing for the entire day. Now he found himself walking again behind the Sheriff's men and in front of the sailors, feeling the loathing that radiated from his crew. O'Donnell straggled at the rear of the party, staying as far away from him as possible. He sweated, and his head ached. One of the Sheriff's men took something from his pocket and put it in his mouth – a biscuit? a piece of dried fruit? – and Gubby fought hard to resist asking for a bite of it.

The lane curved, and the harbour came into view. The *Wasp* looked like a refuge of sanity in a landscape of madness. Gubby still could not bring himself to look back at the sailors, or to share a moment of relief. One of the island men on the road behind shouted, *Get on your fecking boat, you bastards! Leave us alone!*

Three sailors with rifles were standing watch on the *Wasp*. To Gubby's surprise, the Sheriff stepped aside to let him board first. He turned to look at the eviction detail. The dispirited men were glaring at him, waiting for orders. His throat clogged when he tried to speak. He coughed until he could say, "Bring those logs on deck."

Prescott, who was still on watch by the gangplank, said, "Shall I get you some water, Sir?"

"If you would, please."

The men carried the logs onto the deck and dropped them with a clang by the rail. Gubby climbed the ladder to the bridge. The knot of island men stood on the dock, talking among themselves and glaring at the *Wasp*. Prescott appeared on deck with a tin cup of water, which he handed up to Gubby. He drank it in a gulp.

"Prescott!" he said, relieved that his voice was working again. "Take up the gangplank. We're casting off."

"Aye aye, Sir. Should I tell Lieutenant Armstrong, Sir?"

"Yes, of course." *And thank you, Prescott,* he nearly blurted out.

The metal gangplank screeched across the flagstones of the dock as the men began pulling it onto the deck.

"Lieutenant!"

Gubby saw the Sheriff shouting from the deck. "Yes?"

"The rope!"

The coil of greasy rope with its noose-end lay on the dock where O'Donnell had dropped it. The men who were hoisting the gangplank stopped and looked to Gubby for instructions.

"We need the rope!" the Sheriff shouted.

Gubby looked down at the pudgy little man, the muscular deputies, and the crewmen who were waiting for him to respond. The ugly day swam before his eyes. A torrent of rage and frustration boiled up in his chest, and he shouted, "Get it yourself!"

The Sheriff glared at him, turned on his heel, and jerked his head toward the rope. One of his men stepped toward the gangplank, and the sailors lowered it back onto the dock. The Sheriff strode to the front of the ship and banged on the Captain's door.

≈≈≈≈≈

"You wanted to see me?"

Startled, Gubby whirled to see Armstrong standing behind him. "Yes! Yes, Sir – I – we need to cast off as soon as possible."

"The steam is up. We can move as soon as you wish."

Looking at Armstrong's imperturbable bulk, Gubby felt a wave of despair. "Armstrong," he said, "this has been a – a wretched business..."

"So it appears."

"And I have spoken to the Sheriff out of turn..."

Armstrong grinned. "Perhaps. Or perhaps you should have stood your ground with him earlier. The protocol is not entirely clear, since he is hardly a fellow-officer..."

"But I undercut him in front of his men..."

"You did, and it was not diplomatic, but it may have been the wisest thing you've done all day. You look exhausted, Gubby. Shall I take the wheel back to Westport?"

Gubby swallowed hard and fought off an urge to hug the man in gratitude. "No, Armstrong – thank you, but no. This is my mission, and I will see it through."

"You're certain, then?"

"Yes. Absolutely."

"Very well. I will retire to the engine-room, where there have been some complications in replacing a valve. Nothing that will affect our pleasure-cruise back to the quay."

≈≈≈≈≈

As soon as Armstrong left the bridge, Gubby regretted his choice to stay at the wheel. His guts continued to churn, and his hands were trembling. He thought briefly of telling one of the men to bring him biscuits or a mug of tea, but he worried that a request for food would be taken as a sign of weakness. He saw that Prescott was looking up from the deck, waiting for orders. He said, "Prepare to cast off," grateful that his voice sounded clear.

Prescott said, "Aye aye, Sir," and the men on the deck began the familiar routine of stowing the gangplank and preparing to lift the cork fenders. Gubby swung the handle on the engine telegraph, and the bell rang again as the chief engineer sent back an acknowledging signal. The door to the Captain's quarters opened and the Sheriff stepped out onto the deck. He kept his head down as he walked over to his two men at the rail. Gubby strained to catch any indication of what had transpired in the Captain's cabin. *Had the Sheriff complained? Was the Captain preparing a formal warning?*

"Ready, Sir!" Prescott shouted.

"Right!" said Gubby, relieved by the distraction of duty. "Cast off!"

Two sailors on the dock lifted the lines from the bollards and hopped to the ship across the widening gap. Gubby signalled the engine room for DEAD SLOW power, and the propeller began to turn. He spun the wheel to the left, and the *Wasp* angled away from the dock as it moved forward. The island men moved down onto the dock, shouting and gesturing, but Gubby could not hear their words over the roar of the engines. One of the men threw a rock that clanged off the side of the bridge and landed on the deck. Prescott picked it up and dropped it over the side.

Gubby advanced the telegraph to SLOW, and the *Wasp* began to move toward the mouth of the cove. The steady hum of the engines beneath his feet soothed his nerves, and the air felt cool and refreshing. Perhaps, he thought, there would be no harm in asking to have a plate of biscuits brought up to the bridge. He looked around for Prescott but could not locate him on the deck. He tried to remember the name of the tall, rangy sailor who was replacing the metal panel that filled the gap where the gangplank had been. Where was Prescott? And where was O'Donnell?

He looked up to see three black *currachs* rowing across the mouth of the cove. Piled high with brown fishing nets, the low vessels were dead ahead of the *Wasp*. Gubby's mind raced like a disconnected engine. Do they not see us bearing down on them? Am I supposed to give some kind of signal? The piles of fishing-nets alarmed him. If the *Wasp* crushed or capsized one of the *currachs,* the nets would unroll in the water like giant spider-webs, fouling the propeller for hours. And the angry men still shouted from the dock, with their sticks and rocks...

Gubby spun the propeller hard to the left and signalled FULL to the engine-room. However hard they might row, he could outrun the damned *currachs*. He would show them the power...

A loud clang shot through the vessel. The *Wasp* lurched as the hum of the engine changed to a sickening lump-lump-lump like a broken wheel. Gubby grasped at the telegraph handle to signal STOP, but the engineer had already halted the propeller. The ship began to drift sideways toward the island shore.

The Captain burst from the door of his cabin, looking furiously from side to side. He shouted, "Lower the anchor!" and the chain clanked loudly through the hawsepipe as the huge weight dropped to the sea-floor. The engines stopped, and the silence seemed louder than the noise.

The men came streaming onto the deck from below, even the Cook in his apron. Their shouted questions – *What happened? What did we hit?* – dwindled into silence, and Gubby looked down on a sea of faces that were tilted up toward him. His heart pounding, he felt like an insect in a display-case, pinned and unable to move.

"Armstrong!" the Captain barked.

"Yes, Sir!"

"Give me a damage assessment!" Gubby saw the big man nod and move toward the stern. "And Gubby..."

"Yes, Sir..."

"To my quarters. Now!"

≈≈≈≈≈

"Gubby, are you insane?"

Russell stood ramrod-straight behind his desk, livid with rage. Gubby stood awkwardly before him, holding his hat in front of his stomach like a shield. He saw his own trembling hands, and the sweat-stains that darkened his shirt.

"What were my orders, Gubby?"

Gubby had to clear his throat twice before he could speak. "We were to..." He broke off in a fit of coughing.

"You were to what?"

"We were to cast off after we returned from... After the Sheriff finished knocking down..."

"From the *evictions!*" the captain roared. "They're called *evictions!*"

"Yes, Captain. From the evictions, and we were to make straight for Westport."

"And why, Lieutenant, were my orders not followed?"

Gubby swallowed hard and tried to find words to describe the blur of events in his mind. "I was attempting to follow your orders, Sir. We were making for the mouth of the cove when the – the row-boats came across our bow and blocked our way. There were carrying nets..."

"Nets? What kind of nets?"

"They were – I think they were fishing-nets, Sir, and..."

Captain Russell breathed loudly through his nose. "You saw fishing-boats armed with fishing-nets, blockading the *Wasp*. Is that correct?"

"Well yes, Sir, but..."

"And what exactly did you do, Lieutenant?"

Gubby felt like the walls were closing in on him. "I – I turned the wheel, Captain – to avoid them..."

"Damn you, Gubby!" The Captain slammed his fist down on the desk. "You were at the wheel of one of Her Majesty's *gunboats*, under orders to make straight for Westport, and you turned the *wheel?* To avoid *fishing-boats?*"

Gubby fought hard for breath. "Captain, I had no intent to disobey. I thought it was within my discretionary authority to alter course..."

"Your discretionary authority? To alter course into a submerged *rock?*"

Gubby lowered his eyes, trembling with shame. When he looked up, he was surprised to see that the Captain was no longer glaring at him, but seemed to be standing crookedly, like a man fighting pain. When the Captain looked up, there was sweat on his brow.

"Gubby, I cannot tell you the full dimensions of this – this action of yours. With a damaged propeller, the *Wasp* is only half a ship. Armstrong tells me that we are limited to SLOW or DEAD SLOW. Do you realise what this means?"

"Sir, I..."

"Do you have any idea how long we will be compelled to berth at Westport? How long it will take the Admiralty..." He broke off, and the rage returned to his eyes. "And do you realise what this will encourage the Irish to do? Can you not hear them in their pubs tonight, crowing about how they disabled a gunboat?"

With hot tears threatening to break through, Gubby shook his head.

"Lieutenant?" The Captain's voice suddenly seemed soft, his tone more gentle. "What happened today?"

Feeling small and weak, Gubby saw his future washing away like sand from under a rock. "I was – I was heartsick, Sir."

"Heartsick?" The Captain repeated it like a word that he'd never heard before. "What do you mean, Gubby?"

"Heartsick at our mission today, Sir. Burning those houses and leaving those people in ruins... That's not what I joined the Navy for, Captain."

"Then you've made a damned poor choice of careers, Lieutenant!" The Captain had turned cold as ice. "Her Majesty's Navy is not a Benevolent Society! You have disgraced this ship, and you have disgraced me!" The Captain sat down at his desk. "Prepare a letter resigning your commission, Gubby. Give it to me tomorrow. In another month we will return to Southampton, and I will be watching you closely until then. Whether or not I forward your resignation to the Admiralty will be entirely up to you. Do you understand?"

"Yes, Captain."

"That is all, Lieutenant. Go to your quarters. Armstrong will take us to Westport."

≈≈≈≈≈

SHIP'S LOG
HMS WASP
12 SEPTEMBER 1884

Cast off Westport 0900 hours. Transported Sheriff to Clare Island. Assigned Lt. Gubby to lead assisting work detail of 8 plus O'Donnell. Four evictions. Detail completed 1600 hours. Propeller damaged exiting cove, Lt. Gubby at wheel. Disciplined Gubby. Berthed Westport 1830 hours.

≈≈≈≈≈

*FROM THE PRIVATE JOURNAL
OF JOHN H. RUSSELL, CAPTAIN
HMS WASP
12 September 1884*

I am surrounded by fools. G unfit for command despite his advantages of birth. Propeller irretrievably damaged. I will break G for this. This incident will not remain a blot on the record of my last command.

When to advise Admiralty of my resignation? I want to walk away with my head high, not discarded by a medical discharge.

If I could get my hands on that woman again I would strangle her and throw her diseased body into the Thames.

Book Three

Báidín Fheilimí

Báidín Fheilimí d'imigh go Toraí,
Báidín Fheilimí is Feilimí ann...

Báidín bídeach, báidín beosach,
báidín bóidheach, Báidín Fheilimí
báidín díreach, báidín deontach
báidín Fheilimí is Feilimí ann.

...Báidín Fheilimí briseadh i dToraí,
Éisc ar bord agus Feilimí ann.

Phelim's little boat went to Tory,
Phelim's little boat and Phelim in it...

A tiny little boat, a lively little boat,
A foolish little boat, Phelim's little boat,
A straight little boat, a willing little boat,
Phelim's little boat and Phelim in it.

...Phelim's little boat broke on Tory,
Fish on board and Phelim in it.

Traditional Irish lullaby. It has been recorded
by The Cassidys and by Sinéad O'Connor.

15 September 1884

"Quinn?"

"Yes?"

"I've received some news to share with yourself and Varney. Are you free at 1600 hours?"

"Of course."

Quinn liked the friendly atmosphere that the Principal Keeper encouraged. Edward Corish did not demand the *Yes, Sirs* and other military formalities that some PK's required. Lighthouse-keeping was a shared enterprise, and the Principal Keepers had to perform the same tasks as the Assistant Keepers, adjusting the ventilators, winding the oil-pump, and polishing hundreds of brass surfaces. It was one of the things he liked most about working on the Lights – no one could sit on his arse and issue orders all day.

"And, Quinn – one other thing?"

"What's that?"

"There is going to be a hiatus. I've been given orders to report to the Tuskar by Friday. I must leave here by Wednesday, but my replacement will not arrive here until Saturday."

"Saturday the twentieth?"

"Exactly. And that leaves yourself and Varney short-handed for four days."

Quinn was pleasantly surprised to realise that Corish was confiding in him before telling Varney about the plans. "Well, Edward, I think that Varney and I might manage. We could switch to six-hour shifts for a few nights..."

"I was thinking of Mary."

So that was why Corish had come to him. "I'm sure she'll gladly take a shift, Edward."

Corish smiled. "I hope so. You'll ask her to sit along with us this afternoon?"

"Of course."

"Good. See you then." Corish turned to leave.

"One other thing, Edward?"

"What's that?"

"Who's going to be the new PK?"

Corish hesitated for a second. "It will be Knox. You know him, I think?"

"Yes, I do."

≈≈≈≈≈

He could hear Corish's footsteps clanging on the metal stairway as he descended the tower. Quinn's stomach clenched, and he drank a glass of water. He wasn't surprised at the news, but it always hurt a little. Someone else was being brought in as Principal Keeper, and he would remain an Assistant for the rest of his life.

But why did it have to be Knox, of all people? He had served with Knox on The Bull, a tower on a tiny rock off the south coast. Knox was a cold, isolated soul who knew no *craic*, no life away from his duties. Inspections and reports, criticism and reprimands – Knox would have made a good prison warden. And that's what the Tory Lighthouse compound would feel like, as soon as he took charge.

Varney, he thought bitterly, *will get on well with Knox.*

Quinn walked around the platform that surrounded the massive light and looked out the windows. He was thankful that Corish had forewarned him, and had not surprised him in front of Varney. Early-afternoon sun sparkled on the waves. No ships were visable on the horizon, and there was nothing to enter into the log.

He walked around the tower twice before he sat down. It was the drinking, of course – that miserable year on Valentia when his taste for whiskey had grown from a habit to a craving. It was on his record, and the Elder Brethren of the Lighthouse Service would never put in him in charge of his own station. He didn't even want the damned PK position – filling out reams of reports, assigning schedules, trying to train the thick-headed junior staff. Still, never to be offered the spot – it still hurt.

And Mary. Corish wanted Mary to fill in, to take shifts. She'd done it before, on Eagle Island, when one of the Assistant Keepers had died. The Lighthouse Service had a title for the wives who could step in – Female Attendant Keeper. Quinn was proud of her, but jealous, too. *If she were a man...*

But that couldn't happen. They'd never put a woman in charge.

17 September 1884

Ruairí loved the atlas. While the other copyists and apprentices played an enthusiastic game of football at noon, he leafed through the big clothbound volume while he ate soup and biscuits at his desk. The atlas was stored in a slot at the side of Simmons's desk, but the supervisor had told him to help himself to the book without bothering to ask.

He had tried to find Krakatoa in the book. From the schoolmaster's description of the eruption, he knew the island had been blasted into nothingness, but since the book was dated 1880, he reasoned that the island would still appear on those pages. He knew that Krakatoa was near Java, but he was dismayed to find that a huge swath of the Orient from Sumatra to Japan had been squeezed onto one crowded page. And he could not find it in the index. Most of the places in the world, he realised, were not in the index. Someone, somewhere, had decided which names to list in the index, and which to leave out. What made one place more important than another?

Harris had made a passing remark about Khartoum – *Wouldn't it be grand to go down there and shoot at the blackies with General Gordon?* Ruairí asked where Khartoum was, and Harris, embarrassed at being taken seriously, had said *Oh, you know – down in Africa someplace.* The continent of Africa was also squeezed onto a single page of the atlas, but Ruairí had found Khartoum, a dot where the Blue Nile and the White Nile flowed together, surrounded by the Nubian Desert. There was something thrilling about the remoteness of the place, but Ruairí could not imagine what an English General was doing there.

The door to the copy-room opened, and Simmons came in with the fat officer from the *Wasp.* Ruairí was startled to realise that they were walking directly toward his desk.

"Mullan!" The supervisor called his name with a formal edge in his voice.

"Yes, Sir?"

"You're Irish, aren't you?"

"Yes, Sir, I am."

Simmons turned to the officer. "There you have it, Lieutenant. He's your man."

The Lieutenant said, "Can you..." and then coughed, as though he had choked on the words. Ruairí watched as the blue-coated officer fumbled in his pocket and pulled out a piece of paper. His fingers were trembling, and Ruairí realised that the Lieutenant was not much older than himself.

Gubby cleared his throat, handed the paper to Ruairí, and said, "Can you tell me what this means?"

Ruairí read the words on the paper and grinned. *Aithníonn ciaróg ciaróg eile.* He said, "It means *One beetle recognises another.* Everyone knows that, Sir."

The supervisor said, "What did I tell you, Lieutenant?"

"Right, Simmons. I suppose... I suppose he will need to make some arrangements...?"

"Indeed. Mullan, you live in the apprentice quarters, do you not?"

"Yes, Sir, but what is this about..."

"You know the *Wasp*, the gunboat? Mister Gubby needs you to assist them for – how long did you say, Lieutenant?"

"We're not exactly sure, Mister Simmons. We've – we're somewhat constrained by repairs, and we're awaiting orders..."

"No matter. Mullan, I am seconding you to Lieutenant Gubby to assist the *Wasp* with – with whatever they need. We will continue with your training here when you return."

"But, Sir..."

"I can assure that you'll be well taken-care-of on the *Wasp*. Will he not, Lieutenant?"

"Oh, absolutely. The food is excellent..."

"And he'll be quartered on the ship – is that correct?"

"Yes, we'll need him there..."

The copyists were drifting back into the room, talking to each other and staring at the odd tableau of the supervisor and the officer at Ruairí's desk. Ruairí felt a surge of irritation toward the other apprentices. His attempts to befriend them had come to nothing, and they seemed to be waiting for him to make a mistake. He realised that he had grown to resent them. As far as he cared, they could sit and draw maps until their fingers broke off. He was being offered the chance to experience life on a Navy ship.

"I'll need to get some things from my quarters, Sir."

"Is that agreeable, Lieutenant?" asked Simmons.

"We'll arrange for a cart, and I will take you there and back," said Gubby.

Simmons laughed, and all of the copyists stared. "Well, now, that sounds rather grand, doesn't it, Ruairí?"

"Yes, Sir. I had no idea..."

"Then off you go!"

Gathering his lunch-parcel, Ruairí felt a giddy excitement mixed with a shadow of unease. Did the officer not trust him to go to his quarters and return? Or was this how the Navy did things?

He thought of the day when the *Wasp* brought the seed potatoes to Toraigh, and his mood brightened. What harm could it be to enjoy the hospitality of Her Majesty's Navy? With a sense of pride and privilege, he followed Lieutenant Gubby past the gawking apprentices, out of the map-room, and into what felt like a much-wider world.

≈≈≈≈≈

The *Wasp* rocked slowly in the currents of Clew Bay. The early-afternoon sun sparkled on the water, and swarms of gnats hovered above the wharf. Ruairí heard clanks and rumbles from the concrete building where grain was unloaded from railway cars. As they walked the few hundred yards from the map-school to the wharf, the fat officer picked up the pace and then slowed down, as if changing his mind about how fast to walk. Ruairí wanted to ask dozens of questions – *What am I to do on the boat? How long will I be required? What is your name?* – but the

Lieutenant's stiffness and uncertainty generated a barrier that Ruairí could almost feel. Remembering the easy banter that he'd enjoyed with the sailors as they smoked their evening pipes, Ruairí decided to hold his questions until he found more-relaxed company.

He was mildly startled when the Lieutenant barked, "Carlisle!"

"Yes, Sir?" A man on the deck of the *Wasp* stood to attention. He seemed to be supervising a crew of sailors who were painting the ship's metal fittings.

"We'll need a cart into town and back."

"Right, Sir. I'll send someone right away."

The Lieutenant turned to look at Ruairí for the first time. "I'm taking you to Captain Russell's quarters."

"Yes, Sir," Ruairí heard himself saying.

They strode up the gangplank and onto the deck of the ship. The painting crew paused to look at them as Ruairí trailed the chubby officer across the deck. The Lieutenant walked even more stiffly, and Ruairí realised that he had felt a similar cloud of tension before, with Father Hayes.

They approached a wooden door in a wall between two round windows. The Lieutenant stopped up to the door, raised his fist to knock, and then suddenly twisted to look at Ruairí. "You don't get seasick, do you?"

"No, Sir," Ruairí lied. "I've been on boats all my life."

"That's good. That's very good." Breathing loudly, the Lieutenant turned back and knocked.

A voice rumbled from within. "Who is it?"

"Lieutenant Gubby, Sir, with..." He twisted toward Ruairí again and whispered, "What did you say your name was?"

"I'm Ruairí Mullan."

"...with Rory Mullan, Sir. From the school."

"Come in."

≈≈≈≈≈

Stepping into the Captain's cabin was like stepping into the stone well on Toraigh. The dark air in the cabin felt cooler and thicker than the air on the deck. Ruairí sensed, but could not identify, a hint of a familiar odour. Traces of sunlight peeked through the shutters that masked the round windows, making the darkness seem more gloomy. Lieutenant Gubby stepped inside the door and then stopped, blocking Ruairí.

A bearded man in a white uniform sat behind a desk. He said, "Let the young man pass, Gubby," and the Lieutenant moved aside. Ruairí pulled the door closed and stepped forward.

The man at the desk cocked his head to one side. "You have only one eye."

"Yes, Sir."

"Hmmm. What happened to the other one?"

"I lost it in an accident, Sir."

"And yet you are an apprentice at the map-school?"

"Yes, Sir. It doesn't seem to make any difference, Sir."

"That's remarkable. I would not have guessed... Gubby!"

"Yes, Sir!" Ruairí felt the floor vibrate slightly as the Lieutenant snapped to attention.

"You have made arrangements for Mullan's berth?"

"Yes, Sir! He is being put – that is, I felt that it would be best if he had O'Donnell's berth, Sir."

"Yes, that is sensible. If O'Donnell returns, he will be sleeping in the brig. You have informed Mullan of his duties?"

"Well, no, Sir – that is, I thought that you might want to – if you wish, I can..."

"I will instruct him." The man at the desk turned back to Ruairí, staring at him from deep-set eyes. "I am Captain Russell. I will require your assistance as a Commander's Servant."

"What does that mean, Sir?"

The Captain nodded. "We will go over your duties in detail." He turned and looked pointedly at Gubby. "It is refreshing to work with someone who knows how to ask questions."

"Sir, I only felt..." Gubby began, and then caught himself. "I'm glad that you're pleased..."

"He'll do very well, I think. Show him around the ship and bring him back here in an hour."

"Yes, Sir – and we'll fit him out with a uniform..."

"No!" The Captain spat out the word, and Ruairí could feel Gubby flinch. "He has not qualified to serve in Her Majesty's Navy. He will wear his own clothing."

"Yes, Sir – in fact, I've sent for a cart. We'll collect his things from the apprentice-quarters..."

The Captain waved away Gubby's scattered words. "Make whatever arrangements you need to make, Mister Gubby. Stop at the telegraph office on your way and check for messages. That is all."

Ruairí suppressed a smile as Gubby twisted toward the door and fumbled with the latch. The Captain looked down at a paper on his desk. Gubby opened the door and stepped quickly out onto the deck, nearly quivering with relief. As Ruairí closed the door behind him, he recognised the trace-odour that had hung in the air in the Captain's cabin. Faint but unmistakable, he could smell a tang of urine.

≈≈≈≈≈

It took only minutes to collect his belongings from his shelf at the apprentice-quarters dormitory. Two shirts and two pairs of trousers, a few undergarments and a coat and hat – it all fitted into one carpet-bag. Eithne had collected his setting-out kit from the East Town neighbours. Ruairí knew that one pair of trousers had been Pádraig's. He shook his head as he put his spare eye-patches into the bag. He had more eye-patches than shirts.

He returned to the Westport street where Lieutenant Gubby sat looking uncomfortable in the open cart. He fought back the impulse to ask the fat officer the simple questions – *What am I to do on the ship? How long will it be before I return to the school?* Gubby's air of misery still presented a barrier against all conversation. Ruairí climbed into the cart and Gubby barked an order to the driver, who tapped the back of his dray-horse with a willow switch.

As Ruairí stowed his carpet-bag under the bench, Gubby asked, "Is that all you have?"

"It is, Sir."

Gubby said, "Hmmm," and looked away.

The horse's hooves clopped on the cobblestones as the cart jolted along the road to Westport Quay. The leaves of the trees were turning red and gold, surprising bright colours after the long green months of summer. Ruairí stared at the larches and maples that rose up from behind the wall that ran along the road. It was the wall of a large estate, probably the estate where he had nearly fallen into a fight with the gate-keepers. Even so, he loved the way the leaves looked against the sky. On Toraigh, there were no trees.

The cart approached a block of warehouse buildings, and Ruairí was startled to recognise the alley where he had spoken in the darkness with – what was her name? *The Last Rose of Summer...* He twisted around in his seat to try to look into the narrow passageway between the buildings. Would she be there in the daytime? He could see nothing beyond the shadowy shapes of barrels and shipping crates – nothing moving, no one calling out *I won't bite, you know.* He wondered about her baby. Had she spent his sixpence for milk? It couldn't be good for the baby, sleeping in a box in the cold alley.

He was surprised to hear Lieutenant Gubby saying, "Mullan?"

"Yes, Sir?"

"It is Mullan, isn't it?"

"That's right."

"What are you looking at?"

Ruairí felt embarrassment sweep over him like a wave of steam. "I was just looking around..."

"You were looking down that alley, weren't you? Is that where the apprentices go?"

His embarrassment evaporated, and Ruairí found himself staring at Lieutenant Gubby. The officer looked suddenly boyish, asking a question that revealed more than it took in. The driver of the cart seemed to be listening, too.

"I don't know what you mean, Sir."

Gubby said, "Hmmm," and looked down at his boots.

As the cart rumbled its way back to the wharf, Ruairí wondered if he had made a deep mistake in agreeing to work on the *Wasp*. Had he, in fact, agreed? Simmons had not exactly given him a choice. Avoiding Gubby's eye, Ruairí looked at the Lieutenant's hands clutching the edge of his bench. The awkward officer seemed to be clenching and releasing his fingers again and again, the way the Assessor had squeezed his chair.

As clearly as if he had been shown a photograph, Ruairí could see Gubby standing among the crates and puddles of the alley, bringing his lonely, awkward self to Rosie for comfort. *But she was so tiny,* he thought, *and he...* Ruairí tried to push the grotesque image from his mind. The cart bumped its way along the tree-shaded streets in the September sunshine, and Ruairí wondered what kind of world he was being drawn into.

≈≈≈≈≈

He was relieved when Gubby handed him over to Petty Officer Carlisle for a tour of the ship. Carlisle climbed smoothly down the steep steps to a large room full of tables below the deck. He showed Ruairí a cubbyhole where a bundle of white cotton was stowed. "That's your hammock," he said. "You'll fix it up between here and here." He pointed to two eye-bolts in the walls over a table. "Have you slept in one of these before?"

"No, Sir."

"Call me Mister Carlisle. You can save those *Sirs* for the commissioned officers."

"Who are they, Mister Carlisle?"

"Well, there's the Captain, and Evans and Armstrong. You'll recognise them. And Lieutenant Gubby, of course." Carlisle looked at Ruairí with a twinkle of mischief in his eye.

Ruairí said, "I've met Lieutenant Gubby," trying not to grin too broadly.

"Yes, I see that you have." They stood together quietly for a few seconds. "Well, come along then," said Carlisle. "I'll show you the old scow."

≈≈≈≈≈

Eoghan had carried so many barrels of oil up the lighthouse stairs that he could do that chore in his sleep. The barrels were not heavy – not for him – but they were too large to carry more than one at a time. He wondered briefly whether he could rig up a sling to carry one barrel on his back while he lifted another in his arms. Could you make a sling out of ropes? Leather? It became too complicated to think about. *Ruairí could figure it out,* he thought. *If he was here.*

He missed his brother. He missed Ruairí's laugh, his stories, his ideas for pranks. Ruairí had always been with him, as much a part of his life as the Toraigh landscape or the wind from the sea. Or Aunt Eithne. Eoghan felt like a man with a missing limb.

He could hear Mister Quinn's footsteps at the top of the lighthouse. He was trimming the wicks of the lamps, Eoghan knew, and adjusting the ventilators that circled the tower. It looked like a tricky business, letting in enough air to keep the lights burning, but closing them down when the wind kicked up so that the drafts wouldn't blow out the lights. Mister Quinn and Mister Corish took shifts during the night to keep an eye on the lights. He wondered what it would be like to sit in the tower all night, with only the rumble of the waves and the moaning wind for company.

"Is that you, Mullan?"

"Yes, Mister Quinn."

"Bring up four more barrels today. The nights are getting longer."

"I will, Mister Quinn."

He knew the Keepers would be busy, even during the middle watch that began at midnight. The massive lamp with its dozens of wicks consumed oil like a bonfire, and the Keeper needed to tap a new barrel every hour. He'd slide each barrel onto a swivelling rack, remove the plug, and tip the rack to pour the oil through a funnel into a tank. Then he'd wind the clockwork mechanism that pumped the oil to the lantern-room where the lights burned through the night.

In the shadowy room below the lantern-room, Eoghan placed the metal barrel at the end of a curving row that sat inside the circular wall, making sure that the plug-hole was at the top. Empty barrels sat in a loose cluster on the other side of the room, waiting to be carried back down to the warehouse. He wondered for the hundredth time why they didn't put the pump and the tank at the ground level. He would ask Ruairí the next time he saw him – but then he heard Ruairí's answer as clearly as if he were standing next to him. *Sure, Eoghan, and if they put the tank down there, why would they need a big garsún like you to carry the barrels? The day they do that, they'll turf you back out into the fields and you'll be scratching your bum with Pádraig.*

He could have sworn that Ruairí's voice was echoing from the stone walls of the room. Was that possible? He would ask Aunt Eithne.

≈≈≈≈≈

"Do you know what it means to be a Commander's Servant?"

"No, Sir."

The Captain nodded. "I like your attitude, Mullan. I wish that everyone on this ship could be as forthright." He gestured toward a box in the corner of the room. "Your first assignment is to wind the chronometer."

"May I take a look at it, Sir?"

"Of course you may."

Ruairí lifted the lid of the box, a cube of waxy brown wood with polished brass fittings. Gold numerals engraved on the lid read *1845*. Deep inside the box he saw the face of a clock, white with Roman numerals. The clock was suspended on swivels, and he could hear the faint whirring of a mechanism behind the face.

"You'll wind it with the key on the right," the Captain said. "It will run for fifty-six hours on a single winding, but I will expect you to wind it every morning."

"May I wind it now, Sir?"

"Go ahead."

Cautiously, Ruairí turned the key. He could feel a light, well-oiled ratcheting in the clockwork. He thought of Mister Geraghty – *clocks have been designed by a new breed of man.* He wanted to lift the mechanism out of the carefully-crafted box and examine it.

He looked up to see the Captain twisted in his chair, facing at the wall. He started to say *Are you well, Sir?* but he stopped himself. The man's rigid posture was like a brick wall with a KEEP OUT sign.

After a few seconds the Captain seemed to relax, and he turned to his desk. Ruairí could feel the gentle rocking of the ship under his feet. "I am responsible for everything that happens on this ship. Mullan," the Captain was saying. "If all goes well, the Admiralty simply nods as if to say *As it should be.* If anything goes wrong, they leap out of their chairs like hounds on the scent, and they will not relent until someone is punished and disgraced. Do you follow what I am saying?"

Ruairí said, "I think so, Sir," but his mind drifted to his Uncle Sean inspecting cattle and building his *currachs*. He could not imagine anyone leaping out of a chair to punish him.

"I am not at liberty to confide in others," the Captain continued. "I want you to remember that above all." He exhaled loudly and drummed his fingers again.

Ruairí realised that the Captain was waiting for him to respond, even though he had not exactly asked a question. "Can you not share your thoughts with anyone on the ship, Sir?"

"The men would take it as a sign of weakness. And my fellow-officers would have my guts for garters. Mullan, do you know how to keep your own counsel?"

"I'm afraid I don't understand, Sir..."

"Can you keep a secret?"

Ruairí began to see where the Captain was headed. "Well, Sir, as far as I know, I will only be with the ship for a short while. I have no reason to tell anything to anyone..."

"Good! You seem like a sensible young man." He turned back to look at Ruairí directly. Ruairí felt the power of the Captain's stare, but he also saw that the man's eyes were dark with pain. "Do you enjoy the craft of map-making, Mullan?"

"I do, Sir. Although I'd like to see a great deal more of the world while I'm drawing pictures of it."

"Indeed!" The Captain seemed to turn over a thought in his mind. "You could be a Navigator. You might be the first Irish Navigator in Her Majesty's Navy."

The Captain lowered his head. Ruairí said, "That would be..."

"No matter – we will discuss that further. But for now, I want you to remember that you may have splendid opportunities, if you will do exactly what I say."

Ruairí resented the implied threat, but he decided not to let it show. "I'll try, Sir."

The Captain drew a deep breath, as though he were going to give a speech. "In two months, Mullan, the *Wasp* will sail to Southampton – do you know where that is?"

"I do, Sir. It's in England."

"Right. And when we dock there, I will be resigning my commission."

"What does that mean, Sir?"

"I will be retiring from the Navy. And I mean to walk away on my own two feet."

Ruairí was at a loss for words. "Why – why would it be otherwise, Sir?"

"I am plagued by medical problems. I..." The Captain seemed to wince with pain, but then he continued, "The nature of my condition is no one's business but my own. But it requires me to take unusual measures, and to seek assistance from someone I can trust. Can you be trusted, Mullan?"

"As I said, Sir, I will not be long on the ship..."

"Right. And while I have little choice but to confide in you, I think I may be fortunate." The Captain stared at Ruairí again. "Do you see my eyes?"

Ruairí looked into the Captain's deep, squinting eye-sockets. "Yes, Sir..."

"They have grown terribly sensitive to sunlight. When my cabin door is opened at midday, it takes long minutes before I can recover from the intensity. It feels like needles in my eyeballs. And I can no longer distinguish the colour red."

"That's terrible, Sir..."

"Hear me out! If that were the only manifestation... Mullan, if you betray me, I will have you flogged..."

"I have no reason to – to betray you, Sir..."

"Of course. That's quite correct." The Captain sat still for a moment, nodding to himself. "It is also affecting my legs."

The Captain rose up from his chair and stepped to the side of his desk, trailing his hand along the top. "Do you see that it will require two steps for me to move from this desk to the door of my sleeping-quarters?

"Yes, Sir..."

"Step over here, Mullan. There will be times when I need to place my hand on your shoulder to move across the room. Unless I hold onto something, my steps are quite unpredictable."

Ruairí moved to the Captain's side. The short, quivering man put his hand on Ruairí's shoulder as he walked across the room. "Now that I can touch the door-jamb, I can steady myself. But turn with me now – I will step back to the desk."

Ruairí glanced at the Captain's feet as they re-crossed the small cabin. His toes dragged lightly across the steel surface, making a rubbing sound. The Captain released Ruairí's shoulder when he touched his desk. "My mobility varies greatly from day to day, Mullan," he said. "Today is quite difficult."

Seating himself in his chair, the Captain drummed his fingers on the desktop. When he spoke, he sounded like someone reciting a memorised speech. "I will require you to be my eyes and ears on the *Wasp*. And my legs. I will assign various duties which will take you throughout the ship. But in the process of each assignment, I want you to listen."

"Listen to what, Sir?"

The Captain sat up straight in his chair. "I want you to listen to what the crew are saying. I want you to listen to the officers, especially if you hear them speculating about my condition. I want you to listen and remember – and come back here to tell me exactly what they say. Can you do that, Mullan?"

Ruairí felt a gloomy burden settling on his shoulders. "I can try, Sir."

The Captain stared for a few seconds. "You do not seem comfortable with this instruction."

"I do not think that the crew will confide in me if they know..."

"Of course they won't! Do I need to reinforce what I said earlier about keeping your own counsel?"

"No, Sir. I think I understand."

"O'Donnell – your predecessor – seemed to relish his role as my eyes and ears. And if he ever felt the need to consult with anyone other than myself, I believe that he sought out Hatton."

"Hatton, Sir?"

"The cook. Hatton has served with me for many years, and he has my confidence. Now, you may as well begin your duties. In my sleeping-quarters, you will find a wicker basket containing my clothing. You will take that down to Phillips in the laundry. Then I suggest that you stow your gear and familiarise yourself with the ship. Hatton will have my breakfast prepared at 0600 hours – you will bring it to me then. You have been assigned O'Donnell's berth, have you not?"

"Yes, Sir."

"There is a voice-tube in the wall next to your hammock. I will use it to contact you if necessary during the night. Is that clear?"

"May I ask you a question, Sir?"

The Captain stared at Ruairí, looking for signs of insolence. "What is it, Mullan?"

"Why..." He stopped and started over, trying to find a simple way of asking the hundreds of questions that were flooding into his mind. "Sir, I thought I might have been brought here to help with maps or navigation. Perhaps for a voyage or two. I know nothing of being a Commander's Servant, or about acting as a go-between..."

The Captain smiled and interrupted him. "And so what perverse fate brought you to this ship? Let me assure you, Mullan, that you will not be needed here for long. The Admiralty has promised to assign a permanent replacement for O'Donnell, but with their usual efficiency they refuse to indicate when he may arrive. They have also promised to send a replacement propeller for the *Wasp*. We might amuse ourselves by wagering on which replacement will appear first."

"And so when my – when the replacement arrives..."

"You will be free to go then, or soon thereafter. Although I understand that you have other skills we may need."

"What skills, Sir?"

"This is quite enough, Mullan. Retrieve the basket from my sleeping-quarters and carry on. We will speak more in the morning."

"Yes, Sir."

The Captain's voice dropped to a cold, formal level. "*Aye, aye, Sir*, is the proper form."

The words stuck in Ruairí's throat. He took a deep breath and forced himself to say, "Aye, aye, Sir."

"Very good, Mullan. That is all."

≈≈≈≈

The Captain's laundry stank of urine. Phillips in the laundry room accepted the wicker basket without comment, but without attempting any friendly banter. Ruairí climbed the steep stairs to the open deck and took deep breaths of the cool, misty September-evening air. A knot of sailors were smoking by the railing, but he turned to the other side of the ship and walked toward the foredeck. He already had too much to think about.

The ship's cat sat on a coil of rope, licking its paws. Ruairí sat beside it and offered it his finger to sniff. Unhurried, the cat examined his finger and then returned to giving its own forepaw an elaborate cleaning. Ruairí probed the soft fold behind the cat's ear, and it purred loudly.

What had he fallen into? How could he have drawn maps in the morning and become a delivery-boy for piss-stained laundry by evening? And a spy for a sick man?

It didn't make sense. Someone named O'Donnell had deserted, but hadn't sailors deserted ever since men had put out to sea? If the Captain only wanted someone to run his errands and help him on his unsteady legs, there were other men on the ship – why not one of them? He had heard the stories about the Press Gangs in the old days – sailors who kidnapped healthy-looking boys from the harbour towns to work on the ships. But they were abducted to do dirty, dangerous work – not to be Commanders' Servants. And he hadn't been kidnapped – not exactly, but...

The cat rolled onto its back, and Ruairí stroked its belly. It stretched its legs, extending its claws like knives.

He hated the idea of spying. To gain someone's confidence, and then to betray it – it would be unthinkable on Toraigh. And beyond that, if the crew had any secrets, would they be foolish enough to share them? *Say, mate – be sure to eat a good breakfast. We've scheduled the mutiny for noon tomorrow.* Had O'Donnell been ordered to snitch on his fellows?

"Pleasant evening."

Ruairí spun around to find a heavyset man in a white apron smoking a pipe by the rail. His thinning hair was grey, and he looked older than the other crew-members – even older than the Captain.

"Hello, Sir."

"Ah, don't call me Sir. My name's Hatton."

"So you're the cook!"

"That I am, such as I am. I'm not one of your French chefs, but I haven't starved anyone yet."

"My name's Ruairí Mullan. I'm glad to meet you."

"So you're with us until we get a replacement for O'Donnell, are you?"

"Well, that's what I... Can I ask you something?"

"Of course." The cook seemed worldly and imperturbable.

"What happened to O'Donnell?"

The cook looked out over Clew Bay and puffed on his pipe. "O'Donnell was very young – I'd say that he was not much older than yourself, but he seemed younger. He was more like a mascot than a crew member – like Hodge, there."

"Hodge?"

"Your friend the cat. He seems to have taken a liking to you. He won't let everyone stroke him."

"Is that his name?" Ruairí rubbed his knuckle under the cat's chin, and it stretched out its claws again. "But what about O'Donnell?"

"You must understand a few things about Commanders' Servants," said Hatton. "They are not universally admired on a ship. Some of the men resent them. They think they have soft duty."

Ruairí stroked the cat in silence, wondering if the sailors would be as unwelcoming as the apprentices. Was everywhere going to be this lonely?

"O'Donnell made it a point to join in the work-details with the men," Hatton continued. "I have seen him holystoning the deck, and sometimes he would peel spuds in the kitchen."

Ruairí looked gratefully at the stout man who was giving him friendly advice. "Where is O'Donnell now?"

The cook paused before answering. "No one knows. The Captain sent him to the telegraph office and he never returned."

"Was he Irish?"

"That's an interesting question, my friend. He had an Irish name, but I gathered that he was raised in England. Are you thinking that he might have relatives here?"

"I wasn't thinking anything," said Ruairí. "I just wish I could talk to him."

"Well, you seem like a bright enough fellow to sort things out for yourself. And unless I miss my guess, the *Wasp* won't be going anywhere for a while."

"No? Why?"

"Her propeller has been damaged. Today she could scarcely out-pace a man on a bicycle."

"What caused the damage?"

"You might find it interesting to ask that question around the ship. However, I would advise you not to approach Lieutenant Gubby about it."

Hatton turned his pipe over and rapped it on the top of the metal skirting. Embers fell into the water with a quick soft hiss, and the cook tucked the pipe into his apron-pocket. "If O'Donnell is still nearby, you might be able to locate him. You'd have a better chance than the rest of us, at any rate."

"Why is that?"

Hatton smiled. "For one thing, you're not in uniform."

The cook nodded and strolled away. Invigorated, Ruairí gave the cat a quick belly-rub and stood up, brushing off his clothes. Of course he'd have a better chance of finding O'Donnell – with or without their uniforms, the crew of the *Wasp* would signal their Englishness with the first words they spoke, and no one would tell them a thing.

The sun was setting behind Clare Island on the western horizon. Ruairí walked back toward the gangplank. Sailors were leaning against the metal skirting and sitting on the deck, whittling, smoking, playing cards. One of the card-players nodded as he passed. "Nice evening."

"It is." Ruairí hesitated, eager to go searching for O'Donnell but not wanting to act aloof.

"I seen you on the quay, haven't I?"

Ruairí did not recognise the man. In their blue uniforms and flat white hats, the bearded sailors looked a great deal like each other. "Sure, I come along here just about every day."

"I thought I knew who you was. That eye-patch, you know."

Ruairí smiled. "I come by it honestly."

"You're the Captain's new man, aren't you?"

The other men had started to listen. Ruairí made a decision and said, "Yes, I am. For a few days. Some other bloke is on the way, and when he gets here I'll be going back to the map-school."

Someone said, "You're Irish, aren't you?"

"I am."

The men nodded to each other and turned back to their cards and whittling. Relieved, Ruairí stepped toward the gangplank.

"Got a pass, mate?"

Two sailors stood near the gangplank with rifles slung over his shoulder. While they seemed relaxed, they clearly weren't lounging like the others.

"What's a pass?"

The taller sailor said, "You need a pass to go ashore. From the Captain."

"Just to walk around the quay?"

"That's right. Just to walk around the quay."

Frustration flooded over Ruairí like a wave of dirty water. He wanted to shout *I'm not in the fecking Navy*, but he could feel the men watching behind him. "Well, then," he said, "I'll take a walk around the – ah..."

"The deck."

"Yeah. Around the deck."

The sailors nodded at him with relief, and he walked back to the prow of the ship. He sat on the same coil of rope and kicked at it with his heel until his frustration and rage settled down. The ship felt small and claustrophobic, like a cage.

He took deep breaths until his insides settled down. He thought of Simmons, only hours before: *Well, now, that sounds rather grand, doesn't it, Ruairí?* Did he know? Could Mister Geraghty have foreseen this? Why hadn't anyone told him?

Rain began to spatter down. He could hear the footsteps of the men as they headed below decks. There was no sense in getting himself wet as well as miserable. He stood up, wondering where the cat had gone. Had it headed for shelter like one of the Toraigh animals when it sensed that rain was coming? It was probably as well that the creature had made itself scarce, Ruairí thought ruefully. If he'd seen 2the cat a few minutes earlier, he'd have been tempted to throw it overboard.

≈≈≈≈≈

Eithne snapped awake. The dim light made the walls of the cottage seem soft and indistinct, as though she had found herself sitting under water. She knew she had been dozing. Sleep had always come easily to her, a welcome relief from the river of thoughts and feelings that flowed through her waking hours. Now she found herself napping several times through each day, weary when awake, ready to drop into unconscious oblivion. Some day, she knew, she would simply not wake up.

But her dream had startled her, and she sat tingling with energy. In her dream the sky had lowered like a heavy blanket, threatening to smother her. She was in a place of walls and corridors, grey and clammy to the touch. When she tried to shout, only a blurry sound reached her ears, like the groans of an injured animal.

She closed her eyes and drifted back into the feeling of the dream, the sense of being trapped in a thickening glue that would not let her move. Her body resisted the enveloping pressure, the stifling fog that had pushed aside the air...

Ruairí. She sat up with a terrible certainty that something had happened to Ruairí. He was slipping by degrees into a sink-hole, a trap. She looked out the window toward the western end of the island, past the lights of *An Baile Thiar* and beyond to the western fields and the sea. The last rays of the sunset had subsided, and the glow from the lighthouse silhouetted the rocky north cliffs. She wished that she could summon her nephew back to the deep certainties of Toraigh, to the island that was settling itself to sleep like a large, sturdy creature. She tried to convince herself that her dream grew out of something else – a worry, a half-forgotten misadventure of her own – but she knew better. Whatever she had glimpsed in her dream, it would be Ruairí's to grapple with – if it had not already overtaken him.

18 September 1884

He sat on a compartment-lid on the deck of the *Wasp*, eating the porridge that Hatton served the crew for breakfast. The Captain's breakfast-tray had included rashers and eggs, baked beans, and two kinds of pudding. The stack of bacon rashers was spilling off the plate onto the tray, and Ruairí wondered if Hatton had added extra slices for him to steal.

The Captain, fully dressed and sitting at his desk, had accepted the breakfast-tray without comment. Ruairí had waited for instructions, but the Captain had said, "Carry on, Mullan. We'll see to your duties later."

As he finished the porridge, he watched a horse-drawn dray-wagon bumping over the cobblestones on the quay. It stopped near the gangplank, and one of the sailors on guard duty stepped onto the dock. The driver pulled a wrinkled paper from his coat-pocket. The sailor on the dock gestured to his guard-duty companion, who turned and spoke into a voice-tube.

Armstrong and Carlisle emerged from below and hurried across the gangplank. The driver stepped to the rear of the wagon and began loosening the ties on a tarpaulin that covered a stack of boxes and crates. Carlisle returned to the ship and sent three sailors to join Armstrong at the side of the wagon.

The wagon-driver said something to Armstrong and the men. They lifted the crates onto the dock, digging something out of the centre of the stack. Ruairí moved to the skirting to watch.

The driver extracted a flat crate the size of a bicycle-wheel and handed it to Armstrong, saying "That 'un's yours, Sir." Armstrong looked at the shipping-label on the crate and laughed loud enough to be heard in Westport.

≈≈≈≈≈

A sailor carried the flat crate onto the deck and placed it beside the door of the Captain's cabin. After Armstrong signed the wagon-driver's documents and stepped onto the deck, he called out to Ruairí, "You're the Captain's new man, aren't you?"

"I am, Sir."

"Let him know that our shipment has arrived. And stand back when he sees it."

Ruairí knocked on the cabin door, and the Captain growled "Come in!" He entered and closed the door behind him. The Captain was writing at his desk, with the breakfast-tray and dishes stacked neatly to one side. "What is it, Mullan?"

"There's a shipment here, Sir."

"Finally!" The Captain pushed his chair back and stood up.

"Do you want me to help you, Sir?"

"That won't be necessary, Mullan. I'm doing well today." The short, intense man stepped around his desk, touching the furniture lightly with his fingertips as he moved. He squinted and opened the door.

Armstrong stood beside the flat crate, and a semicircle of sailors had gathered behind him. The Captain blinked, staring at the crate. "What is this, Armstrong?"

"It appears to be a cock-up, Sir. It's supposed to be our propeller."

"Sweet suffering Christ. I want you and Evans in here in five minutes."

The Captain closed the door, bending like a man who had been hit in the stomach. Ruairí moved to his side, and the Captain grasped his shoulder. "I need to sit."

"Yes, Sir."

They moved together to the desk, and the Captain eased himself into his chair. "I want you to stand by, Mullan. This bloody business is not my doing!"

≈≈≈≈≈

Ruairí sat at the side of the room while Evans and Armstrong pulled their chairs close around the Captain's desk. Although he could not catch everything that they were saying, he heard a rhythm to their talk – long minutes of sober discussion punctuated by outbursts from the Captain. *What are those lazy fools in Southampton thinking of, sending us this pin-wheel? Do they imagine that the Wasp is a row-boat?* Evans and Armstrong would sit quietly for a few seconds, and then the rumble of discussion would begin again.

The three officers handed papers back and forth, making remarks like *...that should have been clear enough.* Ruairí heard the word *sabotage* followed by silence, and he realised that for a few seconds the Captain had been staring at him. But Evans said *That could hardly be possible, unless it happened at the other end,* and the officers turned their attention back to each other. Then someone said *...possibly mis-keying the order,* and someone else said *...or a copy of the telegram, to be certain.*

"Mullan!"

"Yes, Sir."

"Do you know how to find the telegraph office?"

"It's in Westport, Sir. By the river."

"That is correct. I want you to go there with..." The Captain pulled a sheet of paper from a drawer and began writing with a scratchy pen. "...with this message. I want records of my communications with Southampton for the past three weeks. I want you to bring them back here as quickly as possible."

"Will I need a pass, Sir?"

"Right! Here..." The Captain scribbled on another sheet of paper. "Get started now. I'll be waiting for you to report back."

Ruairí said, "Aye aye, Sir," and he thought he saw a glimmer of amusement pass between Evans and Armstrong.

≈≈≈≈≈

The three officers sat in silence after Ruairí closed the cabin door. After a few seconds, Evans broke the silence. "Is this wise, Sir?"

"What do you mean, Evans?"

"Was it not on a mission to the telegraph office that O'Donnell disappeared?"

"It was."

"Would it not therefore be more prudent to send one of the crew?"

"Ah, but I have you there, Evans. As long as the faintest possibility of sabotage remains in the air, who among the crew can be trusted?"

"Surely Carlisle, or Hatton..."

"...or yourselves?" The Captain sat up taller in his chair, suppressing a smile at his own sarcasm. "No, gentlemen – young Mullan has not been on board before yesterday, so he cannot possibly be involved in anything that went before. He is the one and only man I can trust. Other than myself."

Evans and Armstrong exchanged glances but said nothing. The Captain said, "We'll allow matters to stand at that, for now. Armstrong, I want you to consult the manuals and prepare a detailed description of the replacement screw that we require. List the unit, and specify the page numbers of its documentation. We will apply the kind of pressure to Southampton that they regularly apply to us."

"Very well, Sir."

"Thank you, gentlemen. That is all."

After the subordinate officers left, the Captain sat silently at his desk. Where was the requisition for the propeller? Had he failed to write out a copy? He had not made a mistake like that in years. There should be a copy at the telegraph office – there had to be. And it was imperative that he read it before anyone else could, to be absolutely certain that he had not created this ridiculous situation. And if he had – the less evidence, the better.

≈≈≈≈

The air on the Westport Road smelled fresh and bracing. Ruairí walked exuberantly, feeling like a man released from prison. Orange and yellow leaves crackled under his feet. He picked up chestnuts from the gutter – brown, waxy nuts that looked like the eyes of animals peering out from spiky green split-open shells.

Had the schoolmaster ever seen chestnuts? he wondered. *Sure, he must have seen them – he was from Sligo.* With a pang, Ruairí realised how much he missed the tiny man, and a flood of Toraigh memories washed over him. The schoolmaster pointing at maps with a stick nearly as tall as he was, Eoghan playing football like a boulder crashing down a hill, Eithne measuring out her herb-packets – his home island never seemed so sweet.

He wished that he could talk with the schoolmaster, to ask him about the *Wasp* and its strange Captain. What would he ask him, if he could? *How do I get back into the map-school? What will the Captain expect of me?* The answer to that particular question, he realised, would not come from the schoolmaster – but it could be at hand, in Westport, if he could find O'Donnell.

He walked over the crest of the hill and into Westport Town. Horse-drawn carriages congested the streets, and merchants had painted signs of all sizes to attract business. Large wagons were stopped on every street, unloading beer and collecting empty barrels. Ruairí thought of Eoghan hoisting the oil-barrels up the lighthouse steps, and he wondered how his brother was getting on with the Keepers, and with the endless routine of the job.

At the telegraph office he waited in line while a well-dressed Englishwoman sent a telegram to her daughter in India. Over her shoulder Ruairí glimpsed a few words – WILL YOU COME HOME FOR CHRISTMAS STOP – and wondered what it must feel like to be rich – rich enough to sail halfway around the world for a holiday. Would he be able to return to Toraigh for Christmas? He had not thought about it.

The clerk behind the counter read the Captain's note several times, eyeing Ruairí between readings. He took off his glasses and said, "Where's the lad who usually brings these?"

"O'Donnell? I'm looking for him, too."

"And who are you?"

Ruairí looked at the telegraph clerk's thinning hair and too-busy mannerisms. "I'm the Commander's Servant now."

"Where's your uniform?"

"I don't have one."

The bell on the office door jingled as a businessman entered. The clerk looked at the Captain's note again and said, "I can't look for these records right now. You'll have to come back."

"The Captain says he needs them today," Ruairí said, enjoying the chance to press the grumpy little fellow.

"I'll get them! But not now! I have to take care of this man now!"

Ruairí left the office, humming.

≈≈≈≈≈

There were drinkers in the pubs, even before noon. Old men with deeply-wrinkled skin, and young fellows with bloodshot eyes. Quiet men, keeping to themselves.

Speaking Irish, Ruairí ordered a pint. One of the old men at the bar glanced at him for a few seconds. The publican filled the glass within an inch of the top and then released the tap-handle. No one said anything while the bubbles rose from the stout.

The publican topped up the glass and presented it to Ruairí with a small flourish. He suppressed a smile at the man's well-practised flair, making a show of his pint-pouring skills for the early-morning drinkers. He dug into his pockets for sixpence. Taking a sip, he realised that there were two weaknesses in his plan – he would soon run out of money, or get drunk. Or both.

Speaking Irish, someone said, *I've seen you around the town.*

He looked at the wispy-haired old man who sat two seats away. The man's skin looked pale and transparent, like Aunt Eithne's. Ruairí said, *I've been here for a few weeks.*

Working here, are you?

I'm in the map-school, down on the quay.

The old man nodded. *I've heard about that place. You draw the maps, do you?*

I do.

What do you think of it?

I like the map-making. I don't like the others there.

They both took sips of their pints. The others in the pub were listening, even if they tried to show no sign of it.

The old man said, *But you're roaming the town today instead of drawing the maps?*

I'm looking for a bloke who ran away from the Navy ship.

Ruairí could feel the tension in the room rise a notch. He took a sip before continuing, *He's English, but he's got an Irish name.*

Will they pay if someone finds him? asked the old man.

No, it's not that. They want me to do his job. I want to know why he ran away.

Without looking, Ruairí could feel the men in the pub exchanging glances. It would be the same on Toraigh, he thought – if a stranger appeared and started asking questions, no one would tell him a thing until they knew more about him.

You're not from around here, are you? asked the old man.

No. I'm from Toraigh Island.

Up north?

That's where I'm from.

They say there aren't any trees on Toraigh. Is that right?

That's right. No rats, either.

I heard about that, said a man at the end of the bar. Some kind of dirt keeps them away?

It's a special clay. From a grave.

Something in the atmosphere of the pub lifted, and the men relaxed in their seats. Ruairí heard footsteps and a door opening and closing behind him.

Have you got any of that clay with you? asked the man at the end of the bar. *There's some English rats that we'd like to get out of Westport.*

Ruairí hesitated, not sure how to respond. The old man said, *Do you know the story about Granuaile's grave out there on Clare Island?*

No, I haven't heard that one...

The man at the end of the bar interrupted. *Tell him about the time she shot the Turkish captain...*

The old man launched into a complicated story about the Irish pirate queen who gave birth to a baby while her men fought a battle with a Turkish ship. Taking a sip of his pint, Ruairí wondered how soon he could ask about O'Donnell again. There was a rhythm to these conversations, and he knew that if he pressed too soon for an answer, the drinkers would withdraw into silence.

A door opened and closed. Although he was only half-listening, Ruairí could tell that the old man had stopped his story in mid-sentence. The publican leaned over the bar and tugged at Ruairí's sleeve, gesturing toward a dark alcove at the back of the bar. *There's someone here,* the publican said, *who wants to talk to you.*

≈≈≈≈≈

The man sat in the corner of the snug with his back to the window. From his silhouette, Ruairí could see that he had a full head of hair and a flowing beard. His deep-set eyes were barely visible in the craggy lines of his face. The light from the window fell on the man's work-stained hands and thick wrists on the table. Ruairí sat across from him on a wooden bench.

After a few seconds, the man said, *Where are you from?*

I'm from Toraigh Island. Up north of Donegal.

The man seemed to study Ruairí for a time. *They tell me that you're looking for someone from the Navy ship.*

I am.

Is there a reward for finding him?

No, they don't even want him back. I'm the one that wants to find him.

And why do you want to find him?

It's what I told those other fellows before. They want me to do his job. I want to know why he ran away.

The man looked long and hard at Ruairí. His stare felt as cold as the Captain's. *If you find him, what exactly will you say to him?*

Resenting the question, Ruairí said, *Then you know who I'm talking about.*

I do.

Ruairí weighed his words. He had no reason to trust this man. Still...

I want to know what they made him do. And what was it that made him run away. I want to know before I get into deep waters.

If you're on the ship, the man said, *you're in deep waters already.*

Ruairí felt a weight bearing down on his shoulders again. *Will you tell me where he is?*

If I tell you where he is, will you tell me what the ship's orders are?

Ruairí laughed. *I don't know that myself.*

But if you take your man's job, you will. We need to know where that ship is going. And what orders it receives.

Ruairí felt a force radiating from the man, like the push of the wind against the side of a *currach*. He asked, *Why do you need to know that?*

The man snorted. *Where have you been living all your life?*

On Toraigh. Why?

You really don't know, do you? About the way that people are being treated by the police? About the evictions?

I know that life is not easy...

And it benefits some people to keep it that way.

Ruairí let the thought sink in before he asked *Have you talked about this with the boy from the ship?*

For the first time, the man seemed to pull back. He turned his head slightly, and Ruairí could see a jagged scar on the side of his nose. *He is English. And he seems to be interested only in drinking.*

If you tell me where to find him, I will try to talk him into going back to the ship.

And you might well persuade him. But if you take up his duties on the ship...

The man let the thought hang in the air. Ruairí said, *What if I do?*

If we knew that evictions were planned...

What would you do?

The man started to say something, but he seemed to change his mind. *We need someone on that ship.*

You do not know me, and I do not know you. Why do you trust me?

Should I not trust you?

Ruairí thought of the schoolmaster, and his brother in Mountjoy Prison. He slid across the bench to the entrance to the snug. *You are asking me to risk a great deal. If you will not help me find O'Donnell, then I must continue looking...*

The man exhaled loudly, as if disappointed. He said, *The Forge.*

I do not understand...

There is a pub named The Forge at the edge of town. He will be there, drinking away his money. Tell him that he will not receive any more.

Surprised, Ruairí said, *Thank you for telling me...*

I have not told you anything that you would not discover for yourself. But there is one thing I want you to remember.

What is that?

After you see the – the duties that the ship performs, you may change your mind. I suspect that you will. If you come looking for me, we will talk again.

Will I find you here?

I will know if you come looking for me. Go now.

≈≈≈≈≈

The Forge was quiet in the early afternoon. The barman who pulled Ruairí's pint walked with a limp, and his left arm hung uselessly at his side. Foam sloshed over the rim of the mug, and he made no attempt to wipe it off. He pocketed Ruairí's sixpence and turned his attention to a ragged newspaper.

Ruairí took the dripping pint and walked to the table near the rear door where O'Donnell was half-hidden in shadows. Three empty mugs sat uncollected on O'Donnell's table, and he was drinking from a fourth. O'Donnell looked like he had slept in his clothes – a dirty shirt and pants, not a Navy uniform. He glared at Ruairí with red-rimmed, glassy eyes. "Who are you?"

"My name's Ruairí Mullan. I'm from the *Wasp*."

O'Donnell jumped up in alarm. "You ain't here to take me back, are you?"

Ruairí shook his head. "If I wanted to take you back, I wouldn't come here all by myself." He grinned at the thought of trying to drag O'Donnell, half-drunk and trying to escape, through the town of Westport and down the mile-long road to the Quay.

"Whadya want, then? Who are you, anyway? I don't remember you."

"They got me onto the ship to do your old job."

O'Donnell looked up in genuine surprise. "Takin' care of the Captain?"

"That's me."

He shook his head and looked back down at the table. "I ain't never going back on that ship."

"What are you going to do when you run out of money?"

"Who says I'm gonna run out of money?"

"The man who gave it to you told me he wasn't going to give you any more."

O'Donnell shook his head, bewildered. "If they ever find me, they'll put me in the brig."

Ruairí leaned across the table. "C'mere, O'Donnell. How long have you been in the Navy?"

"About a year, I guess."

"So what do they make you do? On the ship?" O'Donnell reached for his pint, but Ruairí put his hand over the mug. "Come on, mate. Tell me before you get too drunk to talk."

O'Donnell put the pint down, pulled a handkerchief from his pocket, and blew his nose loudly. "I don't have to talk to you."

"What have you got to lose?"

The boy hesitated, and Ruairí realised how lonely and frightened he was. O'Donnell said, "It was easy on the ship. I run errands for the Captain. *Do this. Bring me that. Tell So-and-so to come here.* He didn't keep me busy. Half of the time, I'd be lookin' for things to do."

"Did you have to help him walk?"

"Sometimes. He was crippled or something. Sometimes he didn't need me to help him."

"Was there ever any funny business? Did he ever try to mess around with your wanker?"

O'Donnell looked genuinely surprised. "No, nothin' like that."

"Then why did you run off?" O'Donnell reached for his pint again, but Ruairí grabbed his wrist. "Listen to me. They got me onto that boat, but nobody will tell me what they want me to do. And I think they told the crew not to talk to me, or keep away from me, or something."

O'Donnell tried to pull his arm away. "Leave me alone."

"Either you tell me or you ain't going to be alone for long. Those people who been helping you ain't going to help any more.

I can be back here with a gang of sailors as quick as anything. What do I have to do to get you to tell me?"

O'Donnell jerked away from Ruairí's grip and knocked an empty mug onto the floor. The barman looked over briefly but turned back to his newspaper.

"It was those evictions. I swear to Jesus I didn't know what they were headin' out to do."

O'Donnell took a deep drink from his pint, and Ruairí did not try to stop him. "Tell me what happened."

"Okay. I'm in the Captain's cabin. We're about to sail out to Clare Island, and then Tubby comes in and says he wants me to go along with him."

"Tubby?"

"Lieutenant Gubby. Somebody told him that I could speak Irish, an' he wants somebody that knows how."

"Can you speak Irish?"

"I jus' know a little. My Ma and Da, they're from Monaghan, but they come over to England for work. They used to talk a little Irish at home. I learned how to cuss in Irish. *Póg mo thóin.*"

Ruairí laughed. "Kiss me arse."

"Yeah. My mates thought it was funny, on the ship, you know. Anyway, Tubby comes to the cabin, and the Captain tells me to go along with 'em. They took along a whole bunch of us, the crew I mean."

"Who was they?" asked Ruairí. "Who was telling you what to do?"

O'Donnell took deep swallows of his pint. "The Sheriff. And there was two deputies with him."

"Is that how it goes? They just send you off with somebody and you have to do what he says?"

"No, Tubby went along too. But he just told us to do what the Sheriff said."

O'Donnell breathed heavily, looking down at the table, remembering something. Ruairí said, "So what did they make you do...?"

"I'm gettin' to it, you one-eyed son of a bitch. You come in here and push me around..."

"Hold on..."

"I ain't holdin' on for nothing. He marches me up to this house where this woman is living, and she come out with a baby, and he says to me, *Tell her to pay the rent or get out!*" O'Donnell glared at Ruairí. "You know how to say that in Irish?"

"Is that...?"

"You want to teach me how to say that in Irish? So I can go back to the ship and knock down some more people's houses?"

"Knock them down...?"

"Bust the door down. Throw everything they got into a pile..."

"Jesus, O'Donnell..."

"...and then they set the house on fire so they can't go back. Everybody's screamin' and cryin', and that fat-ass Sheriff is yellin' at me..."

"I didn't know..."

"No, you don't know. Nobody knows." O'Donnell chewed his lip. "I'll tell you what I can't get out of my head. After they broke that door down, a little boy come runnin' out. He can't be more than ten years old. He's got a fork in his hand, and he's cryin', and you can see he's tryin' to protect his Ma. He goes right at the Sheriff, but one of those deputies sticks out his foot and trips him. And while he's down, they kick him and step on his hand." O'Donnell looked at Ruairí. "He was the only one with the guts to try to fight. And they laughed at him."

A fly buzzed against the windowpane of the pub. Ruairí said, "It's not right, what they asked you to do..."

"Asked? You don't get asked nothing in the Navy. They *tell* you what to do."

"I don't suppose there was nothing else you could do, was there?"

"I thought about that every day since then. I wish I was that little boy. At least he tried to do something."

They sat in silence while a horse and wagon clopped past the pub. O'Donnell said, "That day, out there, I couldn't think at all. I just stood there like my feet was stuck to the ground. Then one of my mates comes up and hands me a cook-pot from out of the house and says *Here – come on,* and I follow him out to the road. Then they set the house on fire, like I told you. And then we went on to the next one."

Half to himself, Ruairí said, "I won't do that."

O'Donnell snorted. "Yeah. You sit here and tell me how brave you're goin' to be. Wait till you go back to the ship. They can lock you up. I seen it done."

"I've got to get out of there."

The dreary, empty pub felt like a mausoleum. Ruairí looked at the dregs of his pint. "When did you know this was going to happen?"

"Like I told you, it was the same day. The Captain don't usually say what he's going to do until it's time to do it, so nobody knows. Unless..."

"Unless what?"

O'Donnell hesitated, and a moment of clarity seemed to slip away. "I don't know for sure about this. The Captain writes in a book..."

"What book?"

"He writes in this book when he thinks nobody's around. Then he slips it under his desk, where you can't see it. I took it out and looked at it once, but..."

"But what?"

"He writes it in some other language, I guess. I can't read much. But I bet that if somebody could read what's in there, he'd know what was going to happen."

O'Donnell looked a little like Eoghan when he'd had a few pints. Ruairí leaned across the table again and grabbed his wrist again. "Listen to me," he said. "I don't know anything about evictions, or about taking care of a sick captain, or getting locked up. I come here to Westport to go to a map-school, and I don't want to have nothing to do with knocking people's houses down.

You're the one who's in the Navy. You've gone and run off for a few days, and you got yourself into some kind of trouble, but they won't hang you or make you walk the plank or whatever they do."

O'Donnell nearly sobbed. "I ain't goin' back if I have to do those evictions."

"But now they know you don't speak Irish, don't they? And the Captain needs you to take care of him."

"I don't know..."

Ruairí pushed his chair back from the table. "They'll find you sooner or later. Come on back to the boat where you belong and take whatever licks they give you. Then I can go back to the map-school where I belong."

O'Donnell hung his head. "You ain't gonna tell on me, are you?"

Ruairí stood up. "It'll be better if you walk in on your own hin' legs than if they drag you in. You know that, don't you?"

"I'll think about it..."

"Don't think too long, O'Donnell. I'm in trouble, too."

≈≈≈≈≈

The man at the telegraph office said, "Where you been? I thought you wasn't coming back ..." but he handed Ruairí a fat envelope. "You can tell your Captain he's got a new message in there, too."

Ruairí walked unsteadily along the Westport streets, blurred by the pints and by O'Donnell's story. He could almost see the sailors in front of the eviction-house, the crying woman, the fat Sheriff. *Tell her to pay the rent or get out!* Was there an Irish word for rent? It didn't matter. He wasn't going to translate anything for anybody, if it meant throwing people out of their houses.

He realised that he was nearing the quay, and he hoped that he wouldn't run into any of the crew members on the road. He slipped into the side-door entrance of the map-school building, his mind whirling with questions. He walked up the fourteen steps to the copy room and paused at the doorway. "Mister Simmons?"

The copyists and apprentices looked up from their desks, gawking. Simmons said, "Mullan?"

"Can I ask you something, Sir?"

The supervisor made a sour face and got down from his stool. The copyists watched as he walked stiff-legged to the door. Ruairí wished he had waited till later, perhaps catching Simmons as he left the building in the evening, but he could not be sure that he'd be free to leave the *Wasp* at the right moment.

Simmons stepped into the hall and closed the door behind him, breathing heavily. Ruairí said, "I'm sorry to bother you, Sir..."

"What is it, Mullan?"

"Am I – am I in the Navy, Sir?"

Simmons snorted with exasperation. "You came here to ask me *that*?"

"I mean, Sir, will I be coming back to the map-school?"

The supervisor stepped back and looked at Ruairí. "I take it you're not happy on the ship."

"No, Sir, it's not that. I was just wondering how long..." Ruairí's voice trailed off in misery, fearing that he was losing his once-friendly mentor.

Simmons took a handkerchief out of this pocket and wiped his nose. He looked through the distorting glass of a hall window at the *Wasp* berthed a few hundred yards away along the Westport Quay. "The Lieutenant said that he needed someone who could speak Irish. As far as I know, you are the only copyist who qualifies."

"But Sir," Ruairí said, his voice nearly breaking, "am I required to follow orders, or..."

"Let me tell you something, Mullan." Simmons drew a deep breath. "This enterprise – this school – is an unprecedented gesture on the part of the Admiralty. These maps could be made in London, and men would queue up to work on them. But someone, somewhere, has decided to distribute this work to the far corners of the Empire. And I have been assigned to oversee this school."

"Are you in the Navy, then, Sir?"

"I am on the civilian staff of the Admiralty, and I have no illusions about the authorities I work for. If Captain Russell requested that all the copyists in this school report for duty as powder-monkeys, I would send them all to the ship without a blink."

"So you have sent me to be in the Navy, then?"

"I have sent you to work with the Navy," said Simmons. "For a time. These arrangements are temporary courtesies." The supervisor unfolded and re-folded his handkerchief. "We have stretched our policies to bring you in as an apprentice here, Mullan – stretched them considerably. Are you telling me that I have put my confidence in the wrong individual?"

"No, Sir! I appreciate everything, Sir. But if there are more evictions..."

"I see." Simmons put the handkerchief back into this pocket and looked up at the ceiling for a moment. "I suggest that you look at it this way, Mullan." He gestured toward the copy-room. "Our craft grows more valuable every year. You are a talented draughtsman, and you may look forward to a comfortable career. But we pay a price for everything we receive."

"I appreciate that, Sir..."

"I expect you to assist the Navy in carrying out its orders, however distasteful you may find them. If you do not, it will reflect poorly on you, and on this school, and on me. I advise you to see this through, Mullan. Otherwise, whatever your talents, you will not be welcome back here."

≈≈≈≈≈

I have confidence in you, and I know you won't let me down.

He stood in the alcove of the map-school door, almost hearing the tone of Mister Geraghty's voice. What would the schoolmaster say now? Surely he would not want him to help with evictions – but would he need to? The Captain said that a new Commander's Servant was on the way. What if he walked away from the *Wasp* and abandoned his spot at the map-school, only to find out that his replacement had shown up the next day? He could never look Mister Geraghty in the eye again.

But if O'Donnell was telling the truth, the Captain wouldn't give the orders until it was time to carry them out. Would he find himself being ordered to join an eviction-party, surrounded by armed men? There might not be a chance to slip away.

He realised that he was thinking in extremes. What had Mister Geraghty said – something about finding a middle ground? He took a deep breath and tried to relax. As a Commander's Servant, he was in a good position to see what was coming. He would be able to watch the Captain closely – what he said, and what he didn't say. His spy-missions would offer clues to the Captain's thinking. And, unlike O'Donnell, he could read.

≈≈≈≈≈

Sailors were carrying boxes of provisions from a wagon on the dock up the gangplank and into the ship's hold. Ruairí waited for a break in the flow of men and materials before he stepped into the gangplank. A tall sailor with a rifle moved toward him. "Are those orders you got there?"

Ruairí didn't recognise the sailor, and he didn't like his attitude. "This is for the Captain."

"You didn't look at 'em, did you?"

"Are you going to let me on board, or not?"

"Ah, come on." The sailor nodded sideways with his head. "We just want to know what they're goin' to make us do." Ruairí stepped forward, and the sailor sniffed at him like a dog. "Hey, mate – you been drinkin'?"

"I been doing what I was sent to do." Ruairí stepped past the sailor and onto the deck, wishing that he had thought to read the packet. The late-afternoon sun cast long shadows of the men and the boxes they carried. He could feel the sailors stealing glances at him. Did he smell like beer? He was too tired and angry to care. He crossed the deck and knocked on the Captain's door.

"Who is it?"

"It's Ruairí Mullan, Sir."

"Come in, Mullan."

He stepped into the Captain's quarters and closed the door. A lamp was lit in the bedroom, and Ruairí heard the Captain clear his throat twice and spit something into a metal cup. "Shall I come in there, Sir?"

"No, stay where you are. Do you have the records from the telegraph office?"

"I do, Sir."

"I want you to go through them and find the ones that refer to the replacement propeller. Can you do that, Mullan?"

"Yes, Sir, but I wonder if..."

"If what, Mullan?"

"Could I get something to eat first, Sir? I haven't had nothing since breakfast."

"Right. Hatton will see to you. But I want you to come back and go through the correspondence tonight."

"Yes, Sir. I'll just leave it here on the desk..."

"Put it on the chair outside this door."

"All right, Sir." As he stepped across the room, Ruairí glimpsed the Captain sitting in his bunk bed wearing a nightshirt. He placed the packet on the chair and stepped back to the door. "Is there anything else, Sir?"

"No, you may go. But I want you to review the telegrams tonight and separate out the ones regarding the propeller. Do not knock, because I may be sleeping. You may light the desk lamp. And Mullan..."

"Yes, Sir?"

"Not a word of this to anyone. You may go."

Ruairí heard himself saying, "Thank you, Sir," as he left the stifling cabin. *I'm beginning to sound like a real servant,* he thought. His stomach grumbled as he descended the steep metal stairs to the galley. Nothing seemed to add up neatly. Review the telegrams tonight and separate out the ones regarding the propeller... Was the Captain setting some sort of trap for him? He knew at least one thing – the Captain had ordered him to leave the packet by the door to his sleeping-quarters so that he wouldn't have to walk the three steps to his desk.

In the galley, the sailors who would be on late-night guard duty had already strung up their hammocks. The sleeping men formed lumpy bean-like shapes in the cotton slings. Ruairí remembered the claustrophobic feeling of sleeping in the hammock the night before, tangled in a tube of sheets, less able to move with every passing minute.

He was glad to find Hatton in the kitchen. Looking up from the table where he was writing in a ledger, the cook said, "You're back."

"Did you not expect me back, Mister Hatton?"

"Well, O'Donnell didn't come back. But you appear to have more sense than him. Are you hungry?"

"I'm starving, Mister Hatton. I haven't had anything to eat since breakfast."

"Well, then," said the cook, "this will be your second breakfast of the day."

As Hatton fried rashers and eggs, Ruairí knew what he would do. He would review the Captain's telegrams after he ate, but before he twisted himself into his hammock he would write to the schoolmaster.

≈≈≈≈≈

18 September 1884
Dear Mr Geraghty,

I am sorry to be writing to you like this but I need some advice. Mr Simmons from the Map School has sent me to work on The Wasp, which is an English gun boat in Westport, the one that brought the potatoes last spring. The reason they want me is because they are doing evictions, and they want some one who

speaks Irish to talk to the people. Mr Simmons says I cant go back
to the Map School until the Captain of The Wasp says I can go.

I dont want to let you down Mr Geraghty, but I dont want to
do evictions. You always have good ideas that I dont think about.
Can you see a way out of this for me?

Is mise, le meas
Ruairí Mullan

He had addressed the envelope before he realised he had no stamps. And how could he mail a letter from the ship? He walked back to the galley. "Mister Hatton?"

"Yes?" The cook looked up from the steaming sink where he was standing.

"How can I post this?"

"Give it to Lieutenant Gubby. He handles the Royal Mail."

"And where can I get a stamp?"

"You won't need one." Hatton chuckled. "The Navy will generously send that for you. Do you know where Gubby's quarters are?"

"I do. Thank you, Mister Hatton."

He walked past the dining tables where men sat writing, playing draughts, and whittling pieces of bone. He could see Gubby's shadow on the thin curtain that hung across his alcove. He paused beside the curtain and said, "Lieutenant?"

"Who is it?"

"Mullan, Sir. The Commander's Servant."

Gubby's chair scraped against the steel deck, and the curtain shot open. "Does the Captain want to see me?"

"No, Sir. I wanted to ask you about posting this letter."

"Oh – very well." Gubby took the envelope from Ruairí and peered at it. "You need to write the ship's name on the back."

"Yes, Sir. Do you have a pencil I could use, Sir?"

Gubby groped at a pigeonhole in the small writing desk beside his bunk. Ruairí thought he saw crumbs of cheese on the desk. Gubby found a pencil stub and handed it to Ruairí, who wrote *The Wasp* on the back of the envelope.

"It's *H.M.S. Wasp*," said Gubby. "And add *The Royal Navy.*"

Ruairí crossed out *The* and wrote *H.M.S.* above it. Gubby inspected the envelope again and placed it in a slot on his desk where other envelopes were sitting. "Is there anything else?"

"No, Sir. Thank you."

Gubby said, "Very well," and pulled the curtain.

Seething, Ruairí climbed the steep stairs to the main deck. He brushed past the men who were lounging near the gangplank and hurried to the prow of the ship, as far away from the others as possible. Hodge, the cat, looked up and slunk away from the coil of rope where he'd been napping. *Smart cat,* Ruairí thought. *He knows when somebody's mad enough to kick him.*

Ruairí leaned against the steel skirting-rail and performed half-pushups until his neck ached. The cat peeked out from behind a capstan. Ruairí laughed, stood up, and said, "Come here, you little bugger." He held out his finger until the cat came over to nuzzle. "I'll tell you something," he said as he stroked Hodge's ears. "I'm not staying on this boat one day longer than I have to. You can stay if you want, but I'm getting off."

He wondered how soon he might hear from the schoolmaster. If Gubby posted the mail tomorrow – that would be Friday, and then how long would it take to get to the north coast of Donegal? When would Ben Rodgers sail over from Toraigh to the mainland to collect it? He didn't make the trip every day, and in rough seas he wouldn't try. It could take more than a week, even if Mister Geraghty wrote back immediately. And if he didn't...

≈≈≈≈≈

Censoring the mail, Gubby knew, was part of his duty as a Royal Navy Officer. The world was rebuilding its navies into ironclad fleets, and it wouldn't be beyond the Frenchies or the Germans to plant spies among Her Majesty's crews. Still, he found it to be a miserable task to read the men's letters to their wives and mothers. It was no secret that the job fell to him – the crew of the

Wasp knew that he as junior officer would read every word they wrote, and gave them another reason to resent him.

He opened Mullan's letter. The boy hadn't even attempted to seal it with wax. He looked at the inside surfaces of the envelope, where the men sometimes wrote words that they didn't want him to see. Nothing was written there. He opened the page and read. *Dear Mister Geraghty...*

Gubby was surprised at the clarity of Mullan's writing. Most of the letters from the crew were scrawled, half-hearted things – *Mary I mis you how is the Boy?* Where had this Mullan been educated?

...I cant go back to the Map School until the Captain of The Wasp says I can go... Can you see a way out of this for me? Gubby thought of his own rambling letters to his father, and he envied the clear, simple tone of Mullan's plea. Sometimes he wondered if something had passed him by in life, if others had been taught lessons that had been withheld from him.

And then it struck him. *Can you see a way out of this...*

Mullan was disloyal. He was trying to evade responsibility. Gubby knew how highly the Captain hated the slightest hint of disloyalty, or even indifference...

It was what he had been hoping for, his chance to re-establish himself in the Captain's good graces. He would be in the Captain's cabin, fully prepared, at first light.

19 September 1884

At first he thought the windows were dirty. Quinn scrubbed them with vinegar and ammonia until they squeaked, but nothing changed – when he looked out at the passing ships at night, or at the stars, he saw a dim halo around every light. The moon seemed to be surrounded by a faint glow, even on cloudless nights. He had always been proud of his clear, far-sighted vision, and it frightened him badly to think that it might be slipping away

He checked the clock and hurried down the stairs with the water-pitcher. The tank, he knew, held enough oil to supply the beacon for another ten minutes. He could wait for the ten minutes and then descend to the galley after he'd opened and tipped in a new barrel of oil, but his throat clenched with a craving for water. The metal stair-steps rang underfoot as he hurried to the base of the tower. As he filled the pitcher, the handle of the pump in the galley sink felt cool and slippery in his hand. He gulped water from the side of the pitcher, spilling it on his shirt. He refilled the pitcher and hurried up the stairs to open the next barrel of oil.

The neck of his shirt felt clammy where he'd spilled the water. He was glad that he was alone. That was one of the advantages of the middle watch. From midnight until 4:00 am, no one else was awake to see.

It was the craving, the damned feeling of hunger and need, that bothered him most. He had always prided himself on his endurance, his ability to stick with a job while other men grew tired and dropped away. But something inside him had shifted, and the simple feeling of being thirsty had been replaced by a powerful urge to glut himself with water. A growing tension threatened to seize his throat. Water – ordinary, unexceptional water – glistened and beckoned in his imagination. When it wasn't at hand, he could think of little else but where to find it. *He craved it as desperately...*

He laughed at the thought. Now he craved water almost as desperately as he had once craved whiskey. What would Mary say if he told her? In those terrible old days, when the bottles of whiskey and beer inflamed his imagination, Mary would tell him, *Drink some water, Paddy. Drink it slow, you'll feel better.* What would she say if he told her he was now craving water? Would she urge him to drink some beer?

After he wound the clockwork that pumped the oil up to the lamps, he poured and drank another glassful. No, he wasn't going to tell her, or anyone. This was a temptation, he thought, a bit of deviltry that he would overcome by himself. He climbed the stairs to the lantern room, sat on the hard wooden chair, and looked out over the sea. In the privacy of these dark hours, he felt proud and stubborn and alone, and he knew that he could count on himself to sort out nearly anything. But he could not avoid the thought that there was a small, malicious imp in his soul who tried to knock him off-balance with temptations. While he carried out his daily work, the imp would distract him with fantasies of idleness, of women, of the freedom that the passing ships represented. The imp had almost conquered him with the alcohol – if Mary had not stood by him, he might well be sleeping in a gutter instead of standing watch in a lighthouse.

With a stab of annoyance, he realised that he had to urinate. Like the galley, the toilet sat at the base of the lighthouse tower, a tiresome number of stairs below the lantern room. Again he checked the clockwork pump before he started to descend. There was no urgency this time, he realised, but he seemed to be making more piss-runs, and more urgent ones, with every passing month.

As he climbed down the stairs, he wondered for the hundredth time if the others would pass any remarks if he brought a chamber-pot to the lantern room. But it would feel like an admission of weakness. He also knew that his urine had developed a sweet pungent smell that would be embarrassing. No, it was better to make the climb.

He felt a wave of dizziness as he stopped to check the clockwork pump, and he poured himself another glass of water. A vicious circle, he thought – hurry to piss, work up a thirst, drink the water, need to piss more... It would be five more years before he could retire, and it was beginning to feel like a prison sentence, with hard labour. *But no,* he told himself, *I will not let this defeat me. I can manage this. As long as they leave me alone.*

≈≈≈≈≈

"Come in, Gubby."

Stepping into the dim cabin, Gubby was surprised to find Ruairí Mullan sitting across from the Captain at his desk. A tall stack of paper sat on the desk between them, and the Captain seemed to be explaining something to the red-haired boy. Without looking up, the Captain said, "What is it?"

"May I – have a word with you in private, Sir?"

The Captain shot an irritated glance at Gubby. "Very well. Mullan, get another pot of tea from Hatton and bring it up here."

Ruairí said, "Yes, Sir," and left the cabin without looking at Gubby.

Gubby felt an uncomfortable thickening in his throat. "This may take a few minutes, Sir..."

"Not if you get to the point, Gubby. What is it?"

"It's – it's Mullan, Sir."

The Captain put down the piece of paper he had been reading, and he stared directly at Gubby. "And exactly what about Mullan do you want to discuss?"

Gubby felt a trickle of sweat running down his back. "It's this letter, Sir." He fumbled at his coat-pockets. "He wrote a letter that I thought..." A wave of panic began to rise in his stomach until he found the envelope in an inside pocket. "I thought that I'd – I thought that it should be brought to your attention."

The Captain snapped the letter from Gubby's fingers and pulled it from the envelope. He wiped his eyes and took a magnifying glass from his desk drawer. Gubby said, "It seemed to me..."

Without looking up, the Captain snapped, "What did it seem to you?"

"It seemed to me to – to raise questions of loyalty, Sir."

The Captain put down the magnifying glass and stared at Gubby. "You are an extremely poor judge of character, Lieutenant. Do you realise that?"

"Sir, I only wanted you to..."

"I can see what you wanted. You wanted to improve your standing with me by besmirching someone else."

"I was only reading the letter as a matter of routine..."

"Mister Gubby! This letter only shows that young Mullan is aware of his situation. As we all are! And he is making a sensible request for advice."

"Sir, I had no intention..."

"You led a bloody eviction-party yourself! And you came back from that mission so... How did you describe yourself? So *heartsick* that you could not use your intelligence to steer the ship! Why didn't you ask for help?"

Gubby looked away as tears welled up in his eyes. He heard himself saying, "I'm sorry, Sir..."

The Captain leaned over his desk and massaged the bridge of his nose. "If there is disloyalty in this letter, then I will need to enlist an entirely new crew. Go back to your duties, Lieutenant."

Gubby felt unable to move. "Sir?"

"What?"

"Sir, I confess that I am trying to find my way back into your favour. I had no intention..."

They heard Ruairí's footsteps across the deck. There was a rap on the cabin door. The Captain said, "If you want to impress me, catch a deserter."

"Do you mean O'Donnell, Sir?"

"It would weigh heavily in your favour if you foiled a deserter, whether O'Donnell or anyone else. It wouldn't surprise me if Mullan has already found O'Donnell."

Gubby started to leave but turned back. "Shall I mail the letter, Sir?"

The Captain replaced the letter in the envelope and tucked it into his own coat pocket. "Leave it with me, Gubby. I'll have a word with this young man."

≈≈≈≈≈

The cabin door opened. Gubby brushed past Ruairí, jostling his arm, and a splash of liquid from the metal teapot splatted onto the deck. Gubby crossed the deck with quick strides, not looking back. Ruairí wanted to throw the pot at the Lieutenant's clumsy figure.

"Come in, Mullan."

The cabin door was still open. Ruairí closed it and placed the teapot on a trivet next to the Captain's desk. "Shall I pour you a cup, Sir?"

"No, not now. Please sit down."

Ruairí returned to the chair where he had been sitting across from the Captain. Something had changed – the Captain was leaning back in his chair, drumming his fingers on the desk. They sat in silence until the Captain said, "Did you understand what I was telling you before?

"I think so, Sir. You're searching for a request document..."

"A requisition."

"...a requisition document. For a propeller. And you want me to bring the folders over here for you to read and then replace them in the cabinets."

"That's right, Mullan. I also want you to scan through them yourself. With fresh eyes, you may see something that I don't."

Ruairí wondered briefly if the Captain was needling him with an insult. But the Captain cleared his throat and spoke in a soft, unexpected tone. "How are you finding it, here on the *Wasp*?"

Sensing a trap, Ruairí said, "I'm – I'm not sure that I'm cut out for the Navy, Sir."

"In what way?"

"I've always lived on my own, Sir. I lived on an island where I could go everywhere. I'm not used to being... Not used to staying in one place."

"Being confined, I believe you were about to say. I imagine that most of the men felt that way at first. Have you spoken with anyone about this?"

"No, Sir. I barely know the men."

The Captain stared into space. "Indeed, you've only been with us a few days. But when you get to know the crew, you'll find that most of them were not much older than yourself when they signed on."

"Is that what I've done, Sir? Signed on?"

"Well, not precisely... But are you regretting that you chose to work with us?"

Ruairí looked down at the desktop, choosing his words. "Mister Simmons explained to me that it was important for the map-school..."

Loud pounding on the cabin door interrupted his words. "Captain! It's Armstrong, Sir!"

"Come in, Armstrong."

The Gunnery Officer burst into the room, waving a telegram. He glanced at Ruairí and hesitated. The Captain said, "What is it?"

"John Adair was shot by the Fenians last night!"

"Here in Westport?"

"No, the ambush was in Donegal. But, we're to implement..."

"Was he killed?"

"Apparently not, Sir. But we're to implement isolation-and-security measures."

"Oh, for the love of God..." The Captain pressed his thumb and forefinger against the bridge of his nose. "Are we provisioned for isolation?"

"I believe we've plenty of food, Sir. But we've still not received that shipment of coal."

"Right." The Captain looked at Ruairí. "Mullan, find Evans and tell him to come up here immediately. Then stand by below. I may need you later."

"Aye aye, Sir."

≈≈≈≈≈

Blinking in the morning sun, Ruairí stepped out onto the deck and closed the cabin door behind him. He hurried down the steep metal stairs to the galley and through the passageway to the Officer's Mess. Evans looked up from a map that was laid out on the dining-table. "What is it, Mullan?"

"The Captain wants to see you immediately, Sir."

"Right. Put this back into my quarters, will you?"

As Evans hurried from the Mess and down the passageway, Ruairí noticed that he was limping. He looked at Evans's map. *Wales*, it read, *Western Coastline, Southwest Quadrant.*

"Did you draw that map, Master Mullan?" The cook stood in the doorway, wiping his hands with a towel.

"No, Mister Hatton. I'm just putting this away for Lieutenant Evans."

Hatton looked at the map and craned his neck to read it. "Perhaps that's where we're going next."

The thought sent a shudder of alarm through Ruairí. "Are we leaving Ireland?"

"I have no idea. Evans may be studying his ancestral homeland." He tucked the towel into the belt of his apron. "You're in the best position to overhear where we're going."

Ruairí hesitated until he remembered that the Captain had expressed confidence in the cook. "Mister Hatton?"

"Yes?"

"What are isolation and security measures?"

The cook looked up sharply. "Is that what's coming?"

"I'm not sure, Sir. I just heard it this morning. What does it mean?"

"It means," said Hatton, "that you're going to eat a great deal of porridge and very little meat."

≈≈≈≈≈

Ruairí stood at the stern of the *Wasp*, looking at the fishing boats on Clew Bay. How far from land would the ship need to move to be isolated and secure? A mile? Fifty miles?

"Mullan!"

Ruairí spun around to find Lieutenant Gubby squeezing between the rail and a ventilator hatch. "What is it, Sir?"

"A word with you, Mullan." The Lieutenant wheezed and pulled a handkerchief from a pocket to mop his brow. "Stand easy."

Ruairí had not been standing at attention, but he found himself shifting his weight to acknowledge Gubby's words. The Lieutenant's raspy breathing was loud enough to be heard over the cries of the gulls.

Gubby replaced the handkerchief in his pocket. "Mullan, do you know where I can find O'Donnell?"

"O'Donnell, Sir?"

"Your predecessor. You know who I mean, don't you?"

Ruairí hesitated. "I'm afraid I don't know him, Sir."

"I think you do, Mullan. And it would weigh heavily in your favour if you helped me find him."

A wet droplet had formed on the end of Gubby's nose. Ruairí watched the quivering white pearl of moisture, and his stomach felt queasy. *I don't care what he says*, he thought. *I'm not going to tell this arse-wipe anything.*

Gubby pulled the handkerchief from his pocket again. "You aren't refusing to cooperate, are you, Mullan?"

"No, Sir. I don't know what to say..."

"It isn't because he's Irish, is it? You wouldn't conceal evidence because he's a countryman of yours, would you?"

"No, Sir, that never occurred to me..."

"Then where is he?"

"I imagine he must be on the mainland, Sir."

Gubby stared over the rail at the bay. His eyes were puffed, and he looked like he was on the verge of crying. Ruairí said, "Sir?"

"What, Mullan?"

"What would you do with O'Donnell if you found him?"

"I'd clap him in the brig. We have a fine brig for deserters."

"What if he came back of his own accord, Sir?"

"I'd still clap him in the brig. Until the court-martial. We'd hold a court-martial." Gubby's eyes snapped into focus, and he turned to glare at Ruairí. "You *do* know where he is, don't you?"

"No, Sir, I only asked because I wondered..."

"What did you wonder, Mullan?"

"If he came back, I wondered if I could go back to the map-school."

Gubby snorted in disgust. "There's a war going on, and you people are shooting at decent Englishmen, and you're worried about going back to your map-school?"

Ruairí said, "That's what I want, Sir."

Gubby sneered in disgust. "That will be all, Mullan. You may go."

Ruairí looked at the fat, posturing Lieutenant and came very close to saying *I was here first, Sir*, but he could tell that Gubby was itching to lash out at someone. And he couldn't make any plans if Gubby clapped him in the brig. As quietly as possible, Ruairí said *Aye-aye, Sir* and stepped away from the stern, leaving the Lieutenant to stare over the rail.

≈≈≈≈≈

"Gubby, you are proficient in Morse, are you not?"

"Yes, Sir, I – that is, I won an award at the Midshipman's Academy..."

"And semaphore?"

"I am, Sir."

"Good! Are you aware that we are implementing isolation-and-security procedures?"

"No, Sir, I hadn't heard..."

The Captain thought *...and you're probably the only man on this ship who hasn't*, but he stopped himself from saying it. Gubby shifted uncomfortably in the silence that lapsed between them. The Captain pressed his lips together and shook his head before continuing. "We have received orders to take an armed position away from shore. I am assigning you to serve as Land Signal Officer for the duration of the emergency."

"Land Signal Officer... What am I to do, Sir?"

"You will be our link with Southampton and Whitehall. Their orders will be issued by secure telegraph through the Castlebar barracks. They will be brought to you at Westport House, and you will relay them to the ship."

"At Westport House, Sir?"

The Captain smiled. "Yes. We have a long-standing agreement with Lord Browne to use one of his towers as a signal station. You and three of the men will be required to sleep on the Westport House linens and partake of their hospitality. Do you think you can manage that, Gubby?"

"I'm – I don't know what to say, Sir."

The smile faded from the Captain's face. "You will be expected to relay all orders immediately, not after breakfast. I will also be issuing communications, so you will need to establish a rotation of watches. However, I expect you to receive and transmit all messages personally. If this means rousing you in the small hours, so be it. Are you following me?"

"Yes, Sir."

"And, Gubby, there is one thing that I want to impress upon you. If you receive sealed orders, you will bring them to the ship, unopened."

"Yes, Sir. Unopened. "

The Captain raised his eyes from his desk to stare directly at Gubby. "Your success in this mission will weigh significantly on your future, Lieutenant. Ask Evans to assign three reliable men to work with you. I hope I'm not making an error in entrusting you with this."

"No, Sir. I appreciate the opportunity..."

"That will be all, Gubby. You may go."

Amused, the Captain watched Gubby hurry out the door. He anticipated that the isolation-and-security orders would be rescinded in a few days, as they usually were. The young Lieutenant would throw himself into the signalling routines that others would find tedious and confining, even within the comforts of Westport House. And it would be a relief to get the miserable fellow off the ship.

≈≈≈≈≈

Ruairí leaned against the iron skirting-panels that surrounded the deck. The *Wasp* was snugged against the quay, rubbing against the cork fenders that cushioned the steel hull from the stonework of the dock. He could step across the gap. Anyone could.

The men standing watch at the gangplank were talking to each other. Ruairí wondered what they would do if he stepped onto the land. Shoot him? They had live ammunition – he'd seen the rifle-shells laid out like brass jewellery in the munitions-room. He wondered if he could make his way to the railway switch-yard before they noticed him. They'd spot him if he ran, but if he walked casually...

He was startled as Lieutenant Gubby emerged from the hatch near the gangplank, followed by three sailors. The men on guard duty snapped to attention. Gubby showed them a white paper from his pocket, and they stood aside to let the party pass. No wagon was waiting for them on the quay. They walked toward the Westport road but then turned toward the gate of the mansion that overlooked the quay. Ruairí wondered if the same blokes were manning the gatehouse, and for a moment he wished he could join Gubby's detail and march past the arrogant bastards.

He realised that the Chief Petty Officer was also leaning on the metal deck-skirting. "Mister Carlisle?"

"Yes, Mullan? Rory, is it?"

He thought briefly about trying to correct the Englishman's pronunciation, but he decided to let it pass. "That's right, Sir."

"Save that *Sir* business for the officers. Call me Carlisle. What's on your mind?"

"What's this all about? Is there a war starting?"

Carlisle snorted. "Hardly. Someone took a pot-shot at Black Jack Adair, and now Whitehall is over-reacting as usual. We'll be out there bobbing around like an armoured cork until someone decides we can relax. Then we'll return to picking our noses here at the quay."

Ruairí smiled at Carlisle's exasperation. "Who is this Adair?"

"He owns a huge estate up in Donegal. They say he owns a cattle-ranch over in America, too."

"So why are they shooting at him?"

"You're asking me to explain that to you?" Carlisle looked Ruairí full in the face. "You aren't taking the piss, are you?"

"No, Sir – I mean Mister Carlisle. I don't know anything about any of this."

Carlisle looked out at the horizon, choosing his words. "Adair is the kind of landowner who gives landowners a bad name. He's an arrogant cock, from what I've heard. He wouldn't speak to the likes of me, and he might not even speak to the Captain."

Ruairí grinned. "So he wouldn't speak to me, either?"

"No, my Irish friend, he wouldn't. Unless he was evicting you."

Ruairí pulled back into himself as their air of camaraderie evaporated. "Is he behind the evictions, then?"

Carlisle looked down at the deck, also sobered. "He's not the only one. But he's one of the worst. He tore down forty-six houses up around Derryveagh, just to get those tenants off his land. He got the police to help him. They still talk about the 'crowbar brigade.' That's why your people are shooting at him."

"My people?" Ruairí hesitated, wondering what Carlisle saw when he looked at him. "Has the *Wasp* ever done evictions for him?"

"I don't know," snapped Carlisle. "And I choose not to know. If anyone asks, we never had this conversation."

The Petty Officer turned and strode away, and the engines of the *Wasp* began to rumble underfoot.

≈≈≈≈≈

Evans directed the launch. A team of sailors lifted the gangplank and stowed it along the bulkhead that supported the bridge. Other men loosened the mooring-ropes from the bollards on the quay and jumped back onto the deck. Evans telegraphed DEAD SLOW to the engine-room, and the deck-hands lifted the cork fenders as the ship began to pull away from the dock.

Ruairí stood on the deck, half-wondering if he should report to the Captain's quarters. His feet felt like lead weights. For a few long minutes he knew that he could still jump overboard and swim to shore, but that idea faded as the *Wasp* drew further away from the dock. He could see the entire panorama of the Westport Quay – the merchant-ships moored along the dock, the grain elevator where the railway cars were unloaded, the grey granite map-school building, the Westport road, and, high on the hill, the towers of Westport Manor. The land receded until the people and wagons and horses seemed small as ants.

He had never felt more lonely. He turned from the railing and climbed down the steep stairs to the galley. He sat at a table, listening to the men's footsteps on the deck above and fearing that he had missed an irretrievable opportunity. If Carlisle's guesses were right, the *Wasp* might well be back in its berth on Westport Quay in a few days. If not...

He tried to shake off his sense of dread. How, he wondered, would Mister Geraghty's letter find its way to him? There had to be some sort of ship-to-shore traffic – a pilot-boat, perhaps – but what if the *Wasp* did not return to Westport?

And what of his own letter? Ruairí hurried down the length of the empty galley, stepping quietly to avoid drawing the attention of Hatton and his crew in the kitchen. He stood outside the cloth curtain that screened Lieutenant Gubby's alcove. He checked to see that he was still alone, and he pulled back the curtain. He looked in at the table where the Lieutenant kept his pens and papers and the men's letters. The letter-rack was empty.

Relieved, he returned to the chair where he had been sitting. If the Captain wanted to summon him, he was within earshot of the voice-tube. He was doing the right thing, he told himself. He would bet that Carlisle knew what he was talking about. And with a broken propeller, it wasn't likely that they'd be going anywhere.

≈≈≈≈≈

The *Wasp* dropped anchor at the mouth of Clew Bay, a mile beyond Clare Island. Evans drew up a rotation of double watches, assigning guard to men who did not customarily work together. Armstrong organised a detail to polish the spotlight lenses and test the carbide lamps that produced brilliant beams of light.

The Captain fell heavily into his bunk. The busy day of isolation-and-security preparations had energised him, and he had walked around the cabin and out onto the deck without hesitation or support. The men had seemed to pick up the pace in response to his energy. He had even devised a way to use Gubby – a challenge, he thought, for any Commander. He felt decisive and in control, with his instincts at full alert. But rain began falling in the late afternoon, bringing an early sense of dusk, and the Captain's energy evaporated.

He breathed heavily as he lay on his back. His limbs felt like burdensome lead weights. He rolled onto his side to slip his arms out of his coat, letting it fall to the floor. He knew that he needed to remove his shoes. If he did not remove them, they would drag filth into his bed – but his legs felt impossibly distant. A muscle in his chest had knotted painfully, and the centre of the pain throbbed alarmingly near his heart. Unless it *was* his heart...

No, he thought, he would not permit this. In two months he would walk ashore in Southampton, terminate his career with the Navy, and retire to take good care of himself. He would get the exercise he needed, eat nourishing food, allow himself the pleasures of reading and study. He would not be cashiered out, discarded into a hospital like a defective mechanical part. His body might fight him, but his will would conquer.

As he drifted into unconsciousness, something from the day nibbled at the back of his mind. Something he had committed to do, some action he had intended... The throbbing near his heart grew more painful, and he rolled onto his side to try to relieve it. He squeezed back tears of frustration that threatened to well up in his eyes. Whatever had slipped from his memory, he decided, could wait until tomorrow.

20 September 1884

He woke with a fierce itch in his eye. He pulled himself from his bed and lit a match to his reflection in the mirror above the shaving-basin. A large white stye dangled from his left eyelid, irritating and blurring his vision.

Why, for God's sake, why? The Captain cursed his deteriorating body. Others seemed to stroll through life without handicaps. Why was he singled out to be bedevilled by illnesses and irritations? And what time was it, anyway? The idea of struggling over to the chronometer seemed exhausting. It had to be sometime in the middle watch, the bleakest hours.

His hand shook as he tried to grasp the swollen cell between his thumb and forefinger. The involuntary muscles of his eyelid jerked and twitched, and the sty slipped away. He was torn between the urge to pinch the damned thing off and a painful desire to urinate. His hand shook as he dried his fingers with a towel and tried to grasp the stye again. Forcing his eye to remain open, he pinched again. A spasm jerked through his body, and he jammed his thumbnail into his eye.

Clenching his teeth to prevent crying out, he fell back into his bed. He wadded up a corner of the sheet and held it against his throbbing eye. Tears of frustration ran down his face, and he realised that he was flooding his bed with hot urine. He had never felt so hopelessly alone.

≈≈≈≈≈

Eoghan opened the cottage door slowly, hoping the hinges would not creak. Eithne was asleep, and he could see the blanket on her bed rising and falling with her breath. He was halfway into his sleeping-room when she cried out, making a soft yelp like a rabbit in a snare. She sat up in bed, her small features surrounded by a halo of white hair.

"Sorry, Aunt Eithne. I didn't mean to wake you..."

She was breathing rapidly "It wasn't you that woke me, Eoghan," she said. "I was dreaming about Ruairí."

"About Ruairí? What's he doing?"

Eithne shook her head. "It's not that kind of dream. But I know..." Her voice trailed off.

"What do you know, Aunt Eithne? I want to know, too."

"He's drifting. He's in some kind of trouble, and he's drifting."

"You mean he's swimming?" Eoghan asked, remembering the day when Ruairí fell out of the row-boat.

"No, I don't think so. I can't tell you exactly, Eoghan..." She looked at the bulk of her nephew silhouetted in the doorway. "I'll think about it and try to sort it out in the morning."

"I got something to tell you, Aunt Eithne. I can tell you now if you're awake."

"Tell me now, Eoghan." She lifted the glass chimney from the oil lamp and lit the wick with a match.

"The reason I come home late tonight is because Mister Corish left the lighthouse today, and Missus Quinn is taking his shifts. Till the new man comes on Saturday."

"Missus Quinn is tending the light?"

"Yes, Mister Corish asked her. She knows how to do everything, Aunt Eithne. Even the signals to the shore. The only thing she can't do is lift the oil barrels."

"So they want you to do that, to help her with the barrels..."

"Yes, all this week. They want me to sleep over there, too. Until this new man arrives."

Eithne smiled. "I wonder if women would run a lighthouse different from men..."

"No, she's not running it. Mister Quinn and Mister Varney..."

"I don't mean now," said Eithne. "I mean someday."

"Then they'd need me all the time. For the barrels."

Eithne shook her head and smiled. "I wish your Da was here to see you, Eoghan. He would have liked you."

"I wish Ruairí was here."

"Is that what you wanted to tell me? That you're helping Missus Quinn?"

"No, it's what Mister Geraghty said. Or what Pádraig *said* he said."

"And what was that?"

"Mister Geraghty heard that they're going to come to Toraigh to collect the rents. With a Navy boat."

His aunt made the whimpering sound again, like a struggling rabbit. "Are you all right, Aunt Eithne?"

"Now I know what my dream means. I saw a house on fire..."

Eoghan sat in silence, frightened by the worry that he felt radiating from her. "Do we have to pay rent, Aunt Eithne?"

"They say everyone has to pay," she said. "They say we're supposed to send money to a man in England. But no one on Toraigh ever does."

"What happens if we can't pay? We don't have any money, do we?"

"People who can't pay get put out of their houses."

Eoghan looked around at the walls of the cottage. "They'd put us out of here?"

"They could."

"They pay me for what I do at the lighthouse..."

"It's not enough."

Eoghan stared into the flickering flame of the oil lamp. "I won't let them do it, Aunt Eithne. I'll get Pádraig, and the others, and we won't let them..."

"They have guns, Eoghan."

"Sean Rodgers has a shotgun..."

"Eoghan, I want you to do something." Eithne looked directly into his eyes. "The first thing tomorrow morning, I want you to tell Mister Geraghty that I need to see him. Will you do that?"

"Sure I will, Aunt Eithne..."

"And if Pádraig told you, he's probably told everyone on the island by now. I want you to tell me everything you hear. Tell me what they talk about at the lighthouse. And if the lads say anything about taking up arms, you come and tell me right away. Will you?"

"Yes, Aunt Eithne."

Eithne rose from her bed and looked out the window. Clouds rolled across the night sky, and the lighthouse beam was dimmed by rain. "I hoped I wouldn't live to see this, Eoghan."

"Don't say that, Aunt Eithne."

"I hope that what Pádraig told you is wrong, or that he is only being a brave storyteller. But send Mister Geraghty here tomorrow."

"I will."

"You'd best get some sleep, Eoghan. You'll need to be up early."

Eoghan fell into bed, his mind spinning. If they came to collect the rent, he and the others would fight... The only place to dock was the East Port Pier, at the foot of a steep cliff. If a boatload of soldiers tried to land, they would shower them with rocks... But what if they made a landing in the middle of the island, on the shallow beach? They'd wait until the landing-party had left the boat, and then they'd knock holes in it, and scuttle it... They'd come at them from all directions...

"Eoghan?"

"What, Aunt Eithne?"

"We can't fight them. There aren't enough of us."

"Was I talking out loud, Aunt Eithne?"

Eithne hesitated before speaking. "A bit, Eoghan. Enough that I could imagine what you're thinking."

Eoghan lay back in his bed, feeling exposed and vulnerable. He was almost certain that he hadn't said a word. Through the doorway of his room he could see Eithne staring out the window, her hair glowing in the lamplight.

≈≈≈≈≈

Ruairí smelled the ammonia-like stench before he knocked on the Captain's door. He found the Captain sitting at his desk with his back turned, hunched lower than usual in his chair. Ruairí placed the breakfast-tray on the desk and waited. Without turning, the Captain said, "Mullan?"

"Yes, Sir?"

"Take the laundry-basket to Phillips and tell him that I want it given priority. And try to avoid the other men on your way there."

"Are you not well, Sir?"

The Captain whirled around in his chair, and Ruairí was surprised to see that his left eye was covered with a white gauze bandage. It was a clumsy dressing, one that he must have fashioned for himself. "I am fully capable, thank you, Mullan. Do not ask me again."

"Sorry, Sir, I did not mean..."

"There is something that I want you to do." The Captain shoved a piece of paper at Ruairí. "Can you read this?"

The paper was covered with columns of handwritten numbers in a grid. Most of the numbers were written in a copper-coloured ink. Ruairí said, "It appears to be a page from a record-book, Sir, but I can't say that I understand it."

"It is not necessary for you to understand it. You see that this is not a requisition, don't you?"

"It doesn't say what it is, Sir."

The Captain pulled back the paper and exhaled loudly. "Mullan, I do not know you well, but I feel that I can rely on you. And now I must. I have injured one eye, and my other eye is not strong enough for reading."

"Do you not have spectacles, Sir?"

"No. I can read a page or two, but then the strain becomes – difficult. Consequently, I must leave it to you to locate the propeller requisition on your own. Do you understand what I am saying, Mullan?"

"I think so, Sir..."

"I must sleep to let this injury repair itself. You are to work by yourself at this desk, lifting the files, reviewing them, and replacing them. Until you find my requisition for the propeller. Is that clear?"

"Yes, Sir. But is there not a special file for the requisitions?"

The Captain shook his head and managed a half-smile. "There is, Mullan. And I have looked at every document in it. The one that I need is not there. But your question confirms that you are the right man for this job."

Flattered, Ruairí said, "Thank you, Sir..."

"Tell Hatton to have your meals sent up here. I want you to spend all of your time here until you find it."

Ruairí hesitated. If any of the men saw him sitting at the Captain's desk...

"What are you thinking?"

"Nothing, Sir."

The Captain drummed his fingers on the desk. "Mullan," he said, "I know that you are not happy here. I do not expect that you will enjoy examining these files. But I will tell you this – if you find my requisition, I will see to it that your posting on the *Wasp* will be as short as possible. Even if I must be without a Commander's Servant for a time."

Ruairí looked at the Captain and wondered how they would appear to an outsider – two one-eyed men, a naval officer with a gauze bandage and an island boy with an eye-patch, staring at each other across a desk stacked with papers. "Sir," he said, "I'd be pleased if I could return..."

"Good! That settles it. I will sleep now. If anyone comes with a message for me, tell them I am not available except for emergencies." The Captain stood and shuffled to his sleeping-quarters, closing the door.

Ruairí sat looking at the desk and the empty chair. Was he really to look at every scrap of paper in the files? He heard a rattling sound at one of the portholes. Pulling aside the cloth curtain with his fingers, he saw rain lashing across the glass, and sailors in wet-weather gear patrolling the deck in the gloom.

There were worse jobs, he realised, than sitting in a padded chair and sorting through stacks of paper. At least until the weather broke.

≈≈≈≈≈

"That isn't what I said, Eithne."

"Then what did you say, Mister Geraghty?"

The schoolmaster ran his fingers through his hair in frustration. "We were talking in the pub. We were talking about how someone tried to shoot John Adair, and what a foul specimen of a landlord he is. Then we were talking about evictions. And then I said that I've heard that some of the Englishmen who own the Irish islands – who claim that they own the Irish islands – have enlisted the Royal Navy to help collect taxes."

"And to help with evictions?"

"Yes. Evictions."

"And are they coming to Toraigh, Mister Geraghty?"

The schoolmaster shook his head. "I did not say that."

"Pádraig told Eoghan that you did."

"Pádraig wasn't even there."

"I'm not accusing you, Mister Geraghty." Eithne said. "And what you said or didn't say makes little difference. But the whole island must think by now that they're coming for us."

The schoolmaster rubbed the bridge of his nose. "I was a damned fool for even discussing the subject."

"Perhaps not, Mister Geraghty. What do you know with certainty?"

"I was told that landlords were enlisting the help of the Navy some time ago. And I heard recently that they were involved in evictions on Clare Island."

"And where did you hear this?"

"I was speaking with Constable Gormley. In Magheroarty."

"He confides in you, does he?"

The schoolmaster hesitated. "Ah, the man talks too much. And I regret that I listened."

"But you will let us know, won't you?"

"Let you know what?"

"If you hear that they are coming – the police, or the Navy, or any of them – you'll tell us, won't you?"

"Absolutely, Eithne. I swear that I will."

They sat in silence for a long moment. The schoolmaster looked at Eithne, who was fingering her braided necklace and staring into space. She seemed to be lost in her own thoughts. "Eithne?"

"Yes?"

"What would you do if you heard they were coming?"

"I don't know, Mister Geraghty. I truly don't. Perhaps I would pack my belongings."

The schoolmaster looked around at the smoke-stained stone walls of the cottage. To think of Eithne being evicted was to imagine a tree being uprooted. "I can't envision you living anywhere else, Eithne."

"Neither can I, Mister Geraghty. Neither can I."

≈≈≈≈≈

Ruairí leaned back in the chair, his eye blurred with watery exhaustion. He stood up and walked around the small cabin, stepping quietly to avoid waking the Captain. His leg muscles were stiff from sitting. His neck was sore, and he had to piss.

How could anyone sit at a desk all day? It was torture. He had used a draughtsman's board in the map-school, but he'd sat on a tall stool, half-standing, and he'd made regular trips to the cupboards for paper and ink. He'd felt like he was accomplishing something. But this – reading at a desk, examining a mountain of documents – this felt like idleness in fancy dress.

He had started with the cabinet marked REQUISITIONS, suspecting that the impatient Captain might have missed something. He was impressed, and then bored, by the endless lists of supplies that the fifty-six men on the *Wasp* consumed. *Food. Water. Coal. Munitions. Clothing. Tools. Soap. Spare parts. Paper. Medicine.* He had lifted the folders out of the drawers and removed the drawers from the cabinet. He'd found a few yellowed pages that had fallen under the bottom drawer, but none was a requisition for a propeller.

It had taken the guts of the morning to review the Requisition files. He had heard soft snores from the Captain's quarters, and occasional footsteps, but the door remained closed. He had moved on to other cabinets and files, leafing through the folders with dwindling interest. Shortly before noon he found himself staring at a page that, after he focused his attention, he discovered that he was holding upside-down.

He needed to get away from the confines of the cabin. He stood and stretched, spread a napkin over the scraps on the Captain's breakfast-tray, and opened the door. Sheets of drizzling rain swept across the deck. He hurried to the hatch and climbed down the steep stairs with the tray.

Hatton and three of the men were preparing the midday meal. The cook looked up and half-smiled. "You're a bit damp there, Mister Mullan."

"Not as wet as the fellows out on guard duty."

A stocky sailor held up a potato and a knife. "We've got a lorry-load of these to peel. If you're lookin' for summat to do, of course."

Ruairí cringed at the friendly gesture. "I'd rather do that than what I'm doing," he said. "but the Captain's got me on a mission."

The sailor shrugged. "Oh, well, then."

He put down the tray and hurried back to the cabin. He would make a point of working with the men as soon as he could, he told himself. He closed the slats on the cabin windows. He'd be mortified if the sailors saw him mucking with papers at the Captain's desk.

Two stacks of file-folders sat on the desk. Ruairí couldn't remember whether he'd already read them, or if they were waiting to be read. The futility of his assignment began to gnaw at him. Somewhere in those reams of records, a requisition for a propeller had been misfiled. Without a new propeller, the *Wasp* could only creep around like a coal-barge. And the Admiralty had sent out the wrong replacement, unless...

Unless the Captain had buggered up the request. And the Captain seemed distracted enough to write down a wrong number, or to stuff a piece of paper in the wrong file. And he didn't want anyone else to find out that he'd made a mistake, and so he had assigned...

Someone knocked on the door, and Ruairí jumped up from the desk. The stocky sailor who had invited him to join in the potato-peeling was standing in the rain. He looked over Ruairí's shoulder. "Where's the Captain."

"He's in his bunk. His eye was injured last night."

"Mmm. Does he want his food brought up here?"

"I'll come and get it when he rouses. What's your name?"

"McLaren. You're Mullan, aren't you?"

"That's right. I'll be with you on kitchen duty one of these days."

"Don't hurry yourself. It's bloody tedious."

Ruairí leaned close and whispered, "So's this."

McLaren grinned. "Right, mate."

Ruairí took a deep breath and returned to the desk. Peeling potatoes, plodding through stacks of paper – the work didn't matter if he could find a touch of comradeship now and then. And he didn't need to read every page – the requisitions all looked alike, and they looked different from everything else. If the damned request for the propeller was there, he'd find it. And if he did, and if the Captain would keep his promise...

≈≈≈≈≈

The men on guard duty saw the preliminary flashes from the Westport House tower. They alerted Armstrong, who climbed to the bridge in wet-weather gear. He lit the carbide lamp and adjusted the valves until a bright steady flame burned with a throaty roar. Flicking the brass shutters of the lamp, he sent the counter-signal READY TO RECEIVE.

The tower light flashed a series of short and long bursts. Armstrong was amused and impressed by Gubby's skill with Morse code. For a man – Armstrong had to remind himself not to think *boy* – a man who could barely find his way from one spoken word to the next, the young Lieutenant was quick and confident in Morse. He made a mental note to compliment Gubby on his skill.

The text of the message was blunt. RECEIVED SEALED ORDERS.

Armstrong flashed the response RETURN TO SHIP and climbed down to the main deck. He knocked at the door of the Captain's cabin. Instead of the usual challenge, he heard a scuffling of feet, and Ruairí Mullan opened the door. Armstrong said, "I need to speak to the Captain."

"The Captain says he's only to be disturbed in case of emergency."

"Then tell him it's a fecking emergency!"

He heard a cough from the direction of the Captain's quarters. A voice said, "What is it, Armstrong?"

"Sealed orders, Sir." said Armstrong.

"Have they arrived?"

"Gubby's bringing them from the mainland. He should be here in thirty minutes."

"Very good. I'll meet with you and Evans when they're here."

≈≈≈≈≈

As he watched the mail-boat approach the Port Doon pier, Quinn wished that he'd listened to his wife's advice. *Why don't you take the shift?* she'd said. *I'll go to meet Mister Knox.* But his pride had swelled like a stubborn lump in his throat. *No, Mary, I'll meet him.* He didn't want to look weak in her eyes, and he suspected that Knox might take it as an insult if he sent his wife on the errand of greeting. He had sat for an hour in the pony-and-trap on the pier with Liam McClafferty, wishing that the mail-boat would sink and take Knox down with it.

Quinn could see a gaunt black-clad figure bent over the stern of the boat. While the man unfolded himself and wiped his face, spitting brownish shreds into the water, the boatman dropped the fenders over the side and tossed a line onto the dock. Quinn caught the line, looped it around the bollard, and pulled to bring the boat snug against the landing.

Knox staggered out of the boat and up the stone stairs. He glared at Quinn with red-rimmed eyes before he looked away. "Those are mine," he said, waving toward two steamer trunks on the boat. He pulled a handkerchief from his pocket and wiped his mouth, turning away to spit again into the water.

Bristling with resentment, Quinn made his way down the stone steps and took the first steamer trunk from Ben Rodgers. He wrestled the boxy trunk up the steps and slid it onto the dock. McClafferty lifted it onto the pony-cart, and Quinn noted with satisfaction that he had trouble lifting it, too.

He let McClafferty and Rodgers struggle with the second trunk as he turned to Knox. "We have your quarters ready," he said, suppressing the impulse to say *Sir*. He heard himself adding, "The compound is on the other end of the island."

"I know," said Knox.

"Mister Quinn!" Ben Rodgers was calling from the deck of the boat. "There's a box here for you! I mean for Missus Quinn!"

He stepped to the edge of the dock and lifted the small wooden crate from Rodgers's hands. The word LEMONS was scrawled on the top, and he could see the the yellow fruits between the slats. Knox peered at the crate. Quinn heard himself saying, "They're for my wife," and immediately regretted offering an explanation that no one had asked for. Knox looked away and climbed onto the seat of the pony-cart.

Quinn hoisted himself onto the rear of the cart and sat facing backward with his legs dangling. McClafferty shook the reins to start the pony. As they rode along the bumpy road in silence, Quinn wondered how a man like Knox who suffered from such wretched seasickness could have risen in the ranks of the Keepers. He remembered that when they had been stationed together on the Tuskar rock-light, Knox had always landed on the island with the same grey-green pallor, choking back the last spasms. He would take to his bed for two days before he would rise, cold and unavoidable as a north wind, to bully the Assistant Keepers with his authority. Quinn despised him and made no effort to conceal it, but Knox did not appear to notice. Quinn wondered if the man thrived on the contempt of others.

As an experiment, Quinn had once arranged to accompany Knox on the boat from the Tuskar lighthouse to the mainland. Knox had looked miserable but had not grown ill, even though they had both eaten a substantial lunch of beef stew before the trip. It was on the return trip, after a three-week duty-break ashore, that Knox suffered his bilious spasms. Quinn was certain that the man had spent his leave-time drinking heavily.

McClafferty's cart bumped to a stop in front of the lighthouse compound gates, and Knox climbed out. Looking at a spot over Quinn's head, he said, "Where are my quarters?"

"The detached house. On the left."

Knox turned and pushed open the gate. Quinn and McClafferty looked at each other, and Quinn shrugged his shoulders. Together they lifted the trunks from the wagon and carried them to the front door of the Principal Keeper's dwelling. Knox let himself in and shut the door behind him.

≈≈≈≈≈

The rain had slowed to a drizzle by the time the steam-powered pilot boat pulled alongside the *Wasp*. Ruairí watched from the deck as two of the sailors on the boat grasped the dangling rope ladder. Gubby climbed the jacob's-ladder hanging from the side of the ship, unwisely grasping the horizontal ropes. *If I was on that ladder with him,* Ruairí thought, *I'd step on his fat fingers.*

Gubby hoisted himself over the metal skirting and stood unsteadily on the deck, gasping for breath. Ruairí said, "The Captain wants to see you right away."

The boyish Lieutenant said, "Right," and fumbled in his coat. He pulled out an envelope, took a deep breath, and walked to the Captain's door. Without asking, Ruairí followed him.

The Captain's voice rang out before they reached the door. "Is that you, Gubby?"

"It is, Sir."

"Come in."

Ruairí started to follow Gubby into the Captain's quarters, but the Captain snapped, "Mullan!"

"Yes, Sir?"

"Tell the pilot-boat to wait. Then return to your quarters. I'll send for you when I need you."

"Yes, Sir." Ruairí caught a brief glimpse of the Captain at his desk, with Evans and Armstrong sitting in the low chairs across from him. They all stared at him until he closed the door. The formal ranks of the *Wasp's* officers had snapped back into place like iron gates.

≈≈≈≈≈

"Bloody hell!" shouted the Captain. "Who do they think we are?"

Evans and Armstrong looked at each other without saying a word. Gubby looked at the floor. The crumpled telegram lay on the desk.

REPLACEMENT PROPELLER AT MOVILLE DRYDOCK PROCEED IMMEDIATELY ESCORT MOVILLE SHERIFF PROPERTY RECOVERY AND FORCIBLE EVACUATION INISHTRAHULL MONDAY 22 SEPT DARLINGTON

"Bloody Armchair Admirals! Ship the bloody propeller to Moville, and then order us to race there and perform an eviction before we can get our hands on it!"

Armstrong ventured, "We could request extra time, Sir..."

"That's just exactly what they want us to do! To embarrass ourselves by asking for extra time!"

"We may not have a choice, Sir," said Evans. "I'll check the distances, but I'll warrant that at SLOW speed we'll not be able to reach Moville by Monday."

"Even if we had the coal," added Armstrong. "Which we may not."

"We could sail."

Evans, Armstrong, and the Captain all turned to look at Gubby. He looked surprised, as though the words that were hanging in the air had come from someone else's mouth. The Captain said, "What did you say, Gubby?"

"We could sail, Sir. There's a strong southwesterly wind..."

The three senior officers looked at each other. Armstrong said, "We haven't deployed the sails for months..."

"Is there anything wrong with the sails?" asked the Captain.

"No, Sir, I imagine that they're in good enough repair. It's the men I'm thinking of. They're likely to be rusty on the procedures..."

"But you can supervise them, can't you, Armstrong? How much coal do we have?"

"We've roughly a day's worth..."

"That will be enough to steam us out past Achill Head and into open water. Then the southwesterlies will carry us to the north coast. We'll pick up a strong westerly at Tory Island, and that will take us to the mouth of Lough Foyle. Once the sails are set, we'll scarcely need to adjust them. Gubby..."

"Yes, Sir."

"Are you quite certain that the southwesterlies will sustain through tomorrow?"

"I think so, Sir. They've been steady..."

"Do you agree, Evans?"

"Well, Sir, it's anyone's conjecture..."

"But you don't disagree, do you?"

"No, Sir."

"Good. Gubby, return to the mainland and go straight to the Castlebar barracks. Send this message." The Captain groped in a drawer for a sheet of paper and a pen, craning his neck to compensate for the bandage on his left eye. He scribbled furiously on the paper and handed it to Gubby. "Can you read this?"

"Yes, Sir. WILL RENDEZVOUS MONDAY 22 SEPT 0900 MOVILLE TO ASSIST SHERIFF REQUIRE 3 DAYS BERTH FOR REPAIRS AND PROVISIONING."

"That's right. Then come directly back to the ship. We wouldn't want to leave without you, would we?"

"No, Sir. I mean *Aye aye, Sir.*"

"Carry on, Gubby. Well done."

Gubby jumped out of his chair and nearly ran from the cabin, slamming the door behind him. The Captain looked at his Lieutenants. "Well, gentlemen?"

"May I speak my mind, Sir?"

"You always do, Evans."

"You're putting a great deal of faith in the wind, Sir. We've always had enough steam power to push against a typhoon if we needed to. Sailing is another matter entirely."

"I'm aware of that, Evans. But I believe that Gubby is right in this case. The southwesterlies have been steady since August."

"Then we'd best set sail this evening, Sir. Perhaps even now. It will do no harm if we reach Moville a day early."

The Captain twisted his mouth into a smile. "And leave young Gubby behind? I wouldn't dream of it. You and Armstrong, select a rigging crew and drill them this afternoon. And when Gubby returns, move us out to anchor off Achill Head. We'll hoist the sail at dawn. Any questions?"

The subordinate officers sat in silence for a long moment that verged on rudeness before Evans said, "No, Sir."

"There's one other thing. Don't tell the men about the eviction. Not until we get to Moville."

"May I ask why, Sir?"

"It's a morale issue. Just tell them that we're going to be fitted with the new propeller. That will be all for now, gentlemen."

≈≈≈≈≈

Evans and Armstrong walked to the stern rail and looked out at the pilot-boat chugging back toward Westport Quay. Gubby was barely visible, his coat a blue smudge of colour on the distant deck. Evans toyed with a box of matches and put them back into his pocket.

Armstrong broke the silence. "This is bloody ridiculous, you know."

"Hmm. He'd do anything to avoid saying *No* to Southampton."

"Can we get there in twenty-four hours?"

"It's possible. We will, or we won't. If someone has to pay the Sheriff or the deputies for an extra day, they'll be shitting their pants. But we'll have tried."

"And then the Captain can start a row about how we'd have been on time if the Admiralty had sent us the right propeller..."

The light in the Clare Island lighthouse began to shine in the dusk. Armstrong said, "What do you think about the eviction?"

"I'm not leading any damned eviction detail. Gubby can lead it."

"Do you think the Old Man will let him?"

"Gubby didn't have any trouble with the Clare eviction. He made a balls of steering the ship."

Evans leaned against the skirting and rubbed his knuckles up and down his spine. Armstrong said, "Is your back bothering you?"

"Is it noticeable?"

"It is."

Evans shook his head. "I slipped on the bloody bridge-ladder yesterday. I'm afraid I twisted something."

"You might want to take some rest, you know," said Armstrong. "I'd be hard-pressed to run this ship by myself."

"I'll manage."

The two career-men looked at each other. Evans said, "I suppose we'd best get started."

"Right," said Armstrong. "Sailing to Moville to collect our propeller."

≈≈≈≈≈

"Mullan!"

"Yes, Sir?"

The Captain appeared to be shrinking inside his uniform. Ruairí could not see an exact change, but the Captain appeared to be less forceful, more exhausted.

"What progress have you made in the files?"

"I've been through the *REQUISITIONS* cabinet from top to bottom, Sir. I didn't find anything there."

"Then what?"

Ruairí gestured around the room. "Then I went on from one cabinet to the next."

"And where are you now?"

"At *KL*, Sir."

The Captain shook his head. His eye-bandage looked grubby, as though he had been fingering it. "There are two things I want you to do, Mullan. I have been informed that our propeller has been shipped to Moville, and I have given orders that we set sail to collect it there."

"That's good news, Sir..."

"I want you to dine with the men and spend the evening with them. I want to know how they respond to the news that we are proceeding by sail."

Ruairí thought for a moment. "I don't exactly understand, Sir. What would they..."

"Most of them have never served under sail. We may be rousing them from their hammocks to climb the masts in the middle of the night. And if the wind shifts..." The Captain sighed. "It can be an exhausting discipline. I want you to take the pulse of the crew."

"Very well, Sir."

"And then tomorrow I want you to redouble your efforts to find my requisition for the propeller."

"But Sir, if the propeller is in Moville..."

The Captain sat bolt upright in his chair. "We have no bloody idea what we will find in Moville! They may have sent us a wheel for a donkey-wagon! I want you to keep searching until you find it!"

Astonished by the Captain's outburst, Ruairí heard himself saying, "Aye aye, Sir."

"Now go. Keep your ears open, and report back here at first light."

Ruairí found himself on the open deck, closing the cabin door behind him. The smell of food wafted up from below decks and he felt deeply hungry, as though he hadn't eaten in days. As he hurried down to the galley, he was surprised at how the Captain's fury had rattled him. But regardless of what had triggered the Captain's outburst, Ruairí felt sure that he was not being told the whole truth.

≈≈≈≈≈

"So you're joinin' us for tea and crumpets, are you?"

The stocky sailor was sitting at a table with two other men. He nodded at an open seat. Ruairí carried his food tray to the table and sat down. The other men didn't look up from their soup and bread. The sailor said, "So what's the Captain dining on tonight?"

"I don't know," said Ruairí. He took a spoonful of his own soup. "I bet it's not this."

"No, it ain't. I took his tray up a while ago. He don't give you his scraps, then?"

"I been eating the same as you." He looked the sailor in the eye. "And that's a fact."

"So how come you don't eat down here with us?"

Ruairí took a deep breath. "They sent me here three days ago, and they been keeping me busy ever since. They say when my replacement shows up, they'll send me back to school. Right now I'm just a pimple on the arse of this boat." One of the sailors chuckled, but he didn't look up. "So no offence meant."

The stocky sailor grinned. "All right, mate. None taken. What's your name?"

"Ruairí Mullan. What's yours again?"

"McLaren. What they got you doing up there?"

"Paperwork."

One of the other sailors looked up from the table. "You get to read the orders, then?"

"No. They got me reading the old files."

"But you know what the orders are?"

Ruairí thought for a second before answering. "They tell me we're going to Moville."

The sailor nodded and turned back to his food. Ruairí guessed that he already knew, and he didn't feel like answering questions like a schoolboy. Turning to McLaren, he said, "What do you do?"

"Everything. Nothing. That's what Able-Bodied Seamen do."

"Whatever they need?"

"Summat like that. You seen me peeling spuds the other day. Tomorrow we'll be climbing around in the rigging. What'll you be at tomorrow?"

Remembering the Captain's outburst, Ruairí said, "More paperwork."

"I suppose it wouldn't do to have you up there on the masts. I mean with one eye and all."

"No, that's right. I'm a piss-poor judge of distance."

An awkward silence settled over the table until Ruairí asked, "So why did you join the Navy?"

McLaren mopped his soup-bowl with a piece of bread. "I seen what happened to my father. I wasn't going to let it happen to me."

"What was that?"

"He worked in a foundry. Ever been in a foundry?"

"We don't have those where I come from."

"He worked in a foundry where they made pumps. You know those long-handled water pumps they have in the town squares?"

"I think I know what you mean."

"He made those."

Ruairí tried to imagine how that could be done. "Did he use a hammer, or..."

"No, he was an iron-moulder."

"What do they do?"

"They take foundry-sand, they soak it in oil, and they put it in a box. Then they press a wood shape into it, and it leaves a cavity. My Pa would take a bucket of hot iron, pick it up with tongs, and pour the iron into it."

"Melted iron?"

"That's right. You have to pour those handles in one go. He was good at it."

"Did he ever get burned?"

McLaren shook his head. "You should have seen him. He had scars all over his arms. And a big one on the side of his face, where it splashed once."

"Is that why you joined the Navy? So you didn't have to work with the iron?"

"No, the Navy's got plenty of ways to mangle you. But I seen what the air did to him."

"The air?"

"Aye, the foundry air. That place was like hell with the lid off. You have the furnaces, and the coal-smoke that comes out of them. Then there's the dust from the sand, and the fumes from the oil. My Pa got all that shite in his lungs every time he drew a breath. He came down with the black lung, like the miners get. It killed him."

One of the other sailors said, "The engine-room ain't much different."

"No," said McLaren, "it ain't."

Ruairí looked around the galley. The sailors were like the Toraigh farmers and fishermen – rough, direct men who didn't have many choices in life. He could imagine choosing to enlist in the Navy and to make a life on the ships. It would be better than working in a foundry. But if orders came down to open the arms-cache and shoulder a rifle...

He finished his meal while McLaren told stories about his boyhood in Leeds. He knew he could make friends with the men over time, working with them as O'Donnell had. He wondered what the Captain would ask him in the morning. No matter what questions he might be asked, he would feel better about lying to the Captain than spying on the crew.

≈≈≈≈≈

Armstrong gave the order to stoke the engine at 1900 hours. A long spiral augur fed the coal from the bunker to the engine-room, and the pressure-gauge on the boiler began to rise slowly. It took an hour to build enough steam-pressure to drive the ship.

≈≈≈≈≈

The Captain knew the coastline by heart. North of Donegal Bay lay the Bloody Foreland, where the Armada had wrecked. That had been three hundred years before, when maps were crude sketches and distances were guesswork at best. And the Spanish fleet had been wrecked by a massive, unexpected storm. The Spaniards might have been the first to reach the New World, he mused, but their ambitions had outrun their luck when they tried to mount an assault on England.

He took a map from his desk and began calculating the bearings, first north and then north-east. The coastline was circled with lighthouses, unmistakable beacons that were easy to see and steer by. He set a course to skirt the land, first north to Eagle Island, then across the mouth of Donegal Bay toward the Rathlin O'Birne Island lighthouse. North-east from there, well clear of Tory Island, and then due east toward Malin Head and Moville. It would be a simple passage, never out of sight of land.

≈≈≈≈≈

Evans stepped onto the deck and sent a sailor to ask Armstrong to join him. He studied the sails and rigging. Lit by the lingering sunset, the masts made the *Wasp* look like a square-rigger from the glory-days of Cook and Vancouver. Ruefully, Evans realised that he had become a man of instruments and numbers, and that he had not even looked at the graceful spars and furled sails for weeks. He shook his head and reminded himself to concentrate on the mission at hand.

Armstrong emerged from a hatch, and the two officers walked together to the stern. A sailor who had been standing guard duty at the rail moved away as he saw them approaching. They waited until he was out of earshot before they spoke.

"How much coal do we have?" asked Evans.

"Enough," said Armstrong. "But just enough. After we anchor off Achill, we'll have – oh, about twenty hours of steam."

"And we'll need it to manoeuvre in Lough Foyle, land in Moville, and then fetch the bloody deputies out to bloody Inishtrahull." Evans was surprised to hear the anger in his own voice.

"And bring them back."

"Yes. And bring them back. So there's no choice but to sail."

The two men looked at the sea-birds wheeling over a fishing-boat off Clare Island. Evans said, "I don't trust the wind."

Armstrong rubbed his hands together. "The men seemed enthusiastic when we ran the drills this afternoon. And the Captain is likely right – once we get the sails set, we'll not need to change them until we pass Malin Head."

"And so we sail. There's no real choice."

"Not if we're to get there by Monday." Armstrong looked at his fellow-officer. "Is that what you wanted to hear, Evans?"

The Navigator looked out across the water. "To tell you the truth, Armstrong, I'm not entirely sure what I want. I don't like this mission, and – and I suppose that I want to say so."

"I don't care for it, either. How many more years for you?"

"Five will do it for me. What about yourself?"

"Closer to ten. You'll be a gentleman farmer in Wales while I'll still be firing twenty-one-gun salutes."

"Oh, you'll have your own command before then."

"You will too, I expect."

"So then we can both patrol the Irish coast, and we'll reminisce about the good old days on the *Wasp*."

Armstrong punched Evans lightly on the shoulder. "Let's get some sleep. We'll need it tomorrow. And watch that back of yours."

≈≈≈≈≈

Ruairí felt the rumble of the engines under his feet. The deck resonated with the clank of the chains as the windlass pulled the anchor up from the sea-floor. Released from its mooring, the *Wasp* drifted and rolled in the swells. Ruairí heard the bright metallic ring of the telegraph as Evans sent the signal for SLOW speed. The ship pushed forward and stabilised as it cut through the water. The damaged propeller created its own vibration underfoot, a *lump-lump* throb like a wagon wheel rolling over a log-road.

The *Wasp* headed a few degrees north of the setting sun. Ruairí watched Clare Island receding, and he wondered for the hundredth time whether he should have tried to swim away while he had the chance. *No*, he told himself, *I have a plan. Now is the time to wait.*

The sunset cast a red sheen across the water. Ruairí knew that the days were growing shorter, and that the summer and the winter would soon graze the backs of their hands as they passed each other. He wondered if Aunt Eithne would light a candle, and a sob threatened to well up in his throat. Had it been only half a year since he had gone egging and lost his eye? It felt like three lifetimes.

The Captain had said that they were sailing to Moville. No matter which course they followed, they'd need to sail close to Toraigh. *How close?* Ruairí wondered if they'd pass along the south coast, and if he'd be able to see Aunt Eithne's cottage. And if they were that close...

He watched the bright edge of the sun slipping into the water, and his eye hurt. Too many documents, too much reading – he longed to do something active, to scramble in the rigging with McLaren and the crew. But he could finish the files tomorrow, and weren't they going to reach Moville by Monday? He squeezed his eye shut to relieve the ache. This day, he decided, had gone on long enough. He would rig up his hammock.

≈≈≈≈≈

The Captain bent down to reach for the journal under his desk, but a rush of blood-pressure surged into his head. He sat upright and clenched his teeth. If he could reach the damned book, what would he write? *This propeller débâcle is not my fault? Mullan must find the document?* No, he decided, he would not dignify those thoughts by writing them. They sounded like the ravings of a desperate man.

As the pressure subsided, he saw himself clearly – a man beset with illnesses, straining to carry on a life that was slipping beyond his grasp. Evans and Armstrong, he knew, were running the ship. He was lucky to have them, but their patience would soon wear thin.

He would see the *Wasp* through the Inishtrahull mission. Then, while the ship was in dry-dock, he would request relief and early retirement. And he would confide his plans to his subordinate officers. That would provide the dignified exit that he so desperately wanted.

He unwound his eye-patch and threw the grubby bandage into the waste-bin. His eyelid still itched and stung, but he hoped that meant it was healing. There was nothing more for him to do. He would sleep.

21 September 1884

Gubby woke before dawn. He pulled on his uniform and hurried up to the bridge. The deck was deserted except for the sleepy men on night-watch. He was relieved to feel a steady breeze from the southwest. He could imagine how the Captain might react if the wind had died in the night.

He had barely been able to sleep. It still astonished him that the Captain had been so quick to pick up on his idea to proceed under sail – and it *was* his idea, even if he had blurted it out as a half-formed thought. If the wind held, they could reach Moville before nightfall.

And might the Captain tear up his letter of resignation? That hope had sustained him through the strange days of his assignment to Westport House. He had been offered a sumptuous officer's bedchamber with down pillows and a feather mattress, but he had insisted on sleeping in the servant's quarters with the men. He had organised six-hour watches and had assigned one to himself. He'd ordered the men to wake him immediately if signals were flashed from the *Wasp* or if messages arrived from the military telegraph at the Castlebar Barracks. The men had made jokes at his expense – *He'd sound the alarm if a goose shat in the bay* – but he had pushed himself to maintain discipline and perform his share of the work.

When the sealed orders arrived, he had chosen to bring them personally to the Captain. His return trip to transmit the reply from Castlebar had taken an agonizingly long time, and at one point he had wondered if the whole business was an elaborate prank – if he would return to find that the *Wasp* had sailed away, leaving him stranded like a child who had been tricked into holding the sack in a snipe-hunt. But now they sat at anchorage off Achill Head, ready to sail to Moville.

To *sail*, like Cook or Nelson – and it had been his idea. From below decks he could hear the crew waking, stowing their hammocks, lining up for their breakfasts. He realised that he hadn't eaten a bite since rising. He hurried to the Officers' Mess.

≈≈≈≈≈

Ruairí watched the men scramble up the rope-ladder shrouds to take their positions on the masts. Other sailors stood in teams of threes and fours on the deck, ready to heave on the ropes that dangled from pulleys on the masts and yardarms. For the first time since he'd set foot on the gangplank, the *Wasp* felt like a hive, a vibrant colony with a single purpose, where everyone knew his job. Ruairí wanted to be up in the rigging, sharing in the buzz of anticipation.

From the bridge, Evans blew a complex series of notes on the bo'suns pipe. A windlass on the foredeck began to turn, lifting the bow anchor. The ship rolled in the Atlantic swells, and the men in the rigging shouted taunts at each other as the masts swayed. Carlisle released the stern anchor. When it hit the sea-floor, the *Wasp* swung around slowly to point northeast.

"It's quite something to see – isn't it, Mullan?"

Ruairí was astonished to find Gubby standing beside him. The Lieutenant looked alert, energetic – nothing like his usual dispirited self. For a moment Ruairí wondered if Gubby had a twin brother who was conspiring to perpetrate a hoax. "It's remarkable, Sir," he said.

"I sometimes wonder if morale would be higher under sail."

Ruairí suppressed a smile at Gubby's unexpected officer-like tone. "The men do seem excited, Sir."

"So they are. Take heed, Mullan. You may be seeing one of the last of these exercises."

The bo'sun's pipe shrilled again. The men on deck pulled on their lines, lifting the canvas sails with a clacking sound. Armstrong strode up and down the deck, shouting orders – *Easy over here! Keep it even!* The sails unfolded in stiff accordion-pleats, guided by the men standing on the yardarms high above the deck.

A mainsail caught the wind and ballooned out like the belly of a pregnant mare. The men on the deck staggered back to take up the sudden slack in the lines. They lifted the sail to full height, and the wind stretched it into a graceful curve. As the smaller sails opened and arched, Ruairí felt a complex humming under his feet. Sails, masts, and ship established a balance, and the *Wasp* strained to move forward.

Weigh anchor! The windlass at the stern reeled in the chain, lifting the anchor from the sea-bed. The ship surged forward like a living creature.

Evans spun the wheel, setting the *Wasp* on a northerly course. Armstrong prowled the deck, adjusting the lines while the men on the masts pegged the rigging into place. Ruairí turned to Gubby, but the Lieutenant was gone. He wondered if the confident, well-spoken man had been there at all. He had disappeared like...

...like a cat. Ruairí realised with a small jolt that he hadn't seen the ship's cat in days. Where was Hodge?

≈≈≈≈≈

"That son of a bitch Varney!" Quinn slammed his hand on the kitchen table. "The next time I see that fecker, I'm going to wring his neck."

"You'll do no such thing, Paddy." His wife sipped her tea and looked at him as from a great distance. "And is it him that you're angry with, really?"

"I know what that sneaky little bastard is up to. *RECOMMENDATIONS for the Tory Lighthouse* my arse!" He picked up the crumpled paper that he'd thrown on the floor. "He just wants to suck up to Knox. And make me look bad."

"He's an ambitious man, for sure." Mary Quinn rubbed her eyes. She had taken the morning watch from 0400 until noon, and she felt those hours sitting like lead weights on her bones. "How is Mister Knox, anyway?"

"Still sick as a parrot. He looks like boiled shite."

"Did you talk to him today?"

"I can't be arsed. You'd have better *craic* with a dog turd."

Mary Quinn heard herself saying, "It wouldn't hurt..." but she stopped herself.

Her husband glared at her. "What wouldn't hurt, Mary?"

"Sometimes I think you're your own worst enemy, Paddy. It wouldn't hurt for you to try to show some sympathy to Knox. Or at least be civil..."

"Oh, right. Be civil to a cold-blooded fecker who's going to make my life miserable for the next three years..." Quinn stood up and stormed around the kitchen, massaging his neck where he'd pulled a muscle lifting Knox's trunk. He picked up Varney's paper from the table. "I suppose you think I should write him one of these."

His wife looked away with a sour expression on her face. "What does it say, Paddy?"

Quinn scanned the page with its neat copperplate handwriting. "*Replace the oil pump. Convert to a coal-gasification system. Install a rotating beacon.* Hell, that's my idea! I told Varney we ought to install a flashing beacon!"

His wife looked at him without saying anything. Quinn stared at her until she said, "It may be your idea, Paddy. But it's his name that's on the paper."

"Bloody hell!" Quinn felt tears of frustration welling up in his eyes. "Is that what you want me to do?"

"I don't want you to do anything, Paddy..."

"Maybe you should move in next door with Varney."

"Stop it, Paddy."

"You could take the girls with you..."

"Stop it! I mean it!" His wife stood up and glared at him. "I thought it would be nice for us to see each other for a few minutes. Now I wish I'd gone straight to bed!"

"I wish you had, too!"

"Oh, I hate you when you're like this! I'm going to sleep!" She rubbed her eyes. "And you can cook for yourself, too!"

"Don't worry. I know how."

She stormed out of the room. Quinn wadded Varney's paper in his hands, opened the lid of the cooker, and threw it onto the fire. He hated the lonely, empty feeling in the room. Trembling, he sat on a kitchen chair and cradled his head in his hands.

≈≈≈≈≈

As the sails ruffled and snapped in the wind, Evans turned the wheel to adjust for a slight eastward drift. There *was* something extraordinary, he thought, about sailing before the wind. It reminded him of riding a horse, of finding the balance between exerting command and following the creature's instincts. He would have a horse on his farm in Wales – yes, and more than one, because they were social animals and would not thrive without each other's company.

He could hear Gubby's footsteps banging across the deck, then the clank of his boots on the ladder to the bridge. Evans kept his gaze forward while the young officer caught his breath and said, "You sent for me, Sir?"

"I did, Gubby. How are you keeping this morning?"

There was a slight hesitation. "Fine, thank you, Sir."

"Has the Captain assigned you a task for today?"

"No, Sir – I'm going to check the rosters, and I – I've been studying the rigging..."

"How would you like to take the wheel?"

There was a pause before Gubby spoke. "I – I'd be grateful, Sir."

"Step up here." Evans moved to the side. Gubby stepped forward and grasped the spokes of the wheel. "It will feel different from running under steam."

"Yes, it does..."

"You'll sense the wind and the currents more. They used to call it *steering by your balls.*"

"Really?"

"The Captain has set us on a northerly bearing. Stay with that. The Old Man can smell it if you change course." Evans gestured toward the glass-topped tray where the Captain's orders were detailed on tracing-paper and overlaid on a map. "I'll relieve you after we pass the Rathlin O'Birne lighthouse, around noon."

"Yes, Sir!"

"Carlisle is on the foredeck watch, so you'll be well-informed if there's any trouble. But your best advice will be to stay the course." Evans clapped a hand on Gubby's shoulder as he stepped to the ladder. "And by the bye, Gubby – Armstrong tells me that you're a fair hand with Morse."

"Thank you, Sir..."

"That's good to know in case we need it. Over to you, Lieutenant."

Gubby trembled as Evans descended the ladder. He had never felt so happy in his life.

≈≈≈≈≈

Ruairí closed the last folder and returned it to the file-cabinet labelled *WXYZ*. He lifted the drawers from the cabinet and looked into the dusty interior. Two rusted pen nibs lay at the bottom, along with a faded ticket from a London concert.

He replaced the drawers without bothering to remove the long-lost items. He'd found no misplaced requisitions for propellers, or for anything else. Feeling the kinks of inactivity in his legs, he stretched and walked around the cabin. He checked the chronometer and was disappointed to see that it was not yet noon. He promised himself that he would not sit in the cabin all day. Carlisle or Hatton could point him toward a job that involved moving about. He might even climb up into the rigging on his own.

The Captain's desk was the last place to search. He stretched to relieve the ache in his back, sat back in the chair, and opened the top centre drawer. A half-dozen maps of the Irish coastline, a sheaf of gridded tracing paper, pens, and an inkwell – the drawer reminded him of the map-school. He picked up a pen that felt well-balanced and comfortable in his hand. *Before long,* he thought, *I'll be back doing something I enjoy.*

He opened the other drawers. One was stuffed with the Captain's personal letters. Another was packed with medicines in bottles and jars, some labelled and some blank. He was dismayed to find that a large drawer contained file-folders, but he made himself pull out the files one by one and review each piece of paper individually. One folder contained plans for an estate, with gardens and walkways.

Ruairí removed all of the drawers from the desk and looked at the dusty interior. Spiders had spun egg-sacs in the corners of the woodwork, but the sacs looked old and abandoned. He replaced the drawers in the desk, and he sat back in the Captain's chair. *That's that,* he told himself. If the Captain had kept a copy of his requisition for a propeller, it must have – what? Blown overboard? Stuck to the bottom of a meal-tray, discarded with the food-scraps? Wherever it was, it wasn't misfiled in the ship's records.

Ruairí looked down at the mahogany drawer-fronts and saw that the desk sat on stubby feet. There was a one-inch gap between the bottom of the desk and the floor. He remembered what O'Donnell had said – *He writes in this book when he thinks nobody's around. Then he slips it under his desk* – and he felt a flutter of excitement. He pushed his hand under the right-hand side of the desk and felt the edge of a leatherbound book.

He looked around the gloomy room and listened. He could feel the hum of the sails, and he could hear the steady rhythm of snores from the Captain's sleeping-quarters. He crouched on the floor, slipped his fingers into the narrow space, and pulled out the book. It was a wide, flat volume filled with ink-lined paper, printed with rows and columns for numbers. But instead of numbers, the pages were covered with handwriting that appeared to be in a foreign language. Some were unpronounceable clusters like *pftx*, and others ended in odd letters like *q* and *j*.

The dates between the paragraphs were written in English. The last entry was dated 14 Sept 1884. *Sunday,* he thought. *Seven days ago.*

He froze when he heard the Captain cough and roll over in his sleep. *I'm doing nothing wrong,* he reminded himself. *He told me to search everywhere.* He lifted the book and shook it, holding the covers apart. An envelope and a telegram fell out on the desk.

He unfolded the telegram. REPLACEMENT PROPELLER AT MOVILLE DRYDOCK PROCEED IMMEDIATELY ESCORT MOVILLE SHERIFF PROPERTY RECOVERY AND FORCIBLE EVACUATION INISHTRAHULL MONDAY 22 SEPT DARLINGTON

He read the message again.

ESCORT MOVILLE SHERIFF.

FORCIBLE EVACUATION INISHTRAHULL.

They were going to evict the people who lived on Inishtrahull.

Tara and Feargal.

The conversation with O'Donnell came flooding back to him. *The Captain don't usually say what he's going to do...*

MONDAY 22 SEPT

Tomorrow.

He turned over the envelope and read the address. It took a few seconds for him to recognise his own handwriting:

> *Mr Peter Geraghty*
> *The Schoolhouse*
> *Toraigh Island*
> *Co Donegal*

He shoved the chair back from the desk and stormed from the room. The bright sunlight on the deck nearly blinded him. He ran to the railing and looked across the water at the distant shore. *How far was it? A mile? Five miles?* Tears of frustration blurred his vision. *Why do I have to be a one-eyed freak who can't tell how far away anything is?*

He hunched down between two coils of rope. He had suspected it from the beginning – why he had been recruited, how he had been kept off-balance with half-truths. And he had drifted along, trying not to make a fuss, convincing himself that there would always be a way out. Now they *had* him – the lying bastards had him cornered. And he had let it happen.

Bastards. All of them. Lying bastards.

He wrapped his arms around his knees and drew himself into a ball while waves of helpless fury washed over him. He wanted to lash out at the *Wasp* with a hammer, smash the compass and the telegraph, batter the smug mahogany file-cabinets, set fire to the Captain's piss-smelling cabin and fan the flames into an inferno. A hot ball of misery burned in the back of his neck until his muscles ached. As he loosened his grip and began to breathe, a cold anger began to grow in the pit of his stomach. He clenched his fists. He remembered the night that the gate-keepers had harassed him, and how he had nearly gone back to fight them. They would have hurt him, yes, but he could have done some damage.

The gloves were off now. No one knew that he had seen the orders. The men thought that they were sailing to Moville for repairs, to spend a few comfortable days in dry-dock and install the new propeller. But he knew.

ESCORT MOVILLE SHERIFF. Would the *Wasp* dock at Moville to pick up the Sheriff? If they docked, he was sure he could slip ashore. But what if the Sheriff sailed out on a pilot-boat to meet the ship in deep water?

One thing was certain – he could not wait until the *Wasp* reached Inishtrahull. On that tiny island there was absolutely nowhere to hide.

His thoughts were interrupted by shouts from the bridge, and the sound of someone banging on the Captain's door.

≈≈≈≈≈

"Lieutenant Gubby!" The hollow sound of Carlisle's voice came out of the voice-tube.

"What is it, Carlisle?"

"We're approaching the Rathlin O'Birne Island, Sir."

Ahead of the *Wasp*, a small island sat in the water off the coastline, less than half a mile from the shore. "I can see it, Carlisle."

There was a short pause before Carlisle's voice came back through the tube. "Don't you want to adjust course, Sir?"

Gubby checked the compass. "The Captain has charted a bearing, and we're on it."

There was another pause. "We're going to run too close to the island, Sir."

"I'm sure the Captain took that into account when he wrote the orders."

He heard the Petty Officer mutter, "Bloody hell..." The forecastle shelter door opened and Carlisle stepped out onto the deck. He hurried to the door of the Captain's quarters and knocked loudly.

Gubby shouted, "What are you doing, Carlisle?" but the Petty Officer ignored him. He looked ahead at the approaching island. Rathlin O'Birne sat high above sea level, as though a giant had placed a thick flat rock in the sea. There was open water dead ahead, but they would pass within a hundred yards of the steep cliffs of the island. He checked the compass. *The Old Man can smell it if you change course...*

Carlisle continued pounding on the Captain's door. The door opened, and Gubby could see Carlisle talking excitedly. From the doorway, the Captain looked up at the bridge. Fighting tremors of panic, Gubby checked the compass again and looked over the prow of the *Wasp*.

"Give us the wheel, Gubby!"

Evans had appeared from nowhere. Gubby stepped back, and the Navigator spun the wheel to the left. The *Wasp* heeled away from the island, and its prow pointed toward open water. Gubby looked down at the deck and saw the Captain gesturing for him to come down.

As he descended the ladder, he saw Evans turn the wheel to re-set the ship on its northeasterly course. His legs felt weak as he crossed the deck to the door of the Captain's cabin. The Captain looked fierce and angry. "Gubby!"

"Yes, Sir."

"What course were you keeping?"

"North-east, Sir." A trickle of sweat ran down his spine.

To his astonishment, the Captain said, "You're absolutely right, Gubby." He turned to Carlisle, who was looking down at his feet. "Now tell me your objection again, Carlisle."

"Sir, our heading was too close to the island..."

The three men looked across the starboard rail. The *Wasp* was skirting the steep cliffs of Rathlin O'Birne. A woman in a black shawl looked down at them from the cliff-top, and a brown-and-white dog ran barking along the edge.

"We don't seem to be running aground, do we, Carlisle? Or would you prefer to chart a different course from mine?"

"No, Sir," Carlisle stammered, "I don't mean to presume... But our margin for error..."

"You're studying navigation, then are you?"

"No, Sir! I was only thinking..."

"*Mister* Carlisle," the Captain said, "I suggest that you mind your own business. That will be all, Gentlemen."

As the Captain closed the cabin door, Gubby looked up at Carlisle. Shaking, the Petty Officer glared at him with furious impotence before he turned away and stormed back to the foredeck. With nausea welling up in his stomach, Gubby crossed the deck and climbed the ladder to the bridge. He tried to convince himself that he had won the encounter, but his trembling insides told him that something was terribly wrong.

Evans stood at the wheel, holding the course as the *Wasp* ploughed through the choppy near-shore waters. As they passed the northern tip of Rathlin O'Birne, the sea returned to a pattern of rolling swells. Gubby stood in agonised silence until he heard himself blurting out, "Did you hear what the Captain said, Sir?"

Evans did not move a muscle, except to make small adjustments with the wheel. "It's too far from here to hear the exact words," he said, "but I think that I followed the thread."

Gubby's thoughts raced as he remembered how Evans had taken command of the wheel from him. "Do you think that Carlisle...? Was I right in holding the course...?"

Evans slowly turned his head to stare at Gubby. "I told you to hold the course, yes. But I didn't tell you to run into the bloody island."

Against his better judgement, Gubby heard himself saying, "But you told me that the Captain would know if I – if I didn't..."

Evans turned his back on Gubby. "Captains can be bloody fools," he said. "They can sit with their maps and their calculations until hell freezes over, but it's still up to *us* to be sensible. That means adjusting the course when we've drifted within fifty yards of the bloody cliffs."

Gubby fought the tears that welled up in his eyes. "I must go and apologise to Carlisle..."

"No! That isn't done. And haven't you been vindicated by none other than our Captain?"

"Yes, but..."

"I don't think that Carlisle would care to see you just now. I cannot imagine what he is thinking. But then again, I cannot imagine what our Captain is thinking, either."

Awash with misery, Gubby could barely speak. "What do you think that I..."

"Go to your quarters, Gubby. Get some rest. Think about the difference between obedience and slavishness."

"Yes, Sir..."

"And here's something else that you might ponder on. While our Captain was speaking with you and Carlisle, did you notice what he was wearing?"

"No, Sir, I didn't..."

"A nightshirt. He'd pulled on his coat over his nightshirt. While he is belittling one of the finest Petty Officers I've ever served with, he has clearly been lingering in bed, or he is too lazy to dress."

"Could he be ill?"

Evans shook his head. "God only knows. I cannot imagine where this is all going to lead."

≈≈≈≈≈

Ruairí stood at the rail, gripping the white-painted metal plate as the island receded into the distance. The ship's wake broke against the sheer cliffs. The dog on the heights seemed to be barking at the *Wasp*, but they were already too far away to hear it.

And too far to swim, he thought bitterly. They had been close, tantalisingly close... If only Carlisle had not wakened the Captain – but no, he realised, someone would have seen him, and they would have sent a lifeboat back to fetch him. And throw him in the brig. High noon was no time to escape.

Night would be the right time. He would wait until dark – near land, after nightfall. Where would they be? Somewhere along the north coast of Donegal, near Malin Head, near the long shoreline of the Inishowen Peninsula...

Near Toraigh? He looked at the full-bellied sails and felt the ship surging before the wind. They would pass Toraigh too soon, in daylight, unless something could slow the *Wasp*...

This was no time, he knew, to do anything out of the ordinary, anything that would arouse the slightest suspicion. He walked slowly back to the Captain's door and stepped inside. His heart raced when he could not see the journal on the desktop, but he found it on the floor where he'd dropped it when he bolted from the room. He replaced the letter and telegram inside the front cover and slipped the journal under the desk. His stomach twisted with nervous hunger, and he remembered the Captain's orders about eavesdropping on the crew. *I'll go to the galley, all right,* he thought, *but I'm no fecking spy. I'll give them something to chatter about.*

≈≈≈≈≈

For the hundredth time, Father Hayes told himself that it made no sense to hold two Sunday masses on Tory Island. Only a handful of devout old women attended the early service, while most of the islanders dragged themselves and their families into the pews for the noon Eucharist. When he had voiced his thoughts about offering mass only once on Sundays, the men had protested vigorously – they had animals to feed, they said, and children to dress and bathe. The women who frequented the early masses were equally adamant about not giving it up, and the priest knew that their support was a vital ingredient in his uneasy relationship with the islanders.

Standing at the sacristy door, Father Hayes looked across the fields that sloped upward toward the north shore of the island. Through the open door he could hear the islanders shuffling into the pews, murmuring restrained greetings to each other and seating themselves. He felt a sudden urge to walk away from the chapel, to hurry across the fields, to stride to the edge of the cliffs and watch the endless pounding of waves on the rocks. The power of his urge alarmed him, and he lowered his eyes to the scrubby weeds in the back garden of the church. This, he reminded himself, was his parish – the weather-beaten houses and the fragile souls of Tory, not the anarchic clash of the elements.

As he turned to enter the sacristy, he stole another glance toward the cliffs. A bank of dark clouds was forming on the western horizon, and he entertained the thought that a rainy afternoon would reduce his temptation to seek solace in cliff-walking. A glimpse of white caught his eye. It moved along the north cliff-edge at a steady pace, not in the jumpy rhythm of a hare or a bird. He watched the tiny, distant shape – silhouetted against the dark clouds, framed by a gathering storm – for a long moment before he realised that he was looking at Eithne Mullan.

A cold spasm of anger made him clench his teeth. Eithne, who claimed that her infirmities kept her from attending mass – *You know I'm not able, Father.* Eithne, who undermined his authority by holding the islanders in thrall to ancient practices and pagan superstitions. What was she doing? She moved unhesitatingly along the cliff-edge. Even at a distance, he could sense the purposefulness in her stride.

He had seen the other women making circuits of the island, involved in some deviltry that no one would explain to him. Some offered transparent excuses – *"We're doing the Stations, Father."*

"If that's what you're doing, you should do them in the nave. That's what the chapel is for."

"But we did the Stations around the island before the chapel was built, didn't we, Mags?"

The women had stopped when he'd challenged them, but he suspected that they continued making their circuits when he wasn't watching. Eithne's timing was well-planned, he realised – he would be busy serving mass when her circuit brought her near the church. He would chastise her later, but she would protest with an innocent-eyed explanation that would make him even more angry. But this time he would press her, he promised himself – he'd had quite enough of her veiled insolence.

As he closed the door it struck him that Eithne was not following the path of the other women. Whatever she was doing, she was making her pilgrimage in reverse.

≈≈≈≈≈

Ruairí saw McLaren sitting with Cobb and a handful of other sailors talking in low, anxious tones over the noon meal. He took a seat at their table without being invited, and the conversation died quickly. Cobb glared at him, but he ignored it. He looked at the bearded men, seeing the deep lines around their eyes and the resigned set of their mouths. From inside he felt a surge of grim energy. After a few hours, he would never see them again. He said, "Hullo, Cobb," with a hint of challenge in his voice. "Hullo, McLaren."

McLaren looked at him with worried eyes. "Did you see how bloody close we come to that island?"

"I did," he said cheerfully. "We could have pissed in their boots."

"You think it's funny, do you?" said Cobb. "You'd like to see us run up on those rocks, I'll bet."

"That wouldn't do me any good, would it? If you sink, I sink too."

"I'll bet you think some fisherman would pull your Irish arse out of the water."

"I know fecking well *you* wouldn't."

"Take it easy, you two," said McLaren. He turned to Ruairí. "I know that *he's* a right bollocks," he said, nodding toward Cobb, "but what's got into you?"

Ruairí chewed on a mouthful of beans before he answered. "Something I read."

After a few seconds, McLaren said, "Are you going to tell us?"

Ruairí looked around the table. "Where do you think we're headed?"

"To Moville," said one of the men.

"And before that?"

"Listen, you little Irish prick," said Cobb. "Just because you wipe the Captain's arse doesn't mean you can come here and talk down to us..."

"So you don't want to know..."

"There's a lot of accidents can happen on this ship..."

"Hold it!" snapped McLaren, turning to Ruairí. "I been telling everyone that I thought you was all right. I hope you ain't lording it over us."

Ruairí put down his fork and looked McLaren in the eye. "You know Inishtrahull Island?"

"Aye, there's a lighthouse up there."

"And people. There's about forty people living there."

"Yeah, I seen the houses," said one of the men. "We put in there once."

"Then get ready to see them again," said Ruairí. "We're going to evict them."

"Oh, shite!" said McLaren. "You sure of that?"

"I seen the orders. We meet up with a Sheriff at Moville, and then we go back out to Inishtrahull."

"Bloody hell!" A ripple of murmurs ran through the galley. McLaren said, "So it ain't true about the propeller?"

"No, that's true. But we won't go there till after the eviction." Ruairí turned to Cobb. "So you can meet some more Irish people."

"Feck it," said Cobb. "It's all the same to me."

"I think some of them have guns."

"Mullan!" Ruairí looked up to see Hatton leaning over the table. The cook was glaring at him. "Come with me!"

He stood up and followed Hatton along a passageway. When they were out of earshot of the galley, the cook turned and glared at him. "What in the hell do you think you're doing? Trying to start a mutiny?"

Ruairí's bitter confidence evaporated. "I'm just telling them the truth."

"And you're absolutely sure that's the truth?"

"I read the orders."

The cook took a deep breath and looked away. "I wondered why we were in such a damned hurry... Do you remember who the orders were from?"

"Somebody named Darlington."

"Hmm. From the Admiralty, then..."

They stood in silence in the empty passageway. The hum of chatter from the galley had dwindled, and Ruairí wondered if the men were straining to overhear them. Hatton glared at him and turned away. He felt half-ashamed, as though he had betrayed a friend.

A murmur rose from the galley, and Ruairí felt a change in the rhythm of the ship – instead of surging through the sea like a horse, the *Wasp* seemed to be rolling side-to-side. Hatton said, "Now what the hell's going on?" He strode back into the galley. The men had left their plates on the tables, and the last of them were crowding up the steep stairs to the main deck.

Ruairí followed Hatton up the stairs. Mist and drizzle surrounded the ship, and the sails hung loosely from the masts. From the bridge, Evans shouted *Drop anchor!* The crowd of men listened in silence as the chain rattled out through the hawsepipe and splashed into the sea. The entire length of chain unspooled.

The ship drifted until a dull thud shuddered through the deck. The *Wasp* began to turn slowly to face into the ocean swells. Armstrong gestured, and two sailors followed him to drop the fathom-line over the bow.

"This is not a display for your entertainment!" From the door of his cabin, the Captain's voice cut across the deck. "Every man to his duty station. Officers to my quarters. *Now!*"

≈≈≈≈≈

"Who is responsible for this?"

The Captain sat bolt-upright in his chair, staring at the three officers who stood in front of his desk. Evans and Armstrong exchanged glances while Gubby stood a step behind them, staring at the floor.

Evans broke the silence. "We are becalmed, Sir."

"I can see that, Evans. Do not patronise me."

The Navigator drew a breath but decided to say nothing. The Captain shifted his gaze to Armstrong, who had been staring at him intently. Armstrong lowered his eyes, but more slowly, the Captain thought, than usual. "What is your opinion, Armstrong?"

"I can only tell you what I see, Sir. We took a risk by initiating this mission under sail. We were able to take advantage of a favourable wind this morning, but now that wind has died."

The Captain looked at the floor and bit his lip. "And what is the state of our coal reserve?"

"We have ample coal for twenty-four hours, Sir. Our problem is the propeller. If we exceed SLOW speed, the vibration will damage the ship."

"Yes," said the Captain, lifting his eyes and staring at Gubby. "The propeller."

In a strangled voice, Gubby said, "It was my idea to proceed..."

"Please do not attempt to tell me something that I already know, Mister Gubby. Listen to me carefully. I want you to establish our precise position."

"Yes, Sir. But I'm afraid that the skies..."

"Mister Gubby! I don't care if you use a sextant or a divining rod. Use your head, man! Use every resource at your disposal to establish our position! Then report back to me."

"Aye aye, Sir..."

"That is all, Gubby. Get busy."

Muttering more *Aye aye, Sirs*, Gubby hurried out through the cabin door. Evans and Armstrong glanced at each other and looked away, amused at the thought of Gubby trying to fit out a work-party with a sextants, telescopes, maps, and sounding-lines. Evans nearly said *That should keep him busy, Sir*, but he restrained himself.

The Captain sat silent for a long moment, drumming his fingers on the desk. His eyelid itched. He took a handkerchief from his pocket and dabbed at his face around around his left eye. He thought of stepping into his sleeping-quarters to dab cold water on his eye, but did not trust his legs for the few necessary paces. He could hear his own breathing in the silent cabin, and the creak of a chair as Armstrong shifted his weight.

"I have half a mind to inform you..." he began, but stopped himself. He looked at the two officers who sat in front of him, realising how much he had come to rely on their quiet strength, and their loyalty. They were like himself – not high-born fops with titles and connections, but solid, determined men who were trying to carve out decent lives for themselves. As phrases formed in his mind, he realised how much he wanted to confide in them. He could say *This will be my last command... I am beset with ailments which are impairing my mobility, and my judgement..*

"Sir?"

"What is it, Evans?"

"I didn't hear what you said, Sir."

"I – I need an assessment... What are our options with respect to secondary ports?"

"Right, Sir. We were half-an-hour past Rathlin O'Birne when the wind died. It would not be inconceivable for us to reverse course and make for Killybegs."

"Are you suggesting that we abandon the mission?"

"I'm simply saying that Killybegs is a strong candidate as a secondary, Sir. They maintain deep reserves of coal. And we could telegraph Moville from there."

"Remind me of the signal-stations on our course. If we proceed northwest."

"Our best bet will be Tory Island. They monitor the Atlantic shipping route. I'm not sure what response we can expect from the smaller harbours on a hazy Sunday afternoon."

The Captain pushed down on the arms of his chair, trying to relieve the ache in his legs. "Tell me, then – if we proceed under steam, how soon can we expect to contact the Tory lighthouse? And what distance will remain to Moville?"

Evans stood and ran his finger along the coastal map on the desk. "Well, Sir, if there is any wind at all to augment our SLOW pace – and Armstrong, it may be prudent to reassess our coal reserves – we can progress along the Bloody Foreland..."

As Evans and Armstrong outlined their options, the Captain found his mind drifting to his unreliable legs, his irritated eye. He knew that his officers were fully capable of sailing the *Wasp* without him. He also suspected that they knew his misery, his incapacity – and that they had been quietly covering up his lapses in attention for some time. He found himself wondering what they would say if he interrupted them to announce *I wish to relinquish my command.* Would there not be some sense of relief? He could imagine them saying *We'll respect your decision, Sir. The men don't need to know. Then after we complete this mission...*

The cabin door flew open and Gubby burst in, his words spilling over each other. "The barometer is falling, Sir! We'll have all the wind we need!"

≈≈≈≈≈

"Can I have a word with you, Father?"

Eoghan Mullan stood at the door of the sacristy, fumbling with his cap and shifting his weight from one foot to the other. Father Hayes locked the altar-wine cabinet and turned to the boy. "I didn't see you at mass, Mullan."

"I been working, Father. At the lighthouse."

"Surely you can arrange your schedule..."

"It's my uncle, Father."

"Sean Mullan?"

"That's him, Father. He must be real bad sick. Aunt Eithne thinks he's dying."

Staring into the boy's eyes, he said, "I saw your aunt this morning."

"Yes, Sir. She come to the lighthouse to tell me."

"Why didn't she come to tell me herself?"

"I don't know, Father."

Father Hayes felt his stomach rumbling and thought of the noon meal that was waiting for him. "All right, Mullan. I'll attend to your uncle. You'll be coming with me, won't you?"

"No, I can't, Sir. I got to get back to the lighthouse, Father."

"Oh, very well. Go on, then!"

Eoghan hurried away, half-running with relief. Father Hayes locked the sacristy and walked across the back garden to the rear door of the rectory. He hurried past the dining room where his housekeeper had set out the serving-dishes of roast beef and vegetables, resisting the temptation to eat a few bites. From the cabinet in his bedroom he took a bible and the leather pouch with the viaticum and oils for the Last Rites. The housekeeper knocked at the open bedroom door. "Is anything wrong, Father?"

"It's Sean Mullan, Mrs. O'Kane. I'm told that he's ill."

"Oh. I'll cover the food, then."

He said, "Yes, thank you," regretting that he had forfeited any chance to feed himself.

As he left the rectory, he paused on the road to collect his thoughts. It would take at least half an hour to walk to Sean Mullan's cottage at the east end of Tory Island. Surely someone would have a horse and cart – but the only parishioner he could think of was Liam McClafferty, who lived farther away than Mullan. He could see no one on the West Town streets – *eating their noon meals,* he thought – and he was was struck by the dead quiet of the day. The hazy sky had diffused the sunlight into a dim brownish murk, with no breath of wind.

Father Hayes shook his shoulders and started on the long walk across the island. *I cannot let my imagination run away with me*, he told himself. *I will not join my superstitious parishioners in searching for omens under every rock and pebble.* The clammy air felt too thick to breathe.

≈≈≈≈≈

No one answered when Father Hayes knocked on the door of the cottage. He knocked again and called out *Mullan!* His voice seemed to be muffled by the heavy afternoon air.

With growing dread, he lifted the latch and let the door swing open. Dim coals glowed under the ashes of a hearth-fire, and breadcrumbs lay scattered across the small handmade table and onto the dirt floor. The priest ducked his head as he stepped through the low-ceilinged room. He pulled aside the cloth that hung in the doorway to the bedroom. Shirts and undergarments were scattered on the floor, and a pipe and matches sat on the bedside table. There was no one in the bed, sick or well.

He stepped outside and looked around the cottage. The skeleton of a half-finished *currach* sat upside-down on stones, near a pile of animal hides and a bucket of pitch. From the rear of the cottage a path led eastward, toward the sea-cliffs. An ugly thought occurred to Father Hayes – had the sick man ended his own life and condemned his immortal soul to hell?

"Good afternoon, Father."

The priest whirled around to find Sean Mullan standing at the front gate with a walking-stick in one hand and a coil of rope in the other. His heart was pounding, and he was sure that Mullan could see his alarm. "Where have you been!"

Mullan smiled and sat down on a crate and began to remove his boots. "Myself? I've been up in the cattle-pasture. Have you been here long, Father?"

How many minutes, he wondered, had he been standing like a statue in Mullan's back garden? The priest said, "I was told that you were ill. Gravely ill."

"Well, Father, I'll confess that I've had better days. But I don't think that I'm ready for the Extreme Unction just yet. Will you come in for a cup of tea?"

"No, I..."

"I'll be making one for myself, and I have some buns. I'll be grateful if you'll join me."

His head spinning, Father Hayes looked down at the bible and the leather pouch that he carried. "Thank you, Mullan," he heard himself saying. "I would like to ask you a few questions."

≈≈≈≈≈

The schoolmaster resolved for the hundredth time that he would begin doing a better job of feeding himself. His Sunday lunch had been a sorry cold-plate of ham and potatoes, the leftovers of his Saturday night dinner. He had once heard a Wexford man refer to leftovers as *manevolens,* a word that he'd not heard again. It sounded vaguely French. He would ask about it in the pub. Whether anyone had heard of *manevolens* or not, it would be good *craic*.

Hoping that fresh air would soothe his indigestion, he stepped out the front door of the schoolhouse. He was surprised to see a cluster of islanders walking along the road toward the lighthouse, still dressed in the clothing that they'd worn to mass. He caught the eye of Ben Rodgers, who seemed to be leading the group, but the boatman looked away without acknowledging his wave.

Geraghty moved to the side of the schoolhouse and looked across the sweeping flat fields that covered the west end of the island. Groups of men and women were making their way toward the lighthouse in a steady, ragged procession. He wondered briefly if he had forgotten a funeral, but he could not see a casket or wagon. Or a priest.

He retrieved his coat from the foyer of the schoolhouse and followed the knot of islanders at the rear of the long silent line. One of the women looked back at him and then looked away quickly. He felt a wave of loneliness, half-tempted to ask someone where they were going, half-wondering if he was trapped in a strange delirium. The windless sky was overcast with a brown haze, and the air felt thick and sticky. The black-and-white lighthouse tower looked like a faded photograph in the dim light.

Mass hysteria. Following at a distance, the schoolmaster fought back the thought that some terrible compulsion had gripped the islanders, urging them to march like the lemmings of Norway and drown themselves in the sea. *Nonsense. These are my people. The parents of my students. My friends.* Still, the cold silence of the procession disturbed him deeply. He felt the stirrings of something remorseless and ancient, and his imagination served up images of bloody human sacrifice.

The islanders turned from the main road and followed a path that led around the lighthouse compound and down to the rocky shore. The schoolmaster hesitated and held back, standing in the marram grasses at the edge of the beach. The islanders formed a circle around a long, flat stone that was as thick as a sarcophagus. Another stone, round and flat, sat on the top surface of the sarcophagus-stone. It was the size of a small wagon-wheel, and thick as two fists.

Eithne Mullan stood with her hand on the wheel-stone. She waited until the islanders stopped shifting around before she spoke.

I wish no harm to anyone. Her voice cut through the still air like a small, sharp knife. *No harm. No pain. I have tried to relieve pain wherever I have found it. I have always tried, but sometimes I have failed. You know that, and I know that.*

She looked out over the mossy rocks at the sea, quiet at low tide. *We have lived here longer than any of us can remember. Our grandmothers and grandfathers lived here, and so did their grandmothers and grandfathers. It is not an easy life on Toraigh. We cannot always feed ourselves as much as we need. And sometimes the sea takes us. We do not need long memories to know that.*

We only want to be left alone. But now men are coming to drive us away. Men with guns and clubs and fire. They think they own our island. Eithne swept her arms in a circle. *How can they think that? How can any man think that he owns our island? We live here and struggle here, but we do not own Toraigh. No one does.*

She looked into the sky. *We don't tell the old stories any more. We tell stories about Columcille, but we don't tell the old stories about Balor. The people who write down the stories say that he was cruel. They say that he demanded tribute.*

But the people who write down the stories are the same people who demand tribute from us. They call it rent. They call it tax. And they are coming with clubs and fire.

When my grandmother told the old stories, she told how Balor protected Toraigh. She told how his army stands in the sea, to protect us from invaders from the east. And she told how he sent the badly-injured men to live under the sea – to live with the great fish and the creatures of the sea-floor, to strike at invaders from below. When the storms blow I can hear their battle-cries.

And this is his eye. Eithne touched the round flat stone. *His army watches to the east. His eye watches the west.* She ran her hands over the stone. *We have turned his eye to the earth, so he can sleep. But now we need to wake him.*

She stepped away from the stone and walked to where Liam McClafferty was standing in the circle of islanders. She took his hand and led him back to the centre. He stood awkwardly, looking at the ground like an inexperienced altar-boy. *Now,* she said, *we need someone from An Baile Thiar.*

And she looked up over the heads of the islanders to the spot where the schoolmaster was standing. *Please come down, Mister Geraghty,* she said. *We need you.*

He found himself walking without thinking, as if drawn along by a magnet. The islanders in the circle shifted to let him through. Eithne gestured for him to stand on one side of the coffin-stone while she led Liam McClafferty to the other side. The wheel-stone lay between them.

Turn the stone, she said.

Awkwardly, the two men tried to grasp the edges of the wheel-stone to rotate it. *No,* said Eithne. *Turn it over.*

They fumbled with the edges of the wheel-stone, trying to get their fingers under it. Other men stepped in from the circle. They pushed the stone toward the schoolmaster's side until it protruded a few inches over the edge of the sarcophagus-stone. Crouching, the schoolmaster pressed up with his shoulder. He raised the stone a few inches, and the men reached under it to lift it higher.

The men shifted and pulled at the wheel-stone until it stood upright. Then, with their arms entwined like a multi-tentacled sea-creature, they eased it over until it lay flat on the sarcophagus again. As they stepped back, the schoolmaster said *My God.* A nearly-perfect circle of blood-red quartz was embedded in the surface of the stone, with a pitch-black spot in its centre.

Thank you, said Eithne. She touched the side of the eye-stone and then walked away as the crowd of islanders parted before her. They clustered around the stone like bees around a hive, each touching it and then moving away. The schoolmaster stood like a rock in the centre of a stream, feeling the islanders flowing about him. And then the last of them were gone, and he found himself alone on the boulder-strewn shore.

He rubbed his hand on the side of the stone. He could not bring himself to touch the red surface. He would come back again, he told himself – alone, and on another day, to study the vivid formation. As he walked up the path from the beach, he felt the first faint stirrings of a breeze.

≈≈≈≈≈

Evans felt drowsy in the damp, heavy afternoon air. He could feel the thumping of the off-balance propeller under his feet as the *Wasp* made slow progress along the Donegal coastline. It was like steering a coal barge – dull, steady work that left too much time for his mind to wander.

He could not forget the the agony that he had seen in the Captain's eyes. He had served under six commanders, but he had never seen an officer as twisted with pain as Russell. Even Armstrong, who seemed to prefer machinery over people, had noticed.

What's wrong with the Captain?
I've been wondering myself. He looks piss-awful.
Was he trying to tell us something...?

As he turned the wheel to compensate for the landward drift of the ship, the dull ache in his lower back began to flare. He shifted his feet and stretched his neck. Three days in dry-dock, he reflected, would do no harm. There were medical facilities at Moville, and he would organise a rotation of hot showers and check-ups for the entire crew. The evictions, he realised, would provide a perverse logic for the medical inspections – the islanders would surely bring an infestation of fleas and lice onto the ship. How would the Sheriff control a forcible evacuation? Would he restrain the people? Would he seize their animals and bring them aboard?

Evans pinched the bridge of his nose and shook his head. He would seek a transfer, he promised himself, as soon as possible – and far from the landscape of human misery that Ireland had become.

≈≈≈≈≈

Striding furiously up the path to Eithne Mullan's cottage, Father Hayes tried to remember the exact words that her nephew had used. *He's real bad sick, Father?* Or was it *He's terrible sick?* Whatever his words were, the boy had been lying through his teeth. His uncle was as spry as any man on the island, he thought. The young whelp had lied to his face.

What else had the boy said? *Aunt Eithne thinks he's dying.* He rapped loudly on the door of the cottage, grew impatient, and pushed open the door. He heard himself shouting her name. The cottage was silent, and empty.

Had the boy lied about what his aunt had said? Or had the old crone put him up to the whole business? He paused for breath and felt his heart racing. He had seen her – he *thought* he had seen her – from the sacristy door. Eithne Mullan, who claimed to be too weak to attend mass – *where was she?*

He would find the boy and corner him until he told the truth. Or he would shame the boy by bringing him to his uncle's cottage...

Unless Sean Mullan was lying, too. Could all of the Mullans be lying to him?

Desperate for fresh air, he walked out to the front garden of the cottage, his head swimming. He saw a cluster of islanders walking toward East Town along the south shore path, and he wondered why they had chosen that narrow, little-used footway.

Were they trying to avoid meeting him? Was everyone on the island hiding something from him?

A breeze from the west felt cool against his skin. Anger made his stomach churn. He decided that he would eat, and possibly sleep, before he went searching for Eoghan Mullan. And he would question every single islander until he found someone – anyone – who would tell him the truth.

≈≈≈≈≈

The coquettish westerly breeze tormented Gubby through the afternoon, rippling the sails and then falling back to a dead calm. He checked the barometer for the tenth time to confirm that the air pressure remained low. The needle was still dropping. *The wind will rise soon*, he told himself. *People can be unreliable, but a barometer never lies. There must be wind and rain.*

As the *Wasp* chugged through the swells, he tried to pass the time in his quarters by drafting a letter to his father. *I am much hearten'd by encouragement from our Captain. He has acted on my suggestion that we proceed on our mission under sail. Altho my optimism is not entirely shared by my fellow officers...* He hesitated, imagining his father's reply. *And how, young Will, are you guided in your judgement? By reason or by impulse...?*

He put the pen down. The monotonous *thump-thump-thump* of the propeller reminded him of the disastrous day on Clare Island, and of his letter of resignation that sat – where? If the Captain stood ready to cashier him out of the Royal Navy, why would he follow his suggestions? Unless he was correct? Still, the conversation with Evans burned in his memory. *It's up to us to be sensible. I don't think that Carlisle would care to see you now.* Confused and miserable, he sat staring at the sheet of paper, wishing that he could find someone to confide in.

≈≈≈≈≈

At sunset the wind began to stir, blowing away the haze that had shrouded the afternoon sky. In the fading light, Armstrong could see a dark mass of thunder-heads gathering on the western horizon. He turned to the voice-tube. "Carlisle!"

The Petty Officer's voice responded from below decks. "Yes, Sir."

"Come up to the bridge, will you?"

"Aye, aye, Sir."

In a few seconds Carlisle's boots rang on the ladder. Armstrong turned and nodded toward the west. "We need to trim the sails."

Carlisle nodded as one of the jibs flapped in a gust of wind. "Yes, Sir, we do."

"And as soon as we have sufficient wind, I want you to bank the boilers. We cannot continue to burn coal at this rate. You'll see to that, won't you?"

"I will, Sir."

"But Carlisle – a quick word before we pipe the men up here. I heard that the Captain made your life rather miserable this morning."

The Petty Officer looked out at the approaching storm-clouds for a few seconds before he spoke. "He disagreed with my judgement, Sir."

"This happened when Lieutenant Gubby was at the wheel, did it not?"

"It did, Sir."

Armstrong looked the Petty Officer in the eye. "I need to sound you out on an awkward situation, Carlisle. Evans and I had determined between the two of us to bring the *Wasp* into Moville. But Evans has injured his back, and he is not fit to take the wheel tonight. Tomorrow..." He thought for a moment before continuing. "I will need a few hours of rest before – before tomorrow. Consequently I need to assign young Gubby to the wheel again. And I want you to take the watch at that time."

The Petty Officer said nothing. Armstrong continued, "I will make it clear to him that he is to heed your warnings, not second-guess them. I will order him to follow your guidance even if you tell him to reverse course and head for America. And if the Captain says a single word about this, I will take full responsibility. Do you understand what I'm saying, Carlisle?"

"I do, Sir." He paused again, choosing his words. "May I ask you something, Lieutenant Armstrong?"

"Of course, Carlisle."

"Are we to perform evictions in Moville, Sir?"

Armstrong whirled around. "Where did you hear that?"

"The men were speaking of it, Sir. In the galley."

Armstrong shook his head. "Has Gubby been fraternising with the men?"

"No, Sir."

"Carlisle, I do not..." He paused and began again. "I am not at liberty to disclose orders before the Captain issues them. Certainly you know that."

"I do, Sir. I regret that I asked..."

Heavy raindrops began to spatter down on the bridge. Armstrong looked at the Petty Officer and then turned away. "Call up the rigging parties, Mister Carlisle. And hold them on deck until we take the full measure of this wind."

≈≈≈≈≈

It will be simple.

Ruairí grinned as he watched the storm-clouds rolling in from the west. The rain would discourage the men from roaming the deck at night. It would be dark, with only a sliver of a moon. He could move from the cabin to the bridge in a few seconds to snatch one of the ring-floats that hung in the alcove under the structure. With any luck at all, the officer at the wheel would never notice him.

He had slipped back into the Captain's cabin in the late afternoon. As he'd hoped, he could hear resonant snoring from behind the closed door of the Captain's sleeping-quarters. He re-opened a file cabinet and stacked the contents on the desk, ready to invent a progress-report if the Captain woke, or to rub his eye and bemoan his task if anyone else appeared.

The sound of the bo'sun's pipe alarmed him. He moved to the window and watched the men climbing the rigging while others formed into squads on the rain-spattered deck. From the bridge, Armstrong piped signals to the men on the masts and shouted orders to Carlisle, who relayed them to the crew below. The men struggled with the rigging in fits and starts, mis-hearing commands and getting in each others' way.

Raindrops blurred the window, and Ruairí returned to the desk. How many hours would it be, he wondered, before they neared Toraigh? He scoffed at the stacks of files, wondering how he had managed to convince himself to pore through them, page after page. *Was that how other people behaved – plodding along, performing mindless work simply because someone asked them to do it?* It was something he would like to talk about with Mister Geraghty…

The schoolmaster's story about his brother and the gunpowder-recipe letter came back to him with a jolt. If another letter fell into the hands of the police – a letter linking him with a deserter – he would be in serious trouble. Ruairí fumbled under the desk and retrieved the book. His envelope sat inside the front cover, and he slipped it into his pocket.

As he closed the journal, he saw a second envelope sandwiched between its pages. He hesitated for a second and then laughed at himself. Why should he worry about reading anyone else's letter when he was planning to jump ship? He pulled the envelope from the book and opened the folded page:

To Captain John Russell, HMS Wasp:

I hereby resign my Commission as an Officer of Her Majesty's Navy.

> *Signed,*
> *Sub-Lieutenant William Gubby*

There was no date on the letter. Ruairí read the page several times before he re-folded it and replaced the envelope in the journal. He shoved the journal under the desk and sat for a long moment, trying to make sense of the message. *Why would anyone write a letter like that? What kinds of people were these Englishmen?*

The cabin became quieter, and Ruairí felt a shift in the direction of the ship's rolling motion. He crossed to the window and saw the men hurrying below as sheets of rain swept across the deck. The *Wasp* was under sail again, and the engine had stopped. He smiled to himself – with the propeller no longer churning, he could slip over the rail without fear of being chopped to bits. Another obstacle gone. He needed only to wait.

≈≈≈≈≈

"Stay a mile offshore, Gubby. No closer. We're approaching the Bloody Foreland, after all."

Gubby said, "Yes, Sir," with a sense of relief. Armstrong's orders were absolutely clear.

"Steer due north after we pass the Aranmore lighthouse. The drift will push us eastward."

"Yes, Sir. But with these clouds I won't be able to confirm our course by the stars. Is there significant declination between true north and magnetic north?"

Armstrong was impressed. "Good question, Gubby. We've adjusted the compass to compensate for it. Just keep the needle on North until you see the Tory Island lighthouse. Then give the island a wide berth."

In their foul-weather gear, the two men had to shout to be heard. The rain had subsided to a drizzle, but the wind blew across the deck in ragged, bone-chilling gusts.

"One more thing, Gubby. I've assigned Carlisle to take the forward watch."

Gubby hesitated. "Sir, I'm not sure if... That is, Lieutenant Evans said..."

"Hear me on this, Gubby. Carlisle will keep to himself unless absolutely necessary. But if he makes a recommendation, I want you to follow it without question. Is that clear?"

"Yes, Sir. Crystal clear."

Armstrong paused and then said, "I will relieve you at the morning watch, Gubby. Hold the course until then."

"Yes, Sir."

As he climbed down the steep steps and out of the rain, Armstrong shook his head. *Crystal clear.* If a man did not understand when to keep his mouth shut, was it possible to teach him? He doubted it.

Bone-weary, Armstrong threw himself onto his bunk. He wondered if Evans would be fit to take the wheel at 0400. He knew that he could rouse himself if necessary, but his body ached for sleep. *Will old age feel like this?* he wondered. He thought of Gubby standing on the bridge, shivering in his foul-weather gear and doggedly following the compass. The boy would manage well enough, Armstrong reassured himself. Carlisle would see to that.

22 September 1884

Mary had left the lighthouse in irreproachable order. Although the storm pelleted the west windows with rain, she had adjusted the ventilators precisely and the oil-wicks burned without a flicker. Without bothering to look around the lantern room, Quinn knew that he would not find a fingerprint anywhere. She was skilful, he knew, and when she was angry, she could become a perfectionist.

She had not spoken to him since their argument. His shifts followed hers, and she left the tower a few minutes before he arrived at midnight. The log sat on the table, with the names and times of passing ships recorded in her well-formed handwriting. The Mullan boy stayed until Quinn waved him away. That was her only weakness, he knew – she needed help moving the oil-barrels.

This will pass, he told himself. He would apologise to her in the morning, and after a time she would make tea and offer him a cup in the domestic ceremony that he knew all too well. Their daughters would re-emerge from their rooms, and they would talk of commonplace things – the weather, the new school terms, the people they had met on the island.

But Varney – Quinn still bristled when he thought of Varney's list of *RECOMMENDATIONS* in his careful copperplate script. Knox would probably have gravitated to Varney anyway, he realised – the two men held the same cold ambition at the core of their souls. He was not one of them, and he never would be.

His stomach rumbled. He had tried to prepare a Donegal fry for dinner, but he had burned the eggs into a glutinous, inedible mess. He had growled at the children when they complained, and the episode had ruined his appetite. Now, he realised, he was facing into the middle watch, the lonely shift from midnight until 0400, on an empty stomach.

He could make a dash from the tower to rummage in his kitchen for bread or apples, but he would likely find Mary sitting by the hearth, and it would be awkward between them. No, he told himself, he would endure this stormy night on his own. He would inventory the oil-stores in the provisioning rooms, and he might scrub the galley if he needed a distraction.

The sound of water running through the roof-drains made his bladder twitch, and he hurried down the spiral stairs toward the toilet. A wave of dizziness blurred his vision, and he stopped by the oil-pump to squeeze his eyes shut. He walked the rest of the way, holding tight to the rail. It took an uncomfortably long time to relax and let his urine flow. He would need to pace himself, he realised. His night was only beginning.

≈≈≈≈≈

Ruairí stared at the chronometer as the hours of the middle watch crawled by. He read every word on its face – *Thomas Bassnett, 5 Bath Street, Liverpool* – until the letters became curls of paint with no meaning. *Signifying nothing.* He remembered how the Mister Geraghty would chuckle when he taught about kings and queens, or ancient wars. The schoolmaster would conclude by saying, half to himself, *Full of sound and fury, signifying nothing.* It sounded like a quotation, and Ruairí swore that he'd ask Mister Geraghty about it the next time he saw him.

He had seen the lights of Aranmore Island around midnight. He'd copied enough maps of the Donegal coast to know what lay ahead – Owey Island, then Gola, and then a clutch of small islands in Gweedore Bay. Then the next light would be the beam of the Toraigh lighthouse. When he saw the light, he would slip out of the cabin and take a ring-float from the storage alcove beneath the bridge.

But where were they now? He lifted the porthole shutters but could see no light. Could they still be moving along the Bloody

Foreland? Or had they shot past Toraigh hours before, when his attention had drifted? It didn't matter, he told himself – wherever he landed, even on the mainland, he could make his way to Magheroarty, where Ben Rodgers collected the island mail.

He was running out of time. The chronometer read 3:30 am – or 0330, he thought, as the Captain would call it. In half an hour the morning watch would bring men to their duty stations and more eyes on deck. If he didn't move now, he'd be trapped on the *Wasp* all the way to Inishtrahull. This was his last chance.

He put on his coat and hat, and he stepped through the cabin door onto the deck. The sails hummed overhead, and he could feel the surge and buck of the current as the *Wasp* cut through the waves. He looked in all directions for a glimpse of light, but saw none.

A solitary figure stood at the wheel on the bridge, and Ruairí was relieved to recognise the bulky silhouette of Lieutenant Gubby. Evans or Armstrong would have questioned why he was prowling about, but he felt sure that he could stay a step ahead of the young Lieutenant. Or *Sub-Lieutenant*, as he had read in the letter. If he had resigned, why was he steering the ship?

He moved quickly to the alcove under the bridge, where the cork ring-floats hung on brackets. He lifted one and tried to pull it away from the wall. The rope snagged on something, and in the shadowy space he could not see what it was. He pulled at a second ring, and the first one fell on the deck with a loud slap.

Gubby's head appeared at the side of the bridge. "Who's down there?"

"Mullan, Sir!"

"What are you doing?"

Ruairí pulled at the ropes, trying to break the tangle. "I couldn't sleep, Sir. Have we passed Toraigh Island?"

"That's none of your business, Mullan. Go back to your bunk."

Ruairí ignored him and pulled at the floats. He cursed himself for not checking in daylight to see how they were secured.

"Mullan! Leave those life-rings alone! They're only there for emergencies."

The wind lashed a spray of cold rain across the *Wasp*. With tears of frustration stinging his eye, Ruairí struggled with the tangle of cork and ropes. He heard Gubby's boots banging down the ladder. "Carlisle!" Gubby shouted. "Take the wheel!"

Ruairí pulled a cluster of life-rings from a bracket and threw them onto the deck. As Gubby tried to kick them out of the way, Ruairí scrambled to the side of the ship and swung his legs over the metal railing-skirts. The water below looked black and forbidding, like an icy grave.

"Come here, you little Irish prick."

In foul-weather gear, Cobb was standing behind him, pointing a rifle at his back.

≈≈≈≈≈

Mary Quinn never slept well when she and Paddy were fighting. She dozed fitfully and woke from vivid dreams of disaster – Paddy dying of tuberculosis, her daughters drowning in the sea. Worry had been her curse and her salvation. She had imagined thousands of grim events that had never come to pass, but she was seldom surprised by anything that happened. Worry had made her a good Keeper.

The storm rattled the bedroom windows behind the heavy curtains. Paddy, she knew, would be working at some tedious chore in the lighthouse tower to muffle his lonely anger. Had she been unsympathetic with him? Soon after they had married, she'd realised that Paddy Quinn was a hermit at heart, happiest when he could work alone. She sometimes wondered what it would be like to live with a man who teased her or made jokes.

She threw off the bed-covers and decided that she would take Paddy a flask of hot tea. It would be her signal that their stalemate was over, and when he came off-watch they would sit in the kitchen and talk of small things, letting the harshness drift into the past. She entered the kitchen before she realised that the lighthouse tower was dark.

She stood for a few seconds in the doorway, looking at the window over the sink. She ran back to the bedroom, threw a coat over her nightdress, and ran to the door of the bedroom where the Mullan boy was sleeping. "Eoghan! Get up!"

"What is it, Missus?"

"Come to the tower! As fast as you can!"

She ran through the rain across the dark courtyard, fighting an urge to shout for help. A small oil-lamp lit the entrance to the base of the lighthouse tower. She pushed the door open and saw her husband's feet sticking out of the galley.

He lay sprawled on the floor beside a chair that he'd knocked over when he fell. He was gasping for breath, with phlegm rattling in his throat. A stain of blood ran down from his nose and onto his shirt. He looked up at her with unfocused eyes, and his words slurred together when he tried to talk. "Oh, my God, Paddy!" she heard herself shouting. "How could you do this?"

She bent down and touched his clammy skin. Eoghan loomed in the doorway behind her. "Is he drunk, Missus Quinn?"

She started to snap *What do you think?* but she caught herself. She couldn't detect a smell of whiskey – but had he found a bottle of *poitín*?

"Do you want me to pick him up, Missus Quinn?"

"Yes – *no!* Go up and fill the oil-pump. Be quick!"

Eoghan's heavy footsteps banged up the metal stairs. Mary Quinn looked around the galley floor and in the waste-bin, muttering *What have you done, Paddy? Where's the damned bottle?*

She heard the scraping sound as Eoghan dragged a barrel across the floor above. She knew what she had to do. Leaving her husband on the galley floor, Mary Quinn seized a box of matches and hurried up the stairs to the lantern-room.

≈≈≈≈

Cobb stepped closer and cocked his rifle. Ruairí said, "Where the hell did you come from?"

"Stern watch, boy. You don't know much about the Navy, do you?"

"I know you're in it, you piece of shite."

Cobb spat. "I don't know whether to shoot you or stick you in the brig."

Gubby pushed past the floats and lumbered to the railing. "Don't let him get away, Cobb. He's a deserter."

"I can shoot him now and save a lot of trouble."

"No! I want the Captain to see this."

"What the hell is going on?" Carlisle's voice cut through the dark. "We're drifting!"

"Over here, Carlisle!"

"Who's at the wheel?"

As Carlisle worked his way along the railing from the foredeck, Gubby looked up and muttered, "*Oh my God.*"

"What is it, Gubby?"

He pointed at a spot over Carlisle's head. A beam of light cut through the darkness, dead ahead of the *Wasp*.

Cobb looked up at the light, and Ruairí dived into the black water.

$$\approx\approx\approx\approx\approx$$

"*Where did that fecking light come from?*" shouted Cobb.

"*Gubby!*" shouted Carlisle. "*Hard a-port!*"

Gubby struggled up the ladder and spun the wheel to the left. High above the bow of the *Wasp*, the light grew brighter. The ship shifted into a ponderous arc to the left, slowing as the sails flapped in the wind.

Carlisle looked up at the looming lighthouse tower. "*We're too bloody close!*"

The *Wasp* began to roll as breaking waves surged against the side of the ship. Gubby shouted, "*What am I to do?*"

Carlisle shouted "*Signal for power!*"

The deck jumped under Gubby's feet, and the wheel lurched in his hands. Momentum carried the ship forward, lifting the prow out of the water with a screech of metal against stone. The *Wasp* shuddered to a stop, her sails fluttering uselessly.

Gubby grasped the handle of the engine-room telegraph and jammed the handle to FULL ASTERN. The telegraph bell sounded thin and weak in the howling wind.

Men poured onto the deck, pulling on their boots over the long-legged white underwear they slept in, rushing to the railings and looking over the sides. Gubby saw Armstrong push his way across the deck. He looked up at the rungs on the backward-tilting bridge and shouted to two nearby sailors, *"Fetch a ladder!"* He grasped the arms of two other sailors who hoisted him onto their shoulders, and he scrambled onto the bridge.

Gubby sat clinging to the telegraph, fearing to stand on the wet, tilted floor of the bridge. Armstrong looked down at the slumped, moon-faced boy. *"What in God's name have you done, Gubby?"*

"There was a deserter, Sir! Mullan..."

"What are you talking about? What have you done to the ship?"

"The lighthouse!" Gubby shouted. *"We didn't see..."*

"Bloody hell you didn't!"

A ladder clattered against the side of the bridge. Evans pushed through the mass of men on the deck and climbed the rungs. As he pulled himself over the rail, a wave lifted the ship and dropped it back onto the rocks with a bone-jarring crash. Armstrong grasped the wheel, and Evans staggered to maintain his footing. The wind whipped sheets of rain across the bridge.

"Where the hell are we?" shouted Evans.

Gubby shouted, *"I think it's Tory Island, Sir!"*

"You think? You don't know?" The three officers turned as the Captain appeared at the top of the ladder, his eyes blazing under the brim of his commander's cap. *"I expect my helmsmen to know our location at all times!"*

"We haven't seen a light since Aranmore, Sir..."

"And you didn't report this? Who was on the forward watch?"

"Carlisle, Sir."

"Carlisle? Then where is Carlisle?"

"I expect he's on deck, Sir..."

"I want him up here immediately! Help me over this bloody railing, Armstrong."

Armstrong reached over the bridge-rail and hoisted Russell onto the platform. As soon as his feet touched the floor, the Captain pulled away from Armstrong and shook himself violently. "I can stand without your help! What are you looking at?"

"Nothing, Sir..." The three officers tried not to stare at the Captain's old-fashioned night-shirt. The wind and rain plastered the wet cloth against his thin body, exposing his naked feet and ankles. He looks like a rooster, Armstrong thought – a wet rooster who forgot his shoes but remembered his hat. The Wasp groaned as another wave lifted and dropped her.

"Now!" the Captain shouted, "Can someone tell me the situation?"

"We appear to be wedged, Sir!" said Armstrong.

"Have we run aground?"

"No, Sir, we're still twenty yards off. We're pinned between two rocks."

The Captain whirled around to glare at Gubby. "Why did you bring her this close?"

"There was no indication, Sir. We had a deserter..."

Gubby's heart sank as the Captain turned away. "This is madness!"

A voice from the deck below shouted, "Do we abandon ship, Sir?"

"Absolutely not!" The Captain peered down at the men. "Who said that?"

No one spoke as the wind howled over the ship. "The situation is under control!" shouted the Captain. "I assure you of that!" Quietly, to Armstrong, he said, "Full power astern."

"We have no steam, Sir."

"*What?*"

"The coals are banked. It will take thirty minutes..."

"*Bloody hell! Send the stokers to the engine room!*"

Lifted by an incoming wave, the *Wasp* rose again and dropped with a shuddering crash. Armstrong shouted, "*Drury! Fire the boilers!*"

Someone shouted, "*She can't take much more of this, Sir.*"

"*I know what she can take,*" the Captain shouted. "*And I know what she needs! She needs loyalty!*" He began pacing back and forth. "*That is what Her Majesty's Navy needs! Not the coal, and not the provisions. Not the gunpowder, not the guns! It is loyalty!*"

On the deck, the men's faces tilted up like pale moons, following the Captain as he tried to stride back and forth. His feet dragged like half-dead limbs. "*It is loyalty that carries the day! I mean loyalty to the ship! And I mean loyalty to the Navy! And yes, I mean loyalty to the Crown!*"

Gubby sat clinging to the engine telegraph, dazed and fascinated by the Captain's sudden burst of energy. He could not take his eyes off Russell's bony, shuffling feet. As the wind howled and the rain poured down, he felt an odd sense of peace. There would be no more Navy, no humiliations, no more pretence. The worst had happened, and he was free.

As he looked up at Russell, he found himself thinking how the Captain might appear in a portrait, a portrait framed in marble – and it seemed that a slab of marble had appeared behind the Captain, rising from the sea. He knew it could not be marble, but it looked like marble, a wide grey-green slab streaked with black. Taller than the bridge where they stood, the moving shape surged steadily closer, glinting in the glare from the lighthouse. Gubby admired its remorseless beauty, and he felt relieved. It was something for which he could not possibly be blamed.

≈≈≈≈≈

The great wall of water smashed over the ship, driving the prow deeper between the twin pillars of rock that rose up from the sea-floor. It ripped the sails from the masts, twisting the *Wasp* the way a fisherman twists the spine of a trout to break its back. The roar of the breaking wave drowned the groans of the metal and the screams of the men.

The floor of the engine-room lurched, throwing Carlisle against the firebox, burning the side of his face. He dropped onto the platform that surrounded the boilers, his skin throbbing. His shovel clattered as it fell under the metal walkway. When he groped in the bilge-water to retrieve it, he felt a surging current.

"*Carlisle?*" He heard Drury's voice from the direction of the hatch. "Where are you, Carlisle?"

"Over here!"

"Armstrong says we're to fire the boilers."

The Petty Officer pushed himself to his feet. "It's too late! There's a breach in the hull!"

The walkway was covered by rising water. Carlisle sloshed his way through the darkness of the engine-room, his face stinging. "Where are you, Drury?"

"Over here!"

"Keep talking, man! I can't see a bloody thing!"

He blundered into Drury's outstretched arm and climbed through the hatch. The two men tried to shut the hatch-door, but it would not fit into the buckled frame. The ship lifted and dropped again, and a deafening boom resonated though the hull. "Forget the hatches!" Carlisle shouted. "Let's get the hell out of here!"

≈≈≈≈≈

A torrent of water poured down into the galley from the stern access-door. Carlisle and Drury ran up the tilted floor and climbed the steep stairs onto the deck. The men were scattered in the driving rain, clinging to the railing-skirts and the masts.

Tangles of rope and splintered wood sagged between the davits where the lifeboats had hung.

"Carlisle! Up here!"

McLaren stood on a yardarm above the deck, clinging to the mainmast with one arm and a rigging-line with the other. "*Take hold of summat!*" he shouted. "*Another wave and you'll be gone, too!*"

Carlisle swung into the shrouds and started climbing. Drury shouted, *"If that mast goes, you'll be done for!"*

The Petty Officer looked out at the mountainous Atlantic swells. *"I think McLaren's right!"*

"I'll take my chances down here." Moving from one handhold to another, Drury made his way up the sloping surface toward the prow.

Shaking his head, Carlisle climbed to the yardarm beside McLaren. He looked up and saw other boots on the spar above. Wet sails, torn half-loose from the rigging-lines, flapped in the wind while the mast swayed. *Am I insane?* wondered Carlisle. *Is Drury right?*

He looked down at the empty bridge. *"Where are the officers?"* he shouted to McLaren.

"Gone."

"Gone where?"

"Overboard. The wave took 'em. Gone." McLaren squinted his eyes against the driving rain. *"Took half the men, too."*

"My God..." Carlisle looked down at the churning waters that surrounded the *Wasp.* Could anyone swim in that froth? Could a lifeboat float?

Another wave lifted the *Wasp* and twisted the ship as it dropped, swinging the mast out over the water. Carlisle and McLaren clung to the rigging as their feet slipped on the tilting spar.

McLaren shouted, "*This way!*" and scrambled higher up the mast. Carlisle stood dumbfounded until he realised that the mast might be long enough to reach the shore. Following McLaren, he climbed.

≈≈≈≈≈

From the foredeck, Hatton saw Drury clinging to the railing-skirts as he pulled himself toward the uptilted prow. The cook clung to the anchor-chain near the windlass, looking desperately for safer hand-hold – a railing, a rope, anything at all. He could imagine the anchor breaking loose and plunging to the sea-floor, wrenching the chain through the narrow hawsepipe and mutilating his arm. Wave after wave lifted and dropped the *Wasp*, twisting the deck to a sharp angle where footing was impossible. He was on the high ground, but the stern of the ship was already under water.

He cursed himself. The Navy was a young man's world, where muscle and courage and recklessness carried the day. It was no place for an ageing, overweight cook who was painfully out of breath, whose arms ached with the simple effort of hanging onto a chain. He could have taught in a cookery school, or worked in a prison kitchen. What vanity had convinced him to ply his trade on a gunship?

Other men scrambled after Drury, working their way up the tilting foredeck to escape from the waves that poured over the railings. As the wind howled, driving sheets of rain like bullets, Hatton felt a tremor and then an odd sense of peace. He looked at the men the way that he might look down from the top of a lighthouse – calm, remote, almost godlike – and he knew with pitiless certainty that they were all going to die.

Drury was shouting at him when the next wave struck. Hatton felt his fingers burn as the crushing force of the water poured down on him, and he lost his grip on the anchor-chain. As the cascade of water forced him under the surface, his forehead hit something with a hard, sharp edge. He choked with pain, gulping salt water into his mouth. His lungs contracted in spasms of gasping and spitting, and he flailed to push himself to the surface.

He touched something that seemed to be floating. He gripped it and tried to pull himself upward, but the mass sank in his hands, and he realised that he was clinging to the hair of a drowned sailor. With a spasm of revulsion, he shoved the body downward and pushed himself to the surface.

He gasped for air but choked on foam. He could not feel the surface of the water – the sea churned like a cauldron of froth. His lungs knotted with spasms as he tried to breathe, and he could not lift himself out of the choking spume.

Hatton sank back into the freezing water. Exhausted and despairing, he seemed to step outside himself, no longer caring whether he lived or died. He watched his body sink like a convulsing shadow as the sea-water burned in his lungs. He wished that he could see his children again. He had a vague sense of being swept along by an overwhelming surge before darkness closed in and he felt absolutely nothing at all.

≈≈≈≈≈

"That's the oil pump full, Missus Quinn."

Mary Quinn ran down the stairs from the lantern-room. "Eoghan, now listen to me. Take my husband back to our quarters and put him to bed. I need you to do that before Mister Varney comes on watch. Can you do that?"

"Sure, Missus Quinn.."

"And see if you can get him to drink some tea."

"I don't know, Missus Quinn. What if he chokes?"

"I hope he does. Maybe he'll throw up..." She stopped herself and began again. "Just get him to our quarters. And Eoghan..."

"Yes, Ma'am?"

"Not a word of this to Mister Varney. Or anybody else. Can you promise me that?"

≈≈≈≈≈

The masts leaned out at a steep angle from the twisted hull of the *Wasp*. As the mainmast tilted closer to the water, Carlisle and McLaren straddled the spar and inched their way toward the tip. Wet sails sagged over the mast, and the wind snapped the rigging-lines.

One of the men at the the tip of the mast swung down, hung by his hands for a few seconds, and dropped. He disappeared into a shadowy gap between massive boulders on the shore of the island. *"By God it's long enough!"* shouted McLaren. *"Come on, Carlisle!"*

The ship lay on its side in the churning water. A wave lifted the exposed keel, lashing the mast like a whip-handle. Carlisle clung to the flexing timber and watched two other men drop from the tip of the spar and vanish from sight.

McLaren shouted *"This is it!"* and ran along the last ten yards of the mast like a tightrope-walker. A breaking wave hit the shoreline rocks and threw up a thick stinging spray. Carlisle clung to the narrowing timber as the water washed over him. When he opened his eyes, McLaren was gone.

Carlisle started pulling himself frantically toward the end of the mast as a wave dislodged the *Wasp* from the rocks. Free of the vise-like notch, the ship tried to roll upright, and Carlisle fought back panic as he found himself being lifted higher. The keel hit the sea-floor, and the mast began to tip toward land again. Half-blind with salt-water and exhaustion, Carlisle thought he saw rocks below his dangling feet. Instinct told him he was too high for a safe drop, but he could not trust the sinking vessel to bring him any closer. He swung down and released his grip. As the shadowy boulders rushed up toward him, he wondered if it would have been wiser, and less painful, to drown.

≈≈≈≈≈

Quinn tried to wriggle free when Eoghan lifted him over his shoulder, but he slumped after a few seconds. As Eoghan carried the half-conscious man across the courtyard and into his house, he could see a light in the window of Varney's quarters. He couldn't tell if Varney had seen them.

He bent forward and lowered Quinn into an armchair. The Keeper didn't exactly seem to be drunk. Eoghan had carried many men home from the Toraigh pub, and he knew the smell of drunkenness – the stench of whiskey-breath mixed with stomach acid, compounded by an annoying tendency to say the same words over and over. Mister Quinn's skin felt clammy, and his breath didn't stink.

He wished that he could ask Aunt Eithne what to do. He had heard her tell worried islanders, *If you can't bring him here, then wipe his face with a clean cloth and bring me that cloth.* She would smell the rags that were brought to her, ask a few questions, and know what was needed. Could he wipe Mister Quinn's face and then run to East Town with the towel for Aunt Eithne to smell? He could, but it would take a long time, and he'd need to tell Missus Quinn if he was going to do that. What was the right thing to do?

Quinn stirred in his chair and coughed. Eoghan went to the sink and pushed down on the handle of the pump, but it squeaked loudly, and he didn't want to wake anyone. He saw a pitcher of Missus Quinn's lemonade on the shelf by the sink. He poured a glass of the sweet drink, took a swallow himself, and brought the rest to the half-conscious Keeper.

Mister Quinn sat slumped in his chair. Eoghan held the rim of the glass to his lips, but he only coughed and sprayed some of the liquid. Remembering what he had seen Aunt Eithne do with a baby, Eoghan tilted Quinn's head back, pinched his nostrils shut, and poured some lemonade into his mouth.

The Keeper gagged and spluttered, but he swallowed the mouthful. Eoghan waited until Quinn stopped moving around, and he forced him to take another swallow.

Quinn opened his eyes, grabbed the glass from Eoghan's hands, and downed the rest of the lemonade in greedy gulps. He sat breathing heavily for a few seconds, like a man who'd been kicked in a football match. Then he said, "I want more of that."

Eoghan brought him the pitcher of lemonade. Quinn poured and gulped another glassful, looking around the room. "How did I get here?"

"I carried you here, Mister Quinn."

He tried to get out of his chair, but his legs were shaky. "I'm on the middle watch."

"Missus Quinn is in the lighthouse for you."

He shook his head. "Where's Varney?"

"He didn't see nothing, Sir. But I think maybe he's gone over to the lighthouse by now."

Quinn sat rubbing his legs and turning his head from side to side. "Listen, Mullan – you'll say nothing to Varney about this, will you?"

"No, Sir. But I think Missus Quinn wants me to come back."

"Yes. She'll need you over there. Go on, Mullan."

Eoghan left. Quinn's hand shook as he poured and swallowed the rest of the pitcher. He walked around the room for a long time, testing his limbs and trying to remember what had happened to him.

≈≈≈≈≈

Wait until I tell Aunt Eithne. Eoghan ran toward the lighthouse tower. Somehow, by instinct or luck, he had cured Mister Quinn. Nothing like this had ever happened to him before. Could this be his gift?

He stood outside the tower door, trying to collect his thoughts. Both Mister and Missus Quinn had warned him not to tell Mister Varney, and he would keep that promise. But who could he tell? And what would he tell them?

Mary Quinn appeared in the doorway of the lighthouse, startled to see him standing on the pathway. She closed the door behind her and whispered, "I've just done the hand-over to Varney. How is he?"

"He's fine, Missus Quinn. I think I – I think he's cured."

"Cured? What do you mean, cured?"

"I give him some lemonade, and he woke up."

She stared into his eyes. "Lemonade? Did he tell you to say that to me? Did you and he..."

A high-pitched cry cut across her words, and they both turned to listen. She said, "Is that a gull?"

The wind and rain receded for a second, and they heard another wailing sound. "I don't think so, Missus. It sounds like a man."

"This isn't some trick, is it?"

"No, Missus. Do you want me to go look?"

"We'll both look."

Eoghan followed Mary Quinn around the lighthouse. Unobstructed by the tower, the wind blew sheets of rain across the western side of the compound. Eoghan could hear a sound in the roar of the wind – something like a shout, but he could not be certain.

He looked at the six-foot wall that surrounded the lighthouse compound. For all of his life, he and Ruairí and the island boys had prowled around the compound wall like spies surveying an enemy fort. They had boosted themselves over the wall, sometimes landing in Mister Corish's chicken-yard and stirring up a racket of clucking and crowing. On a night like this there could be island boys – Pádraig, or the Rodgers brothers – prowling the cliffs and the rocks outside the compound, possibly hurt.

He thought he heard a shout again, and he and Mary Quinn looked at each other.

"That sounded like it came from down there."

"Yes, Ma'am."

Ducking their heads to avoid the driving rain, they followed the walled path that ran from the compound toward the cliffs at the tip of the island. The wind howled, and lightning crackled across the sky. Mary Quinn slipped on a wet mossy rock, and she reached up to steady herself. She recoiled as something cold and wet jerked itself out of her grasp. A bloody arm was groping over the wall.

She unlocked the gate. Five wet, shivering sailors staggered through the opening. One limped, and another was bleeding badly from a gash in his arm. "Where did you come from?" she shouted.

The limping man said, "The *Wasp!* She's on the rocks down below."

She shot a look at Eoghan. "How many of you are there?"

"There's five of us." said Carlisle.

"Is that the whole crew?"

"Good God, no. There's another fifty or more."

They looked at the forbidding panorama of boulders and crevices between the compound wall and the sea. "Eoghan," said Mary Quinn, "go out there and see if you can find any others. The rest of you come with me."

≈≈≈≈≈

Eoghan made his way across the craggy rock surfaces to the edge of the shoreline cliffs. Looking down, he saw the prow of a ship above the churning water, pointing upward at a severe angle. The ship looked twisted and grotesque, like a drawing he'd seen of a man who'd been hanged. The top of a mast and a tangle of sails and rigging floated nearby. He could not see any sailors on the prow or in the water.

The only places to come ashore, he knew, would be the coves. The waves pounded against the cliffs, and anybody in the water would be slammed against the granite and pulled down by the undertow. What had the sailor said? *Fifty more men?*

He moved to the edge of a deep cleft in the rocks that he and Ruairí called Purgatory Cove. They had scavenged the lobster-trap buoys and flotsam that accumulated in that cleft – narrow at the neck, wider on the inside – a notch that functioned like a lobster-trap itself. Deep shadows made it impossible to see the bottom until a flash of lightning illuminated the notch. A blurry white shape was sprawled on the sand below.

He felt his way down the slippery path. A man lay on his side on the wet, stony sand. Eoghan approached him from behind, looking for any sign of movement. Rain splashed on the man's sodden white shirt. Eoghan found himself trembling as he reached forward and touched the man's shoulder. "Are you alive, Sir?"

Slowly, the man twisted his head to stare at him with glazed eyes. He coughed and said, "Yes, I'm here. I'm here." The man's voice was flat, like someone reading numbers out of a book.

"What – how did you come here?"

"I didn't come here at all."

"What do you mean?"

"A wave came in and left me here. A wave at sea."

Eoghan looked at the blood on the man's forehead. "Did you hit your head or something, Mister?"

"I was waiting for another wave to take me out again...

"You got to come with me up to the lighthouse..."

"...but there wasn't any wave, so I'm laying here..."

"Listen, Mister. I don't know who you are, and I don't care where you're from. Do you want to come with me to the lighthouse?"

The man stared blankly at the water. "I'm waiting for another wave."

"Then *stay* here, for feck's sake! I'm not going to drag you!" Eoghan started up the path, but he turned back. "Come on, please. Missus Quinn will make you some soup or something."

The man turned his head. "Is there soup?"

"Yes, she'll make soup, and we'll get you dry..."

"I'd like some soup."

The man made no attempt to move. Eoghan looked at him sprawled in the rain. "Your mates are up there, Mister."

Coughing, the man tried to push himself up. Eoghan reached under his arms and pulled him to his feet. The man staggered, but he kept his balance. "Can I have some soup?"

"Come on. I'll take you to the kitchen."

Like a large, obedient child, Hatton followed Eoghan up the path and across the rain-slick granite, stumbling toward the lighthouse compound.

≈≈≈≈≈

Ruairí felt like his skin was covered with a layer of gelatine. He clawed his way to the surface of the cold black water and saw the hull of the *Wasp* sliding past, her sails silhouetted against flashes of lightning. He gulped a deep breath and dived again, fearing that Cobb might take a pot-shot at him. He stayed beneath the waves until his lungs were bursting.

When he surfaced, the stern of the gunboat moved away from him into the darkness. As he dog-paddled in the wake of the ship, he could see only sheets of rain. A clutch of panic welled up in his chest. His clothes felt like sodden weights, dragging against every movement. He thought of the tangle of life-rings lying on the deck of the ship and he felt small, like an insect flailing to stay afloat.

He pulled off his shoes and let them drift away. He slipped out of his coat, and he felt wonderfully lighter. He picked at the knot in the rope-belt of his trousers, but it had jammed into a stubborn tangle that refused to yield. He groped in his pockets for something that could pull it apart. His fingers found only a few coins that he released into the sea. Why hadn't he brought a knife? What had he been thinking?

He paddled with his feet to keep his head above water while he fumbled at the knot with his fingers. With agonising slowness, he pulled one strand away from the tangle, and then another. The rope-belt yielded its grip, and he slipped off his trousers. Released from the drag of the wet cloth, he felt light as a cork.

He tied knots in the waterlogged legs of his trousers, and he re-tied the belt. Holding the waist open, he lifted the raggy garment out of the water and whipped it down onto the surface to capture an air-bubble. The pant-legs filled with air like two wet balloons. He slipped his arm between the legs and let the improvised float carry his weight. It hissed with leaking air, but it held him up.

He stopped kicking, grateful to rest. His half-numb sense of warmth began to fade in the deep chill of the water. He would need to keep re-filling his pant-leg float with air, but he could keep doing that much longer than he could swim. But where was he? And where was the shore?

As he rose and fell in the swells, he glimpsed a flicker of light that seemed to be moving away from him. It had to be the Toraigh lighthouse, he knew – no other beam could penetrate the driving rain. And the lighthouse absolutely could not move. *He* was moving, but in the wrong direction. A current was carrying him away from the island. In the Sound, he'd be drifting toward the south beaches of the island, but he wasn't. He was being pulled by the current that swept around the rocky west coast of Toraigh and surged toward the mainland.

Air sputtered out of his float, and it collapsed into the water. Ruairí lifted the wet pants and captured two more air-bubbles. His legs felt heavy when he tried to kick. His eyelids drooped. *No*, he told himself, *stay awake*. He could not let himself doze, even for a second. Sleep was a trap, a lure – a sweet invitation to surrender to an icy death. He was not ready to die, not yet. He would not let himself die until...

Until what? Clinging to his leaking float in the black bitter ocean, he looked up and saw nothing but roiling storm-clouds and rain. He wondered where Eoghan might be on this ugly night, and he realised that he had answered his own question. He would not let himself die until he saw his brother again.

≈≈≈≈≈

The sailors sat shivering in the Quinns' sitting-room, wrapped in blankets and trying not to spill the mugs of tea they held in their trembling hands. Mary Quinn sponged the blood from their cuts and abrasions, tearing the bed-linens into strips for bandages. The men were badly scraped and bruised, but she could not detect any permanent damage. The Petty Officer had twisted his leg badly, but he did not seem to have broken any bones.

As she watched her husband feed wood into the cooker, she forced herself to think of his half-conscious body on the galley floor, slurring his words and unable to stand. What had happened to Paddy? An empty pitcher sat on their table, near scraps of bread from the sandwich that he must have made for himself. Now he moved quickly in the kitchen, building the fire to heat kettles of broth for the injured men. She could still see the splotch of blood on his shirt – or had that come from one of the sailors? Nothing in this night made sense.

"Hatton! Is that you?"

Eoghan Mullan ushered a heavyset older man into the sitting-room. The man looked dazed and breathless, and blood oozed from a cut on his forehead. The sailors made space for him on the couch near the hearth. The man said, "I want some soup."

"I think he's knocked his brains loose," said Eoghan.

Paddy said, "I'll get him some dry clothes. You get some too, Mullan." He turned to find Varney standing in the doorway.

Varney looked around the room. "What in God's name is going on here, Quinn?"

No one spoke for a few seconds. "There's been a wreck," said Mary Quinn.

"On your watch?"

"It must have happened when we were handing over. I heard them when I left the tower."

Varney scowled. "Why didn't you report this to me?"

"They're injured, Varney," said Paddy Quinn. "They need patching up before we do the paperwork."

"And what about you, Quinn? I thought you were sick."

"He was, Mister Varney," said Mary Quinn. "That's why I relieved him."

The three Keepers looked at each other. "We'll take care of these men," said Paddy Quinn, "and then I'll come up and make an entry in the log. What brought you down here anyway, Varney?"

Varney pointed at Eoghan and at the glassy-eyed cook. "I saw *this* one bringing *that* one down the path from the gate. I wonder what Mister Knox is going to make of this." He turned and left the room.

Paddy and Mary Quinn looked at each other. "Eoghan," she said, "get yourself some dry clothes. Then I want you to go and bring Father Hayes back here."

"Do you mean wake him up and bring him now, Missus Quinn?"

"Yes, Eoghan. I mean now."

≈≈≈≈≈

The weak sun did nothing to warm the icy Atlantic waters. Rain-clouds rolled endlessly across the sky, driven by a fierce wind that churned the swells into white-capped storm-waves. No sea-birds ventured into the wind, not even the hungry ones, sensing a force that was strong enough to snap their bones.

Ruairí drifted onto the rock as the first dim light appeared on the horizon. His numb feet dragged across the submerged surface until a barnacle cut his ankle and a bright flash of pain shot up through his leg. Shocked alert, he groped under the water with his hands. The rock angled upward until it emerged from the sea. Joyfully, frantically, Ruairí dragged himself onto the solid surface.

His muscles ached as the cold wind blew across his wet body. A wave washed over the rock, and he wondered if he could stand. His legs felt like heavy lumps of meat, resisting his efforts to move. He clung to a crack in the wet stone surface, his heart pounding.

The cut in his ankle stung in the salty sea-water. He wondered if the tide was rising or falling. If the sea was ebbing, he'd have a better chance of staying on his solid perch. If the sea was rising, he'd need to catch air in his float again...

His float had drifted away.

≈≈≈≈≈

"Why did you lie to me yesterday?"

"I didn't lie to you, Father."

In a foul mood, the priest peppered Eoghan with questions as they hurried through the darkness and rain toward the lighthouse. "You told me your Uncle Scan was sick. Why did you tell me that?"

"Aunt Eithne told me to come and tell you."

"I went to his cottage, and there was nothing wrong with him. Why did she tell you to lie?"

"I wasn't lying, Father..."

"And now you tell me there are injured sailors at the lighthouse..."

"There's been a wreck, Father. They come out of the sea..."

"Eoghan!"

They turned to see the youngest Rodgers boy running to catch up with them. He splashed to a stop and hesitated. "Hello, Father."

The priest scowled at the boy. "Why are you out at this hour, Danny?"

"Miss Mullan asked me – Eoghan, your auntie wants you to come home right away."

The priest whirled and glared at Eoghan. "Did your aunt send you to wake me?"

"No, Father. Missus Quinn told me to come and get you..."

"You tell Eithne that if this is one of her lies, I'm coming straight to her house. Do you understand?"

"Yes, Father." The priest turned on his heel and continued toward the lighthouse compound. Eoghan ran toward East Town, with the Rodgers boy trailing behind him.

≈≈≈≈≈

He could see land. As the rain subsided to a drizzle, he could see other rocks protruding above the surface of the water and, in the distance, a shoreline. How far away was it? He rubbed his eye and tried to focus. He couldn't tell. A hundred yards? A mile?

Exhausted, he shivered in the wind and ached for sleep. Like the overcast sky, he felt trapped in a grey in-between zone, not asleep and not awake. *At least not dead*, he thought. His legs hurt when he moved.

The waves no longer washed over the rock where he lay. *Lucky*, he thought. *I'm lucky. Bone-lucky.* It was possible, he thought, that his tiny island of rock might still be above the surface of the water when the tide came back in, but he doubted it. It was far more likely that the incoming tide would lift him from the surface, and he knew that he couldn't swim ten strokes. He thought of the schoolmaster, and the pictures he had drawn to show how the gravity of the moon pulled at the oceans of the world. *There are tides in the air, too*, he had said, *but we cannot see them*. Ruairí had sat dumbfounded at the thought of the oceans being pulled like hot tar as the moon circled the earth. But before he knew the *why* of the tides, he had always known the *how*. Twice each day, as every islander knew from birth, the ocean would rise.

As the clouds and drizzle distorted the gloomy light, he strained to get a better view of the land. If anything at all would float within reach, he would grab it. It wouldn't have to be a life-ring or a buoy – any floating thing would help hold his head above the surface. Oars and planks washed up on the Toraigh beaches and rocks every day. Where were they now?

Something moved on the distant shore. He blinked and squinted, hoping that the shifting light wasn't deluding him. Two figures seemed to be moving along the shore. They looked tiny, and he wondered if they were children. But, he realised, it didn't matter. If he could see them, they could see him.

He pushed himself up onto his knees and waved. The figures seemed to stop in their movement, and he sensed that they were looking at him. He shouted, but his voice sounded strangled and weak, and he knew that they were too far away to hear.

He waved his arm. The figures stood motionless, and he wondered if he had deluded himself. What if he was waving at trees or rocks? He waved frantically, hoping for any sign of recognition.

The figures on the beach appeared to merge into one, and then they separated again. They began to move, but without haste. Frantic, Ruairí waved both of his arms. The figures moved slowly until they disappeared behind a pile of boulders.

Please! Please! He heard himself shouting hopelessly across the expanse of water. The wind rose, and curtains of rain obscured his view of the shore. Despairing, he collapsed back onto the wet, flinty surface that had become his world. What had Uncle Sean said? *Your Da kept wavin'... but then the tide come in... He was wore out...* Ruairí could almost hear his uncle's voice. *Over there they think it's a curse if they save a drownin' man. They think if you save your man, you cheat the sea, and the sea gets you.*

The wind and the rain closed in on him, and a penetrating chill made him curl into a ball. He knew that no one could see or hear him – and what would it matter if they did? He was utterly alone, and in a few hours his body, like his father's, would be lifted by the tide and washed onto that superstitious and indifferent shore.

≈≈≈≈≈

Eithne sat by the dying coals in her hearth, sobbing. Everything had gone wrong, more terribly wrong than she could imagine. She had never felt as many screams, as much desperate struggling for air, as much black despair as in the waves of death that had swept through her that night. They were young men, not much older than Ruairí or Eoghan. Ordinary men, not greedy or cruel men. She dreamed of men in a churning cauldron, men who knew they were trapped and doomed.

The gift is also a curse. It was one of the few things she could remember her grandmother saying. Even as she recited the invocations to staunch a wound or to ease a birth, Soinbhe told her curious granddaughter *It is not in the words.* Old Soinbhe, who seemed to touch and steer events by her mere presence. Soinbhe, who remembered the days when there was no priest on the island.

Eithne pulled a shawl over her shoulders. Her grandmother's world was gone, swept away like an old *currach* that had outlived its seaworthy days, whose ribs and beam had dried to brittleness. Were people different then? Did they believe more, and worry less about knowing? Was it better then, or now?

If she had found someone – anyone – to take her place, she would gladly have taught her about the plant-medicines and the invocations, and the inexpressible half-world behind them. But none of the island girls had expressed the yearning, the spark that signalled the gift. If she'd had a daughter of her own – but she didn't, and even if she had...

Did Ruairí have the gift? He had it as much as any man could, she suspected. But men blundered about, trying to shape things in the image of themselves. A man would never know another's life in his body, unless it was one of the dark root-like tumours that would kill him. How could a man know what it was like to give life? How could a man feel the moon in his blood?

Like a basket of eels, feelings swam through her body, confusing her and clamouring for her attention. She knew that Ruairí had been caught up in some hateful business, but he was far away, and she felt helpless. She knew that Ruairí had been moving toward her, probably on a ship, with bitterness and indecision in his heart. Then Eoghan had told her of the ugly rumours of evictions. Had she confused her protective instincts for Toraigh with her love for her nephews?

So many deaths... She shuddered, yielding to the torrents of despair. She had wakened in the blackest hour of the night by a terror that rolled across the island like a wave. She had not been surprised to see the light in the window of the Rodgers cottage, or to find that the youngest children had wakened and were crying inconsolably. And she had sent Danny Rodgers to bring Eoghan, and Eoghan had told her of the shipwreck. She had nearly heard his words before he spoke them. *A gunship run onto the rocks, under the lighthouse... Six men come ashore, but they say fifty was lost...*

But when Eoghan tried to describe the chaos at the lighthouse – *First there was five of them at the wall, and then I went and got one more up from the rocks* – she found herself imagining a tangle of cork floats. She had tried to dismiss it as a distraction, an idea that someone might babble about to avoid an unpleasant truth. A shipwreck, death and injury, the grief of wives and families – but the sense of the cork and the ropes would not go away. She almost felt the peeling paint under her fingernails – and then she knew.

Eoghan, she had said, *do you remember where your Da died?*

Wasn't it over on the mainland where they found him?

No, I mean where their boat was wrecked, and Uncle Daniel drowned.

Sure, I think I know. Ruairí and I rowed out there. It's by the rocks under the lighthouse.

Now, listen to me careful, Eoghan. I want you to row out there tonight. Then when you get close, let the currach drift.

Why, Aunt Eithne?

Because I think Ruairí is somewhere out there. He's still alive. He was on that ship that sunk, but he must have got off it first.

Do you think he's out there on the rocks, where the ship was?

No. He's in the water. Like your Da was.

And he had gone again into the rain-swept night. Eithne had built up the fire in the hearth, but the wind sent a penetrating dampness through the cottage. Chilled to the bone, she watched the coals flicker and subside. *I will not live much longer*, she thought. *And I do not want to.*

And I should never have turned the stone. She had imagined the curse inspiring a comedy of errors, misdirecting the ship to sail to the Hebrides or to sink in the shallow waters of Toraigh Sound while pompous uniformed officers led an undignified retreat in life-boats. She had not imagined fifty men and boys dying in a stormy, blood-drenched sea.

Exhausted, she looked for any glimpse of dawn. Squalls of rain battered the windows, and she began to doubt the wisdom of what she had told Eoghan to do. Alone, rowing a *currach* on storm-swept waters – was she mad to have sent him? Would she lose everyone she loved?

She hoped deeply that she had not precipitated a further disaster. *Perhaps it is best after all,* she thought, *that I take the gift with me when I die.*

≈≈≈≈≈

Eoghan snapped awake. He had no idea how long he had been drifting. A foot of water had accumulated in the *currach,* and he bailed with a tin cup to empty it over the side. Bailing felt like a futile exercise as the rain hammered steadily down.

He had rowed fiercely to the west end of the island, and when he'd allowed himself to rest, he'd slipped into a half-sleep. He peered anxiously through the rain as the *currach* drifted through the Atlantic swells. The dim morning light revealed no shores or beaches, no rocks or landfalls. His feet felt cold and shrivelled in the bilge-water that sloshed in the bottom of the boat. He felt bone-weary and terribly alone. His stomach rumbled, and he realised that he had not eaten anything since yesterday's dinner. He and Ruairí had once stuffed themselves on a platter of mouldy bread that no one else wanted to eat. Would they ever have a chance to do that again? *Please,* he thought desperately, *don't let Aunt Eithne be wrong.*

Something thumped against the side of the *currach,* and Eoghan picked up an oar. A man in a white under-shirt seemed to be swimming beside the boat. He grasped the shirt by the back of the neck and pulled it up, but the swimmer made no attempt to rise from the sea. Trembling, Eoghan grasped the man's arm and turned him over in the water. The glassy eyes of a bearded sailor stared skyward as his mouth sagged open in the water. His body was a cold, dead mass. Eoghan dropped the arm with a shudder of relief. It wasn't Ruairí.

He pushed the corpse away from the boat with the oar, and it rolled over to float face-down again in the water. Eoghan shuddered, remembering the time he had found a man's body floating near his lobster-pots on the north side of the island. Something had nibbled off the man's lips and eyelids, and the open-eyed grimace of the corpse had haunted his dreams for weeks.

He glimpsed another shape floating in the swells. He slipped the oars between the pegs in the gunwale and rowed toward the body. The corpse, clad in a blue coat, floated low in the water. Eoghan saw a white collar around the back of the fat neck and stopped rowing. Whoever the man had been, he wasn't his brother.

The low sun rose in the east, and Eoghan saw other bodies floating in the water. White undergarments billowed around some of the corpses. Some had been injured, their cuts exposing pink fatty muscles where the sea had washed away the blood. All seemed to slump with resignation – their lives, useful or wasted, joyful or sad, were over.

Eoghan paddled from body to body in the flotilla of death, hoping that he would not see an eye-patch or a thatch of red hair. He wondered if he was looking at the same men again and again, or if other bodies had been swept up by the current. He wished that he could show someone – anyone – what he was seeing. *Look*, he would say, *think about what you're doing. This is what will happen to us.*

One of the corpses had washed halfway onto a rock, its legs twisted at a severe angle. Eoghan reached with his oar to nudge it back into the water, but when he touched its side, it coughed and raised its hand.

Slowly, painfully, the figure turned its head around. An empty eye-socket hung open like a slack hole in its face. Its matted hair was tangled and filthy, and the skin of its legs was a pale, sickly blue. Eoghan stared at the figure – half-frozen, barely alive, and, ridiculously, without any pants.

It coughed again and croaked, *"Eoghan?"*

"Yes! It's me!"

"If you're here, Eoghan," it whispered, *"I can die now."*

"Oh, no, you can't" he growled, reaching to lift Ruairí's limp body into the *currach*. "Aunt Eithne would kill me if I let you do that. You're going to fecking live!"

Aftermath

He slept. Dreams drifted through his consciousness like ocean swells, looming and fading. The Captain leaned on his arm for support, but the Captain's hand became a shackle attached to an anchor-chain, dragging him down into murky depths. A volcano rose from the sea and poured molten lava over Toraigh, setting fire to the cottages while the islanders tried to swim into the sea to escape. A girl's voice beckoned him into a shadowy alley where faceless men threatened to crush him under barrels and crates.

In the brown oblivion between dreams, he felt heat under his arms and on his belly, sometimes soothing him and sometimes building up into a hot flush that made him writhe. He felt layers of earth and seaweed weighing down on him. His feet tingled and itched. When he tried to move, his legs seemed to be caked with wet clay.

At other times he remembered the calm, orderly feeling of the map-school. He imagined that the ship's cat lay on his drawing-desk, curled asleep in a spot of afternoon sun. When he tried to stroke it, it shrank to a dot and vanished. A map of Toraigh lay pinned to the desk-top, and he felt like a sea-bird hovering over it. And he became a sea-bird, a hawk gliding over the island, watching the breakers embellish the north shore with a border of lacy sea-froth. A warm rising current lifted his wings. He soared high above Toraigh and eastward, toward the heat of the sun. Toraigh dropped behind, and another tiny island appeared over the horizon. As he dived toward the speck of land, he saw a girl and a boy waving from the beach.

He snapped awake, sweating. He tried to shout *Tara!* but his rusty throat could only whisper. He pushed at the pile of blankets that weighed down on him, trying to swing his legs onto the floor. He was half-sitting when Eithne and Eoghan burst through the doorway. Eithne wrapped her arms around him and sobbed

My boy! My boy! Eoghan stood awkwardly, turning his cap in his hands.

"Did they go to Inishtrahull?" he croaked.

Eithne drew back and looked at him quizzically with tear-streaked eyes. "No, this is Toraigh," she said. "You're home."

"But I mean..." He fumbled for words, his thoughts a blur. "Did the *Wasp* go to Inishtrahull?"

Eithne and Eoghan looked at each other and shook their heads. Eoghan said, "What are you talking about, Ruairí?"

"The *Wasp*... That ship..."

Eithne's eyes lit up with understanding. "No," she said, "your friends are safe."

"But they were going there..."

"It sank."

Ruairí sat for a long moment. He looked at the rain-spattered window of the cottage. It was his room, his and Eoghan's. How did he get here? "But I was on it..."

"It ran up on the rocks under the lighthouse. Eoghan saved some of the men."

"I didn't save them, Aunt Eithne..."

Eithne smiled at Eoghan. "From what people have told me, one of them is alive because you were there."

"How many of them..."

"Six."

"Just six?" Ruairí thought of the galley – the tables full of men, and the long rows of hammocks strung up at night. "Where did the others... I mean..."

"A few of them washed up on the south shore," said Eoghan. "A lot of them was in the water where I found you."

"You don't mean swimming, do you?"

"No. They was dead."

A wave of exhaustion flooded over him, and he felt the salty sting of tears in his missing eye. He groped at his face. "Where's my eye-patch?"

"I'll make you a new one," said Eithne. "You should go back to sleep now."

"But I..."

She touched his face with her hand. "You need to get well. That's all you need to do now."

He lay back down in the bed, and his aunt pulled the covers over him. "Maybe," he muttered, "maybe I'll just sleep a little more..."

"Sure, Ruairí," said Eoghan. "I'll stay with Aunt Eithne until you wake up."

Nodding to his brother, Ruairí fell asleep.

≈≈≈≈≈

After days of downpour and wind, the silence shocked him awake. Sunshine lit his bedroom window. His back hurt. He swung his legs out of bed and pushed himself up with his arms. He felt weak and awkward, but he could walk.

Eoghan's bed was empty. Ruairí took a deep breath and felt disgusted with the sickroom smell, the stench of sweaty bed-clothing and, he suspected, his own half-washed body. He felt restless. No one was in the cottage. He stripped off the undergarments that he'd been sleeping in and washed himself, using the basin and rags. A new leather eye-patch sat on the kitchen table, and he wondered if Aunt Eithne had recruited Uncle Sean's help to make it. Someone had washed his clothes. When he put them on they felt loose, like hand-me-downs from a bigger man.

The breeze was cold in the late September sunshine. On wobbly legs, he walked out into the garden, looking at the stone cottage that had been the only home he could remember. His head swam in a flood of blurry thoughts. Had Aunt Eithne always lived there, or had his parents lived there before they died? The thatch needed mending. What would happen if men came with rifles and torches to turn them out onto the road? Sickened at the thought, he sat on the wall. His legs were weak, and he realised that he would need to work to build back his strength.

"Ruairí?"

349

His brother was standing behind him. "How long you been back there, Eoghan?"

"I just come back here from the McClaffertys'. I was over there with Aunt Eithne. One of their girls is sick. She sent me back to see if you was all right." Eoghan looked at his brother slumped on the wall. "You don't look so good."

"I feel like somebody beat me with a stick. How long was I in that bed?"

"I think you been sleeping three or four days. I slept a whole day, too."

"You pulled me off a rock, didn't you, Eoghan?"

"I suppose I did."

He thought of the people on the mainland beach. "You ain't scared that you're going to drown now?"

His brother looked puzzled. "Why would I think that, Ruairí?"

"Since you saved me?"

Eoghan looked at him for a long time. "You're talking like that sailor I brought up from the cove. The one that hit his head. Maybe you should go back to bed."

"Wait a minute – what about this sailor?"

"There's six sailors on Toraigh that come off that boat. One of them was down in that cove..."

"Who are they? What's their names?"

"I don't know most of them. The old one's called Hutton or something."

"I know him! Where are they now?"

"They been at the lighthouse, but Liam McClafferty said they come over to Port Doon this morning. Some Navy boat is supposed to come get them."

"Are they still there?"

"I suppose, unless they already been picked up..."

Ruairí stood down off the wall, and the ground felt unsteady under his feet. "You got to help me, Eoghan," he said. "I want to see them."

≈≈≈≈≈

Carlisle sat on the Port Doon pier, watching the *HMS Valiant* riding at anchor. The three-masted brigantine had approached and retreated from Tory Island for four days, waiting for a break in the weather. The *Valiant* was not going to risk her hull, or her crew, by drawing nearer than half a mile offshore. And instead of sending in a lifeboat, her Captain had signalled to the lighthouse for a Tory boat to bring out the survivors. *If we had been half that cautious...* Carlisle thought. *At least they will appreciate the conditions we were sailing under.* He and the others had found themselves sitting for endless hours in the lighthouse compound, staring out through the Keepers' rain-streaked windows and sleeping in their quarters. Now they sat on the dockside, waiting for Ben Rodgers to return from the mainland.

He worried about what was to come. A volume of Morse messages had flickered between the lighthouse and the mainland signal-station, and as the highest-ranking survivor he was responsible to answer them. After two days of inquiries, the orders came – they were to make their way to Southampton for a court-martial. The London newspapers had picked up the story, demanding that Whitehall explain how the Royal Navy had lost fifty men and a gunboat while helping to collect some piddling Irish rents. The Admiralty, he knew, would be under severe pressure to find someone to blame.

He reminded himself that he had nothing to hide, but he felt deeply worried about being tripped up by insinuating questions or legal double-talk. Although he despised himself for thinking it, he knew that he and the others were lucky that no officers had survived to testify. The court-martial would be conducted by Naval officers, and they would be reluctant to convict their peers. But he had no doubt that they would send a crewman to jail. Or to the gallows.

He regretted putting his name on the paper that the priest had pressed them to sign. *The lighthouse was lit as we approached Tory Island.* Was it? Yes, he had seen the beacon before the crash. And the sky had been thick with oily black clouds. But it seemed as though they had sailed for hours in utter darkness after passing Aranmore Island. How would that sound in court?

It seemed that we sailed for hours...

It seemed, Mister Carlisle? Did you not keep a log of those hours...?

The thing to bear in mind, he told himself, was that the lighthouse-keepers would not be on trial. He would.

Ben Rodgers' boat came into view at the entrance of the cove. Hatton, McLaren, and the others stood up and stretched, yearning to move, to break the weary boredom of waiting. Carlisle eased himself onto his feet. His leg still felt fragile, and he wondered if he had cracked a bone.

"Mister Carlisle?"

It was the boy from the lighthouse. "Yes? Owen, is it?"

"My brother's asking to talk to you, Sir."

"Don't call me *Sir*. I don't have time to talk to anyone. I'm getting on that boat in a few minutes."

"He's just over here, Mister Carlisle." Eoghan gestured toward a pile of empty crates.

The men had moved to the edge of the pier. Carlisle said, "Who is it wants to talk to me?" Eoghan reached in his pocket and pulled out a leather eye-patch.

Carlisle said *My God* and hobbled to the crates. Ruairí sat on a wooden box, massaging his legs. "Hullo, Mister Carlisle."

"Mullan! I thought you were dead."

Ruairí shook his head. "No. Eoghan, give me back my patch, will you?"

Carlisle looked away awkwardly while Ruairí pulled it over his head. "What do you want, Mullan? The boat is here for us."

"Who's with you?"

"Hatton and McLaren. And three Marines."

"What about the Captain? Or Lieutenant Gubby?"

"No. They drowned. Why are you asking me this?"

"Because I want to go back to the map-school. And I don't want anybody coming back there for me..."

"Mullan, let me tell you something. You aren't going back to any Admiralty map-school."

"But if they're all dead..."

"Listen to me close. You were never on the *Wasp*."

"But you *know* I was..."

"I know a lot of things, Mullan. A lot of irregular things have been done out here in this godforsaken corner of the world. And one of them was bringing you on board the *Wasp*. You had no business being there."

"But the Captain told me..."

"The Captain was sick. I knew it, and I think Evans knew it. If a doctor had seen the Captain, he would have reported it, and someone else would have been put in command. But that didn't happen. We all kept the ship running, because we knew he wouldn't last forever. But then he brought you on board."

"Because I speak Irish?"

"Carlisle!" McLaren shouted. "They want to catch the tide! They're going to cast off!"

Carlisle grabbed Ruairí by the arm. "I'm being ordered to Southampton for a court-martial. I'm not volunteering a bloody word about this, but if your name comes up, I'll testify that you demoralised the crew, and that you jumped overboard. They'll think you were a Fenian. Do you understand me?"

Ruairí sat stunned, unable to collect his thoughts. Carlisle said, "You'd do everyone a favour, Mullan, if you'd just disappear."

≈≈≈≈≈

Eoghan followed as Ruairí stumbled painfully home. He didn't understand his brother, but he would not embarrass him by offering to help. He shifted the parcel from the mail-boat from hand to hand, wishing that Ben Rodgers had not asked him to take it.

They walked up the steep road from the Port Doon pier and down the sloping path toward the cottages. Ruairí paused near Uncle Sean's gate, breathing heavily as he watched the Rodgers boat cut through the swells toward the English ship. Eoghan wanted to ask a hundred questions, but Ruairí's grim attitude made him hesitate to speak.

Ruairí finally broke the silence. "What are you carrying there, Eoghan?"

"Ben asked me to give it to Father Hayes," he said. "It's some books and a newspaper. There's supposed to be something in it about the wreck."

"Let me see that."

Ruairí unfolded the newspaper and scanned the long grey columns of print. He skipped past the stories of court proceedings and the dispatches about the fighting in Khartoum. The story of the *Wasp* was on page seven, starting near the bottom of the page:

The Derry Journal
Wednesday, September 24, 1884
THE WRECK OF THE WASP

The long and sad story of evictions in Donegal has received yet another shade of sorrow. The record, already all too dismal, has now added to it an occurrence of a melancholy and whelming character. Usually the eviction scene affects but so many poor Irish peasants, who are to the manner born, and know how to endure greatly. To-day the grief is carried into many an English home, to shadow the happiness and embitter the life of parents, wife and mother. The gunboat Wasp, sent by the Admiralty to convey an evicting party to Inistrahull, has gone down off Tory Island and fifty of the crew are dead beneath the wave. The crew, we believe, are nearly all English, and their death in the circumstances will cause a grave sensation in their own country. The Wasp was sent round on sheriff duty, and was to put into Moville to take that official, as well as the Resident Magistrate, the bailiffs, and the police to evict some wretched creatures in the island of Inistrahull. The gunboat was on her way, bound for Moville when, caught in the storm at Tory, the disaster occurred. It is a most touching and calamitous event. These poor fellows never entered the British service to do the work of the agent and bailiff. The impulse that stirred them to brave the dangers of the deep, and of battle if necessary, was a higher one than a desire to form part of a sheriff's escort. This consideration makes the occurrence all the more melancholy. We can anticipate the indignation that will arise in England over the sacrifice of these lives, and we mistake greatly if the occurrence be without its influence in hastening legislation. In this catastrophe "the message of death" is more than a figure of speech. It is a dread and lamentable reality.

"The feckers," said Ruairí.

"What's it say?"

"Listen to this. *Usually the eviction scene affects but so many poor Irish peasants, who are to the manner born, and know how to endure greatly...*"

Eoghan looked away, and Ruairí knew that he was struggling to understand. "It means that if they come around and feck us out of our houses and treat us like dirt, that's all right. But if something happens to their Navy boys while they're fecking us out..."

Eoghan didn't say anything. Ruairí said, "Don't you see? They don't think we're *people*! But look at what they say here. *We can anticipate the indignation that will arise in England over the sacrifice of these lives..*" He thought of Cobb. "I'm glad the bastards drowned."

Eoghan said, "But Ruairí..."

"But what?"

"But you was on that ship *with* them."

"What are you getting at, Eoghan?"

Eoghan groped for words. "I was up at the lighthouse this week, working. Some of them give me a hand with the oil and supplies."

"So?"

"They're just – *blokes*. Like me and Pádraig, I mean. Maybe not..." Eoghan looked away and said, "Maybe not like you."

Ruairí looked at his brother and saw the steady, decent man that Eoghan was becoming. Light-headed and ashamed, he grasped his brother's arm. "Eoghan, I'm not thinking straight..."

"I know you understand things better than I do..."

"No! Don't say that, Eoghan! Don't ever say anything to make yourself small." He looked up at his brother. "You got a big heart, you big *garsún*."

"I'm sorry, Ruairí..."

"You got nothing to be sorry about. Will you..."

"Will I what, Ruairí?"

"Will you help me get home? I got to get well. I got things to figure out."

≈≈≈≈≈

Father Hayes sometimes wondered whether God still intervened in human affairs, but he never doubted that Satan did. How could anyone question it? Every newspaper brought fresh evidence of his handiwork – wars, mutilations, debauchery, and wretched stories of starvation and murder. Men were weak, and easily tempted. Over time, Father Hayes had constructed a detailed image of his antagonist, in the same way that a police detective would create a profile of a master criminal. He saw the fallen angel as muscular, clever, cruel – a dangerous adversary.

Pushing the wheelbarrow down the road toward the lighthouse, the priest knew that he was engaging the enemy on his own territory. Had anyone ever seen a clearer demonstration of the power of evil? The islanders – his flock – had dared to summon the powers of darkness, and now fifty men lay dead at the bottom of the sea. Their curse lay like a black stain over the entire island, and he was absolutely certain that any Tory souls who perished now, no matter how devoutly they might have believed and prayed, would surely be consigned to hell.

Liam McClafferty had finally told him, after he had convinced him of the eternal damnation that threatened his wife and children. McClafferty described how the word had raced around the island like fire in dry gorse – the English were sending a gun-boat to collect impossible sums in rent and, if not satisfied, they planned to level every house on the island with artillery. And the islanders had congregated on the beach, where they had taken a stone – a *wishing-stone*, he had called it – and turned it over to try to stop them.

So you invoked a curse upon them, did you?

No, not a curse, Father – you don't understand. We were only trying to protect ourselves.

Do not try to deceive me. I know a curse when I smell one.

Father Hayes found himself pushing faster, his anger growing like steam in a boiler. Now he knew why Eithne Mullan had distracted him with a fool's errand at the east end of the island. And why he had seen a glimpse of her white hair near the cliffs on Sunday morning. He would deal with her, absolutely. But first he would shatter the symbol of the dark power.

He had to slow his pace as he left the lighthouse road and guided the wheelbarrow through the tall heathers and weeds that lined the path to the beach. The nails that protruded from the sides of the barrow snagged the undergrowth, and he wished that he had brought a hammer to drive them back into the wood. It was like everything else on the island – no longer new, heavily-used, needing repair. Was that also happening to him? Was he becoming an exhausted version of himself, his strength deteriorating like this barrow?

He saw the round stone as he wheeled down the path toward the beach. It lay on top of a sarcophagus-shaped rock, staring upward. It was fiercely red – not like the pale rose-tinted marble of an altar, but a circle of brilliant crimson quartz that gleamed in the sunlight around a coal-black centre. An eye of stone and crystal, a warrior's eye. An eye of blood.

He wheeled the barrow to the side of the rock. He clenched and un-clenched his fingers, wishing that he had brought along a pair of work-gloves. Low waves broke on the shore, leaving a tide-line of seaweed. The bodies of eight men, he knew, had washed up on the beaches of Tory Island. No crucifixes had been found on any of the bodies, and he had presumed, in consultation with the new Principal Keeper of the lighthouse, that they were Protestants. Now they lay in a storage-shed within the lighthouse compound, soon to be interred in a common grave near the lookout-point.

Through a series of Morse messages from the mainland, the Royal Navy had announced that they would pay for help in retrieving the bodies, two pounds for each body brought in, or five pounds if the body were put in a coffin and buried. Father Hayes had been surprised at how little interest the islanders had shown. McClafferty had told him that everyone ignored the offer, fearful of stirring up ghosts.

Ghosts. Wishing-stones. Stirred with indignation, the priest tried to slide the round stone from the coffin-rock into the barrow. He could barely move it. He pried and shoved at it, with little effect. The red eye of the stone stared indifferently into the sky. Fighting back tears of frustration, Father Hayes walked to the lighthouse, seeking help.

≈≈≈≈≈

Quinn helped the priest manoeuvre the stone into the barrow, and he wheeled the barrow up the steep path from the beach. "That's a man-killer of a load," he said, catching his breath. "What are you going to do with it, Father?"

"I'm going to cast it into the sea."

Without saying anything, Quinn looked at the waves lapping at the shore a few yards behind them. "No," said Father Hayes. "Not here. They'd only pull it out again. I'm going to drop this heathen thing off the cliff above East Town. And I want everyone to know that it's gone."

Quinn massaged his own shoulder-muscle. "That's a long way from here, Father. Would you want someone to help you?"

"Who are you suggesting, Quinn?"

"We have a lad who helps here with the oil. His name is..."

"No, not him, of all people. I know who he is."

An awkward silence fell between them. Father Hayes realised that he was using Mary Quinn's words: *You've got to help us, Father. You, of all people...*

"Quinn," he said, "are you still tempted by drink?"

"Father, I would be lying if I told you that I am not tempted. But I swear to you, and Mary, and anyone else who wants to know, that I have not touched a drop in ten years. And that includes this past Sunday night."

"I don't doubt you, Quinn. Thank you for helping me with this accurséd thing."

≈≈≈≈≈

He felt every pebble and rut on the road to West Town. He wished that the weight of the stone sat further forward in the barrow, with its centre of gravity over the wheel, but he could not shift it. Under his cassock, sweat dripped from his chest and stomach. His thin shoes provided no comfort to his soft, sore feet. Thoughts turned in his mind like spokes on a wheel. He should have put aside his priestly garments for the day. He should have worn boots, gloves, a work-hat... And yet he was doing this to show that his belief, his will, was stronger than any heathen idol. He wanted them to see the power of a priest, not the labour of a workman.

He was thankful that the sun was dim in the cloudy late-September sky. It was the time of year, he thought, that was most difficult for his faith. He preached of God's bounty at harvest-time, but it was complicated by the feel and smell of the fecund earth that the pagans had worshipped. The rest of the year made sense – celebrating the Lord's birth as a ray of light in the depths of winter, and celebrating His resurrection in the flush of spring. But at harvest-time, people felt the lure of the old dark gods, and there was no Christian festival to divert them.

He stood straighter as he entered West Town. He passed the Tomb of the Seven, where Sean Mullan took pinches of clay and handed them to fishermen and boatmen. He promised himself that he'd soon put a stop to *that* heathen practice. He rolled the barrow and the heavy red stone past the pub and the cottages. The islanders, his parishioners, watched him through their windows but did not come to their doors. With his stride, his posture, he defied anyone to ask what he was doing. No one did.

He did not waver until he had passed the schoolhouse and started down the road toward East Town. He found a level spot to sit the barrow down on its back legs, and he wiped his forehead with a handkerchief. A breeze from the south chilled him, and he felt a vulnerable ache in his throat. He looked down the long, straight road to East Town and thought *One hour. Only one more hour and I will be done with this business.* With aching arms, he lifted the handles of the barrow and pushed ahead.

≈≈≈≈≈

A ribbon of pain shot down his left arm as he made his way up the slope toward the cliffs. His heart hammered in his chest, and his skin felt clammy. He had not remembered the steep angle of the path on the north side of the island – the increasing slope of the fields, as though the Lord had put a great shovel behind Tory Island and tilted it up out of the sea. His throat was sorely dry, but he rejected the thought of stopping to ask Sean Mullan, or anyone, for a drink of water.

The unblinking red stone gazed up into the sky. He staggered when he pushed the wheelbarrow over a rock. *They will remember this*, he told himself. *The day the priest cast the cursing stone into the sea. I will have the last word.*

The grassy walkway ended, and a narrow dirt footpath began. It ran along a narrow granite ridge, inches away from the sheer cliffs on both sides. Eithne Mullan stood at the end of the path.

They looked at each other, saying nothing. He could hear the sound of the waves crashing on the rocks below. He moved forward with the barrow, hesitated, and lowered its legs onto the narrow pathway. Eithne looked at the round red stone that sat in the sagging wheelbarrow. "What are you doing, Father?"

"I'm not going to listen to any of your insolence, Eithne Mullan. You and this hellish thing are responsible for fifty deaths."

Eithne looked down at the sea-birds that circled endlessly over the ocean. "Perhaps they were necessary deaths, Father."

"That is blasphemy, Eithne!"

"Do you know what they were going to do, those men on the ship? They were coming to burn our houses. They would have killed our boys if they tried to resist..."

"They were not coming here! I spoke with them, and they were going..."

"To Inishtrahull. Ruairí told me. Does that make a difference, Father?"

Shaking, the priest pointed his finger at her. "You cannot take these things into your own hands, Eithne Mullan. God will never forgive you..."

"And Toraigh would have been next. What would you do, Father? I've heard stories of priests who have tried to stop the evictions. They have only been brushed aside."

"Oh!" Father Hayes's face contorted with pain, and he rubbed his left arm. "This is madness, Eithne. You have dabbled in evil, and this bloody great idol is evil!"

She looked at the red stone. "'Tis only a rock, Father."

"It is the eye of Satan!" The priest grasped the handles of the barrow and pushed it forward with a lurch. A burning sensation shot down his arm, and the muscles of his left hand lost all power to grip. Wood groaned and cracked as the barrow fell on its side and the stone slid over the cliff-edge. Falling, it seemed to drift in mid-air as it tumbled down the granite face like a red blinking eye. Shooting spray in all directions, it plunged into the sea.

Father Hayes dropped to the ground, his chest and arm flaring in agony. As he gasped for air, he saw sunlight shining through Eithne's hair. He felt her hands on his face, and then on his chest. She seemed to be speaking, but her words sounded deep and muffled, as though she were under water. She was saying something over and over. He could not raise his head, but she leaned closer to his ear. *"Breathe, Father,"* he heard her saying. *"Breathe. Breathe."*

Eithne ran her hands over the man's forehead. He kept shuddering, and his left arm lay limp at his side, but he seemed to be relaxing into some sort of peace. She put her ear to his chest. She felt the struggles that surged within him, the endless conflicts between his mind and his body, between his stunted feelings and his stubborn will. If he did not die, she would lead him back to her cottage and prepare a tincture of foxglove. He could live for many more years, she knew, if he used it wisely. Or perhaps not – but she would offer it nonetheless.

The sea-birds still wheeled and cried, startled by the crashing and the spray. Eithne wondered where Ruairí was. *If he had not gone egging on the cliffs...* She shook her head at the worlds of possibilities that rose up like misty wraiths. What if he had chosen to become a priest? What if his father had lived?

She knew that she might never see Ruairí again. But wherever he was, she felt his sense of purpose, of destiny. What would he do now? She was curious to know, and that was a good reason to stay alive.

≈≈≈≈≈

The pub in Westport seemed to be like a waxwork, a changeless diorama of dim morning light and quiet, solitary men. Ruairí took sips of his pint and sat by himself at the end of the bar. He knew he would not order another, because he needed to think with absolute clarity. And he had only a few more coins in his pocket.

He overheard two of the men exchanging recollections of a football match in bored tones. How many days, he wondered, would they sit in the same gloomy light, consoling themselves with inconsequential chat? He had enjoyed his share of evenings in the pub on Toraigh, relishing the unhurried company of farmers and fishermen rewarding themselves with a few hours of leisure. Did the Toraigh pub even open its doors in the mornings?

The publican walked to a spot opposite Ruairí and wiped at the surface of the bar with a rag. When Ruairí finally looked at him, he nodded toward the snug by the back door.

≈≈≈≈≈

So you've come back.

The man with the scar on the side of his nose sat with his back to the window. The blinds were drawn, and the air felt thick as water. Ruairí said nothing.

The two men looked at each other. The man with the scar said *Were you on the ship when it sank?*

I jumped off before it ran onto the rocks.

And did you have anything to do with the wreck?

No. I found the orders, and I knew they were going to do evictions. I just wanted to get away.

So you don't know why she went down?

No.

The man ran his hand through his shaggy hair. *I wondered if there was a mutiny.*

Ruairí started to say *No* but he hesitated. Had he touched off something in the galley, something that had flared into a revolt?

The man shifted in his chair. *So you come back to draw maps for the Navy, did you?*

No. I couldn't if I wanted to.

Then why are you here?

As much as he resented the question, he knew that he was being tested. *When I was here before*, he said, *you told me about how some people get rich from other people's misery.*

363

The man stared at the table and said nothing. Ruairí said, *I've seen that now. I want to do something about it.*

Without looking up, the man drew a circle on the table with his finger. *You got onto that ship,* he said, *and you stayed there. You ate there and slept there and stayed until you got orders that you didn't want to follow. What if that happens again?*

I didn't know what they'd tell me to do...

Do you think you know what we'll tell you to do?

Ruairí sat up straight and looked the man in the eye. *I'm not going to kill anybody, if that's what you're asking.*

Sometimes people get killed in a war.

But killing them doesn't stop anything. They aren't the right ones.

The man rubbed his nose and breathed out loudly. *I suppose you know who the right ones are?*

I've learned this much. The ones that's causing it, they sit in big houses in London and Southampton and send out a bunch of blokes to do their dirty work.

So you want to join us and confuse us, like you did on that ship...

No. I want to do what they done to Captain Boycott, down in Ballinrobe. When they fixed things so that nobody would talk to him, or pick his crops, or deliver his mail. When they had to send the soldiers in to harvest his potatoes.

Where did you hear about that?

The sch... Somebody told me about it. He said it cost the government ten thousand pounds to pick potatoes that wasn't worth three hundred quid. That's when things change, he told me. When it costs them money.

The man rubbed the back of his neck. *That wasn't far from here, you know. And it wasn't all neat and clean like you make it sound.*

Are you saying you don't want me...

No, I'm not saying that at all. But sometimes you have to follow orders. Can you live with that?

Ruairí looked the man in the eye. *I should be dead right now.*

What's that supposed to mean?

I almost died on a rock, out in the ocean. I promised myself that if I lived through it, I'd never take orders from anybody again.

The man looked down at the table. Ruairí said *But I also promised myself that I'd do the right thing. That's why I'm here.*

The man shook his head. *This won't be easy, you know.*

I didn't think it would be.

They sat in silence, listening to the clip-clop of draught-horses in the street outside. Someone in the pub ordered another pint. He would work with the man, Ruairí thought, as long as he could learn from him. But he would choose his battles, and his own tactics. His life was his own.

Author's Note

Reliable information on the shipwreck of *HMS Wasp* is hard to find. The *Wasp* sank near Tory Island a few minutes before 4:00 am on Monday, 22 September 1884. Forty-six crewmen and four officers drowned. Five men scrambled up the mast and dropped to safety on land when the ship keeled over, and the cook, the oldest crew-member, was washed ashore.

The *Wasp* had been ordered to proceed to Moville to assist the Sheriff and deputies in forcibly evacuating Inishtrahull Island. At the time of the wreck, the *Wasp* was running under sail with a young officer at the wheel. The engine-room fires had been banked, and she did not have sufficient boiler pressure to manoeuvre herself off the rocks. The court-martial dismissed the event as "navigational error," and the records of the hearing have disappeared.

Since 1884, the *seanchaí* of Tory Island (who are "brave" storytellers) have filled in the gaps in the story with an Irish stew of speculations and surmises. *The Cursing Stone* is another recipe for that concoction. I have not attempted to match the events of *The Cursing Stone* precisely with the events, ships, and systems of 1884. Sadly, however, the quoted article from the *Derry Journal* is transcribed word-for-word.

Many individuals have contributed information and ideas for the story of *The Cursing Stone*. I would like to thank:

Patsy Dan Rodgers, King of Tory Island, R.I.P., for providing newspaper clippings, engravings, and other documents related to the *Wasp*, and for sharing his thoughts and speculations at length in several interviews.

Father John Boyce of Tory Island for his insights into the long-standing tensions between Celtic Christianity and Roman Catholic doctrine.

Frank Pelly and Captain Owen Deignan of the Baily Lighthouse Museum for their generosity in organising tours and discussing lighthouse systems and procedures.

Brian Leyden, author and Writer-in-Residence for the Sligo Library System, for reading excerpts of the work-in-progress and recommending changes to bring out the rougher side of Ruairí's character.

Heather Corish, Andy McLaren, and Eugene Perry for reading and sharing their thoughts on early versions of the manuscript.

Above all, I would like to thank Monica Corish for her support, enthusiasm, and thoughtful critique of this novel. She is my Alleluia Chorus, as I am hers.

When Monica and I visited Tory in 2009, a number of people assured us that the Cursing Stone is still on the island. No two islanders suggested the same location, but everyone agreed that the stone has a blood-red streak in its heart.

Tom Sigafoos
Ireland, 2021

Sources

Stories from Tory Island by Dorothy Harrison Therman, 1989 (Country House, Dublin, ISBN 0-946172-14-5). Oral histories often lie flat and lifeless on the printed page, but Ms Therman transcribes and formats them into lively folk-poetry.

Donegal Shipwrecks by Ian Wilson, 1998 (self-published, ISBN No. 094815456 X).

The Waves of Tory: The Story of an Atlantic Community by Jim Hunter, 2006 (Colin-Smythe Ltd., Bucks UK, in conjunction with the University of Ulster, ISBN 0-861 40-456-4).

Memoir for the Wasp by Enda McLaughlin, 1989 (The Glendale Press Ltd, Sandycove, Co. Dublin, ISBN 0-907606-55-5).

Lighthouse by Tony Parker, 1975 (Eland Publishing Ltd., London, ISBN 0 907871 585).

The Royal Navy: An Illustrated Social History 1870-1982 by Captain John Wells, 1994 (Alan Sutton Publishing Ltd, in association with The Royal Naval Museum, Portsmouth, ISBN 0-7509-0833-5).

The Royal Navy: An Illustrated History by Anthony J. Watts, 1994 (Arms and Armour Press, London, ISBN 1-85409-124-7).

For the Safety of All: Images and Inspections of Irish Lighthouses (National Library of Ireland, ISBN 0907328369).

The author on the egging cliffs of Toraigh Island. Photo by Monica Corish.

Tom Sigafoos has lived in northwest Ireland since 2003. His short stories and creative nonfiction have appeared in *The Quiet Quarter Anthology, Crannog Literary Magazine, The Cathach Literary Journal, The Leitim Guardian, The Irish Times, *82 Review, Authors Publish Magazine, Trasna, The Ekphrastic Review* and *Loughshore Lines*.

The first chapter of *The Cursing Stone* was excerpted in *The Copperfield Review* under the title *Egging*. An early version of his historical crime novel *Pool of Darkness: Raymond Chandler in Ireland* was shortlisted for the Penny Dreadful Novella Prize.

A member of the Irish Writers' Centre, the Irish Writers' Union and WORD, he has served as Chair and Public Relations Officer of the Allingham Arts Association.

CPSIA information can be obtained
at www.ICGtesting.com
Printed in the USA
LVHW020025040322
712557LV00012B/1847